COWBOY WITHIN

LIAM LENHART

ISBN 979-8-9913102-4-6 (paperback)
ISBN 979-8-9913102-5-3 (hardcover)
ISBN 979-8-9913102-6-0 (digital)

Printed in the United States of America

PROLOGUE

Luke Anderson's impulsive decision turns his life upside down leading to confined isolation in unfamiliar conditions. His self-inflicted and ill-conceived actions create a situation where strangers control his daily life with chaotic new routines.

Hope is an intangible emotion yet carries people through difficult times. Luke's tragic childhood compels him to abandon this life raft and withdraw behind elusively unprotective walls.

Luke encounters new turmoil, challenges, and an unusually arranged imprisonment on a Dude ranch after an unplanned escape to Texas. Early miseries could lead to happiness with a woman besieged by her own emotional ordeal. Hope Cooper guards her heart after a failed marriage but could hold the key to true love, if she doesn't kill Luke first.

To Megan and Sean.
You inspire and encourage me
To reach for a dream and make it real.

ONE

Sunlight flashes off the silver Peterbilt grill to redirect his eyes from the souvenir program in his lap and witness the horror unfold. Metal collides with metal creating a thunderous boom coupled with a violent spine-tingling screech. Short-lived screams of absolute terror drown out the horrifying sound of steel ripping apart while he's viciously jerked around in the rear seat. Squealing tires scorch rubber when air brakes lock up too late preceding an unholy silence falling upon the scene. The terrifyingly vivid memory wakes Luke abruptly.

"Daddy! Mom!"

Luke whimpers in the dark room and wipes beads of sweat away from his face. Fear grips his soul to cause uncontrollable trembling and his nostrils to flare open. He attempts to meditate to reduce his racing heart. His eyes search the room for anything familiar while recurring thoughts surge through his angst-ridden mind.

'Why can't I stop this nightmare? Why did this happen? Am I being punished for something I did when I was young? Why does life hate me so much?'

A horse whinnies to interrupt his thoughts and force him to refocus on the persistent scent of manure wafting through the open window. Reality sinks in and generates a strongly annoyed statement.

"Great. It's not a nightmare within a nightmare. This is real."

Luke Anderson concedes the reoccurring nightmare waking him in his Chicago apartment won't be happening for an unspecified amount of time. The warm, muggy mid-March air confirms the change is real and he's trapped somewhere he never imagined possible.

'How could I let this happen? I'm stuck in redneck hell here. Maybe I should've let her shoot me.'

Luke's struggled to shut his emotions down since his pre-teen years to avoid further agony and heartbreak. Reality continually stomped on his plan so he's found it impossible to bury his feelings permanently. Life often worsened after he'd lose control of his temper under duress. Hope and a happy future vanished when Luke was ten and sad memories have fractured his soul. The broken road he travels has been built from misguided choices and a misdirected and unreceptive attitude.

One young woman had shown Luke what real love felt like before he pushed her away for the wrong reasons. Others tried convincing him to break his self-imposed chains to live a full and rewarding life. One influential and supportive man in particular nearly reached Luke until fate tore it all apart. Luke's past experiences forced him to think people couldn't understand him. Occurrences, memories, and emotions from the previous several days flood Luke's mind. Especially the spellbinding woman he's just met under harsh conditions.

Luke won't admit he's responsible for turning his life upside down after another regrettable decision. His current long-term relationship just imploded like a dying star to form a vacuous black hole causing unwelcomed consequences yet again. Luke's presently trapped on a ranch as the result of his life crumbling again over the previous three months.

One particular December day in Chicago initiated the end of all that had been familiar to Luke. The scene plays out like a movie in his mind. Luke had expected a different outcome to a specific question until it turned sour and forced him from his bedroom. The rejection creates a frown and saddened eyes to distort his chiseled features and slumps his shoulders. He stands in his small sparsely decorated living room covered only in sweat. His short brown hair is teased into a

tousled mess. His six-foot one-inch muscular frame is deflated instead of celebrating shared happy news.

The weather replicates Luke's swirling emotions. Forecasted flurries have developed into an unexpected blizzard when winds change direction off of Lake Michigan. Whiteout conditions howl with great force and encase the city under a deep layer of fresh snow. Mother Nature seems determined to permanently bury the dirty underside of the city from view. The frigid, unyielding wind rattles a loose window pane in the old wooden frame to create a high pitched whistling sound. Outdoor activity ceases while a bitter, acidic storm brews inside Luke's apartment, again.

A hostile female voice reaches Luke's ears and grows louder when his naked girlfriend furiously stomps after him. Linda makes a point of slamming the bedroom door while her long, straight but now somewhat tangled blond hair flows behind her. She throws a small rectangular pillow from the worn maroon couch at Luke's head. He steps aside and reaches out to catch it so it won't break the old floor lamp behind him.

"Are you kidding me? Are you trying to ruin a whole day of great sex? Is that really why you bought a vanilla scented candle? Not just because it's my favorite. Are you trying to make me leave? I don't want to go out in this storm. I'd rather stay here and be naked with you."

Linda's pale blue eyes icily glare into Luke's hazel shaded eyes.

"It seemed so right."

Linda verbally pounces and crossly replies.

"It's not! We've discussed this too many times already."

Luke eyes Linda's beautiful body which rivals a supermodel with her hourglass figure. The men at her office scheme to steal her away from Luke but she remains loyal to him. She's nearly five foot seven inches tall and loves wearing high-heeled shoes for Luke whenever they go out. She enjoys looking and feeling sexy for herself and for Luke. Her flawless porcelain-hued face resembles an angel's when she smiles, but at this particular moment, the angel had hastily stepped out of the room. Her reddened cheeks indicate the intensity of her anger.

Linda Williams possesses a sharp, intelligent mind with an unstoppable drive to succeed at the marketing firm which hired her.

A college professor contacted a friend to recommend Linda for an internship during her freshman year. At twenty six years old, Linda's finally getting noticed by her new boss. She's determined to achieve lofty goals unlike Luke who never mentions any goals.

"Luke, your decision-making skills still lack maturity and timing. I'm not ready to get married. I'm building a career and I don't want to be tied down."

Linda catches herself after witnessing Luke's wounded expression while the words leave her full, rose-colored lips.

"That didn't come out right. I do love you. I'm not ready to get married. Stop pushing our relationship in that direction or I'll begin pulling away. I'm trying to balance you and my career so I can have a better life than my parents have had. College forced them to keep working since I didn't get a scholarship."

Linda's reference to her parents causes Luke to flinch after hearing yet again about their sacrifice for her.

'People don't know how lucky they are to have parents who care.'

Luke's asked Linda to marry him three times now and feels hesitant and insecure instead of hoped for elation. They've dated for over four years so he wasn't expecting to get turned down this time since it felt right. The previous times evoked a discussion followed by a long passionate exchange but Linda's far more agitated this time. Linda's voice lacks love resonating while speaking and appears distinctly unfriendly about their future.

"I'm finally getting recognized for my ideas at the office and I know I put work first at times. It's so competitive and people will step all over you if you don't fight for what you want. You're a sweet, loving man and I appreciate what you do for me, but I want a bigger life, full of adventure and enjoyment. Succeeding at work is the only way I'm going to get there."

"I know. You've told me everything was a struggle until this new manager."

Luke has taken a back seat at times to support Linda's desire to climb the corporate ladder. This latest rejection stings deeper and Luke wonders how Linda would react if she knew more about his struggles. Would she stay or leave him like so many others had throughout the years? Fear prevents him from sharing that information and risk knowing the real answer.

"I know this has been hard on you and I appreciate your support while I pursue my career goals. I'm serious about pulling away if you keep pushing for marriage. I'm not ready. I'll let you know when I get to that point. I have a good chance for a promotion because my new boss likes my ideas for the concepts we're working on."

Linda recognizes Luke's rejected state when he looks down and into her eyes again. She unexpectedly flashes a devilishly wanting smile. She views Luke's perfectly sculpted body unashamedly and feels a hunger for his physical touch again. Linda knows it's impossible to return to her own apartment and chooses to make the best of the situation. She bites her lower lip ever so slightly while taking a small step towards Luke.

"Should we go back to the bedroom and enjoy each other some more?"

Linda's question surprises Luke.

"You're not leaving?"

Linda lets her hands wander where she wants to put them and feels Luke's body eagerly respond to her fingertips teasing touch.

"How could I leave this when we have nothing but time together?"

Linda looks down where her hands are seductively playing before looking into Luke's eyes with hopeful anticipation.

"Unless you want me to leave?"

"Yeah, maybe you should leave."

Linda's shocked expression speaks volumes.

"Are, are you kidding me? You really want me to leave?"

"Um, uh, I don't know."

Luke pauses and then responds enthusiastically.

"Of course I want you to stay here all day!"

His lips reveal a fiendishly mischievous grin.

"Wow, for a second I thought you were serious, I was worried you didn't want me anymore."

Linda opens the bedroom door.

"Come with me. My orchid's wet and I want you inside me. Pollinate me again."

Luke smiles while eagerly mounting Linda's willing and sexy body and listens to her moan loudly in obvious pleasure. Linda wraps her legs around him to keep him in place and lets out more animalistic moans to express the wondrous ecstasy she's experiencing. Linda readily surrenders herself to sexual pleasures with Luke and becomes more excited after he whispers dirty wishes into her ear.

TWO

Unbeknownst to Luke, a newly met stranger also reflects on life's recent and previous occurrences. She's determined to find a workable solution while he's imprisoned in strange new surroundings doubling as a jail cell. Luke struggles with a fading will to live and feeling even more disconnected.

Hope Cooper wrestles with troubling thoughts on her patio in the mild mid-March predawn outside Austin, Texas. Disruptive ideas and unanticipated tensions from a newly unwanted encounter prevent her from relaxing. Hope's concerned about uncontrolled circumstances at the ranch during the past twenty four hours. Her lifelong suspicious nature is on high alert. The song 'Tin Man' by Miranda Lambert and Jack Ingram plays to match her mood. Early morning darkness normally sooths her apprehensions but she's bewildered by a recently etched reoccurring memory. Hope scrutinizes it for meaningful clues but it's baffling her emotions with alarming clarity. The previous day's events change the complexion of her memory to give it potential new meaning and Hope's unsure how to handle the transformation.

'What's happening to my life? I can't lose control of my plan for how life should be. There's nothin' or anyone permitted to change my plans one bit. Especially someone I hate.'

Hope grapples with particular events to unravel the timeline and find any logic to explain it all. She seeks where an unnoticed shift took place and her attention drifts back to one specific December day. The sights, sounds, and conversations have mysteriously stood out in her memory for no apparent reason until now.

'Is this when everything began changing?'

Rusty metal hinges creak loudly before the iron chute's hollow gate clangs against the fence ahead of a dust cloud rising. Several men frantically yell warnings to get out. They shout over the loud, angry snorts from an evil tempered horse and the sounds of hooves kicking the fence.

"Damn, this bronco's definitely an Outlaw. Y'all're lucky ya didn't get freight trained by that beast, Jake. He came at you fast like a bullet. In fact, I think that's what we're gonna call this here mustang."

"Yeah buddy! If it ain't broke, ride it. Ain't that right Ben?"

"I wouldn't know, Jake. I jumped off a broke horse to wrestle a young bull, I don't take on the big guys. Bulldoggin' was my main event. Calf ropin' was my other event. I never lost my sanity like y'all have. As far as I'm concerned, the only reason to get on a cantankerous bull is to meet a nurse or the Good Lord above."

The commotion at the practice corral interrupts the conversation between Hope, Chester Kinkead, and his farrier, Sam Peterson. They're strolling out of the riding barn and wait for everything to settle down.

"Chester, the foal should arrive mid-March or thereabouts."

"Alright, new life is always welcomed at my ranch. It'll liven up the place. Which reminds me, Hope, why don't you and Faith join me for dinner tonight?"

"I appreciate the offer. I've been so busy I haven't restocked the fridge."

Sam adds to the conversation.

"Hey darlin', it's a beautiful day, maybe we can ride together and talk about the future now that our work's done for today."

"I'm not your darling, Sam. We have no future. I'm not interested in you. I have no plans on dating anyone so drop it. I already have someone special in my life to keep me busy and happy."

Chester listens to Hope's sweet as honey, soft, yet husky southern drawl become hard and monotone while expressing her disinterest. Sam speaks defensively in his slow Texan drawl after Hope rejects him again.

"Well now darlin', maybe y'all shouldn't push me aside so quickly. We have common interests and neither of us is gittin' any younger. You ain't had a man in your life for so long I think you might just've forgotten what that can be like."

"If you call me darlin' one more time, I'll punch y'all into next week."

Hope turns away and folds her arms to ignore him. Chester observes her eyes narrow to a seething, ireful appearance and her thin unpainted lips flatten because of Sam's comment. Chester's glad he's never thought of saying anything to Hope about not having a man in her life after witnessing her present reaction. Sam realizes he won't get a positive answer so he finishes his conversation with Chester.

"Mr. Kinkead, I'll be back tomorrow to finish with the other horses."

"That's fine Sam, I trust you to do what's needed for my stable when it needs to be done."

Sam disgustedly heads for his truck after another quick dismissal for a date with the Texas beauty.

"Hope, someday y'all might find the right guy, if you haven't already. Maybe you can give someone a chance to bring you happiness. You deserve it."

"Sure Chester, like someone'll drop down from Heaven and land here at the ranch for me to date and fall in love with. A hot-tempered, slitherin' canebrake's got a better chance of finding love before I do."

"Just remember what I've taught y'all. The right person's someone you make yourself better for while they already accept you for who you are. Someone makin' themselves better for y'all without bein' asked, that's a person you can spend your life with happily, not someone you change to suit you, or who you become less yourself for."

Hope's well-meant response drips with sarcasm.

"Gee, thanks for the pep talk, Dad."

"You're welcome. Daughter."

THREE

Hope's thoughts return to the present stress-inducing situation developing at the ranch until another song gets her attention. The male singer's first lines express his desire to kiss his lover but want a deeper connection with her. Hope looks down at her phone to see who sings the song.

"'I See You.' By Jonny Houlihan and Brittany Clarke. No guy's ever seen me like this singer. And I've never felt the way she feels towards him. I thought I did once, maybe twice."

Uncontainable sensations range from anger and suspicion to doubt and uncertainty and mix together regarding what may happen next. Chester's ranch has been a sanctuary for Hope throughout her life. She's felt peace and comfort along with healing after being abandoned there as an infant. Hope never knew her real parents and bitterness deepens its grip when she thinks about that part of her life. She's never wanted to seek them out and no longer wishes to be found either even if questions linger without answers.

Chester and his wife, Millie, were Hope's surrogate parents and dealt with the constant challenges her tornadic emotional reactions created. Hope was surrounded by ranch hands and grew into a tomboy until her teen years as a barrel racer and a young bull rider shifted her interests. The guys taught Hope how to care for horses, mechanical skills like repairing the tractor, and how to hunt and fish. They regretted teaching Hope how to fight since she would punch them when they got out of line. It wasn't unusual for Hope's knuckles to be skinned and bloodied. Millie attempted to guide Hope towards more feminine choices such as dresses and applying make-up to replicate Holly's choices. She resisted dresses since it restricted playing with the guys. Chester was a steadfast and supportive father figure who mixed a certain level of strictness with allowing Hope to explore boundaries without consequence. It became evident Hope would rather accomplish goals with her mind instead of using feminine charms like Chester's grand-daughter.

Hope's deep-seated trust issues with men emerged while she was young but excluded the men on the ranch. They were dependable and trustworthy because ten rules of the Cowboy Code guided them through life. Hope learned tough lessons not every man was raised like a cowboy which resulted in heartache and disappointment growing up.

Hope's daughter, Faith, enjoys the ranch and riding horses while gaining similar guidance from positive influences. Faith and happy childhood memories carry Hope through tough days. Faith's a tremendous blessing for Hope and puts a smile on her unyielding lips and gritted teeth during hard times. Holly and Hope became sisters but Holly's presence also provided trying and troubling times for Hope to deal with.

Hope surveys her backyard garden until her eyes settle on a bed of yellow roses bathed in the full moon's light. It reminds her of the middle school boy that gave her a single yellow rose for Valentine's Day. He was too timid to hand her a red rose and reveal his crush in case she rejected him. The boy only called Hope his yellow rose when they were alone. He began courting the pretty blonde who asked for help with her homework after finding out Hope was smarter than he was. She'd reward him with plenty of attention to spite Hope. Hope's imbedded cynicism and owariness developed further and the boy's actions strengthened her distrust. Her penchant to guard her heart evolved further from that occurrence.

'I wish my life had worked out differently. I wonder if I made different choices in the past which would've created a better, happier life today. More like Chester and Millie's.'

Hope brushes those memories aside and recalls the most recent Valentine's Day conversation she had at the ranch. A cool, rainy evening kept everyone indoors except for the guys barbecuing dinner. Chester surprised Katie and her husband with a reservation for a romantic dinner. Hope decided she and Faith would stay indoors instead of feeding apples to the horses. She felt happy and relaxed until Billy brought up a sore subject with one simple question.

"Hope, how come you ain't out on a date with Sam? I know he's been askin'. Or Colt? You haven't dated since your divorce"

Hope's eyes narrow and eliminate her contented expression.

"Mind your own biscuits. I'm not interested in Sam, or anyone else for that matter. You're not on a date either."

Billy retreats to avoid Hope's retaliatory punch.

"I asked someone but she had a family obligation. I know how y'all are feelin'. I've been through dark times, you know that. Now I'm dating, happy, and living life again, you should too, that's all I'm tryin' to say. I love you like the sister I've never had. I care about you and Faith. I wish you'd open yourself up, take a risk again. There might be a knight in shining armor waiting to sweep you off your feet somewhere out there."

"Billy, you've got three older sisters."

"True, but they're mean, you're not. I can talk to you when somethin's botherin' me."

"They're mean because you still tease them like a six year old. I'm not ready to risk gettin' hurt. I'm not sure I'll ever be ready again. Heartbreak like that hurt so much, still does when I think about it. I've accepted I might could be alone for the rest of my life, except for Faith, and all y'all here on the ranch."

"You deserve true love, Hope."

Hope laughs at Billy.

"True love? Hush up. Chester and Millie are the closest experience to what true love looks like. No guy has ever shown me what true love is. A guy said he loved me just to take my virginity and dumped me the next day. Ben found out and severely beat him to send a message. Ben's actions are the closest I ever had to a knight in shining armor."

Billy sighs and musters a half smile knowing he's upset Hope for the remainder of the evening. Hope returns home with Faith and settles her into bed but cringes after hearing the distant sound of thunder. Faith's eyes reveal her fear before Hope turns off the light and closes the door. A short time later Faith enters her bedroom.

"Momma, I'm scared. I don't like thunderstorms, they're scary"

'It's gonna be a long night for both of us. Neither of us'll sleep much tonight.'

"Come here. Let's see if we can sleep through the storm, okay."

Hope returns to her early morning rumination while thoughts trail off to questions without answers.

'Is there something wrong with me? Why can't I find true love? Are there any good men left? Maybe I don't deserve to be loved by a good man. How would I even know if I meet a good man? The guys at the ranch are like my brothers and love me like a sister, isn't there a man in this world who could be kind and caring like them, but want to love me for more? Why does it seem so wrong to reach for my dreams and make them real? Did I make the wrong choices? Is a lasting relationship just not in the cards for me? What kind of man would abandon his daughter?'

Hope's equine veterinary practice has been grown with passion and dedication and her reputation is well known in the region. Love's the one component which remains out of reach after her envisioned forever love turned out to be a false image. Hope clings to the idea she has complete control over her life and emotions. Men are captivated by Hope's natural beauty however a wounded and skeptical heart mistrusts any potential suitor's intentions. She ignores any attempts to gain her attention to avoid heartache.

Hope shares a close lifelong bond with two girlfriends and the trio remains inseparable unless and until boys enter the picture. One would drop out of the circle until a break-up happened. The pretty blonde in middle school was quite adept at stealing another girl's boyfriend merely by batting her eyes at them. Hope watched both friends also fall victim to the evil temptress. The attractive seductress manipulated older boys as well to irritate many more girls in the process. Holly's a couple years older than Hope but acts far less mature with her seductive nature around the male population. Hope's often reminded of the young immoral blonde because of Holly's flirtatious behavior which made her both a sister and a thorn.

FOUR

Luke's second night on the ranch is a greater struggle since the first which was a drunken blur. Uncharacteristically heavy drinking erased any idea what happened. The deafening silence between occasional crickets chirping is unsettling due to the absence of perpetual city noise. Luke finds himself missing the blaring horns, sirens, and people shouting to ease his tensions. The ranch seems soft and gentle compared to the ruthless world he left behind. Luke fears falling asleep and the return of his nightmare while pondering the next sound he hears.

'What was that?'

A lone coyote's howl livens up the night-time symphony.

'Oh, maybe a coyote. They live here? Wait, they live everywhere.'

Luke's stumped when another sound blends in with more whinnying. He finally recognizes an owl's hoot calling into the darkness and fascinates him until a familiar but distant sound triggers anger and sadness. The train's muted and desolate horn revives an old rage.

"I hate trains. Why did he have to die? We could've moved. More questions without answers."

'God, I hate my life!'

Luke's physically and mentally exhausted by the previous two days activity and too paralyzed to make proper decisions. He labors to consider his next move after his life and heart have been shattered once again and winding up far from home.

'I wonder if the door's locked.'

Luke remembers the creaky hinge before turning the door knob and slowly pulls the door open.

'That would be too loud at night. I'm surprised the door opens. I thought I was under house arrest.'

Luke peers through the crack into the dark hallway and listens for any noise before soundlessly slipping out towards the stairway. He stealthily walks downstairs to the outer door and repeats the process to slowly nudge the door open. Luke listens for sound in the area surrounding the bunkhouse. Years of intensified training heightens his senses to prevent unexpected surprises and anticipate what may happen next. Most of the time. Luke touches his puffed lower lip.

Luke's shocked no barriers seem to exist to keep him on the ranch while stepping out into the inky night. The mild, moist air wraps around Luke like a comforting blanket in the darkness while scanning the pitch-black canvas overhead. He marvels at the multitude of stars glowing and dimming and twinkling and changing colors and admires the full moon as well.

'That's an impressive sight even if it still smells like horse everywhere. Chicago's lights block all this out. I've never seen so many stars before.'

The awe inspiring sight makes Luke forget his predicament temporarily while breathing in fresh air tainted by horse manure. He reluctantly returns to the isolation of his room.

'Damn that asshole for taking my wallet. I'd try getting out of here if I had it. I don't even know where I am.'

A cagey pair of eyes has watched Luke from a shielded location nearby while holding a Winchester rifle to prevent any attempted escape. Luke lies down on the lumpy mattress and yawns with hopes for undisturbed sleep before, well, he has no idea what the day will bring. His first day went terribly wrong from the start. He dozes until a muted voice disturbs his peaceful slumber.

"Get up!"

Fatigue prevents Luke from reaching consciousness.

"I said get up!"

Luke mumbles incoherently after hearing the vaguely familiar voice and accent.

"I'm tired. I don't want to get up yet. I need more sleep."

"Fine Laddie, take your own sweet time. I'm gonna enjoy doin' this."

Luke starts falling asleep while footsteps travel away from the room until the sound of running water penetrates the veil of nodding off. Luke's mind is unable to comprehend the noise or its intention. The footsteps return ahead of the shock of an icy wet sensation unpleasantly waking Luke. Any chance for sleep vanishes. Luke attempts to jump up but the drenched sheet clings to his body and causes him to fall hard to the floor. Luke's loud angry swearing combined with the unexpected thud wake people below. He shivers from the sheet's cold restrictive grip before finally escaping its cold embrace. Luke furiously confronts this loathsome oversized Leprechaun cackling in front of him.

"That'll feckin' teachya to get up when you're told."

"You dumbass! Why did you do that?"

"That was a lotta fun. Rather satisfying way to wake ya. I'll invite the guys to watch tomorrow if I need to do it again. Maybe we'll record it and post it for the world to see. I hope you've enjoyed the ranch so far 'cause it's gonna get much tougher."

Luke glares after Scooter's ominous message.

"I doubt you can make life any tougher than it's been for me already."

Scooter's bushy red eyebrows rise up.

"You don't want to challenge us here. You're gonna get beat like a rented mule. Every day is tough around here."

Luke recalls Scooter's rude treatment from the previous day before getting his marching orders.

"Get dressed. We've got work to do. Meet me downstairs right quick."

"I've got nothing to change into so you're on your own. Pretty stupid to throw water on me."

Scooter chuckles on the way out and returns with jeans and shirts and drops the pile on the floor.

"Find something and report downstairs. Be ready in two shakes of a lamb's tail."

Scooter's Irish expression confuses Luke.

"I mean now, this instant, pronto!"

Scooter laughs and shuts the door. Luke doesn't understand until sorting through the clothing and finds none of it will fit him properly. It's all either too large or too small. Luke's agitated by his wet clothing which forces him to change while trying to make Scooter wait as long as possible. He exits his room wearing an oversized long-sleeved button down shirt hanging on him while the jeans are falling down because the belt won't close tight enough around his waist. Luke's pulling on the belt to keep the jeans up while walking down the stairs. He forcefully swings the door open to find Scooter furious with his late appearance. Luke's attempt to intimidate Scooter fails miserably.

"I can't work like this. I can't do anything like this. What's with the oversized clothes again?"

Scooter grunts and pulls out his pocket knife and opens the main blade.

"We'll fix that right now so you can work to your heart's content."

Luke's wary of letting Scooter approach with an open weapon. Scooter has no idea he's putting himself into possible danger before harmlessly punching a hole at an appropriate spot. Luke's prepared to defend himself against an aggressor's threat. Scooter's amused by the extra length of belt swinging back and forth.

"Quit standing there like a fence post."

Scooter heads for the main house.

'Thank God, we're going to get food first.'

"Follow me, Laddie. Quit dawdling so we can finally eat!"

Luke trails behind Scooter to the house and watches him open the screen door and unlock the inner door. He motions Luke to enter first and leads him to the roll top desk to remove the American flag from the drawer.

"Let's go. We raise the flag to start the day. Then we take care of the horses."

Scooter's announcement surprises Luke.

"Wait. We don't eat first?"

"The horses eat before we do. Move it, I don't want this to take any longer than it's gonna."

Luke's frustrated he can't eat first.

"I'm hungry. Fine, let's get this over so I can eat."

Scooter lets Luke exit first and quietly closes both doors. Luke notices Chester on the deck in his peripheral vision while sending the flag up the pole. Chester smartly salutes the flag before re-entering the house. Scooter then leads Luke towards the two large barns.

"We really feed the horses first?"

"The horses get fed first. The sooner we finish the sooner we eat."

"Why can't the horses wait until after we eat?"

"Because we wouldn't be here without them. It's our job to care for them."

Luke hesitates near the first barn under several trees until Scooter places his hand on the pistol strapped to his waist. Luke has no idea worse is yet to come.

"Hurry up, dipshit. I'm hungry!"

Scooter watches two male Robins' chase a female to the ground and all three squabble until a third male swoops down to chase the first two males away and fly up to a tree branch with the female. Luke hears the horses inside the barn and smells the heavy stench. He'll become very acquainted with both over time.

"I'm not going in there. I don't like horses."

"You are going in there and I don't give a shit if you don't like horses. I hope they don't like you either."

"They don't, trust me."

Scooter moves closer to stand toe to toe with Luke and looks up.

"I don't trust you. Not after yesterday. You'll work as told or face the consequences of Chester's deal with the sheriff. Go open that gate. Today's starting off like a herd of turtles."

Luke responds with a defiant snarl.

"Their deal means nothing to me. I didn't do anything wrong. I just want my wallet back so I can leave."

Luke attempts to hide his fear of horses while the thought of getting bit again crosses his mind. The thought triggers memories of his parent's deaths while opening the gate. Several cats purr and mew while scattering to other areas of the barn.

"What's with the cats?"

"They catch mice in the barns."

Luke approaches the stalls but jumps back when a horse loudly snorts.

"Go stand in the tack room until I tell you to move."

Scooter pulls a second gate across the open area near the tack room before pulling on a lever. It simultaneously opens every stall so the horses can happily trot into the pasture. Chester created the system to keep the cowboys safe when dealing with the wild horses. Scooter re-opens the inner gate and hands Luke a ten-tined manure rake and a pair of rubber boots.

"Close the outer gate and start mucking stalls on that side and I'll start on this side."

Luke's blank stare indicates he doesn't understand Scooter's order.

"You want me to do what?"

Scooter rolls his eyes.

"Rake the stalls out! Bring everything to the center and I'll take it from there."

The stench emanating from the stalls affects Luke and it worsens once he steps into the first stall and causes him to gag. He runs from the barn and throws up into several small bushes around the corner. Scooter turns the corner to see Luke heaving into the bushes and hysterically laughs until Luke's finished.

"Are ya done yet? Get back in there and get going."

Luke reluctantly returns and clears the first stall and begins the second. The ill-fitting rubber boots slow his progress even more than his normal pace would be. Luke finishes the third stall only to find Scooter's cleaned the rest already. Barn Swallows begin acrobatically flying in and out of the barn repeatedly peeping to add to the activity. Scooter makes it crystal clear Luke's inability to clean stalls frustrates him.

"Dear God, keep me standing long enough to get me breakfast so I don't die from starvation. Alright, get out of my way so I can push this out so we can feed the horses and move to the next barn. Then we get to eat."

Luke happily escapes the barn while an engine sputters to life on the other side. Scooter appears on a green tractor belching black smoke while pushing manure to a larger pile off to the side and repeats the process twice more. Scooter shuts the tractor off and curses at how rough it was running.

"Shit. I thought they were gonna fix that yesterday."

Scooter instructs Luke how to set out fresh hay and oats for the horses before leading him to the second barn which houses the riding horses. Scooter orders Luke to open each stall individually and watches him grow more panicked with each horse he releases from its stall. Scooter finally announces its time for breakfast after the task is completed. The stench of horse manure and throwing up has erased Luke's appetite and diminished his defiant attitude. Scooter opens the screen door and enters the living room first only to angrily spin around when Luke lets the door slam shut. It creates an earsplitting sound which echoes through the house.

"Hold the door when you close it. Don't let it slam shut."

"Sorry, no one told me."

Luke's apology is distinctly sarcastic and insincere.

"Mr. Chester'll be madder than a hosed down hornet's nest if you do that again."

'I'll remember that. If it aggravates Chester, it'll make me feel good.'

Luke's unfazed by the obnoxiously loud slamming door.

'Maybe the door annoys everyone.'

Scooter heads to Chester's office to report the morning's events.

"That boy moves slower than molasses and knows how to air his lungs."

Luke enters the kitchen to sit at the table but his stomach's still unsettled so he merely picks at his plate. Katie's given Luke a full plate knowing Chester plans to work Luke extra tough and becomes dismayed when he doesn't heartily eat breakfast like he had at supper.

Katie works on a knitting project while Luke washes dishes but stops when Luke shares pointed observation with her.

"Hope has a Superman complex, doesn't she?"

"How do you mean?"

"She thinks she's tougher than she is, like she's invincible."

"I don't follow you."

"Hope acts like nothing can hurt her."

Katie withholds her initial thoughts while Luke continues his idea.

"I knew someone like Hope once before."

"Really? What happened with her Superman complex?"

"She got mugged in a place she never should've been."

Luke's revelation shocks Katie.

"Was she okay?"

"No, she died from internal injuries."

Luke's blunt delivery and emotionless eyes nearly mask the hint of despair regarding the woman's arrogance putting her in an avoidable situation.

"She lost her chance to live a long happy life. Superman's not real."

He finishes washing dishes and leaves Katie to ponder new thoughts.

'Has Luke seen something about Hope we might be missin'? Luke has a strong presence when he speaks.'

Luke returns to the rodeo barn for his next task unaware the guys have been rounding up the broncs for Hope. Luke's disheveled appearance generates more snickers from everyone. He's more alert to other smells in the barn. The odors of sweaty leather, hay, and pine shavings mix with the ammonia smell which sickened him earlier. Luke's startled when a horse kicks its stall and bolts outside and jumps over the metal fence. Scooter immediately shouts out to him.

"Get back on this side now!"

Luke's unsure why until looking into the pasture to see two riders pushing a lone brown stallion towards the barn. The wild bronc charges straight at Luke while he freezes where he stands. The untamed mustang closes rapidly before slowing to a trot and approaches Luke. The horse breathes on Luke and rests his head against Luke's chest. Scooter quietly utters two words.

"Leapin' Leprechauns!"

Luke's terrified while Bullet gently nudges him. Scooter speaks softly.

"Slowly bring your hand up and rub his nose and move back to his ears also."

Bullet's calm behavior with Luke confuses everyone. He's lowering and raising his head to show submissive signs of bonding before trotting into his stall.

"What gives? Bullet's been stomping us into the dirt."

Luke's unaware yesterday's occurrence kept him on the ranch instead of getting hauled off to jail during this second amazing moment. Bitter memories of his experience with the pony sadden him while the guys speculate what's happening. Scooter clears his throat and orders Luke to return to work.

"Alright, back in the barn with ya."

Luke's demeanor changes while his energy level drops quickly before he can regain his composure. An inner rage explodes from deep inside when anger replaces fright.

"That's it. I'm done with this place. You can all go to hell! I'm leaving."

Luke exits the barn with a determined stride and heads for the long, red-gravel driveway. He passes the main house and hears Chester holler while the distance grows.

"Stop where y'all are or I'll drop you right there."

Luke's ears identify the sound of a cartridge being loaded before Chester aims the rifle at Luke and issues another warning.

"You ain't gonna make it through the main gate, not alive anyway."

Luke raises his left hand above his head and extends his middle finger. Linda's rejection has emotionally devastated Luke leaving him unconcerned if Chester shoots him. The impact of a single shell explodes in the gravel by Luke's left foot. He continues walking undeterred by the threat.

'Go ahead, shoot me. I wish Hope shot me yesterday. Maybe this asshole will end my pain today.'

Luke's been plagued by thoughts of ending his life due to the guilt of being alive when his parents are not. It's never occurred to Luke he's more afraid to live than to die.

'Just pull the trigger already.'

A familiar pick-up approaches and slows near Luke's position. Hope lowers her mirrored sunglasses to reveal her glare. Luke's hatred and rage is redirected at her when their eyes meet. Hope pulls past Luke to a safe spot and exits with her gun drawn. She's unknowingly blocked Chester's line of fire and can't understand why he's frustrated when he barks his order out.

"Shit! Hope, git outta the way."

'I'll end this mistake right now.'

Hope's attempt to match the intensity of Luke's intimidating stare fails when she blinks because of his hateful glare. Hope recalls their first encounter from the previous day.

'Luke's expression seems more terrifying today.'

Luke has his own thought.

'Hope's trying to be Superman again.'

Hope's unaware what Luke's actually capable of if forced to react.

"Turn your worthless ass around or I'll shoot you right now. I saw Ben last night. I saw what you did to him. I'll even the score for him."

Hope's puzzled by Luke's initial silence.

'Why are you getting my full attention? I can't stop looking at you. You're the most beautiful woman I've ever seen but I don't want anything with anyone after what I've been through. You sure seem to love that dirty old cowboy hat.'

Hope would be surprised to know Luke's thoughts while he gazes into her vivid green eyes which she finds unnerving. She breaks the unsettling silence.

"I'll put a bullet in y'all and rid this ranch of a dirty rat. I mean it."

'Can I really shoot him? I do hate him for hurtin' Ben. He's not one of the guys here so I don't trust him one bit. But what is it about this guy that seems different. I can't put my finger on it.'

Hope's disturbed when Luke laughs after her second threat to shoot him.

"I doubt you will since you couldn't yesterday."

"I hate you so much."

"Yeah, you mentioned that yesterday."

Hope begins squeezing the trigger after Luke's irritating challenge. Luke keenly watches her finger and knows the gun will fire with any more pressure.

'He can't win this time.'

Hope's shot terminates the stand-off silence. Luke's still standing but notices an intense searing sensation on his left side. His shirt has a new hole from the bullet passing through which is being stained by a sticky red solution.

'She shot me. But she didn't kill me.'

Luke unexpectedly steps in Hope's direction after grasping the round merely grazed him before turning towards the barn. Hope shudders when Luke passes within ten feet with an unblinking stare and an evil smirk.

"I can't go anywhere anyway. That dumbass has my wallet."

'What did I just do? I could've killed him. I didn't train for this reason. He didn't even react.'

Hope sighs after removing her finger from the trigger once Luke's close to the barn. She draws in a deep breath and lets it out to regain her composure before continuing up to Chester.

"Dammit, Hope, you blocked my shot. What were ya thinkin'?"

Hope's stunned by Chester's harsh rebuke.

'I don't like disappointing Chester. How did I let him down?'

"How'd you make Luke to return to the barn?"

"I'm not sure. I did warn him I'd shoot if he didn't go back to the barn. He said something about you having his wallet."

Chester grins.

"I knew that was a good idea. I don't get this guy. A horse terrifies him but he don't flinch at a gun. Could you shoot him? You didn't yesterday."

Hope's uncertain about actually shooting Luke.

'I did wing him.'

"I'll shoot him, or someone, if the reason's right."

Hope's underlying message is understood.

"Let's pray that never happens."

Hope nods and heads inside to talk with Katie and exits when Scooter's escorting Luke to the house. Luke coldly stares at Hope while passing her as she heads for the barns. She ignores him up close but glances back several times once he's behind her. Chester observes her uncharacteristic behavior from the deck before addressing Hope.

"I've got your list of chores to do 'round here. You're gonna pick weeds, move hay bales and feed, clean gutters, washin' garbage cans out, cleanin' windows, sweepin', dustin', and stuff I ain't thought of yet. Oh, and ya'll're gonna wash everyone's truck too."

"I'm not your maid. Find someone else to do all that. Let Hope do that, most of it sounds like woman's work anyway."

Katie Thompson overhears Luke's statement and storms out of the house.

"How dare you! Y'all are bein' ugly. Just so's y'all know, a woman can outwork any man at any job anytime she wants to. How dare you think such a condescending thought let alone say it out loud. And just so y'all don't get confused while you're here, Texans can build anythin', break anythin', fix everythin', 'cause we ain't afraid of nothin'."

"I'm sorry ma'am, I didn't mean to insult you. I just don't think I should be forced to do things that are beneath me."

"Beneath you?"

Luke shrinks away when Katie angrily steps forward to confront him which confuses Chester.

'Why would Luke back away from Katie but stand up to Hope and her gun?'

"Nothing's beneath a Texan. We take on all chores and challenges because we can. Apparently, they don't teach that up north. You're about to get a long overdue education about life on this ranch."

Luke's quiet after Katie's stinging rebuke and physically retreats from her continued scolding. Chester remembers what day it is and decides to change things up after sending Luke back to work.

'That was fun to watch but I hope he doesn't make Katie go flyin' off the handle like that again. It ain't fun when she's madder 'n a wet hen. I have a call to make.'

FIVE

Scooter supervises Luke while he cleans garbage cans and washes windows until Chester steps outside and motions them into the house. Luke moves ahead of Scooter and wickedly grins while reaching for the screen door. Luke swings the door wide open and lets it slam shut to allow the ear-piercing whack resound throughout the house. Scooter cringes.

'That boy's gonna be the death of me. I just know it. Chester's gonna chew him out, then he'll be comin' for me.'

Luke's pleased when Chester heatedly responds.

"Stop letting that damn door slam!"

Chester recognizes Luke's set a trap to enjoy his irritated reaction and announces the next task with a smile.

"Change your shirt. We're running an errand."

Luke's grin fades.

'Is he taking me to jail? Or a one-way trip to the middle of nowhere?'

"Where are we going?"

"Someplace that'll give ya a better perspective on life. If that's possible."

Luke repeatedly asks where they're going while considering dire possibilities and becomes noticeably fearful when Chester pulls alongside semi-trucks. Chester uses silence like an intellectual tactic against Luke to show power and authority. The Marines taught him the mind can convince the body to overcome obstacles and knowledge is stronger than muscle. Chester finally speaks when they pull into a parking lot.

"You're gonna meet someone who's gonna change your bad attitude. Me, I'm already wantin' to shoot your ass off."

Luke groans after reading the entry sign.

"A retirement home? I don't need any more old smelly people to bore me. I've already got you."

Chester angrily shakes his finger at Luke.

"Show me the respect I deserve. I own your ass till I decide y'all can leave. These people've earned the same respect."

"You haven't earned my respect."

Chester's glare warns Luke not to say another word while they enter the building. Chester's greeted by several people who pull him to one side for a quiet conversation. He's subdued walking down the hallway with Luke in tow.

"This might straighten y'all out."

Chester stops at a dark brown wooden door with a light green metal sign marked only with a large red number one. A smaller sign with the same olive drab color hangs below with a statement written in bold black lettering.

'No Mission Too Difficult. No Sacrifice Too Great. Duty First!'

Chester pauses before knocking and opening the door to a gruff greeting.

"You're late! Just like a typical Marine. Y'all get lost again?"

Chester scoffs at the playful insult and waves Luke into the room also.

"Ol' Hank here served in the army but I don't hold that against him. He wasn't strong enough for the Marines."

Hank McIntyre rubs a tear away before responding with mock arrogance after Chester's introduction.

"Shit, we've been showin' all y'all how to fight, drink, and pick up girls so you wouldn't look so pathetic in uniform."

The two men share a laugh until Hank notices Luke observing his right sleeve pinned against his shirt.

"Lost my arm in W.W.2. Maybe you've heard of it."

Hank examines Luke's disheveled appearance.

"Who've we got here today?"

"This here's Luke. He's an unexpected guest at the ranch who's gonna pay off a debt he owes me."

Luke's aggravated sigh fills the room.

"Y'all don't seem happy 'bout that. Could be a good experience. Even adventures have troubled times."

Hank's a Texan through and through like Chester. His slow, steady drawl is emblematic of the iconic cowboy on the range.

"I've heard of World War Two. They have these things called history books. Oh, and there's the internet, maybe you've heard of it?"

"Alright dipshit, don't git smart with Hank."

Hank raises his hand.

"Chester, why don'tcha go bother the nurses 'n vets for a while?"

Chester nods and leaves the room. Hank understands Chester has reasons for everything he does even when it doesn't make sense to anyone else.

"Y'all are in deep trouble if Chester's brung ya here, aren'tcha?"

Hank listens to Luke's defensive tone.

"Why? What did that bastard say? He lied to you."

"Son, this ain't my first rodeo with the likes of you. I've seen your type before."

"My type? What do you mean my type?"

Hank's scrutinizing Luke's responses.

"I'm being blamed for something I didn't do. His dumbass farm boys started something they couldn't finish."

"Let's get somethin' straight, Chester's wranglers deserve respect for bein' the cowboys they are. Secondly, no matter who started it, you obviously decided wrong and need to be held accountable for it. Don't be tryin' to sell me snake oil."

"What?"

"You're tryin' to sell me a bag of dog shit, understand that? Bein' accountable for all your actions is something you don't seem to get.

Y'all need to remember every action has an equal and opposite reaction. Newton taught that lesson to the world. Back in my day…"

Luke's weary-eyed expression reveals his disinterest.

"Oh, have ya heard that before. Tough, you're gonna hear it again."

'Why did Chester bring me here? Who is this guy?'

"I reckon y'all ain't from these parts are ya?"

Luke remains silent.

'I'm not talking to this guy.'

Hank recognizes Luke must think he's working with Chester so he'll be unwilling to disclose personal information. Hank shifts gears to share portions of his life with Luke to open avenues of conversation.

"I fought from Normandy through the Battle of the Bulge durin' the war. Shrapnel during a tank fight injured my arm. The field medics did what they could but the hospital sawbones amputated my arm so I could live."

Luke's uncertain what reason Hank could have to tell him anything.

"Cancer took my wife, Sally, my oldest son died in a car wreck, my youngest son died from a bee sting, and I've outlived my daughter as well as my brothers and sisters. I'm the last of my family."

Luke shudders after Hank reveals his own personal tragedies.

"I've known a loneliness that doesn't heal. I've kept livin' for them even when I wanted to die. I prayed to God for strength to keep me goin'."

Hank strikes a bitter nerve within Luke by mentioning praying which produces a hostile interruption.

"Praying has never worked for me. God abandoned me! He stole my parents when I was ten. He took my uncle and someone else, too. My family turned their backs on me and threw me out on the streets as soon as they could. My girlfriend cheated on me. I tried praying on the bus bringing me to Texas and look what that's brought me. I'm stuck here like a prisoner, treated like a criminal for a crime I didn't commit and being made to feel like I don't have any worthwhile abilities."

Hank listens to the familiar agony Luke's voice projects while revealing personal details.

'Luke sounds just like Chester and I did after the war. So full of hatred.'

"God didn't steal your parents. He may've called them home and put you on the path you're meant to be on. You just don't know why yet."

Hank's assessment perturbs Luke but hearing Hank lived similar challenging life events seemingly lifts a weight off Luke's shoulders.

'Is it possible someone else could understand what I'm feeling?'

"I don't know why I told you any of that. I don't share my life with anyone. Don't tell Chester any of that, I don't want him to know."

Hank shares one conclusion with Luke.

"You'd rather be a closed book? Usually a closed mind and heart goes along with livin' life that way."

Hank initially plans to disclose Luke's information with Chester until his expression discloses another thought developing.

"Alright. I understand. Y'all don't wanna share anything yet. I walked in your shoes long ago. Mind if I share more old man wisdom with ya?"

"Do I have a choice?"

"Nope."

Luke recalls a man from his past who failed to help with his problems.

'Why does it feel safe to talk with this guy? Hank seems different somehow.'

Luke's tortured past has remained hidden for so long but he doesn't feel alone in this room with a man with a relatable past. Another man had once extended a helping hand intending to encourage Luke to heal himself from within with a philosophical approach. Luke thoughtlessly rejected his gesture and regrettably didn't recognize it for what it was. Hank breaks into Luke's thoughts.

"Emotions are part of life and can't be avoided. Holdin' everything in will bury ya quick under the weight. It's important to live in the moment. Feel what ya need to feel even if it's sadness, or anger, or even grief."

Luke's stunned expression informs Hank he's sending the right message.

"I'll keep your secrets under one condition."

Luke's immediately suspicious.

"What's that?"

"Have y'all ever been in love? The type that controls every fiber of your body."

Hank's question confuses Luke.

"I just told you I loved my girlfriend a lot but she left me for another guy."

Hank smiles slyly.

"I asked if you've ever been in love, not if y'all loved someone. There's a huge difference. Being in love is much different than simply loving someone."

Luke processes Hank's explanation before speaking up.

"Jini Hu…"

"I don't want names. Only if you've ever really been in love."

"There was someone once. We were both about twenty and after dating for a few months I could see myself with her for the rest of my life. My heart beat faster when she was around. It was magic when she held my hand. One day while we were miniature golfing, she let me know she was engaged to someone else. He'd moved away for work and she was supposed to join him. Then she met me and everything changed for her. I thought I was doing the right thing when I told her she should go be with him to find out how she really felt, if what they had was true or not. I didn't understand she already knew how she felt, what she wanted. It was me. I broke her heart when I pushed her away. I broke my heart when I let her go. Looking back, I should have fought for her, told her to stay with me. But I was stupid."

Hank hears deep sorrow while Luke recounts the painful memory.

"You had morals. You were young. You did what you thought was right even if it turned out to be the wrong choice. Things happen so we recognize a good opportunity when it presents itself again, maybe even a better opportunity. Keep your eyes and your heart open. I was dating another girl when I met my wife. It didn't take me long to figure out who I should be holdin' on to. I loved the girl I was dating, but I fell deeply in love with my wife. Time stood still when we were together and it passed too slowly while we were apart. Love'll hitcha when ya least expect it."

Chester had shared how Hope had punched Luke with Hank.

'Hate hits harder.'

Hank finds it curious that Luke touches his puffed lip after his comment while Luke re-examines his relationship with Linda.

'I was in love with Linda, right? I've been more closed off than I realized after losing my parents, uncle, and Jini from Hank's explanation.'

Luke's shut down has been influenced by other events as well.

"Luke, happiness is both external and internal. External happiness is like a cold beer in one hand and barbecue in the other. Internal happiness is a whole nuther situation. You can't be truly happy unless you're happy with yourself. That's something no one else can give you. Someone else who understands you could help you look inward honestly. Like Hope."

"Hope? No way! What's Chester's story?"

Luke attempts to catch Hank off guard with the question.

"That, son, is for Chester to tell, not me. Chester's a bit of a hard-ass, like the Waylon song, 'Lonesome, On'ry, and Mean. He has his reasons. Believe it or not, y'all could learn a lot from him. My advice to you is this, don't go lookin' for a fight, you'll find one every time. What did you do for work up north?"

"I've worked in a pet store for the past five years and at a bar for the last eight years to make ends meet."

"You're still working two jobs? That ain't gonna getcha anywhere. Y'all ain't got a pot to piss in, do ya? How old are you?"

"I'm thirty four."

"Luke, it appears you've lacked proper direction in your life. Make better decisions and stick with 'em."

"Mister, I'm a broken man and I think some parts are missing."

"I'm sensin' y'all've been on the wrong path. Who are you? What do you stand for? What are your goals in life? Let's consider y'all a work in progress and shake on turning you around."

Hank reaches out and shakes Luke's left hand.

"How do I know I can trust you?"

"We just shook on it. In Texas, that's as good as a signed contract. I won't say anything to Chester unless you force me to. You have my word."

Luke's distracted and misses Hank shoot a knowing wink to Chester when he returns.

'I don't look for a fight anymore, but they still seem to find me.'

SIX

Chester deviates from the route to the ranch and passes through a neighborhood with small houses and trailer homes.

"I knew it. You're dumping me somewhere, aren't you?"

"You ain't that lucky. Whaddya see here?"

Luke coldly shares his observation.

"Run-down homes and people."

"The people aren't run down. Down on their luck maybe, until something better happens with hard work and determination."

"Good luck, you stay here once you fall this far."

Luke thinks about the people in his low-rent apartment complex who have been there for years since life has beaten them into submission. He watches a young blonde woman angrily kick the door of an old white jeep. It looks like a dairy cow with black splotches covering repairs to rusted areas. Chester ponders Luke's negative outlook.

"I nearly lost the ranch twice early on and could've wound up like these people. But they could still achieve success like I have. My dad was good with the herd but lousy in business. I inherited his debts but kept plugging away with a new plan after asking questions and pulling myself up by my bootstraps. I became successful because of those results."

Luke scoffs at the notion these people could find success like Chester.

"It starts with a proper attitude. You've got a real bad one. Nothin' good's gonna come to you that way."

Luke rolls his eyes and looks out the window.

"I'd like to visit Hank again."

Luke's request surprises Chester.

"Thought y'all didn't wanna spend time with more old folks?"

Luke's answer lacks any attitude.

"I think he liked my visit. Maybe having a younger person around is what he needs."

Chester contemplates Luke's reasoning.

'Hank did seem happy to talk to Luke. He lost his best friend and fellow vet last night.'

Chester spots a red Corvette and a second pick-up parked next to Hope's truck once they return to the ranch.

"Someone's here to work and someone came to visit Hope."

Chester heads to the rodeo barn to check in with his farrier. Luke follows since Chester hasn't mentioned his next task yet but hesitates at the door after learning Hope's inside the barn. The horses trigger sadness and fear from constant memories revolving around death again. Hope stands next to Sam Peterson and an unknown man who puts his hand on her waist while saying something to make Hope laugh. Luke approaches slowly while trying to conceal an overpowering terror consuming him. Sam sees him and comments.

"Y'all still here? I figured the sheriff would've hauled you off by now."

Luke scowls at Sam and struggles with confusing emotions regarding the Texas beauty's presence.

'Hope just draws me in, why? She did technically shoot me.'

Luke glances at Hope whenever possible despite her annoyed expression aimed at him.

'It's impossible not to look at Hope.'

The newest visitor speaks with a demeaning tone after Sam's comment.

"Oh, you're the asshole who hurt Ben. Big tough man, hit a guy from behind with a two by four, huh?"

Luke sneers.

"I didn't use a two by four."

Luke's upset while answering.

"Right, it just showed up outta nowhere, is that it?"

'Obviously no one can tell the truth here.'

Luke realizes the altercation with Ben has been distorted already while assessing this stranger. He's about Luke's height with a military-styled high and tight haircut and wears an expensive looking suit.

'He looks military and seems to be in shape.'

The man moves closer to Hope but Luke remains quiet since Chester's present and Hope's armed. Hope notices a glimmer of life in Luke's piercing gaze each time their eyes briefly lock onto each other. She's still furious Luke injured Ben and turns to address Chester.

"Let's talk in your office but first let's visit the foal. I can't stand bein' 'round the disgusting vermin that hurt Ben. You need a mountain lion for larger rats."

Chester nods and turns to Luke.

"Wait here and stay outta trouble."

Chester leaves Luke in the barn since he's afraid of horses.

'What better punishment?'

Chester and Hope reach the door at the same time a new visitor walks in and share a quick conversation.

"You remember Hope? Look around and let me know what y'all think. One or more of my buckin' broncs may fit the bill."

The man begins inspecting the horses for possible purchase for another rodeo circuit. Luke's fear builds to near panicked levels although he tries suppressing it so these men don't discover his emotional distress. Sorrow impairs his attempt to retain his composure and prevent his body's urge to convulse and release the terror. Sam's already proven to think too highly of himself and now this well-dressed stranger appears to be quite arrogant as well. He decides to put Luke in his place after observing Luke's focused scrutiny.

"Nice outfit. You shop in back alley dumpsters? Bring us a pitcher of sweet tea and be useful."

Luke's eyebrow rises after the order.

"I'm not getting you anything. I don't even know who you are."

"My name's Colt, my friends call me CJ, but you can call me sir. Your name don't matter. Get us Katie's sweet tea, now."

"Your name is Colt? Your parents named you like a pretty little pony? Or maybe a defective unicorn."

Colt's indignant expression precedes his condescending response.

"No asshole. I'm named after the famous gun. You're just a stupid Yankee city slicker so you wouldn't know that."

"I'm smart enough not to be named after a pretty little unicorn pony."

Colt's face reddens after the repeated insult.

"Shut your mouth or I'll shut it for ya."

Luke grins while sizing Colt up which infuriates him further.

"I could use a minute's worth of exercise."

Sam pulls Colt away from Luke.

"Hey, let's talk over here."

Holly walks up behind Luke and comes around to plant a kiss on his lips.

"Howdy, lover boy."

Sam and Colt laugh and joke with each other.

"The buckle bunny strikes again."

"Holly, y'all'd be lowering the bar too low with that one."

"Y'all never complain how low I go."

Holly simply smiles and runs her hand up and down Luke's chest before walking off. Luke's able to hear the two men talking while the horse buyer keeps some distance from the three men. Sam switches the conversation to Hope.

"I'd like to knock boots with Hope."

"Sam, y'all don't have a chance with Hope. She's too much woman for ya."

"Hey, I make good money. I own my business. I've worked with Hope on a bunch of ranches. We know each other pretty well."

"Sam, you give horses a manicure, or is it a pedicure. I fly wealthy businessmen around the country in my own plane and teach people to fly. It's a great way to pick up fillies. I grew up with Hope and took her flying in my Cessna trainer. I let her take control of the stick. I have another stick she could take control of, if ya know what I mean."

Sam nods before Colt adds another thought.

"Hope' a serious MILF but I don't wanna deal with someone else's kid."

"Yeah buddy, her kid's okay, but you're right, not mine, so I don't care."

Luke listens to Sam and Colt talking dismissively about Hope and Faith.

'These guys are supposed to be her friends?'

Luke's feeling conflicted about being upset for Hope's sake.

'I don't like Hope but she deserves more respect from people she knows. Hope can hate me but I can't stay quiet on this.'

Colt notices Luke's distressed expression.

"What's the matter, asshole? Can'tcha handle adult conversation?"

Sam chimes in.

"Hey, maybe he likes Hope? No, she nearly killed him yesterday. Or he's tryin' to be a gentleman 'n defend Hope's honor."

Colt laughs at Sam's evaluation.

"Maybe he's thinkin' the same thoughts we are. He's just jealous he can't have her. Y'all got a stiffy over there?"

Colt laughs before speaking again.

"I'd've already made a move on Hope except Chester might shoot my ass off if I do her wrong. Or truthfully when I do her wrong over and over."

"Yeah, I don't think Chester'd be aiming at your ass."

Colt snickers at the implication.

"That's one rockin' body I'd like to get between the sheets, or on top, or anywhere else."

"I wouldn't mind lockin' lips with her, but she keeps turnin' me down."

"I have my own stable of girls already, my fillies, to bed down with. I'll make Hope one too someday. At least until I'm bored with her. They're gone once I'm bored of 'em."

Luke's heard enough and confronts them.

"I don't like Hope but she definitely doesn't deserve friends like you. She's still a person, and a mom."

Colt fake yawns to show disinterest.

"I've had enough. It's time to shut you up. You're braying like a desert canary."

Luke detects Colt's easily signaled punch as he steps forward until Luke stops him with a lightning fast strike to his face. The crushing blow violently snaps Colt's head backwards and knocking him unconscious before falling to the ground. Sam attempts to surprise Luke with his horseshoe puller only to receive a paralyzing front kick to his chest. The force from Luke's kick reverses Sam's direction nearly ten feet before he crumbles in silent agony while gasping for air. He's barely hit the ground when Hope returns to retrieve her phone and witnesses the devastation Luke's dispensed to her friends.

"What the hell did you do?"

A horse snorts while Hope draws her pistol before reaching for her phone.

"Bob, it's Hope, get over to the Twisted Live Oak now."

Luke sighs during Hope's angered request knowing who she's called and what will happen next. Chester also re-enters the barn to find Colt and Sam lying on the ground while Hope's pointing her gun at Luke. She speaks without turning around.

"I've already called Bob."

"You did what?"

"This piece of shit just attacked Sam and CJ. He's going to jail to rot forever."

Chester checks on the potential client and he indicates he's fine while Hope steps closer to Luke.

"You have the brainless reactions of a damaged Pit Bull. You fight before thinking like it's all y'all know how to do."

Sheriff Fisher arrives and cuffs Luke to lead him out to the squad. Luke watches Hope tenderly caring for Colt's bloodied nose before following Bob out with a satisfied smile to watch Luke put into the squad. Chester's annoyed by this unwanted development and waits for Bob's call once Luke's booked.

"Luke was non-compliant the entire time so he's in a cell with several other repeat offenders."

"Fine. I'll stop by tomorrow morning so he can continue paying his debt here."

"Y'all sure he shouldn't stay here? He's more of a menace who doesn't follow rules."

Chester contemplates his next move.

"Alright, he can sweat in jail until the afternoon."

Chester hangs up and calls Hank.

"What'dya you think of Luke?"

"Chester, he's fightin' demons like we did after the war."

"What do you mean?"

Hank's careful what he reveals.

"He'll be a handful. I saw a look in Luke's eyes similar to someone else from the ranch."

Chester leans back in his chair.

"You're talkin' 'bout me, right?"

"No sir, I'm talkin' 'bout Hope. She's had that same rebellious, but lost and forlorn look in her eyes."

Hank's revelation surprises Chester.

"Huh, I've never considered Hope that way."

"They're in an emotional battle to find peace. From what I learned about Luke today, he might help Hope and she could help him if they can give each other a chance. Luke has intangibles he ain't got a clue are there. The proper outside influence could help him that."

"Y'all ain't still tryin' to find love for Hope? She ain't lookin' or wantin' that and you know it."

"Hope won't admit what she wants and needs to herself or anyone else. She's convinced herself she doesn't need love. Luke seems to be hidin' behind walls just like Hope. Frederick Douglass said it's easier to raise strong children than to repair broken men. Hope and Luke have strengths but are also broken."

"Y'all remember Millie and I raised Hope after her mother abandoned her on my doorstep, right? She's dead set against Luke even bein' on the ranch. Hope just had Luke arrested for fightin' Colt and Sam. Changin' that woman's mind's like turnin' a battleship on a dime. Ain't gonna happen. Have ya forgotten yesterday's events between Hope and Luke already? Luke did ask to visit you again."

"Hmmm, interesting. Hope and Luke may not've hit it off yesterday but don't misjudge the situation. Luke acts one way but may surprise everyone with who he really is. He's basically quit life but there's fight inside him if the right somethin' frees it up. He's smarter than he lets on. Chester, y'all never have explained how Hope wound up at the ranch and why you raised her instead of some other family member. Where's her dad been? Or grandparents?"

A prolonged silence is Hank's only answer.

"I'm gonna find out what makes Luke tick, Hank. And I'm gonna break him."

"Yeah? You? Remember what else ticks."

"Yup, a clock."

"Nope, a bomb."

"Luke's no bomb."

"I hope you're right, Chester."

"Adios, Hank."

Chester's contemplating their discussion until his phone rings.

"Howdy, sorry about earlier today. Do you have more questions? Oh, you have information for me, okay."

CHAPTER

SEVEN

Luke's teen years included several experiences in jail for small time theft but only for a few hours to make a point. He would be released to his grandparents who scared him more than the time behind bars. Now Luke sits on the cold cement floor in the corner and stares through the cell's bars.

'If Hope's successful this time could be a longer jail sentence. Can this day get any worse?'

Seeking serenity through meditation is thwarted by his cellmates and evil memories. Three men sit on the two benches and create more adversity for Luke on this second day after trying to talk to him.

'I don't need any more trouble today.'

Luke does his best to avoid engaging the men.

"Whatcha in fer?"

Luke remains silent.

"I asked y'all a question."

Luke glances at the men.

"I was in the wrong place, at the wrong time, and met the wrong woman, again."

The men burst into laughter at Luke's implied crime.

"We've all been there, right amigos?"

All three laugh again.

"Whatcha really in fer?"

Rage fuels Luke's rebuke.

"None of your damned business!"

"Oh, a tough guy, huh? You look more like a Momma's boy 'cuz ya sure can't dress yourself. Your momma wouldn't letcha hug or kiss her like that."

"I'm definitely not here for hugging or kissing your mom. Your dad probably didn't kiss her either."

The biggest guy lunges at Luke only to be stopped by the other two.

"Whoa, Chico, not the time or place. We'll deal with him later."

Chico grunts in agreement.

"They best letcha outta here first. I'll crush y'all like a gnat."

"I'm not scared of you. You won't even touch me."

Luke's arrogance agitates the thugs.

"You best watch your back and sleep with one eye open."

Luke replies smugly without making eye contact.

"Why, there's only three of you."

Luke glances at Chico's face.

"What's with the teardrop tattoo by your eye?"

The men grin slyly before Chico answers.

"It might could mean I killed someone."

Luke scoffs to further infuriate his cell mates.

"Oh, I thought it meant you flunked Clown College."

Chico lunges at Luke but gets stopped again. Luke's relaxed and doesn't flinch after insulting him. He studies them from the corner of his eye when they huddle together and mumble back and forth. The hours pass slowly and uneventfully until a maintenance worker walks by with a step ladder and calls out to the guard.

"Hey, remember we're taking the cameras off line later tonight for an upgrade, you won't have video for a while."

The guard's irritated the news gets broadcast in front of prisoners.

"You wanna draw them an escape map? They don't need to know what you're doin'."

The worker's sheepish expression acknowledges his verbal blunder. The three men glance at each other before looking at Luke and watch him turn away as if he doesn't have a care in the world.

Hope's engaged in a tense conversation with two best friends' miles from Luke's incarcerated location.

"Why're you so worked up, Hope?"

"Yeah, what's with the conniption fit?"

"Chester's still gonna keep that vile asshole at the ranch after everything he's done."

Hope's seething while her friends exchange confused looks since she hasn't been so riled up since her divorce.

'Hope doesn't swear around Faith so this must be bad.'

Chester oughta leave that good-for-nothin' shithead in jail where he belongs. He hurt Ben, CJ, and Sam."

JeniMay Mitchell and Jubilee Williamson listen to Hope's furious protest of Luke's presence at the ranch.

"Is it true y'all nearly shot him dead yesterday? Holly said somethin'."

"Yes, JeniMay, I nearly shot him yesterday. I was making a point. I grazed him earlier today. I know it hurt him but he didn't even flinch."

Jubilee's curious to hear Hope's answer to her next question.

"What was your point?"

"To do as he told and stay outta my way. He was under foot everywhere I went in the barn. And the smug look he gave me when he told me to go home to Faith really irked me."

"Holly says this guy's one hot hunk. She called him a tall drink of iced tea. Is he?"

"What? I don't know. I didn't look that close."

Hope looks down after her last statement.

"Oh, come on. You didn't notice if he's good looking or not. I find that hard to believe, even for you, Hope. You notice everything."

"Can we talk about anything else? I'm not interested in discussing the asshole problem at the ranch anymore."

"Fine, what should we talk about then?"

JeniMay and Jubilee know Hope won't share any juicy details about the stranger at the ranch which means they'll have to visit the Twisted Live Oak themselves.

Night quietly displaces the prolonged daytime confinement at the police station. People settle in to read or and wait for the possible overnight mayhem. An unsympathetic desk officer sporadically checks cells and walks away as if he's reviled by their presence. Luke makes occasional observations of his cellmates and notices they've dozed off on the benches. Time slowly ticks off and Luke realizes no one's checked on the cells for quite some time.

'I guess they stopped caring if we exist.'

Luke shifts positions for comfort but also to stand quickly if necessary. The lighting flickers before some main lights buzz loudly which wakes Chico before everything goes dark. Emergency lighting activates while Chico nudges his two companions.

Luke springs to his feet before chaos ensues when Chico's first to charge at him. Chico's surprised by Luke's rapid response to deliver a savage front kick into his chest that pushes him back against his friends. They fall onto the bench in a pile and regain their balance individually which allows Luke to inflict painful blows singularly. Ruthless impacts from his fists, knees, and elbows dispense agony in the near dark conditions. Luke's full rage is unleashed against these legitimate criminals and his expeditious attack leaves his cellmates unconscious, severely injured, and bleeding. His last vicious act is to slam Chico's head into the bars and permanently mark him. Luke sits on a bench and struggles to rein in his emotional eruption while waiting for someone to arrive.

'They don't care what we do to each other in here.'

Luke swings his legs around to bring his knees to his chest and rests his head on his arms crossed over his knees. Luke's dissatisfied stare at the human carnage on the floor causes him to additional past events including the crash that killed his parents.

'Life took so much and left me so bitter.'

The drunken semi-truck driver stumbled from his damaged cab to see Luke motionless in a state of shock. The man unsteadily walked to the exposed rear seat of the vehicle he's split in half. Luke's staring into the driver's blood-shot eyes lacking any sign of remorse. They look towards the location Luke's eyes had been fixated on to see the crushed front section of the family car turned into a coffin. Second by chilling second of the semi colliding with the car and shredding it apart is vividly imprinted in Luke's mind. It has never left him and seemingly never will allow peace to return. The driver sped through the red light while searching for a dropped beer can and hard braking caused the truck to jack-knife after slamming into the car. The front half became lodged under the trailer's tires and further splintered apart. The impact shattered the car, Luke's family, and life's idyllic ways of his youth. The driver was arrested and jailed for life but Luke also began serving his own life sentence that fateful day. Luke's sister became his worst tormentor and destroyed his self-confidence and tore him down to create the low self-image Luke's carried for years.

Sylvia Anderson is older by seven years and had also been in the car but reading a magazine at the time of the crash. She was traumatized as well but soon began finding ways to blame Luke for the tragic incident. Sylvia had asked to go to a movie but their parents went with Luke's request to go to a circus outside the city limits. Sylvia's hatred deepened that day but it started after Luke was born because she believed he ruined her special bond with their parents. Luke received plenty of attention since he was unexpected even though Sylvia still got an abundance of parental attention for school accolades and extracurricular accomplishments. Her only child mindset created negative reactions when she wasn't the center of attention. Sylvia hid her ever-growing hatred from their parents during family time but was ruthless to Luke once they were alone. Sylvia became Luke's ultimate thorn after the accident and the never-ending salt in his psychological wounds.

Their grandparents refused to take Luke in after the accident and revealed they always loved Sylvia more. His uncle, Jack, chose to sell his lucrative business in Florida to move to Illinois and care for Luke since it seemed best to keep Luke in familiar surroundings. Three years later Jack stepped in front of an oncoming train to end his pain. His suicide note explained he couldn't cope with losing his brother combined with living in a northern climate and a failing business. Luke was moved into his grandparents' house even though they blamed him for another death in the family and lost contact with his friends. Sylvia's attending college nearby and living with their grandparents and leads even worst accusations against Luke.

"Our parents and Uncle Jack are dead because of your selfishness. You know that, right? If you didn't always get your way Mom and Dad would be alive and we'd still visit Uncle Jack in Florida."

Sylvia persisted to hurl the untrue but hurtful claim at Luke every day until he believed it to be factual. Her continued torment was coupled with his grandparents' constant threat to throw him out once he turned eighteen. Luke's teachers in middle school and high school wrote him off as lazy and unmotivated to learn. Popular kids taunted Luke since he was new and quite withdrawn. He was put into therapy to keep him from slipping through the cracks of the system. The psychiatrist was more interested in collecting money than helping Luke. He sat silently inside his own cocoon to protect his emotional state during each session. Luke ended the sessions after the man said something he thought was complete garbage and worthless advice.

"You need to live life and get hurt again in order to heal. Pain will help heal your emotional wound. You may not understand what I'm saying today but hopefully someday it makes sense."

"You're full of shit."

Luke wouldn't give those words another thought until Hank reignites the memory. His self-imposed barriers couldn't keep the world out and would lose his temper and start fights. Luke's uncontrollable inner rage resulted with many trips home with bloodied noses, lips, and occasionally a black eye as well. Staff members finally caught Luke tripping the school's fire alarm after getting away several times and faced expulsion. His grandparents forced him to apologize in front of the whole school for making poor choices. Sylvia would try to keep Luke in jail longer as a tougher punishment after his run-ins with the police.

Luke barely graduated high school and at eighteen was forced out to provide for himself with several low-paying jobs to afford his low-rent apartment and bills. Luke lacked ambition and setting goals or going to college to achieve success. Meeting Jini then losing her set him back emotionally so he quit jobs without notice or concern. Life took a positive turn while Luke cashiered at a department store when a regular customer approached his register to check out. Luke's mood was ill-tempered after the store manager warned him to straighten up and fly right. Luke's dad had used the same expression when he was young and acted up so he mouthed-off after the customer's cheerful greeting. The customer stayed calm and did something unexpected while taking a quarter out of his pocket.

"Try grabbing this quarter from my hand."

Luke tried and failed miserably so the man gave Luke the coin.

"Okay, your turn. See if you can keep me from grabbing the coin back."

Luke doubted the guy could get the coin until his hand moved so fast Luke didn't even realize he didn't have the quarter any longer at first.

"I can help you get where I am if you'll let me. But you'll need to lose the attitude."

Luke grew up as a slow, clumsy, overweight child so he chooses to accept this man's offer if it means he could change into someone else. Luke discovers the man owns a dojo and gym as a sensei and has invited Luke to join his gym for free. Luke's unable to lift much weight initially or move swiftly like others at the gym and becomes discouraged. The sensei focuses Luke's training to lose weight and gain speed, strength, and agility and improvements slowly become apparent. Luke's still controlled by his temper and would lose emotional command when something wasn't working. He took to the gym with a vengeance to build muscle, shed fat, and train for karate tournaments. Luke's sparring partners narrowed to only the sensei and his assistants after too many students suffered serious injuries from Luke's wrath in the dojo. His sensei understood anger drove Luke but couldn't find out why even though he gently coaxed Luke to open up. Luke attacked an opponent during a full-throttled uncontrolled moment in a tournament and was banned from further competition.

Luke's untrusting nature prevents him from explaining anything to anyone and the sensei inadvertently added to that with an announcement. He informed the gym he would be moving to California to open a new gym with a former partner. Luke received an offer to buy into the Chicago gym and dojo but passed on the opportunity. The sensei had been teaching Luke how to run the business to grow him into a new life but Luke refused to reach for new goals.

Tragedy strikes Luke's life again when he learns the sensei had been killed during a botched robbery attempt. The news hits Luke hard which closes him off further until Linda enters his life about a year later. She makes a physical connection with Luke but he remains emotionally aloof. He had been promoted to assistant manager at the pet store and was working at the bar at night. Luke readily took his anger out on belligerent drunks acting like they wore Superman's cape after a few drinks. College kids received his ire easily since they could act the worst. Luke's disciplined enough to keep the boiling rage from fully emerging although his nasty disposition is well known. Luke enjoys fighting since he's able to knock guys out swiftly. He intimidates with his new found size and strength, especially with guys acting obnoxious around women. Luke does worry losing complete control and hurting someone bad enough to get into trouble he can't escape.

'Ben has no idea how lucky he is to be walking.'

EIGHT

Luke's recollections are disturbed when the officer's commanding voice angrily barks questions out.

"Shit. What the hell happened here? Why are they lying on the ground? Did you do this?"

"I wasn't watching. They must've tripped in the dark."

"The captain's gonna have my ass. And the paperwork! Calvin, get over here. Move this guy to another cell."

Calvin opens the cell door and gestures to an empty cell nearby.

"These idjit's need medical attention."

"I should've listened to my dad and become a plumber like him. That kind of shit never gave him any headaches."

Luke enters the vacant cell and lies down on the hard steel bench. Luke's physically and emotionally fatigued from his short time in Austin. Random life episodes continue invading Luke's thoughts. His dad explained Luke's name came from the movie, 'Cool Hand Luke'.

"Luke's a strong name. Be your own man and live by your own rules. But don't do the prison and chain gang stuff."

Ironically, Luke's parent's deaths left him emotionally imprisoned without bars or any chance to escape. Luke and his dad bonded through swimming and movies. His dad loved old westerns as well as war movies and comedies. His dad would often refer to Luke as his little cowboy or Tex even though Luke had decided he wanted to join the navy when he grew up. Luke isolates further after each of life's cruel blows.

Linda's entrance into Luke's life seemed like a positive turning point yet again. Her friends succeeded in pulling Linda away from her studies and noticed Luke caught her eye while they waited in line. Luke's physique had the women swooning so Linda didn't feel like she had a chance. A friend asks Luke if he'd like to meet Linda. Luke nods so Linda shyly walks over to talk and they hit it off immediately. Linda lured Luke into his own bed on their second date. She knew other women eyed Luke continually so she felt she needed to steal him away. Linda's focus remained on her studies and graduated top of her class and moved in with a girlfriend but spent as much time with Luke as well.

Luke and Linda shared a physical attraction but emotionally struggle to connect with each other on a deeper level. Luke resists breaking invisible chains while Linda poured herself into building a career. She struggled to gain a foothold in the company while the manager was an older woman. She was replaced with a younger more supportive male director. Success seemed inevitable for Linda after the changeover occurred.

Robert James was a twenty-nine year old highly motivated young executive greatly admired for his talent and ability to achieve productivity goals for the company. His insight to lead teams and encourage people to give their all and be recognized for it was deeply admired by Linda. She displayed a creative flair so Robert involved her in more of his projects which began a connection yet unseen by either. Linda invited Luke to functions held by the firm and he noticed Linda was happier under Robert's direction. Linda's male co-workers enjoyed embarrassing Luke in front of her to appear smarter and more worthy of her attention. The men compete for Linda's attention because of her beauty and feel she deserves better than a guy working at a bar. One of the firm's partners privately insulted Luke for not being better educated and hungry for success like Linda.

Luke experiences an odd event a couple months after his third proposal failed when a well-dressed man came knocking on his door.

Luke walked past while the man stood in front of his apartment. The hallway is chilly and stinks of stale cigarette smoke. Luke turned the corner and looked back to re-examine the guy until he leaves. He returns several days later while Luke's home and offers him a chance to make a fortune.

"Good day sir, I have an investment deal to make you rich beyond your wildest dreams. If you invest with us we'll grow your money quickly."

Luke flings opens his door to reveal his sparsely decorated apartment.

"Does it look like I have money? Get the hell out of here before I kick your ass."

"But your sister…"

Luke cuts the man off in a fit of rage.

"My sister? That bitch! I should've known she'd be behind this shit. Leave, now! Or I'll send you to the hospital."

The man retreats after Luke's threat at the same time the firm's partners are inviting Linda and Robert to a company dinner to celebrate a major client signing. Linda's excited to ask Luke to celebrate with her but finds him in an extremely foul mood.

"Why do you have to go? Stay here with me."

"I can't stay. Robert and I brought in a huge client. I need to be there but I want you by my side. It wouldn't look good if I didn't show up."

"I'm not in the mood to go anywhere."

"I promise I'll be back as soon as I can, okay."

Linda leaves Luke in an angered state to enjoy the evening with her colleagues. And Robert. Linda begins drinking champagne and starts hanging onto Robert's arm while they walk around together. Linda leans in and kisses Robert during a conversation. She looks into his eyes and leans in again for another longer more passionate kiss. The partner who never liked Luke catches sight of their kiss.

'It's about time.'

Linda wakes the next morning, naked, in Robert's bed, and begins trembling at what's happened.

'What have I done? I've never cheated in my life. Luke's going to hate me. How do I tell him?'

Linda quietly dresses and returns home to shower. She leaves Luke a message with a shaky voice. Linda arrives for dinner but doesn't give Luke her customary hug and kiss and seems rather jittery. After what feels like hours, Linda breaks down and admits what happened the previous night.

"I didn't mean for it to happen, it must've been the champagne, I drank too much. I hardly remember the rest of the night."

Luke recoils in anger and agony when Linda moves closer.

"Don't touch me! I knew there was something going on between you and Robert but I told myself I was wrong. I can't trust you, can I? "

"Luke, there's nothing between Robert and me. I swear."

"I don't believe you. You can lie since I'm not around because I work so much."

"You could find a better job."

Luke's expression informs Linda she's chosen the wrong words to say in the moment.

"I'm sure Robert makes a lot of money. That's what you're interested in most, right?"

"No. I mean, yes. I want a good life and travel. You know that though, I've never made that a secret. I've always been honest with you, even now."

"So you think you can cheat on me and make it alright just by being honest about it? I need to be alone to figure this out. You need to leave."

"I want to stay and talk about this. I love you."

"You have a strange way of loving me, by sleeping with another guy. Get out. Now!"

Linda bursts into tears.

"Luke, I really do love you. I didn't mean to hurt you. Please, can we talk about this?"

"No. Just go! Now!"

Linda's sobbing while she leaves and her heart aches knowing she's hurt Luke. She calls her mom for advice only to hear something she wasn't expecting to be told.

"Honey, I think your heart's trying to tell you something. When you talk about Robert, well, you seem happier than when you talk about Luke."

Luke lets a week pass by without calling Linda so she reaches out to him.

"I still don't know how I feel or what to do. I'll call when I'm ready to talk."

Linda's assistant is fully aware of her situation and perceptive to Linda's elated reaction in Robert's presence since they've started working on projects together.

"Maybe this is a sign. You should give Robert a chance, you both have a lot in common and you make each other smile, a lot."

Linda hears her mom's voice while shrugging off the suggestion. Two more weeks pass until Luke reaches out to inform Linda he's still unsure how to feel or if he can trust her ever again. Linda decides to ask Robert out for lunch after hanging up with Luke.

'Maybe it is time to explore how I feel about Luke and Robert.'

Robert gladly accepts her offer because he's been waiting for an opportunity to discuss what happened between them. Robert knows they were both a bit drunk and wants to fully win Linda over if possible. Linda began sending signals prior to that night indicating there was more interest below the surface. One of the partners comes looking for Linda during her long lunch with Robert.

"Sir, she's at lunch with Robert, I mean, Mr. James. I think they might be sorting some things out."

"Good. Very good. It's about time they figured out what some of us have already known for a while. Let Linda know I'd like to talk to her about an upcoming campaign when she returns. Oh, but let her know everything's fine, okay."

"Yes sir."

Luke bitterly held onto anger for Linda's actions for the past three weeks but comes to the realization she was upfront and honest and admitted her mistake with sincere regret. He decides Linda deserves a chance to repair their relationship and heads over to her office. Luke arrives just as she and Robert return from lunch holding hands and sees Linda lean against Robert and kiss him. She follows their first kiss with another longer kiss. Luke doubles over like he's been punched in the gut and feels sickened by what he's witnessed. His heart shatters and large tears fall while turning away during his aimless walk. Several hours pass before inclement weather forces Luke to return to his apartment. He's reminded of Linda everywhere so he pulls on a hoodie and winter coat and heads back out into the sleety mix to clear his mind. Luke endures the elements into the early morning until his body is half frozen. He shivers in front of a bus station mulling over a thought before entering the building.

'I need to leave. I can't stay around all the shit. I can't deal with it anymore. It's not like anyone'll miss me.'

CHAPTER

NINE

Luke enters the half-lit empty lobby and feels the hot dry air blowing from the overhead vent. Luke studies several destination posters on the wall while a lone woman behind the counter examines him. The middle-age woman is concerned due to Luke's lack of luggage and haggard facial features.

'Is this guy escaping a crime? His appearance, the time.'

Luke resembles the homeless people who attempt to seek shelter inside the lobby but looks more suspicious at the moment. The lighting reveals weather and crying has taken its toll before his voice conveys his inner pain and torment.

"I need a ticket. I don't care where. Anywhere but here, whatever's leaving now to get away from here, from her."

This woman has spent years watching all types of people walk through the doors seeking a ticket out of town. She recognizes Luke's genuine heart-broken tone and agonized expression and decides to process a ticket and points towards the washroom.

"You might want to freshen up before boarding the bus."

Luke doesn't understand until his reflection stares back from the mirror.

"What a sorry sight."

He exits the bathroom and looks at his ticket.

"Texas? I'd rather go to Florida. Why Texas? Nothing but rednecks and hillbillies."

Luke rethinks boarding the bus until the thought of seeing Linda and Robert together merges with an inner impulse to run compels him to get on the bus.

'It can't get worse there, can it?'

Luke walks to the rear of the almost empty bus before it leaves the station to avoid several people speaking with the bus driver. He stretches out on the rear seat and hopes not to be bothered by anyone else during the long drive. Luke searches for peace within the sounds of the engine and wheels while staring out the window.

'Does anyone else feel like I do? Probably not.'

Luke meditates but stays aware of his surroundings while miles and time pass thanks to his martial arts training. He finds it difficult to disconnect from the reality which has profoundly changed his life again. Luke's mind races through disturbing thoughts and memories while seeking elusive comfort in the seat. The engine's steady hum won't soothe his mind, heart, or soul with the vision of Linda kissing Robert burns deeper into his mind's eye. He can't escape his distressed thoughts or rejected feelings due to Linda's actions. Luke's constant companions seem to be agony and despair which creates desperate ideas deep in his soul.

'God, I haven't talked to you in a long time. I don't know if I deserve to now. They say you're infallible but I'm seriously questioning that in my case. Why am I here? Why was I even born? I wish I died instead of my parents. They had meaning and purpose. I'm a broken person like everyone says I am. I stopped praying because you never answered my prayers or gave me a sign you even heard me. I feel worthless and don't matter to anyone. I've been dealt a losing hand so maybe it's time to fold and quit the game. No woman can honestly love me for who I am. I'm defective, unacceptable, and lost. Life's taken so much from me and I don't have much of anything left to give anyone, do I?'

Luke would experience tragedy at the worst possible times in his life. His parent's auto accident began a downward spiral which had the most negative influence on Luke's future. Each terrible event was like an enormous boulder hurtling into a quiet, serene pond. Repercussions create vicious waves which lash out against the fragile shoreline like a hurricane. Positive changes evade Luke since he won't apply himself to work on lasting improvements. His irrational and misguided grudge against life suppresses his ability to solve issues. Luke was deeply hurt when his family abandoned him after repeated hate-filled words and actions furthered his emotional disengagement. He stopped acknowledging family existed after they made him believe he was responsible for people who died.

Luke's happy to learn the bus ride is nearing the end after listening to two women gushing over the floral carpet alongside Interstate 35.

"The blue and white Bluebonnets mix so beautifully with the red shaded wildflowers. Austin is just up ahead."

CHAPTER

TEN

The monotonous isolation of Luke's cell allows him to focus next on his first day in Austin.

Luke doesn't realize he's the only person to put on his hoodie and jacket once the Austin bus depot comes into view. He shocked by hot humid air when he steps off the bus and notices he's overdressed compared to everyone else. Luke's first steps are unsteady as he moves away to take off his coat and hoodie. He stops to stretch the stiffness from his muscles. The heat simultaneously feels oppressive and refreshing and Luke needs time to acclimate after leaving winter conditions behind after the daylong journey. Exhaustion and anxiety press on Luke like cattle herded into a small corral while he considers his options.

'I don't even know where to go.'

Two employees notice Luke's puzzled expression when they step outside for a cigarette break. One offers Luke his pack while they close in.

"No thanks, I don't smoke."

A tall white man wearing a black ill-fitted baggy shirt over his slender frame speaks with a Texas drawl and slow speech pattern.

"Y'all're sweatin' like a sinner in church and look a bit lost. Can we help get ya where you need to be?"

"I don't really have anywhere to go."

Luke's attention is drawn to the guy's large, hawk-shaped nose and pictures the cartoon version of Ichabod Crane in living form. The second man is shorter, somewhat overweight, and resembles a Hispanic version of Johnny Depp.

"Where would y'all like to go?"

Luke hears Linda chastising him for making such an absurd decision and shakes his head to silence her criticism. His focus returns to the present predicament.

"I need food so I can figure anything else out. Is it always this hot here?"

Al, the taller man, answers Luke's question.

"We're fixin' to have a heat wave but it'll change again. It was cooler and wetter last week. We get all four seasons during spring."

"Is there somewhere near here to eat?"

Both men answer Luke.

"Sixth Street ain't far from here."

"Yeah, head over there 'n decide whatcha wanna eat."

Luke's confused.

"What's Sixth Street? Is that a restaurant?"

The two men are baffled that Luke's unaware about Sixth Street.

"Sixth Street is a hot spot in Austin for music, food, and souvenirs. Heck, y'all can even get a tattoo. You've really never heard of it? Where're y'all from?"

Luke hesitates to answer since Miguel's astonished that someone could be unfamiliar with Sixth Street.

"Chicago."

Miguel stares at Luke's coat and hoodie.

"Long bus ride, huh?"

Neither man knows how to solve Luke's dilemma until a woman steps outside.

"Betty's shift is fixin' to end soon. Maybe she'll take ya there."

Betty agrees to help Luke and drops him off at Sabine and Sixth Street.

"Y'all're gonna find a bunch of choices on both sides for several blocks. The east to west streets used to be named after types of trees and the north to south streets are still named after rivers in Texas. Sixth Street used to be called Pecan Street."

Betty directs Luke to walk west on Sixth Street to view the shops, restaurants, bars, and people.

'This isn't what I was expecting. There's pretty women, business men is suits, but where are the cowboys?'

He stops at a restaurant offering Texas barbecue lunch specials and feels revitalized when he steps outside again. The invigorating heat propels Luke onward after taking in a deep breath and slowly exhales. He has renewed energy and a boosted mood since the meal helps push away exhaustion nipping at his mind and body. Luke walks further down the sidewalk while his eyes scan everything around him.

Luke stops at Congress Avenue and turns north to travel through the business district to the Capital building. He observes the structure's stately appearance, upper columns, and dome topped with a statue holding a single star. A nearby tour guide explains the statue is the Goddess of Liberty. The building's pale mixture of reddish and pink hues is attributed to the red granite stone used to build it in the center of Austin. Luke walks around outside the building and notices four monuments honoring the Heroes of the Alamo, Terry's Texas Rangers, Confederate Soldiers, and Volunteer Firemen.

Luke returns to Congress Avenue and walks south and crosses over the Colorado River on the Congress Avenue Bridge. Signage and a sculpture indicate a bat observatory is stationed under the bridge and pulls Luke to the east side to learn over a million bats live underneath the bridge. People watch them fly out to feed each evening from spring through fall before migrating south to Mexico for winter. Luke follows the path down to the bridge and examines the ribbed underside where bats roost and raise families annually. He returns to street level and looks south at the stores, one of which could influence his future someday. Luke crosses over the bridge towards Sixth Street again to explore the western section and notes the diversity of bars and tattoo parlors mixed into the restaurants and stores. The nostril-enticing aroma of basted meats wafts from open doors to tempt pedestrians in to enjoy a meal yet to be ordered. Barbecue is popular but other food choices are available as well. Luke's surprised by a variety of music since he believed only country twang would be blaring everywhere. Traditional country music blends with rock, pop, techno, and one bar has older rap songs playing.

Luke stops at Blanco and Sixth Street after passing a store with a large stuffed giraffe and over-sized gorilla sitting on a nearby bench. He crosses to the south side and heads east towards his starting point. Newer construction blends energetically with older structures on both sides which creates a lively atmosphere.

'Who actually comes here? I really thought I'd see more cowboy hats everywhere.'

The massive infusion of people from other regions dilutes the true Texan flair within Austin's city limits. Several individuals ask for money and food with cardboard signs and receive disgusted looks from well-dressed people passing by. This sight prompts Luke to realize he has no idea where to spend his first night.

'These downtown hotels are probably too expensive.'

Luke has two hundred dollars cash he planned to spend on a special dinner with Linda. Luke's concerned where he'll sleep but not quite panicked yet.

'I really don't have anyone to turn to here.'

Luke feels lost, helpless, and isolated from everything familiar in this strange new city. He leans against a brick wall to reconsider his self-made predicament. The afternoon flows into early evening and his stomach rumbles from hunger gnawing at him again. He steps inside the Iron Cactus Mexican restaurant for dinner and orders a chicken burrito and a beer at the bar. Luke exits later with several guys wearing well-worn jeans, scuffed boots and sweat stained cowboy hats as if they've just ridden in from the range. Their clothing contrasts the newly purchased designer jeans and shiny boots and stylish but flashy shirts worn by others in the crowd. Luke's new friends speak with distinctive Texas drawls and invite Luke to the Blind Pig Pub. They walk upstairs to drink and have fun on the open-air rooftop bar. The crowd's exuberantly singing along with the band to, 'Mamma's, Don't Let Your Babies Grow Up To Be Cowboys'. Luke finds it humorously ironic to listen to Texans heartily sing this song. Luke scans the rooftop area and sees a couple playing over-sized Jenga and walls are illustrated with paintings. A rather drunk girl bumps into Luke while he's looking at one particular picture proclaiming a deeply felt love.

"Y'all're lookin' at murals we have around Austin. Ya wanchur picture with one of 'em?"

"No thanks."

One of Luke's restaurant buddies pulls him away.

"Uh uh. That one's crazy."

Luke joins the group by the railing overlooking Sixth Street and notices the Austin skyline is ablaze in the radiance of the setting sun. Colored lighting along the edges of certain buildings generates a beautiful picture to be appreciated. Luke's attention is drawn to a particular blonde when her long hair swishes effortlessly while she sashays towards the bar.

'Linda? No, Linda's a thousand miles away.'

The eye-catching woman smiles invitingly when her eyes meet Luke's. Her dark blue doe eyes watch Luke after laughing and handing a beer to one of the guys before turning to walk his way.

"Howdy good lookin', my name's Holly, what's yours?"

Holly extends her hand to shake Luke's and looks up at him since she's only five feet five inches tall. Luke's surprised by her grip strength.

'Strong grip but not manly.'

Holly's Texas drawl is sweet and welcoming which captures Luke like a siren's song. Luke notes her pretty facial features include a cute upturned nose and full lips possessing a slight gap begging to be kissed. Holly's long blonde hair curls naturally to frame her beautiful face underneath a black felt cowboy hat.

'Holly's not shy at all.'

Holly's twinkling eyes and luscious lips smiling convey her happy outlook on life. She's surrounded by friends and doesn't appear to have a care in the world. Luke envies her cheerfully boisterous attitude while she accepts a bottle of Shiner Bock from one of the guys.

'I can't even imagine being that happy.'

The band stops playing when an inebriated young woman disrupts the lead singer. Light-hearted boos carry across the room while a staff member escorts her away. People pretend to be annoyed by the interruption until the singer steps up to the microphone again. The lead guitarist stops him and whispers into his ear which evokes a laugh and a quiet remark to the band before starting the next song. The men in the audience erupt cheerfully when the first guitar notes are played. The band chooses Waylon Jennings version of, 'Can't You See' to play off the previous situation. Luke doesn't recognize the song until the lead singer encourages the crowd to join him. The guitar introduction is different than what he's heard up north. Luke's relaxed enough to join the guys serenading the ladies in the group. Holly keeps tabs on Luke while enjoying all the attention. Holly's best friend, a pretty red-head named Laurie makes eyes at Luke along with several other ladies throughout the night. Holly's group adds shots of whatever sounds good in the moment as well as all the beers. Luke recognizes these people want to simply celebrate life together unlike the immature college kids or older people with their list of so-called terrible problems.

Holly's interest in Luke grows and several ideas cross his mind although he doesn't give them much chance. Luke's forgotten the pretty red-head's name even after she's made several passes at him until Holly shoots an angry look her way. She retreats to several friends by the bartender's station but still attempts to get Luke's attention. It's nearing two o'clock in the morning and Luke has no idea fate is rolling the dice on his life. Holly's been talking to a few guys before walking over to Luke at closing time.

"Come join us for more fun. I'd like that, okay."

"Sure. That sounds good."

The effects of lack of sleep and major alcohol consumption affect Luke's thinking ability while crossing the parking lot. He's lost track how much he had to drink before climbing into the back seat of Holly's full-sized pick-up. Luke feels out of place in the mild night air after leaving cold conditions the previous day and doesn't realize he no longer has his hoodie or coat. Holly climbs into the driver's side and turns to ask Luke a suggestive question.

"Are you ready to have a real good time with me?"

Luke's fumbling with the seatbelt but stops to give Holly the thumbs up sign.

'My head's spinning.'

Luke's vision blurs but makes out Holly's warm smile before she starts the truck. They drive northwest from the city and speed down the highway for twenty five minutes before Holly's pulling into someone's driveway. Several other trucks follow behind her and everyone stumbles inside the house to drink, play pool, and listen to more music Luke doesn't recognize. Holly moves closer to Luke and puts her arm around him.

"Let's dance."

"I can't dance, I don't dance. Dance with the other guys."

Holly's persistent.

"We can slow dance. Y'all can do that, right? I'm not interested in the other guys. I want to dance with you."

Holly's inviting, sweet, southern drawl appeals to Luke's inner desires he's thought stayed in Illinois. Holly unbuttons her shirt to further reveal her irresistible breasts and removes her hat and leads Luke to an open place on the floor. He pays more attention to her provocatively short skirt revealing enticing legs in a less crowded setting. Holly leans against Luke's chest and throws her arms around his neck. She rests her head on his chest like it belongs there so Luke detects the tantalizing scent of her fragrant perfume. Her hair brushes against his chin while she leads him through a slow dance. Holly's warm strawberry red lips softly kiss Luke's lips tenderly which tempts him into giving her a second kiss. Holly's hands travel up and down Luke's chest while they continue kissing more passionately. Holly lets one hand go under Luke's shirt and move upward so he feels her gentle touch on his skin while she whispers her seductive request.

"I want to take you home with me."

Luke catches sight of another woman pull her shirt off before fumbling with a cowboy's belt and pull him into another room. Holly lightly bites Luke's lower lip playfully to send a clear message about her intentions. Luke nods eagerly before she slides her hand down the front of his body and continues below his waist.

"You do want to go home with me, big boy."

Holly smiles and grabs Luke's hand to lead him to her truck while Laurie sadly watches the taillights disappear into the darkness.

ELEVEN

Luke shifts his thoughts over to his first chaotic day at the ranch. The screen door slams shut to gain the attention from a group of men at the corral. They watch a stranger nearly fall down the deck stairs. The men dress in jeans, long-sleeved button-down shirts, and cowboy boots. They're leaning against a tall chain-link fence and watch Luke stagger towards them. The excruciating throbbing in his head masks the silence surrounding him. The sun's blinding rays force him to squint through watering eyes and barely distinguish a blurred collection of figures in the distance. Luke's t-shirt is inside out and backwards and he staggers since his gym shoes are on the wrong feet. His tongue feels as if he's licked an old dirty shag carpet several times. Luke's demons normally prevented him from drinking more but now he's severely hung over and regretting the previous night. His thoughts are fuzzy and scattered after a sleepless night and he's unsure where he is or how he got there.

The alcohol's sickening effects are magnified by the hot humid air. Luke's breathing is shallow and labored after leaving the air-conditioned house. Luke stops at a waist high Prickly Pear Cactus surrounded by stately Bluebonnets, bright red-orange Indian Paintbrush along with fragrant yellow Large Buttercups. Luke finds it surreal to be so close to a live cactus and looks at Pecan trees, Cedars, and Live Oaks in full foliage in late March. Luke doesn't recognize anything he's staring at.

Ben Ross, Cody Davis, and Billy Wilson smile and step forward to greet Luke. Jake Jones, his older brother Jesse Jones, Henry Johnson and Jack Wilson, Billy's older brother stay put. Ben speaks with a deep, slow Texas drawl.

"Howdy stranger. Afternoon. Who might you be and what brings y'all here?"

Ben extends a rough, calloused hand to shake Luke's hand. Luke feels the strength of his grip while Ben notes Luke's soft, smooth hand during their handshake.

'Strong grip but baby smooth hands. Probably ain't used to real work.'

Ben's considered country strong and a mountain of a man with a barrel chest. He stands six feet six inches and weighs a very fit two hundred and seventy pounds. The guys joke he'll eat anything that doesn't eat him first. His brown hair and sideburns have touches of gray and his cheerful eyes reveal age lines at forty-three. Ben's recently retired his rodeo spurs since youth has begun to give way to middle-age. He's been a champion steer wrestler, also known as bulldogging, and calf roper in his younger days besides playing football which he now coaches. Nowadays he's the ranch foreman and enjoys working and riding horses every day for Chester on the Twisted Live Oak Ranch.

Ben's alert but relaxed since his pistol's holstered but easily drawn. No one knows why Luke's at the ranch but they all have the same thought how he arrived. One singular person could be responsible for a stranger being on the ranch before the season opens. Luke's first question exposes many truths to the men.

"Where am I?"

Ben glances sideways before answering Luke.

"Surely y'all must know you're at the Twisted Live Oak Ranch, right?"

Ben's deep, slow, thick Texas drawl reminds Luke of the clichéd Texas cowboy in the old westerns. Ben scrutinizes Luke's bloodshot eyes and detects the heavy odor of alcohol emanating from him as Luke weaves back and forth to maintain his balance. Luke replies testily.

"I wouldn't ask if I knew where I was."

Luke struggles to process anything in summer-like heat in his exhausted state. Southerly breezes from the Gulf of Mexico bring an early heat wave to spring. These men don't appeared bothered by the heat and mugginess.

"We'll help ya any way we can but first, we need to give y'all a proper Texas welcome."

Ben glances at the others with a mischievous grin and chooses to have fun with a lost northerner.

"I would appreciate any help you can give me."

"I'll, pardon me, we'll be glad to help you, sir. First, what's your name?"

"Luke."

"Well Luke, we're fixin' to exercise this horse behind me and y'all can help us out. You look like the right height since we have to set the stirrups properly for the intended rider."

Luke's eyes widen when he hears there's a horse nearby.

"I don't ride horses."

"Not to worry. This is the nicest, sweetest horse you'll ever meet. We call him a Bufford 'cause he's so easy to ride. Do us a favor and just sit in the saddle. Then we'll get you anywhere y'all wanna go."

Ben's convincing act works since Luke's clouded mind can't see through the ruse.

"You don't really need to me to sit on that horse, do you?"

"Yes sir, simply get on, then jump off, alright."

Luke has no idea the trouble he's being led into while the others suppress their laughter.

"I don't know."

Ben repeats his request.

"I'm sure y'all can help us."

Luke's doing his best to hide his fear of the horse when he reluctantly nods.

"Alright, climb the chute fence and settle onto the kack, or saddle to y'all, we'll take it from there."

Luke's glancing between Ben and the horse in a small enclosure separated from the actual corral. He hesitates before nervously climbing the fence and studies the undersized saddle.

"Bullet's quite the ride. Take him for a short walk around the arena while we figure out these stirrups."

Luke's impulse is to jump off when Bullet snorts and settles down again. Luke tenses up while Billy steps up to the gate.

'What am I getting into?'

Luke's childhood fear and bitter memories of his terrifying pony ride at the circus grip him deeply. His dad walked beside him until the pony threw him off and bit his right arm. Luke ran through the crowd to escape the horrible beast but his dad easily caught up to comfort him.

"I don't like horses anymore, Daddy."

"It's okay Tex, we can stay away from the horses. You're okay. I'll protect you. I'll always protect you."

Ben's voice snaps Luke out of his recollection.

"Alright, we're gonna open the gate so Bullet can step into the arena. Sit still, hold on the saddle horn, and stay quiet, understand?"

Luke doesn't notice Billy's crouching down as if he's trying to remain unseen once Ben nods and gives Luke a friendly smile.

"Let Bullet loose."

The horse shudders and lurches forward then calms down to step into the arena before all hell breaks loose. Dust clouds the air once Bullet repeatedly jumps and violently kicks his rear legs out behind him. The horse spins one direction and then reverses the other way while Luke hangs on and hears the guys laughing and talking.

"Whoa Lordy! Look at that horse blow up!"

"Now he's startin' to suck back."

Luke grips the saddle horn tighter and keeps his legs firmly tucked against the horse's sides.

"This guy's pullin' leather pretty good."

"Yup, he sure is grabbin' the apple and mashin' up like a pro."

Luke remains on the uncontrollable horse while flashbacks of school kids cruelly laughing at him blend with the men howling outside the fence. After what seems like an eternity to Luke but is only eight seconds in reality, Bullet stops bucking long enough to allow Luke to jump off. He runs for the fence while someone calls out.

"Whaddya know. Bullet's a Union Animal."

Luke scales the chain link fence in one swift motion to flee the wild horse. Luke's overcome by nausea and unsettled nerves outside the corral.

"That guy just rode Bullet for eight seconds. No one's done that."

The ride and residual effects of alcohol cause Luke to unceremoniously throw up in front of the guys. They're entertained at the resulting misery but don't anticipate Luke's reaction to their merciless joke. He catches his breath while Billy drops to his knees with hysterical laughter and double over. Luke's reminded of his tormented past and loses control and charges Ben without warning. No one notices Luke rush in fast and hard to strike lightning fast with a fist to Ben's jaw. Luke's assault ends with an unmistakable thud and grunt being heard before Ben crumbles to the ground and lays motionless. His rapid pace knocks several others over as well. The men believe Ben will stand up and pummel Luke but he remains completely still.

"Ben? Ben? Y'all okay? Hey Ben, Cowboy Up."

Ben usually shook off serious blows in his rodeo days or fights and was always known as a tough hombre. A moment passes and still no movement from Ben has the guys concerned when they notice blood trickling from the corner of his mouth. A reddening mark's developing as well. Luke's glaring defiantly at everyone before growling out a challenge.

"Who's next?"

His clenched fists indicate he's ready to deliver more punishment and his fury is fed by fear and panic. Luke wants to punish all who put him into harm's way but the thundering sound of a gunshot prevents anyone from responding.

TWELVE

Luke continues his jail cell reminiscing about the first day at the ranch.

Chester Kinkead surprises the men with his early return by advancing unnoticed up the long red gravel driveway. Chester witnessed Luke riding Bullet but trees had blocked Luke's assault on Ben. He's perplexed to find Ben lying unconscious on the ground and his men nearby. Luke turns to see what created the explosive sound while everyone else backs off in case Chester fires a second time.

Chester's tall, lean, yet imposing for an older man with a shotgun aimed directly at Luke. One barrel smolders while he stands next to his truck fiercely scowling from under his furrowed somewhat bushy white eyebrows. His gravelly voice gruffly barks out his order while surveying the scene.

"Don't y'all move a muscle or I'll ruin your day!"

Chester prefers a neatly organized ranch and gets irritated to notice a piece of lumber near Ben. He's a tough Marine who doesn't like surprises and especially doesn't like strangers on his ranch. He reaches into his truck for his black cowboy hat and covers his white military influenced hairstyle before pointedly questioning his ranch hands.

"First of all, what the hell's goin' on?"

Chester glares at his men's pale, wide-eyed expressions because they realize they're in trouble.

"Is this what happens when I leave the ranch?"

Chester's rules are clear and they know he doesn't take kindly to anyone breaking them. Period. He approaches Ben to see the deep reddish-purple bruise developing on his jaw and barks out another order.

"Get your truck, Billy. Cody'll help y'all take Ben to the hospital. Jesse, call the sheriff 'n git him here now."

They respond simultaneously.

"Yes sir."

Billy sprints to his truck. Cody steps towards Ben but limps and winces. Chester takes notice.

"Cody, your ankle still acting up?"

"Yes sir."

"Get that looked at if y'all need more therapy."

"Yes sir."

Chester's tone softens addressing Cody before returning his attention to Luke who signals he has no inclination of backing down. His eyes possess the fiery look of a wild mustang and seems unconcerned a gun's pointed at him. A loud whisper is heard from the group.

"Ya think he'll try hittin' Mr. Kinkead?"

Chester heatedly responds.

"He ain't gonna git close enough to hit me."

Luke ignores the double-barrel shotgun during his angered response.

"If you belong to these shitheads then you deserve a beating too."

"I'm fixin' to shoot ya and figure out a reason later unless I have y'all arrested. But first, who are you and why are you on my ranch. Why'd y'all hurt my lead wrangler?"

Luke's stance stiffens after Chester's threat to shoot him.

"You'd go to jail if you shoot me. Go ahead, call the cops. Your boys put me on a horse that nearly killed me."

"Y'all're in Texas. We do things differently here. In case you ain't noticed yet."

Ben's regaining consciousness and moans in agony and reaches for his jaw. He groans louder when he tries speaking so Chester wonders if Ben's jaw is broken.

"Y'all check on Ben."

Luke's indifferent Ben's injured after his horrifying ride on Bullet. Billy arrives with his truck and Cody helps get Ben into the back seat so they can head to the hospital. The guys worry Ben's seriously hurt and won't be able to lead them daily. Chester gives Luke another order.

"Move your ass to the fence."

Luke glances at the fence and Bullet.

"I'll stay here if you don't mind."

Chester angrily growls.

"I do mind. Move! Or else."

Chester motions towards the fence with his shotgun while Luke's fear rebuilds about the horse.

"I'd rather stay here."

Luke seems fearless of Chester and his gun until he menacingly shoves the barrels into Luke's taut stomach.

"Move or I'll cut you in half and feed you to the buzzards."

Chester's intense glare matches his verbal threat. Luke grasps Chester's willing to pull the trigger so he tries to defend himself while backing up.

"They started it. You can't just shoot me."

Chester chuckles while sizing Luke up.

"Stop sounding like an eight year old. You don't understand your situation here, do ya? You're trespassin' on my property. By that right, I can shoot you dead and defend myself in court for protectin' myself and my property. I've got signs posted stating that very warning 'round my ranch."

Luke's alarmed expression precedes Chester's next comment for Luke to ponder.

"Here's some words of wisdom for you to remember, never put a bird feeder where you don't want bird shit."

Luke's dumbfounded by Chester's statement.

"What the hell does that mean?"

"Think about it and the answer'll come to you. Someday. Maybe."

THIRTEEN

Luke watches a sheriff's squad approach Chester's position and the driver's window drop down.

"Howdy, Chester. What's new?"

Chester's focus remains on Luke.

"Just a regular day at the Twisted Live Oak."

"Is that so? How'd you explain the call 'bout a fight 'n shot fired here?"

Luke studies the sheriff when he gets out and notes his pot belly and balding head before he puts a white cowboy hat on. His worn expression and fatigued eyes from a long day and perhaps a long career makes Luke think he's in his sixties.

"I did find an unexpected varmint runnin' 'round my ranch needin' extermination."

"Ya don't say?"

"Yup."

"Maybe we should consider a different option, like relocating the varmint to a jail cell."

Chester glances wordlessly at the sheriff.

"Now Chester, if you go and shoot this fine upstanding gentleman it'll make for a lot of paperwork and I'll miss dinner with the chief."

The sheriff removes his white straw cowboy hat to wipe the sweat from his brow with a neckerchief. He raises both eyebrows which profoundly creases his forehead before putting his hat on again. Luke recognizes this is his chance to plead his case with the sheriff.

"Officer, don't let this guy shoot me. He's crazy. I didn't do anything wrong."

Chester replies indignantly.

"Nothin' wrong? My foreman's headed to the hospital with a broke jaw. Y'all're ridin' my prized buckin' bronc without permission. You're trespassin' on my land. There's a few things wrong here."

Bob Fisher's been sheriff for years and known Chester far longer so they read each other quite well. He decides to infuse a little fun into the situation.

"Chester, I'm gonna make this easy for everyone."

Bob pauses to examine Luke.

"Well, almost everyone."

He unholsters his pistol without warning and aims it at Luke.

"I'll shoot the varmint and we'll bury him where nobody'll find him."

Luke steps back against the fence after Bob's announcement. He's too stunned to have any idea Bob's safety is still set while Chester's shotgun is aimed at Luke. Bullet's presence is forgotten in the moment.

"You'll lose your job if you shoot him."

"Naw. I'll shoot him and we'll feed him to the worms. No body, no crime."

Luke's exhausted state and hungover condition hinders his comprehension for what's transpiring between the two men. His heart rate increases during the troubling seconds and wonders if he'll escape alive.

"I can't letcha shoot him. I'll do it. You're my witness I was defending myself. My men won't say a word."

Luke's frightened state is apparent when he speaks in a stressed higher tone.

"Hold on! Wait a minute! Do I get to say anything or have a chance to run from this crazy place?"

Chester addresses Bob while raising his shotgun and steps aside.

"Alright, shoot him so he don't annoy me anymore. My don't give a damn's just taken the day off."

"No on second thought you're right, Chester. You should be the one to shoot him."

Chester's odd banter baffles his men who wonder what will happen. Luke's very confused when Bob and Chester burst into laughter and watches Chester slap Bob on the back. Luke's worried what could happen when Bob questions Chester again.

"You sure y'all don't want me to shoot him for ya?"

"Bob, Sue, the chief, she'd have our hides on the side of that barn if we did a fool thing like that."

Bob tips his hat upwards and rubs his clean-shaven chubby chin.

"Yeah buddy, she'd definitely have our hides for doin' that."

Bob gets serious and faces Luke.

"Got any ID?"

Luke's hand trembles while giving Bob his license. Bob returns to the squad and waits for any information.

"No outstanding warrants or priors. Mr. Luke Anderson from Chicago, unless you can provide a good reason why you're in Texas, silence is your best friend."

Chester contemplates Luke's punishment while Bob waits for the information.

'Sittin' in jail's too easy for Ben's injury.'

"Bob, can I have a word with you?"

Chester looks at Luke.

"Move an inch and I'll drop your sorry ass where you stand."

Chester's keeping tabs on Luke during his conversation with Bob and stops speaking when a bewildered expression emerges. He removes his hat to scratch his head and puts it on again while watching Bullet lick and bite his lips and slightly shaking his head up and down.

'Bullet's submitting to Luke. He's shown nothin' but contempt for everyone on the ranch.'

Bullet's considered rank or a Honker since no one's able to stay on his back for more than two seconds. Escaping without being kicked or bit is nearly impossible and Bullet claims the distinction as the second meanest bucking horse Chester's ever owned. The meanest was sold to a Stock contractor up north. Chester becomes serious and Bob speaks first whey they approach Luke again.

"Chester, Mr. Kinkead, has convinced me not to shoot you and in fact has also convinced me to allow him to take custody of you. You'll work off your criminal behavior here."

Luke's relieved he's not getting arrested but unsure about staying at the ranch and blankly stares at both men.

"I'm not going to jail?"

"Nope, but you'll want to after a couple days on Chester's ranch."

Luke's puzzled by this odd turn of events.

"I don't understand."

Chester adds to the conversation.

"I'm entertainin' a thought."

Luke replies sarcastically.

"Somehow I doubt I'll find your thought entertaining."

"Shut your mouth and don't interrupt when I'm talkin'. Y'all are gonna stay here on the Twisted Live Oak Ranch and pay your debt to me until I decide when you can leave."

The sheriff clarifies.

"Sorta like house arrest."

"If ya git outta line or think of runnin', you'll end up in jail, or dead."

"This can't be legal, can it?"

"I'm alright with Chester's proposal. Less work for me. You're about to learn a hard-earned, well deserved lesson about goin' where y'all don't belong. Just know this, if I return for anything other than a social visit, y'all are off to jail for assault, trespassin', and whatever else I decide to charge you with."

Bob's stern words match his expression causing Luke to respond the most fitting way possible.

"Yes sir."

"Good answer. I best check in with Sue. She gets rather antsy 'n on'ry if I don't. Here's your license, stay outta trouble."

Chester gets an idea watching Luke take his license back from Bob. Bob heads for his car but stops to look back at Chester.

"Remember, Chester, you can't shoot him unless he does somethin' to justify it."

Bob's malicious laugh and behavior creates an uneasiness within Luke.

FOURTEEN

Chester's studying Luke while the sheriff disappears down the long winding gravel driveway.

'Wonder what this guy's thinkin'.'

"Time to get a few things straight right now."

Chester's rough, gravelly voice imparts a confident assertiveness regarding his decision to keep Luke on the ranch. Chester notices Luke's defiant eyes drift towards the driveway and issues a warning.

"Y'all ain't beating a bullet to the end of the driveway."

Luke glances at Chester but his eyes shift back to the white Toyota Tundra crew cab pick-up driving towards them.

'What are my chances of making it out of here?'

Luke's unfamiliar with guns but believes a shotgun only scatters its pellets so if he gets far enough away he won't get shot. He's unaware of the actual range a shotgun shell can have in the hands of a trained expert.

"The sheriff says I'm stuck here. That's the story of my life. I have no control over it."

"First of all, I need to figure out where your parents went wrong raisin' you."

Chester's clearly irritated by Luke's presence even if it's his idea to keep him on the ranch. The pick-up's arrival is tied to his early return. Luke's defiant stance wilts after Chester insults his parents and deeply strikes a painful chord.

"My family abandoned me. I had no control over that either."

Chester hears Luke's repeated complaint about not having control of his life.

"You do control your life with the decisions y'all make every day. Losing control is mostly an illusion or excuse used by lazy irresponsible people when things go wrong. They blame a boss, or debt, or whatever suits them in the moment. Makin' better choices and decisions builds a better life. That's control."

Luke ignores Chester's message.

'I had no control when I lost my parents when I was ten.'

Chester's concealing thoughts of his own.

'The devil took control from Millie, me, and this ranch.'

"Do you ever picture yourself having control of your life? Have you tried makin' it a reality?"

Luke remains silent.

"I do own your ass and you don't control that."

The truck slowly rolls to a stop under the dark green leafy canopy of several Live Oaks. Chester's blunt statement has Luke wanting to punch him. Luke's mood changes once a tall, stunningly beautiful woman emerges from the truck. Two Mourning Doves flutter to the ground before hastily retreating to a branch above her truck. They gently coo while shafts of sunlight illuminate the woman beneath the lush natural umbrella. Luke's eyes are drawn upward to the commotion before resuming his focus on this woman. Her unexpected presence captivates Luke and Chester notes his irate glare soften. His narrowed eyes widen and his expression turns non-aggressive while his fists unclench. Luke's awe-struck by her appearance which pacifies his attitude.

"Chester, I just saw Bob leavin', is everythin' alright? Who's this?"

Hope Cooper's waist length black hair is pulled into a pony tail and resembles a horse's elegantly styled tail. A worn whitish-yellow straw cowboy hat with a feather protruding from the hat band covers her head. This woman's distinctive almond-shaped eyes possess pronounced suspicion but still pull Luke in. Her eye color is shielded by the hat's brim but lock onto Luke for an entirely different reason. Luke's blinded by her stunning appearance and captivated by her alluring voice during this inescapable moment. He's oblivious to being spellbound by her eyes unrivalled shape and can't shift his gaze away from Hope. Luke forgets Linda's betrayal and his new troubles.

'This woman's gorgeous. Who is she? I've never seen anyone so beautiful in my life. Those eyes.'

Hope lowers her right hand to her nine-millimeter Taurus PT 111 Millennium G2 pistol while Luke's hazy mind struggles with his new reality. Hope's extremely proficient with the weapon. Luke detects her movement without understanding her deliberate action behind the truck's door. Chester points towards the furthest barn.

"Hope, get started, I'll meetcha'll at the barn in a few minutes."

Luke realizes Hope's wearing medical scrubs and carries a black bag. He also notices the pistol strapped to her side.

'Oh, she was reaching for that.'

Hope stares at Luke with distrustful eyes during her departure.

'Why would a vet carry a gun? Why is she staring at me like I stole something?'

Hope's eyes hold Luke's attention so intensely he's forgotten Chester's close by with a shotgun aimed at him.

'I've only experienced this once before.'

Chester interrupts Luke's thoughts.

"How did you wind up on my ranch?"

Luke wipes sweat from his eyes before idly running his hand through his hair while sorting out the previous night's events.

"I can't remember much about last night."

Another woman bolts from the house and hollers at Chester.

"Grand-daddy, what are you doing? He's my guest."

Chester's men snicker knowing they guessed correctly while Chester looks dismayed.

'Hopefully this lady can clear things up and I can leave.'

Luke looks towards Chester to his furious expression.

"Your guest?"

Chester glares at Luke.
"What've you been doin' with my grand-daughter?"
'Oh shit.'
Luke mumbles under his breath.
"Grand-daughter? I did not see that coming."

This new development seems like a far worse situation than the wild horse and knocking someone out.

'So much for getting off the ranch this way.'

Luke swallows hard at the thought that this pissed off rancher thinks Luke's fooled around with his grand-daughter.

'She looks familiar but I can't place why?'

This woman's hair is braided into a pony tail under a burnt orange baseball cap.

'I don't remember doing anything.'

Chester tightens his grip on his shotgun and shoves it back into Luke's belly and reconsiders why Luke's at the ranch.

'Is this guy a con man or hustler? He came here with Holly. The way he looked at Hope. Maybe he's tryin' to swindle Holly from her money. Would he go after Hope? I see why Holly'd go after this guy. She could care less if he's a womanizer.'

The sudden overall silence seems deafening to Luke even though his head still hurts from the prior night's drinking.

'I really can't recall anything.'

"Grand-daddy, he didn't do anything. Really!"

Her voice resonates with disappointment during a quick glance with big blue inviting eyes towards Luke. Luke's focus stays on Chester.

'He's a real threat.'

"I felt bad. He was so drunk and had nowhere to go."

Chester's glaring at his grand-daughter.

"Holly, y'all gotta stop this behavior. You bring a complete stranger here. How many times do I need to tell ya to quit doin' this? Start thinkin' smart like an adult. Your bad decisions are gonna get someone hurt worse than Ben did today."

"What happened to Ben?"

Holly's long glance at Luke again allows him to study her face before she moves between the two men.

"Is Ben okay?"

Chester slides over to keep a clear shot at Luke. The woman's dressed in torn jeans and a plain blue t-shirt.

'She looks vaguely familiar but why?'

Luke takes another long look at the woman.

"Holly? Is that you? You look different from last night."

"Yes, um, uh, Luke?"

Holly's not wearing make-up or skimpy clothing.

Chester's irritated Holly struggles to remember Luke's name.

"This is where I live and work. I don't always dress like you saw last night."

Chester's next comment insults Luke.

"It sounds like y'all can't drink."

Holly attempts to defend Luke.

"He did try to keep up with us, Grand-daddy."

Chester's cross when he cuts her off.

"Go back inside, Holly. I'll take care of this."

Holly's phone rings to prevent her response.

"Howdy, Jazlynn. Can I call ya back? I'm in the middle of somethin'. Okay, thanks."

Chester's aggravated by whose name he hears Holly say.

"That trouble maker ain't back, is she?"

"No, Grand-daddy, Jazzy's still trainin' for body building shows in Florida."

"Thank God. She's a worse influence on you than y'all are on anyone."

"Grand-daddy, be nice."

"That is me bein' nice."

Chester stops Holly from saying anything else.

"You'd best leave now while this guy's still breathing. I need to figure this out."

Chester's frustrated to know Holly's brought Luke to the ranch. It undercuts part of his reasoning to punish Luke. Holly slowly starts to walk away but both men witness her come-hither smile inviting Luke to follow her.

'I'll finish what I started if Grand-daddy don't kill him first.'

Chester's focus is on Luke and Holly until noticing the cowboys dispersing and issues a warning to them.

"There's gonna be a meetin' later to review ranch rules."

Luke's gratified to see fear on their faces but feels shamed by Holly's implication he can't drink.

"I'm not used to drinking that much. I don't even know what I drank last night. Holly and her friends bought a lot of shots and beers."

"My own grand-daughter out drank you? Am I supposed to be proud of her or laugh at you? Holly probably chose Wild Turkey and Tito's to go with the beer."

Chester's berating humiliates Luke which makes him angry.

"I'll ruin your day and the rest of your life if you touch my grand-daughter again. You understand me, boy?"

Chester's shotgun lowers below Luke's belt to make his point.

"Yeah, I guess so."

"You guess so? No. You don't guess so. You know so!"

"Don't touch your grand-daughter, fine. But if she touches me...'

"Holly'll understand not to get within a country mile of you. Or I'll put you six feet under or in jail to make my point."

"Today's definitely ruined. I don't need any more days ruined."

Luke's thinking about Chester's threat before recalling something Holly said.

"Holly said I'm her guest. That means I'm not trespassing which also means I can leave."

"You ain't goin' nowhere. Y'all injured Ben and you rode a horse ya ain't supposed to get near."

"He put me on your stupid horse. It's his own fault he got hurt."

"You're still whining like an eight year old. I need to figure out what I'm gonna do with you while I take care of why I'm actually here for."

Chester rubs his snowy shaded stubble with his thumb and index finger and contemplates his dilemma until someone walks out of the closer barn.

"Scooter!"

The man waves but continues towards the other barn.

"Scooter, git over here and help me out."

The man turns and heads for Chester.

"Yes sir, how can I help you?"

Scooter eyes Luke suspiciously while his words reveal he's not from Texas.

"The tools are sharpened, cleaned, and put away."

His accent announces his Irish roots. He lived in Ireland until a chance meeting with Chester in a pub and subsequently moved to Texas to work on the ranch.

"Take my shotgun and watch this guy while I go check in with Hope and my mare. I also need to have a meetin' to discuss the ranch rules with my wranglers."

Chester reloads the empty barrel and hands the gun to Scooter.

"You want me to hold your gun on him until you return?"

"Yup."

"Can I do it from the deck so I can sit and rest me weary bones?"

"Yeah, y'all can sit and rest, but he stays standing, got it?"

Scooter grins.

"I hear you loud and clear, sir."

"If he gets outta line, you have my permission to shoot 'im."

Luke worries Chester's evil grin could lead to Scooter shooting him. Scooter motions Luke towards the house and settles himself into a rocking chair.

'Chester's got a damn good reason if he's aimin' a gun at someone.'

Scooter emits a loud sigh and rests the shotgun across his lap before taking off his hat. His neatly groomed red beard doesn't match the gray streaked hair on his head growing in different directions. Scooter refers to it as the windswept look while everyone else simply calls it unruly.

Luke inspects the coarse, fresh cut Saint Augustinegrass under his feet and takes in the rich odor of the mowed lawn. The lush green environment is actually teeming with lively sounds and so unlike the cold dead world Luke left behind. Scooter spots Dallisgrass weeds in the lawn to disrupt the clean appearance Chester prefers once guests arrive.

'I'll spray those later.'

The irrigation system is designed to keep specific areas green during the long hot summer months. Several strategically planted fragrant Texas Whitebuds bloom nearby to mask the odor of manure. Luke shifts his focus to his throbbing head and stiff muscles which ache from inactivity before a sound catches his attention. The imposing yet agonized lonesome screech of an unseen hawk reminds Luke how he would scream out in the middle of the night for his deceased parents. Dreadful memories cause his heart to pound while newly created despair forms. Scooter notices Luke shifting uncomfortably from foot to foot and knowingly scans the ground and sees a Fire Ant mound.

"Cead Mile Failte. Although you've already worn out every one of 'em. Move over and get the little buggers off you. Fire Ants sting and bite and a few are annoying but a lot all at once is worse. They won't kill ya but they'll irritate the living daylights out of you."

Luke rips his shoes and socks off while listening to Scooter's brogue resonate with great pleasure. He shakes his shoes and socks and brushes his legs off. Scooter chuckles while whitish spots begin puffing up on Luke's ankles and feet.

"Looks like karma's catching up to you for hurtin' Ben."

"Shut up."

"Pog Mo Thoin."

"Do you know anything about me?

"Nope. Don't care either. You're the asshole that hurt Ben."

"Just remember what you don't know can put you in the hospital or the morgue when you challenge an unknown opponent. So kiss my ass."

Scooter's unsure how to process Luke's threat and wonders if he understood his Gaelic insult or simply stated a common phrase. Luke resents Scooter's insults and being ignored like he doesn't exist but still presses for information about the ranch, Chester, and even about Hope. Birds and insects join the occasional horse whinnying to break up the silence.

Chester met Scooter O'Connor at a pub in Ireland during a business trip to Lisburn and Moira and second honeymoon with Millie. Chester's family lineage led back to Northern Ireland where he discovered the Irish loved horses as much as Texans along with a good drink. Chester intervened after hearing Scooter beg the pub owner for a drink and offer his horse as payment.

"Give the man a drink. I'll pay. Why would y'all want to sell such a beautiful animal for only a drink?"

Scooter's unwilling to share his shame with a stranger but the pub owner explains the situation.

"Scooter trained riders for horse racing until a wealthy owner saw to it he'd never train again after his son was killed while being trained by Scooter."

Chester orders a second drink for Scooter and walks around town to ask people for information and only hears good comments. He learns Scooter's a good man in a bad situation and happens to be one of the finest horse trainers in Ireland. A boyhood friend gave him the nick-name 'Scooter' since he was always under foot and told to scoot out of the way. Chester returns to the pub to find Scooter's finishing the second pint.

"Can I buy y'all another drink and discuss a business proposition?"

Scooter smiles while eagerly accepting the offer for another drink.

"You're the kind of yank I like to see around here."

"I'm no yank, I'm a Texan."

Millie joins Chester to discuss the proposition which Scooter accepts and travels to America with his horse once Chester files the necessary paperwork and helps Scooter become a citizen also.

"There's going to be two parties when I leave. One in my honor and one because I'm leaving."

Scooter laughs at his own joke to show his sense of humor hadn't diminished during the challenging times and piques Chester's curiosity.

"How do you stay so happy?"

"I love God and I know He loves me. I enjoy that He allows me to wake up here and keep our friendship at a distance."

Chester couldn't argue with Scooter's way of thinking.

SIXTEEN

Chester assists Hope during the birth of the foal before heading off to have a heated meeting with the men about breaking ranch rules. A couple hours pass before he returns to relieve Scooter while Hope finishes monitoring the mare discharge the placenta and report the full results to Chester. He waits in his own personal rocking chair which has a matched chair next to his. The other chairs cross pieces differ from each other. Luke asks a question at the same moment Chester catches sight of Hope walking towards him and delivers a sternly worded southern expression.

"Never miss a good chance to shut up."

Chester would rather discuss the foal's birth with Hope than deal with Luke. Hope's clearly repulsed by Luke's presence after Jake informed her Luke injured Ben although his version omitted what initiated the altercation. Luke's spellbound by her beautiful green eyes when she passes him.

'She has a hawk's feather in her hat.'

Luke detects a sweet intoxicating scent blending with the odor of horse.

'It must be her shampoo.'

Hope settles into a rocking chair on Chester's right side so Luke's able to see her disgust. She's appalled Luke's still at the ranch instead of in jail. Hope's scorching hatred sears through Luke while she glares at him even though her eyes also hold his attention. Luke steps back to stretch and loosen his muscles again until Hope jumps to her feet and aims her gun at him. Chester's focus shifts to Luke while she snarls a command.

"Don't move asshole!"

Luke instinctively raises his hands after Hope's unexpected hostility startles him.

"Whoa! Hold on! Hold on! I'm trying to stretch not run. Trust me."

"Trust you? I don't trust y'all any further 'n I can throw you."

Hope inspects Luke more closely. She locks eyes with him before her inquisitive, yet suspicious eyes descend to view how he's dressed. She studies his arms while he holds them up.

'His arms are muscular and he has a scar on his upper right arm.'

Hope re-examines Luke's face and stares into his hazel-colored eyes.

'He's got a predator's deadened gaze, like hiding some cunning thought or deceptive intelligence like Colt. He could be dangerous.'

A thought surprises Hope during her inspection of Luke.

'He's sort of good lookin'. It's a shame this piece of shit hurt Ben. Wait. Why would I even think that? I'm not interested in anyone.'

Luke notices Hope inexplicably bites her lower lip during the moment it takes for her to examine him.

'Linda does the same thing when she wants sex. I'm confused.'

Hope blinks and coldly restates her warning.

"Move another muscle asshole and I'll do what Chester hasn't yet."

Chester's confused by Hope's extended observation of Luke.

'What's up with Hope? She ain't been interested to look at a guy that long in years. She usually ignores 'em all. Do I need to file this away for the future?'

Luke realizes Hope's threat is serious while regaining his composure and lowering his arms. His perplexed stare becomes an intimidating glare to challenge the ferocity in Hope's emerald eyes. She's issued her second threat with unwavering deliberateness in a flattened tone unlike her conversation with Chester. Hope's alluring angelic Texas drawl a man could get lost in has been replaced by a cold harsh tone during her command to Luke.

"Are all you people ready to shoot strangers for no reason? What's wrong with you?"

Hope's finger tightens around the trigger but Luke shows no fear during her ominous action.

"If I keep squeezing I'll put you out of my misery."

'No lady, you'll put me out of my misery.'

Chester watches with concerned curiosity.

'Would Hope shoot someone without proper cause?'

Luke's icy response shocks Hope and Chester while his eyes challenge her to carry out the threat.

"Go ahead. Death doesn't scare me. I've seen the Grim Reaper's face."

Hope shudders after Luke's stone-cold response which softens her angered expression. Luke's defiant until recognizing Hope's finger squeezing the trigger.

"Hope, no…"

Chester starts speaking until the deafening roar echoes across the ranch. Hope inconspicuously shifts her aim so the bullet screams past Luke's right ear and strikes the dirt far behind him. Hope feels her warning shot validates she can enforce her lethal point until Luke sarcastically responds after several seconds pass.

"You missed."

Luke's unruffled retort irks Hope. Chester's impressed by Luke's casual reaction.

'This guy's got gumption, I'll give him that.'

Luke's felt half-dead for so long that he'd welcome actual death to end his pained existence. His will to live has eroded since misplaced guilt and losing Linda to another man suppresses his survival instincts. Oddly, despite his present exhibition, Hope's presence tugs at his heart to confuse his emotional state during this unsettling moment.

'I'd be okay if Hope shot me dead but I also feel lucky to be alive. Why?'

Scooter re-emerges from the closest barn to see Hope aiming her pistol at Luke and shakes his head before disappearing again. Another man exits several minutes later and heads for the house at a slow gait. Chester addresses Hope before the man nears the house.

"Hope, re-holster your pistol, please. I don't think this guy's tryin' to run."

Hope's distinctive, piercing eyes don't leave Luke.

"Y'all don't know that."

Chester stands to face Hope and places his hand on her gun and pushes gently downward.

"Hope, don't do somethin' stupid, alright."

Hope's eyes drift to Chester while her pistol remains pointed in Luke's direction.

"Stupid? Stupid? More stupid than keeping this asshole at the ranch? Instead of lettin' Bob haul him off to jail."

"Somethin' convinced me to keep him here."

Luke interjects his own comment.

"Or shot."

"You can shut up still. Sit your sorry ass down until I figure out what I'm gonna do with y'all."

"Wait, you don't even have an idea yet? Great."

SEVENTEEN

Luke sighs once Hope finally re-holsters her pistol and sits on the steps. Hope's hypnotic green, almond shaped eyes captivate him again. Their elongated contour exudes a sexy allure which appeals to inner desires Luke's trying to bury again. Hope's scrubs cannot fully conceal her overall beauty.

'I don't get it. Hope nearly shot me so why do I feel anything because of her?'

Luke imagines what Hope would look like smiling until she realizes he's staring at her. Hope's threatening expression and irate outburst snaps Luke out of his trance.

"Stop looking at me!"

Chester's entertained when Luke looks away only to glance back at Hope again.

'This guy's gonna get so far out on Hope's bad side she'll punish him far worse than I'm plannin' to.'

Luke's glance puzzles Chester.

'His eyes have an honest spark of interest in Hope that was lacking for Holly. Peculiar. Holly's the one who brought him here for her own shameless pleasure. Hope's pointed a gun and shot at him.'

Chester brings his hand to his face to hide an uncontainable smile after watching Luke rest his head against the railing

'Luke seems to be happy Hope put her gun back.'

Chester acts as if he's seriously considering his next move.

'Luke's lucky Hope's firearm training prevents her from shooting someone without proper provocation. Her suspicions about strangers, especially men, serves her well in most cases. This guy has no idea how lucky he is to be breathing after hurtin' Ben. Ben's Hope's adopted big brother and protector.'

The second man glances down at Luke before gazing up at Hope and climbing the stairs.

"Hope, you're so pretty, you'd make a man plow through a stump."

Luke doesn't understand the southern expression but notices Hope's disgust while rolling her eyes and exhale an irritated nasally huff.

"Sam Peterson, I'm not interested in a date with you. I've told ya that a hundred times already."

Chester speaks to break the building tension after Hope's rejection visibly frustrates Sam.

"Hope, I've got everything under control here, why don'tcha go home to Faith?"

Hope's expressive eyes reveal her agitation Chester's mentioned her daughter in front of Luke.

'I don't need this asshole knowing any information about me or Faith.'

"Don't hesitate to shoot this diseased vermin and feed him to the buzzards if he even sneezes wrong."

Luke glares at Hope after her insulting depiction of him.

"I'm right here and I can hear you."

'Wow, she sounds just like the old guy.'

"You're a shithead. I hate you."

"Hate's a strong word to use on a stranger."

"It fits perfectly in this case."

Chester prevents Luke from replying immediately.

"I can handle this, Hope, don't worry."

Holly reappears in semi revealing denim shorts and a white cropped top which shows off her belly piercing. Hope shoots Chester a disbelieving look.

"I'm not so sure anymore."

Luke glances at Holly before Hope steps forward to walk past him.

"FYI, that's my sister, so back off.

Luke speaks up with unconcealed condescension rephrasing Chester's words.

"Go take care of Faith. We'll be just fine here on the ranch."

Chester knowingly grimaces.

'Aw shit. That ain't goin' over well.'

Hope spins around to bark out her stern order before unleashing her wrath.

"Stand up!"

Hope's bitter command erases her alluring drawl while Luke boldly stares back and defiantly throws fuel onto the fire.

"Why? So you can shoot at me again. No thanks. I'm comfortable here."

'You'd think Hope and Chester were related the way they sound.'

Hope's irritated state furrows her brow and narrows her eyes while she grits her teeth. She despises repeating herself to anyone but her daughter.

"Stand up!"

Chester shakes his head.

'This guy'll be dead before sundown today.'

Chester shakes his head while Sam's pleased to watch the show unfold next to Holly. Luke's annoyed before standing to intimidate Hope with his height but realizes she's almost as tall as he is. Luke's eyes remain more focused on Hope's gun not knowing she has other ideas.

'That's right asshole, keep thinkin' that thought.'

Hope motions as if she's going to knee Luke's groin. He reacts to block her move but Hope surprises him and drives her fist squarely into Luke's disrespectful mouth. Her punch is powered by the pent up rage from a lifetime of heartbreaking memories and years of gym workouts and splits Luke's lower lip. Hope's fierce strike is also fueled by frustrated emotions and forces Luke to step back awkwardly out of reach.

'How was she able to hit me? And so hard?'

Chester and Sam burst out laughing while Holly's mystified Hope punched Luke and stunned him.

'Luke's a physical specimen. How could Hope hurt him?'

Hope's quite capable of defending herself since the guys taught her how to properly fight which they regretted when she turned on them. Millie struggled to calm Hope's terrible temper during her youth and leaned on experience from challenges Chester presented after returning from the war.

Hope's hostility turns to shock due to the ferocity of her violent action and gasps before raising her hands to cover her gaping mouth. Chester wonders why Hope's suddenly concerned and would be surprised she's struggling to come to terms with jumbled emotions.

'He deserved what he got but I've never hit anyone that hard before.'

Chester chuckles after noticing Luke's bloodied lip and chin.

'Gotta love a cowgirl. I knew Hope would punish Luke for injuring Ben.'

Hope's wide, fright-filled eyes dart from Chester to Luke and back to Chester while pondering the intense rage she experienced.

'I'm afraid to feel such uncontrolled anger. Faith would be disappointed.'

Luke's troubled his instincts failed to prevent Hope's punch. His sensei and the assistants challenged his defensive capabilities but he posed more of a challenge to them.

'How come I didn't block Hope's punch?'

Hope cannot see Luke's child-like expression because his back is turned to her until she gently touches his shoulder. He whips around and steps back while Hope softly speaks and attempts to touch his chin.

"Let me look at that, please."

Hope's veterinary commitment to care for injuries overtakes her. Crimson fluid flows freely down Luke's chin and drips onto his shirt and ground when he snarls.

"Get away from me! What's wrong with you?"

Luke touches his lip and looks at the blood on his fingertips before Hope becomes more caring even after nearly shooting Luke.

"I'm so sorry."

Luke retreats further when Hope reaches out again.

"I'll take care of myself. I don't need your help."

Chester interjects with a comment.

"Hope, the man doesn't want your help."

Hope's compassion bewilders Chester.

'Hope's not usually concerned with anyone except the guys on the ranch. No male stranger has seen her caring side in years and no one's ruffled her feathers like this guy has.'

Chester's glad Luke hasn't retaliated against Hope's hostility unlike his reaction to Ben earlier. He wonders why Luke defiantly stands up to Hope and her gun though.

'I figured this guy for a hot-headed trouble maker but he might be a bit more complicated than that.'

Chester's comment regarding Luke's rejection for medical aid changes Hope's attitude.

"Right, why did I think this asshole would want my help?"

"Your help? You shot at me, punched me, and then offer to help me. No thanks. I bet your care makes Frankenstein look worse. Apparently southern hospitality doesn't exist here."

"I promise never to offer you my help again."

"Your husband must hate himself for marrying such a cold, nasty woman."

Hope's glare is beyond description since Luke delivers a verbal dagger to her heart without knowing it. Chester's relieved Hope's not reaching for her pistol again before storming off.

"Goodbye Chester. I'm done here."

Hope stomps to her truck but does glance back at Luke with mixed emotions and less hatred.

'What made me wanna help that asshole after nearly shootin' him for hurtin' Ben?'

Chester's baffled by Hope's unusual behavior and final glance which goes unseen by Luke. She sends up a dust cloud speeding down the driveway.

'What was that last glance about?'

Sam utters a comment while Hope walks away.

"I'd rather watch Hope walk than eat fried chicken."

Chester groans before gruffly speaking to Luke.

"Alright dumbass, follow me, let's fix that lip. Sam, I'll talk to you tomorrow."

Holly's quick to offer to help Luke instead.

"I'll fix Luke up, Grand-daddy."

"Find anythin' else to do somewhere else."

Sam tries bumping Luke out of his way before delivering a slowly spoken deliberate verbal warning.

"Stay in line for Mr. Kinkead 'n Hope or y'all're gonna answer to me."

'This idiot obviously doesn't know I knocked the other guy out, does he?'

Luke repositions himself anticipating Sam's infantile tactic and forces Sam to stumble backwards. Holly adds an insulting statement.

"Sam, y'all ain't strong enough to fight this guy."

Luke smiles despite his split lip before Sam walks off the deck. Chester grunts after Sam's walked out to his truck.

"He's all hat and no cattle."

Chester's comment makes no sense to Luke.

"I'm not answering to anyone on this ranch."

Luke's comment concerns Chester so he shares another southern expression.

"If all his brains were ink, Sam still couldn't dot an 'i'. You ain't that dumb, are ya? Sam's a good farrier but he's a couple sandwiches short of a full picnic basket."

Chester holds the screen door open to let Luke enter first.

"Ya gotta love a woman like that, don'tcha?"

Luke touches his bleeding lip.

"Who? Hope? No way! Love her? I couldn't even like her. I definitely don't understand her. She pulls her gun and shoots at me, punches me, then offers to take care of me. There's no logic anywhere here."

Chester heads for the kitchen and the first aid kit with a wry smile. A strong lemon scent greets them near the kitchen door.

"I've learned you'll never fully understand a woman no matter how long you know her. Women understand us better and quicker.

Us guys, we're a simple breed and easily figured out. Women are complicated 'n I stopped tryin' to figure 'em out a long time ago."

Chester's unable to decipher Hope's inexplicable urge to care for Luke along with Bullet's behavior. Katie Thompson's sitting at the kitchen table enjoying a tall glass of sweet tea after mopping the floor when the two men appear in the doorway.

"Don'tcha dare track dirt on my clean floor or y'all are gonna be moppin' till I say you're done."

Chester halts and stretches his arm out to stop Luke to inspect his boots and Luke's shoes. His action forces a smile from Katie knowing Chester prefers to avoid her ire.

'Millie's gotta be laughin'.'

Katie's overheard Chester and responds to his comparison between men and women.

"Chester, you're absolutely right about us women. We see right through men because y'all don't hide secrets all that well."

Chester proudly grins.

"Yeah, you might be surprised."

Katie good-naturedly retorts.

"I doubt it."

Chester's glad the conversation shifts when Katie notices Luke's condition.

'I don't wanna say anything I'll regret.'

"What happened here?"

Katie's concerned until learning how Luke's injury occurred.

"You're tellin' me Hope did this?"

"Yup."

"I'll get the first aid kit. I'm sorry I didn't catch your name?"

Chester's treating Luke's lip with a Q-tip and listens to Luke's attitude return in his response to Katie.

"I didn't throw it."

Chester reprimands Luke's disrespectful retort.

"Don't git smart. You show some manners in the presence of a woman."

Luke mumbles his name just loud enough for Katie to hear just ahead of Holly stepping into the room.

"Holly, go find somewhere else to hang out."

"Grand-daddy, I'm hungry and I'm checkin' to see what might satisfy my craving."

Katie's watching Chester's irritation grow while Holly gazes at Luke.

EIGHTEEN

Chester returns to the deck once Luke's lip stops bleeding. He rubs his chin whiskers before asking a question with a displeased disposition resonating within his slow, steadily cadenced drawl.

"That tractor's fixin' to get tuned up. Can ya do that?"

Luke shakes his head.

"How 'bout replacin' the torn screen on my door?"

"Nope"

Chester mulls over his next question.

"The house thermostat needs replacin'. Are ya able to do that?"

Luke's uneasy to offer another negative motion.

"My men can do these and a lot more."

Luke rudely responds.

"Make them fix all your broken things."

Luke's attitude irritates Chester before asking a new question.

"Do you have any redeeming qualities? Breakin' my foreman's jaw don't count."

Luke's insecurities rise up.

"I've never needed to fix anything. Someone else did that."

Luke recalls job interviews going poorly for lacking necessary skills and feeling inept and re-examining his purpose for living.

"Are you one of those spoiled rich brats gettin' others to work for you?"

Luke bristles and fiercely responds to Chester's accusation.

"The rich people have made my life miserable. I grew up not needing to learn how to fix things. Is that a crime here too?"

Luke's defensive reaction informs Chester he's hit on a sore subject.

'Luke sure gets prickly about wealthy people.'

Chester carefully measures his next comment.

"Some rich people make life miserable. 'Round here we call 'em politicians. Mostly rich people create jobs and salaries for others to work, succeed, and add value for themselves and the company."

Luke remains silent.

"Y'all're gonna be a sad excuse on my ranch, aren'tcha? You're no more good to me than an eyeless sewing needle and as far as I can tell you ain't worth spit."

Chester pauses so his insults sink in.

"Here's what I know 'bout you so far. Women outdrink you. Ya can't fix a thing. Oh, women can hitcha too. What can I do with that?"

Chester's unflattering portrait of Luke brings about a cutting response.

"Sounds like I don't belong here."

"You're stuck here till I say you leave. Or the sheriff'll be glad to toss you in a cell and lose the key. We'll find somethin' for ya here besides hurtin' my men."

"I was forced to defend myself."

Chester silently concedes Luke may have a valid point after hearing what really happened at the corral.

"Ben didn't deserve gettin' his jaw broke so he can't support his family."

Luke scans the corral and surrounding area knowing he nearly unleashed his full fury on Ben.

'Ben's lucky he's alive and not at the morgue. Stupid horse. Damned alcohol.'

Chester explains details about the ranch so Luke has an idea what to expect moving forward.

"We raise horses for rodeos and riding, and cattle along with maintaining the barns and land 'round here. We fix all kinds of things, 'n hunt 'n fish, 'n growin' food to eat. My daddy learned to fix the machinery and keep the ranch runnin' until I took over. He taught me all those skills. Now we're gonna teach ya to be useful and repay me."

Chester adds another thought provoking comment.

"The Ark was built by amateurs and the Titanic was built by professionals. Don't be afraid to try something new."

Luke doesn't identify Chester's underlying message comparing the two ships.

'How do those ships apply to me on a ranch?'

Chester guides Luke around the wrap around deck surround all four sides of the house during the conversation. Each side has a staircase with the front stairs being the widest after Chester remodeled the house for the large family he planned to have with Millie. Life had different plans.

"Millie and I sit on this deck and watch the sun rise and set over Texas."

Chester looks off to the horizon before resuming their conversation.

"Let me see your wallet."

"Why?"

"Just give it to me."

Luke hesitates but hands over his wallet expecting to get it back.

"I'm gonna hang onto this till you leave. You can't run off this way."

Luke reaches for his wallet until Chester pulls a pistol on him.

"Seriously? You and your guns."

"My guns allow me and everyone here to protect ourselves against criminals. Like you. Maybe you've forgotten the rights this country gives us."

Luke rebelliously rolls his eyes.

"From what I see, y'all got nothin' but what you've got on. Either you're runnin' from the law or somethin' or someone and didn't plan a proper exit strategy."

Luke's regretting boarding the bus and remembers a teacher once telling him the first choice had the highest probability to be correct.

'I think I made a really bad decision this time.'

Luke's predicament leaves him feeling bitter and wanting to remain quiet.

"Listen, learn, pay your debt and you'll be free to get the hell off my ranch."

Luke's focus returns to Chester.

"How long will that take?"

"Don't know. You'll know when I know. Your first task is gettin' squared away in the bunkhouse."

Luke's first image of the bunkhouse riles him up.

"You're sticking me with guys who hate me?"

Chester's peeved Luke would question his intentions.

"Scooter's gonna get you settled into the bunkhouse. Fightin's not allowed on this ranch without good reason, dumbass. Leave them alone, they'll leave you alone. Tell Scooter what you need."

'Like I know what I need. Besides my wallet.'

NINETEEN

Luke's imagination creates possible situations which annoy him while waiting for Scooter to arrive and escort him to the bunkhouse. He visualizes the single open room portrayed in old western movies he and his dad watched. Luke's surprised when Scooter leads him upstairs to his new quarters.

"You'll be bunking here."

Relief washes over Luke to find he gets his own room with bed and dresser.

"The rest of the men live downstairs. Enjoy this time because tomorrow's gonna get rough quick."

Luke's room is located close to the stairway but discovers the hinges squeak when Scooter opens the door. Chester waits on the deck for their return and Scooter infuriates Luke with a parting thought.

"I really thought I'd get to try out my new shovel to bury some shit after hearing Hope's shot earlier. Tomorrow's another day."

Chester barks out his next order before Luke can spitefully reply.

"I want you to lower the American flag so it can be put away for the evening."

"Bring your own flag down."

Chester raises his shotgun.

"Git your worthless ass over there and bring that flag down now. I'll fill ya full of lead and sink you in my bass pond otherwise."

'I'm not this asshole's servant boy. I need to escape this place as soon as possible.'

"Fine, I'll bring your stupid flag down."

"First of all, it's your flag as much as it's mine, dumbshit. The American flag represents all legal citizens in this country and it's why the rest of the world wants to come here. That's why we're the greatest country on earth."

Chester's scathing tone forces Luke to submissively walk to the flagpole. Chester salutes the flag while Luke lowers it until realizing Luke's disrespectfully letting the flag fall to the ground. He moves at a surprisingly fast pace towards Luke while bellowing out.

"Respect that flag. It represents our rights and freedoms. I'll shoot your ass down right quick if you don't."

Luke eyes the flag before looking at Chester.

"We don't treat people like this where I'm from."

Chester sneers and loudly scoffs.

"Y'all come from a place where politicians talk a lot but do nothin' to solve problems. Windy city for sure. The biggest city is a shootin' gallery and no one cares to change it. Those politicians wanna disarm cops and law abiding people instead of the criminals. I laugh every time I hear a yank say I live in the Wild West because they've given up the notion they could carry a gun for self-protection too. I'm safer here knowin' I can protect the people I love with the guns I carry. A good guy with a gun stops the bad guy every time."

Chester touches his Marine issued.45 caliber pistol while formulating a plan to rid Luke of his ignorance, arrogance, and insults without knowing the challenge it will be.

"Do as you're told to get the hell outta here."

Luke continues lowering the flag respectfully and shamefully recalls his dad's service in the navy to defend the country and this flag.

'Sorry dad.'

Luke folds the flag and attempts to hand it to Chester.

"Your puttin' it away to know where it is to raise the flag every morning. You're on flag detail to remember where you live."

Chester leads Luke to an old large cedar roll top desk in one corner of the living room.

"Carefully set the flag in the top left drawer."

Chester's happy Luke's compliant and respectfully puts the flag away.

'This is for you, dad.'

Luke knows Chester's armed and doesn't feel like getting shot at again. He studies the décor around the spacious living room and notes it's tastefully furnished with a Texas ambiance. The walls are white while the ceiling's painted with Palladian Blue to match the ceiling over the deck.

'That must bring the outdoors inside here.'

Luke's unaware a southern tradition is behind the color choice. There is a tan spotted white Longhorn hide located on one wall with a set of Longhorns mounted above it. A large Texas-shaped clock quietly keeps time for everyone to see. It has turquoise hands and Bluebonnets painted across the glossy finished face of a carved piece of Oak. A bronze-plated statue of a cowboy on his horse positioned on its rear legs stands in the far corner of the living room. It appears as if to be running at a fast pace or perhaps jumping. It's set on a black wrought iron pedestal stand to replicate the old west oil derricks which still dot the landscape. A black iron cattle drive reproduction placed over the fireplace on a wide mantle illustrates iconic Longhorn cattle being driven by several cowboys mixed into the herd. A sizeable chandelier covered with groupings of deer antlers is centered at the high point of the room. Two long black leather couches with several southwest patterned blankets draped over the backs sit parallel beneath the lighting. Matching chairs invitingly bracket the couches to welcome people into a reading and conversation area. Twin rectangular coffee tables are positioned in the center with several magazines lying on top. Two large oil paintings hang on another wall, one features the Grand Canyon and the other showcases an open plains landscape with a grayish-hued structure resembling a barn in the distance.

A smaller adaptation of the Texas state flag hangs on a wall surrounded by pictures which pique Luke's curiosity. Most appear to be family photos but two are black and white highlighting a singular person standing at attention in uniform. One seems more updated than the other.

'Is that Chester in both pictures?'

Chester's rolled up sleeves reveal his faded Marine's Eagle, Globe, and Anchor tattoo on his forearm. Luke finishes looking around the room then back at the desk area and instantly recognizes a picture he missed putting the flag away. His dad owned the same picture when Luke was a boy but Sylvia said it was lost in the move to his grandparent's house. Luke believes she threw it out to spite him since it meant so much to him. Chester's house reveals his pride for the state Luke's now trapped in but not in a in a pretentious or arrogant way.

"Outside. I've got things to do still thanks to you."

Chester exits first so Luke lets the screen door slam shut behind him prompting Chester to gruffly scold him.

"Don't let the door slam like that!"

Luke enjoys Chester's irritated reaction.

"I didn't know the door slammed shut."

"Hold the door when you close it, got it?"

Chester notes Luke's smug expression and sarcastic reply.

"I'll try to remember that."

'I see trouble brewin'.'

Chester detects the aroma of dinner.

'I need to plan differently.'

He pulls out a walkie-talkie and calls Scooter to return.

"Scooter, take Luke back to the bunkhouse so he can change."

Chester glances sideways at Luke.

"Wash up. I don't need your stink scarin' the horses into thinkin' wild animals are attackin' the barns."

"I may be stuck here like a prisoner but you're not ordering me around all the time. I didn't do anything."

"I'll order you around all day every day until you leave. I'm a mean-assed son of a bitch Marine. Don't cross me or I'll knock ya into next week or maybe next year. Y'all ain't above us."

Chester's threat provokes Luke's comeback dripping with contempt.

"My dad said the Marines couldn't get anywhere if it weren't for the Navy. They hauled Marine's sorry asses around the world."

"Your dad's an idiot. Marines get anywhere by any means necessary. We're resourceful that way. Marine's navigated the navy ships so they wouldn't go off course."

Scooter walks up and pulls Luke away when he notices Chester's angered state.

"Alright Laddie, let's go."

"Find anythin' for him to change into for supper."

Scooter's hand on the back of Luke's neck pushes him towards the bunkhouse. Luke shakes loose before they reach the building.

"Don't touch me."

Chester's left fuming as he enters the house but he's unaware his insulting comment regarding Luke's dad is a painful blow emotionally.

'That punk wants to push my buttons. I'll push him like a rented mule until he's sure he's livin' in hell.'

Katie comments on Chester's foul mood when he enters the kitchen.

"What's wrong with you?"

"I'm gonna kill that insolent piece of shit within a week. Insulting the Marine's. Not happening on my watch."

Katie's amused by Chester's seething.

"Seems like he's gettin' under your skin and in your head. Ya give him any more ammo and he'll be in charge of you."

"That ain't gonna happen!"

"You sure 'bout that. I just got off the phone with Hope. He's got her hoppin' mad at him too. Why's this guy able to tick both you off so much? He shows up and makes you both spittin' mad like canebrake rattlers under the bottom side of a wagon wheel."

Scooter's ruthlessly searching for clothing which won't fit Luke to embarrass him.

TWENTY

Hope pulls into the Liberty Hill High School parking lot to answer Katie's call after leaving the ranch.

"I saw that crazy dusty departure, Hope. Don't be pickin' Faith up all aggravated. Are y'all okay?"

"I'll be okay. I'm calmin' down and catchin' my breath before gettin' Faith."

Faith's working on a homework project at her one good friend's house. Faith mirrors Hope's behavior to lack trust in strangers, especially men after experiencing a traumatic situation as a toddler. Like Hope, Faith trusts everyone at the ranch but keeps most classmates at a distance. Faith greets Hope with her usual questions.

"Can we visit the ranch? Did the foal get born yet?"

Hope wrestles with lying before answering honestly.

"The foal was born today. He's beautiful. Chester's gonna let you name this one."

"Let's go to the ranch, Momma. I wanna see the foal so I can think up good names."

Hope unintentionally creates a new problem for herself.

"Pecan, there was a mean man at the ranch today so I don't want to bring y'all there. We'll wait until he's gone. It shouldn't be too long."

"But Momma, I need to see the foal. And Grand-daddy misses me."

"Let me talk to Chester and figure something out."

"You promise, Momma? I love bein' at the ranch. Everyone's my friend there. And the horses like when I feed and brush 'em. Why would Grand-daddy have a mean person at the ranch?"

"That's a good question."

'Why would Chester have a mean man at the ranch?'

Hope's unable to offer Faith a suitable answer and remains quiet.

Scooter's sorting through older usable clothing the ranch hands save for the off-season after updating their wardrobe for the next season. Luke freshens up during Scooter's evil quest to find only oversized choices again. Luke's annoyed to discover nothing fits before walking back to Chester's greeting on the deck.

"Time to meet who's gonna be in charge of you besides me."

Luke's discomfort in ill-fitting clothing is clearly evident since Scooter's given him oversized jeans but no belt. Luke's keeping the jeans up by holding onto the waistband. Chester's amused by Scooter's wicked creativity.

'Scooter's hysterical. Luke ain't throwin' punches if he can't let go of his jeans.'

The dining room walls are painted Guiliford Green, a grayish-green shade and the ceiling is standard white. Luke observes an antique China cabinet stands against one wall to display a collection a fine dishware. Chairs surround the large dining room table to indicate many people can eat together.

'How many people live on the ranch?'

The people in the room snicker at Luke's shabby appearance while glaring with pure contempt at his presence. Ben's injury is well known already since he's admired and respected by everyone at the ranch. Ben's firm but fair and never asks anyone to do something he won't do and lives by the Cowboy Code. Everyone enjoys some justice was already served when Hope punched Luke. They're gratified to see Luke's puffed lip since that news also quickly circulated around the ranch.

Chester's goal is to work Luke harder than anyone has ever worked on the ranch before. The Twisted Live Oak Ranch has broken many men over the years and Chester plans to humiliate Luke along the way to breaking him. Billy and Cody are introduced as two people who will supervise Luke and give him orders while managing tasks. Their evil grins bother Luke until Holly saunters in wearing torn jeans and a tight white t-shirt to show off her protruding nipples. Chester's irritated growl causes Luke to look down until Billy speaks up.

"We heard Hope knocked y'all around earlier. She's tougher 'n you and that would've been fun to watch."

"Hey, Billy, what's worse than a woman with a gun?"

"I'm not sure."

"A pissed off woman who's deadly accurate with a gun."

Chester prevents Luke from responding.

"Let's go. You're sittin' in the kitchen."

Chester's still pondering Bullet's reaction and Hope's mixed actions. Luke enters the kitchen to find a single place setting and smells enticing aromas filling the air. Katie chuckles at Luke's shabby outfit. Luke's depressed disposition contradicts the cheerful shade of yellow called Buttermilk covering the wall. Chester hears Luke mutter on his way to the table.

"I wish I hadn't come here."

Chester wittily replies.

"Wishin' works in movies and Disney World. Hard work'll set ya free."

Luke's irritated Chester heard him.

"I hope I escape alive."

"Hope's good but it can lead you in surprising directions."

Chester laughs for reasons only he understands.

"That door's locked so don't think y'all can sneak outta here."

Luke's exhausted, distracted, and hungry and unable to grasp the door unlocks from the inside. Katie serves Luke an overflowing plate of food before joining the others in the dining room.

"I'll check back if'n ya want more."

Holly's boasting had unwittingly filled Katie in that Luke hadn't eaten since arriving with her the previous night. Katie re-enters the kitchen shortly.

"Looks like I'm just in time. Here's a second helpin' and a slice of homemade apple pie as well. Y'all're gonna need it."

Chester walks into the kitchen a short time later.

"You're gonna wash dishes by hand tonight. Dryin' 'em too."

Chester notes Katie's apprehensive expression while laughter's heard in the dining room.

"Relax Katie, y'all sit back but keep an eye on him. He ain't done until you're satisfied."

Chester receives a disapproving look.

"I'll add time if y'all break anything."

"I thought you said I'd start tomorrow."

Katie scrutinizes Luke's exhausted state during Chester's response.

"I lied, so sue me. You start now."

"Chester, maybe he should get some rest first. I don't need dishes gettin' broke."

"He's already on the clock."

Chester laughs while exiting the kitchen with several ideas for Luke to do and joins the others outside.

"You're a very good cook. Thank you for a delicious meal."

Luke's compliment stuns Katie.

'He has manners.'

Katie's always thanked by the ranch hands for great meals but to have Luke thank her seems out of place. He yawns throughout the dishwashing and drying process while the group enjoys a small bonfire and beers. Red flag conditions aren't in effect which allows two younger men to play guitars and sing and entertain everyone. Luke holds the door open for Katie when it's time to report to Chester.

'He's got cowboy manners.'

Katie informs Chester Luke's first task went smoothly while Scooter escorts Luke to the bunkhouse.

"Laddie, today was a picnic compared what's in store for you. The hard work starts early tomorrow morning. You best get a good night's sleep."

Scooter's cackle joins the creaking hinges when he closes the door.

TWENTY ONE

Sheriff Fisher's voice rudely interrupts Luke's review of his first two days in Austin.

"I told 'em to put you in a cell with Chico for a conjugal visit. That would've knocked that attitude right outta ya."

"Chico found out we weren't compatible."

Luke's unwanted reminiscing behind bars has been stressful and tiresome.

'Bad things are still happening to me. Thanks God.'

Chester arrives later than expected after running errands for the upcoming season. He mistakes Luke's despondent expression for being nonchalant inside the cell.

'I knew the ranch was the right choice for this lazy son of a bitch. He's treatin' this like it's his living room.'

Luke's incarceration permits Hope and Faith to enjoy supper at the ranch and visit the foal. Hope gets a call after they've stopped by the ranch before Faith goes to school.

"Go help the horse. I'll get Faith to school."

An emergency call for an injured horse changes Hope's daytime schedule.

"Sorry Chester, we won't be able to have lunch together today."

Chester listens to how calm Hope sounds.

'Hope's calm despite the emergency. She doesn't seem stressed like when she was around Luke. Does he stress her out that much? No one gets to her that much. Lord knows Sam's tried countless times.'

Scooter takes Luke to his task once Chester returns him to the ranch.

"Wash the garbage cans before we work in the barns. Billy 'n Cody'll supervise you."

Luke's frustrated by his task.

"Why should I clean garbage cans? You'll just fill them with more garbage."

Chester answers Luke's question.

"So critters don't spook the horses searchin' for food. And because I said so."

Chester's order informs Luke he won't win his argument. Luke starts alone and barely sprays water into the cans before dropping the hose with immense satisfaction.

"That won't fly with Chester. Use that brush and soap to scrub 'em."

Billy's watched from a concealed spot and reprimands Luke while closing the distance.

"What's the point."

"When Chester tells ya to do something you do it. Don't question him. Or anyone else here got it?"

Billy sneers ahead of Luke's response.

"Remember asswipe, you'll be cleaning garbage cans for that asshole after I leave."

Billy's sneer disappears.

"Clean the damned garbage cans and then go clean stalls."

Luke slowly cleans the cans and whistles thinking he's using up too much time. He's unknowingly set himself up for new troubles in the rodeo barn. Scooter joins Cody and Billy to monitor Luke cleaning the stalls and setting out more feed. Their real reason becomes apparent when Hope enters the barn to examine several horses. Luke finds out there's nowhere to stand not in Hope's way in the barn. She constantly orders Luke to move with an angry tone. Chester's outside leaning against the door to enjoy the verbal ruckus inside. Chester owns the ranch but the barns are Hope's domain. Luke's quickly learning this lesson. Hope's aggravated by Luke's presence because Ben's usually assisting her with this assignment.

'Ben should be here helpin' instead of this asshole standing over there.'

Luke's relieved to get shifted to the riding barn until Hope walks in to check on the mare and foal and continues her personal tirade against him. The guys find it entertaining to watch. Both barns have the horse's names above each stall. Luke has no idea the trail horses names represents country music stars. Chester and Millie chose names of greats throughout the years such as Waylon, Willie, Merle, Jessi, King Bob (for Bob Wills), Dottie, George, Tammy, Roger, Johnny, June, Rosanne, Hank, Reba, Gene, Roy, Barbara, Dolly, Mac, Chet, Buck, Patsy, Charlie, Emmylou, and Loretta. Reba's the mare who birthed the foal and Hope lashes out at Luke for standing too close to her stall.

"Move away from that stall! Someone shoot this filthy rat already. It's gonna infect the horses."

Several cats roam around seeking a way to catch the Barn Swallows zipping in and out overhead while Hope insults Luke.

"Y'all're nothin' but a mangy useless jackass to me, the horses, and the ranch. You're a replaceable monkey here."

Hope's insults have Billy and Cody laughing.

"I have notes for Chester. Keep this asshole away from the foal."

"Yes ma'am."

"Copy that."

Luke's glad Hope leaves but the men don't grasp that Luke hasn't verbally retaliated against Hope like he does with the guys. Billy and Cody grin ear to ear to know Luke's frustrated by Hope when he retreats from her verbal assault.

"I enjoyed that a lot. How 'bout you?"

Cody agrees with a nod and continues supervising Luke until Chester wants him on a different task. Katie's curious to see JeniMay and Jubilee enter the house while Hope's meeting with Chester.

"Hope's meeting with Chester."

The two women act like their searching for someone or something until Hope walks out to greet them with a groan.

"Why are y'all here?"

"We tried callin'. You didn't answer your phone."

Hope instinctively reaches for her phone.

"Dammit, it's in the truck. I need it in case Faith, the school, or a client calls."

Hope retrieves her phone and JeniMay attempts to create an opportunity when she returns.

"Could we all go riding today?"

"I'm busy. Why are you two really here?"

Scooter enters with Luke as if on cue prompting Hope to roll her eyes after seeing their animated reaction to Luke's presence. Chester deduces Hope's irritated retort is connected to their reason for coming to the ranch. JeniMay and Jubilee make eye contact and smile once Luke glances at them. He involuntarily smiles back.

'So there can be happy people at the ranch other than Holly.'

Luke's shabby appearance doesn't dissuade their interest in him. Hope speaks crossly.

"JeniMay, Jubilee, you can ride on your own today."

Both women look at Luke.

"Can we get help with our horses?"

"You've been saddlin' horses for years. The guys are around if y'all need anything. But stay away from that cur dog."

JeniMay and Jubilee are disappointed Luke can't accompany them while Hope faces Chester.

"Why is this vermin still here?"

Luke heatedly responds.

"I can hear you. I'm a person not vermin."

"Your opinion, not my personal observation."

Hope's angered insults amuse Chester.

"Luke's workin' just like you."

Hope glares at Luke.

"I'm done here."

Luke's eyes shift to the clock before mocking Hope.

"Isn't about time to pick up your daughter?"

Chester interjects before Hope speaks.

"Don'tcha go aggravatin' anyone here again."

Holly strolls in to interrupt Chester and show off another skimpy outfit in front of Luke.

"That includes you as well, Holly. Luke, I want all my windows clean so you can't tell there's glass in the frames."

Hope's pleased to hear Luke's next task.

"Is he even qualified for that? Never mind, better him than Katie or the guys."

Jubilee and JeniMay silently observe Hope continue her venomous attack on Luke.

"Get rid of this rat so Faith and I can come here whenever we want and not deal with disgusting shit to scare her."

"I'm workin' on it. Call ya in a bit, okay."

Luke's glad Hope's leaving while her friends head to the riding barn.

"Go clean my windows! I have problems to figure out."

Luke nastily replies.

"You can't be serious. I don't do windows."

Luke recalls Katie's previous scolding.

"Do what you're told. You broke Ben's jaw so clear your debt. Or go back to jail."

Luke recognizes retaliation needs to happen differently.

"What type of ranch is this anyway?"

Chester can't tell if Luke's serious.

"This is a Dude ranch. I raise buckin' broncs for rodeos. We have cattle drives as well. You ain't figured any of that out yet? Should I get a crayon and draw a picture for you? Our season opens soon to showcase our way of life."

Luke's ignorance about the ranch amuses Chester. Luke thinks back to Linda's co-workers tactics to embarrass him and becomes riled up as he walks towards the door.

"Don'tcha walk away until I dismiss you. I'll tell you when you can leave. I'm through with you now. Get the hell outta here!"

Cody greets Luke with paper towels and a spray bottle at the door. Chester repeats his order.

"Y'all clean my windows perfectly. No smudges or smears. Got it?"

Luke swipes the bottle and towel roll from Cody and walks outside. He lets the screen door slam shut so Chester's left grumbling on his way back to his office.

'I'll keep puttin' him around Hope. She's gotta shoot him at some point soon.'

Chester gruffly answers his phone when it rings.

"What! Oh, Hank, sorry. Naw I'm okay, just wantin' to kill someone. Yep, Luke. You wanna see him again. Why? Today? Yeah, that works. See ya then."

Chester calls Hope back.

"Y'all can bring Faith to ride and enjoy supper."

Jubilee and JeniMay return from riding to find Luke still cleaning windows.

"You're the new guy?"

Luke turns around after hearing their Texas drawls.

"I guess so."

"I'm JeniMay, this is Jubilee. Holly told us about you."

"You gonna be here long?"

"I have no idea. I can't wait to leave. I don't belong here."

"Y'all miss the big city, huh? Are the men more sophisticated there?"

"I bet they're richer and drive fancy cars and wear expensive suits."

"And eat at expensive restaurants."

Luke scoffs at their perception of a big city.

'They sound like Linda. It's all about money.'

"Sorry 'bout Hope's behavior earlier. She's not usually so rude."

"I'm willing to bet that's the real Hope."

Jubilee moves closer and wraps her arms around Luke and presses her hips against him.

"Maybe you'd like to take me back with y'all. No one's holdin' me back here."

Jubilee glances at Cody to see a mixture of anger and concern before Chester abrasively disrupts the moment.

"Alright, finish up. You and I are goin' out for supper. We'll leave at seventeen hundred."

Chester thinks using military time will confuse Luke.

"So you want to leave at five o'clock?"

Jubilee and JeniMay feel disappointed Luke's leaving since they find him attractive and datable even if Hope disagrees. Chester examines Cody's angered expression and the ladies ogling Luke.

'What's got Cody pissed off? Great, Holly's got competition.'

"Hope'll be bringin' Faith here so you two ladies are invited to stay longer."

Jubilee pulls close to Luke again.

"I'd like more time with y'all. We're here a lot."

Jubilee's light brown eyes shine while she plays with her long brown hair. Cody's glaring at Luke and Jubilee before walking away which causes her to giggle. JeniMay's blue eyes reveal a hungered desire and her short blonde hairstyle compliments her facial features. Luke's glad to leave the ranch if Hope's returning but he's frustrated while sorting through more ill-fitting clothes.

'What's with these clothes? What's with Hope's attitude? JeniMay and Jubilee seem nice. And Holly, well, Holly's almost too much to take wearing next to nothing and showing off what any man wants to hold.'

Chester's by his truck when Luke exits the bunkhouse while Holly's watching from the deck.

"Where're y'all goin' Grand-daddy? Maybe I should come with you."

"Nope, y'all stay here outta trouble."

The two men depart for an unspoken destination.

'I heard JeniMay and Jubilee flirtin' with Luke. They're not in my league. They don't stand a chance against me.'

TWENTY TWO

Luke's annoyed when Chester pulls into the senior residence parking lot. "This is where you're bringing me for dinner. What's on the menu, mashed potatoes and pudding? I'd rather deal with Hope at the ranch and eat Katie's cooking."

"Shut up. Hank asked to see you. I don't know why but he must have a reason. Or he's lonely enough to want to share time with a shithead like you. Hope gets peace and quiet at the ranch with Faith."

Luke scowls at Chester's belittling reference. Hank's already at his table in the busy dining room.

"I told 'em y'all want extra dressin' with supper, Chester."

"Much obliged old friend."

Luke's quiet during their meal until Chester finally goes to visit the other vets.

"You're first two days have been busy on and off the ranch."

Luke's not sure he can trust Hank and suspiciously scans the room. "Nobody's listenin'."

"It feels like a month already."

"Y'all're gonna need to get along with everyone at the ranch if you plan to ever leave. Chester's gonna run you into the ground during the season but don't take it out on guests."

Luke's unhappy to hear Hank's revelation but his next comment shakes him up.

"You're not replaceable."

"What? Why did you say that?"

"You didn't avoid Hope or Chester shootin' at you. Dyin' might seem like a viable option but someone in your shape's committed to living. Set goals and reach for dreams even if someone says ya can't. Learn that when you stumble or fall you get back up. If life shoves you, push back. Some people spend their entire lives chasin' dreams and never find 'em. Others have their dreams find them in the darndest places. It's time to teach you the Cowboy Code. Your way of thinkin' don't hold water."

"The what?"

"Live each day with courage. That's the first one."

"What does that mean?"

"You'd've been dead a long time ago if you were serious. Why did you stare down Hope yesterday? You ain't goin' through life alone. The good Lord's walked every step next to you."

Luke's eyes can't hide his guilt for being alive.

"Truth can leave a bitter taste for a long time. You've carried an unfair weight for far too long. Believe in yourself when no one else does and rise to the challenge. A more positive outlook erases negatives. You need to find your raison d'etre."

"My what?"

Hank reaches into his shirt pocket and hands a picture to Luke.

"Sally was my everything once I won her heart and love. Sally became my reason and purpose to exist, my raison d'etre. I couldn't win her over until I believed in myself. She knew I brought troubles home from the war and I needed to overcome them if I was gonna live a good life and provide for her. She helped when she could and when she couldn't help or understand, well, let's just say she knew how to use her body to keep me focused."

Hank winks to emphasize his unspoken message.

"I've been misjudged and misunderstood so many times. I'm not sure I deserve anyone anymore. I haven't ever been good enough for anyone. It's not easy for me to open up to anyone."

Hank pays close attention to Luke's self-assessment.

"I'm not sure I deserve a good woman like your Sally."

Hank's heard a similar message from a different person.

"You should talk with Hope."

"Hope? You're kidding, right? She almost shot me. She kind of did shoot me. She punched me. Hope hates my guts. And I don't like her either. I'm not talking to her."

Hank shrugs his shoulders.

"Jini, how'd ya know you were in love with her?"

"I'm not sure."

Luke pauses and recalls his time with Jini.

"Actually, no, I do know. How I felt with her and apart from her. Holding her hand and being with her. How her hugs made me feel safe, like being wrapped up in a comforting blanket."

"What got your attention first? When you first met."

Luke's quick to answer.

"Her eyes. That's what drew me in first."

Hank hears sincere passion in Luke's voice.

"Not her chest? Or her backside?"

"No. It was her beautiful blue eyes."

Luke touches his puffed lower lip with an odd expression that confuses Hank.

'What I noticed first about Jini. That happened with Hope. But Hope shot at me. She hasn't been nice to me for a minute. But it was like that same wow moment I had with Jini.'

Hank pauses before regaining Luke's attention.

'Wonder what he's thinking?'

"You think the world owes you. It doesn't. Being angry won't change a thing. You can control your destiny and direction with every decision or lack thereof. You're the only one who lives your life. Chester recites somethin' y'all need to hear. You can't direct the wind but you can adjust the sails."

'My dad had that expression framed on his desk.'

Luke somberly confesses something he's never told anyone.

"I'm the reason my parents are dead. My uncle, too."

Luke's admission stuns Hank.

"That can't be true."

"My parents took me to the circus I asked for instead of the movie my sister wanted to see."

"That doesn't make you responsible for their deaths. You have a sister?"

"My family told me I was to blame so it must be true."

"You weren't responsible, Luke. It's tragic your family allowed you to think that way."

"They told me my uncle died because he couldn't live in Illinois any more. His new business was failing. I should've moved to Florida but he thought it was better to keep me in familiar surroundings. Losing his younger brother broke him so he stepped in front of a train."

"There was more goin' on than you knew. Nothin' you could be blamed for."

"What's up with Chester? Tell me something about him."

"Nice try, Luke. Accept accountability for your actions. Hurtin' Ben's why you're still at the ranch. You've got a good opportunity to learn new skills. Go to the front desk and read the sign on the wall."

Luke approaches the desk and reads, 'Privacy is Everyone's Job, Not Everyone's Business.'

He returns with a blank stare.

"I don't get it."

"Be patient. Listen to people. You'll learn what you need to know."

"What if no one shares anything? Those people at the ranch don't like me. Why would they talk to me? Why would I share anything either?"

Hank responds sarcastically.

"Ya got any idea why no one likes you at the ranch? Throwin' 'round insults like rocks. You ain't willin' to talk to them so why are they gonna talk to you?"

Hank lets a moment pass quietly.

"Let's continue your lesson about the Cowboy Code. You'll survive better at the Twisted Live Oak. I'll list them off."

Hank slowly explains each one for Luke to absorb.

"Take pride in your work; Always finish what you start; Do what has to be done; Be tough, but fair; When you make a promise, keep it; Ride for the brand; Talk less and say more; Remember that some things aren't for sale; Know where to draw the line."

Luke's focused on Hank while he lists off the code.

"Some are more important for you to know up front. Take pride in your work and make a better impression. Talk less and say more that way. Know where to draw the line. The whole code is important to live by but these'll help ya survive and settle in."

Luke's unsure how to react to Hank's guidance.

"Let's see if there's a cowboy inside waitin' to escape."

Luke ponders his situation and Hank's words.

"Luke, emotions are part of life. Tryin' to avoid 'em means missing out on living. It seems to me you've tried to escape life without allowin' yourself to live in a moment and feel it. Even here, all you wanna do is leave. Opportunity might be knockin' on your door but you're lookin' past it, to what? Nothin'. The unknown. That's great for an adventure but not for livin' your life. You're wastin' time. Holdin' everything inside'll bury you under a mountain of misery and regret. You can't talk about life without talkin' 'bout death. They're intertwined whether you like it or not. One challenges you every day. One's guaranteed. Live every moment feeling what needs to be felt, even if it's grief, sadness, or anger. And remember to feel happiness and love as well."

"You're telling me I'm complicit for my own demise and negative approach, right?"

Hank's smile informs Luke he understands the lesson Hank's teaching.

"One look from the right person's gonna open that closed heart of yours."

Luke's first thought is how Hope's enchanting eyes captured his attention so easily after Hank's comment.

"Maybe I could make some changes. My jobs haven't gotten me anywhere. I'll start when I go home."

"You could start turning yourself into something here. If you apply yourself. There's a big difference feelin' something's beneath you and knowing you haven't reached for your full potential."

Hank chuckles while Luke's expression turns sheepish.

"Yup. I heard you ran into hurricane Katie's wrath. Feel lucky you're still breathin'. Consider you feel how you do because you haven't tried to live a better life. Sometimes when you change how you look at things, what you look at changes. We're capable of changin' and makin' those changes last."

Luke quietly absorbs Hank's summation.

"I think I've shared enough for now. Remember, your actions have you stuck at the ranch. You had control but gave it away. It's okay to fight for the right reasons. Men are built to defend and protect although nowadays that's bein' turned into a bad thing. Act like an alpha male instead of bein' a ninny. Handle situations differently and walk a better path. You're a work in progress. Think about who you are and what you stand for. Alright, this old man needs some sleep."

Luke remains at the table while Chester walks Hank to his room.

"I taught Luke the Cowboy Code. Hopefully he'll shape up for all y'all at the ranch."

"I'm not holdin' my breath."

"Luke's walkin' a thin line between wantin' to live, guilty for being alive, and feelin' like he's died inside already. Like we did when our buddies didn't return from the war with us. Keep that in mind. He's haunted and gutted by his past and guilt has pushed him in unintentional directions."

"You seem to know a lot about Luke in a little amount of time. He's nothin' more than a burr under my saddle."

"Years of practice. And I'm not the one punishin' him. Luke's more like us than you know and sounds like Hope regarding parts of his life. Hope wants to control life and Luke feels he has no control. Life throws curve balls all the time and we either adjust or flounder. Hope's plan is good for raising Faith but she's on an unhealthy path herself. I'd like to talk with her about a few things to see how she responds."

"You're playing with fire, you know that, right? Hope's not lookin' for love."

Hank grins mischievously before entering his room.

"I want to see Hope married before I die."

"Y'all plannin' on livin' to a thousand? You seem rather chipper today."

"Life's given me new purpose."

Luke waits until they reach the ranch to bring up a subject and satisfy his curiosity.

"I've heard people mention your wife, Millie. Where is she? I haven't seen her around."

Luke adds a spiteful remark before Chester responds.

"She's probably at a friend's house to keep away from your grumpy ass."

Luke's shocked when Chester's fist hits his cheek. Chester's initial impulse was to shoot Luke and is unable to conceal his grief behind menacing eyes which are also moistening up.

"You son of a bitch! Cancer stole Millie from me last year after fighting it for three long years. Millie lost her battle with that devil. Don't ever speak her name again. You're not worthy to say her name."

Luke's rubbing his cheek just as Chester attempts a second punch and stops his fist.

"You only get one chance to sucker punch me."

Luke's dumbfounded when Chester discloses Millie's death while retreating to the bunkhouse.

'I don't get it. People talk about Millie in the present tense.'

Luke's emotionally drained and self-conscious about improperly crossing a line regarding Chester's loss.

Katie notices Chester's expression when he enters the house.

'Chester hasn't looked like that since Millie died.'

Chester struggles with soul shredding rage and sorrow and seeks refuge in his office. He unlocks a desk drawer and pulls out a whiskey bottle, glass, and Luke's wallet. He opens the wallet and sees a picture of a couple with a young, smiling boy and a sulking older girl. A second picture of a pretty blonde is also inside along with his driver's license, one credit card, and some cash as well. Chester picks up his phone to send a text and his phone rings a moment later.

"Howdy, I've got some information for you so you can find out information for me in return."

TWENTY THREE

"Wake up, asswipe. Get dressed!"

A male voice pierces Luke's veiled sleep state.

"Get up, get dressed, get breakfast, then we leave."

Luke mumbles but barely stirs.

"I'm tired."

Luke howls out in pain when Cody's boot heel slams against his shin to generate excruciating pain. Luke snarls out his order.

"Get out of my room!"

"Move your ass so we get to church on time."

Luke growls at Cody.

"I don't go to church."

Cody grabs the edge of the bedsheet and firmly pulls it up and yanks it off which sends Luke sprawling over the other side. He watches Luke jump to his feet with clenched fists after the resulting thud makes him laugh.

"I'm sleeping in. Not going to church."

"Everyone goes to church. No one cares if you're tired. We're all tired."

Cody exits Luke's room but re-enters after hearing Luke lay down on the bed again. Cody flips the bedframe with one strong motion as if he's toppling a calf in a rodeo so the frame lands on top of Luke.

"You're goin' to church with or without breakfast."

Cody's harsh delivery informs Luke he needs to get ready so he can eat before being dragged off to church. Word spreads quickly about Cody's adverse encounter with Luke so he receives evil glares at the house. Chester abruptly enters the kitchen to announce its time to leave.

"It's time to go whether you're done or not."

Chester barks at Luke.

"We're never late to church. There's plenty of work to be finished today. Y'all're in Billy's truck."

Church bells commandingly herald the approaching start of services while they enter the parking lot. The deep welcoming notes warmly greet all who seek salvation but induce bitter memories for Luke of a tragic day in his past. His darkest day overpowers him near the entrance. Billy stands next to Luke while Jake and Jesse join the others to enter and find Hope and Faith. Luke has no idea they'll be attending this service also. Billy notices Luke shudder and look as if he's seen a ghost before his eyes well up with tears. Luke suddenly seems weak, vulnerable, and paralyzed to confuse Billy.

'So much for Luke's tough side.'

Chester also notices Luke's rebellious stance evaporate into a saddened slouch.

'I know Luke didn't wanna go to church but is he about to cry over it?'

Luke wipes the escaping tears away with his sleeve only to be replaced by more trickling down his cheeks. Chester reconsiders Hank's assessment of Luke's state of mind.

'Is Hank right? Did Luke go through something terrible like we did? He does remind me how we acted after the war.'

Billy remains with Luke at the back of the church while Chester advances to join Hope, Faith, and the others. Cody motions over his shoulder when Hope realizes someone's missing and waves for Billy to join them with a smile. Her smile disappears once Luke comes into view and glares at him.

'Why's he here?'

"Y'all might wanna move outta sight or Hope might just come back here and shoot ya."

Luke shifts over to be out of sight only to return to peek at Hope again and notices Faith looking at him as well.

"Hope'll drop y'all like a bad habit."

Luke recognizes Billy's pleased by Hope's hate-filled glare aimed his way so he twists the situation around.

"She wants me."

Billy frowns at Luke's attempt to swing the circumstances around.

"Yeah right. She wants you dead."

Billy's smiles.

"She doesn't know she wants me yet."

"Hope knows what she wants. It ain't you."

Billy's irritated to be dealing with Luke's renewed bravado but does notice Luke subtly glance at Hope again.

"Hope'll beat you like a ragdoll again."

Luke's annoyed he's caught peeking at the Texas beauty and slides out of view. Holly enters after services begin and stands next to Luke. Billy amuses himself with a warning to Luke.

"Chester'll come back and shoot you for bein' so close to Holly. Luke slides over only to have Holly move with him and reach her arm around him. Hope's backward glance catches Holly's half hug so she can rest her head against Luke's arm. Hope rolls her eyes before looking forwards but also feels a twinge of jealousy wash over her.

What would make me jealous of Holly? Or him?

Hope's unsettled thought halts when Faith whispers her question.

"Momma, is that the mean man with Billy and Holly?"

Hope considers lying before noting their present venue.

I can't lie here.

"Yes, that's the mean man."

"He looks sad, Momma."

Hope re-examines Luke and realizes she's overlooked something Faith's detected about him. Luke scans the interior of the church and the detailed stain glass windows and misses Hope's scrutinizing glance. Holly remains by Luke's side despite Chester's threat to shoot him if necessary. Luke's focus shifts when the preacher clears his throat to emphasize his sermon's next point.

"Jesus knew each step He would take on Earth before taking the first step. We, His flock, may wander from our intended path without His blessed vision and question what our correct path truly is. What our intended purpose is. We all have purpose and need to live life in order to find it and live to the fullest in His name."

Luke dwells on the preacher's words.

'I don't seem to have a purpose, not a good one anyway. My path is meaningless.'

Memories cloud Luke's mind with two caskets rolling down a church aisle, one draped with an American flag. Luke feels as if the walls have started closing in and hastily exits the building without warning.

'Where's he goin'?'

Billy and Holly follow him outside. Hope also notices Luke bolt outside.

'Good riddance!'

Billy and Holly find Luke shaken and pale just beyond the doorway. Holly's concerned Luke's ill while Billy's simply curious whether Luke's tough guy act is a sham. Hope and Faith use the side entrance to avoid Luke when service ends. Chester assigns Luke to work with Danny and Kyle once they return to the ranch. Damaged sections of fencing continually occur allowing the Longhorn to escape their designated pasture enclosures. Chester believes someone's sneaking onto the ranch to tamper with the barbed wire fencing and create unsafe conditions to shut him down.

"Danny and Kyle are highly skilled at ridin' fences to repair damaged sections. They're good with their guitars too but that's about it."

Luke shreds his hands and arms while learning to repair barbed wire sections. He doesn't complain so Danny and Kyle don't notice and his dark blue shirt hides the evidence. Ben's wife drives fast up the long driveway until she's intercepted by Chester when she reaches the house. Beth jumps out of her truck holding a pistol.

'Ah shit, this is big trouble.'

"Where's he at? Where's the son of a bitch that hurt my Ben? I'm gonna kill him!"

"Whoa, Beth, calm down."

"Calm down? Ben's jaw is wired shut while that son of a bitch's walkin' 'round here carefree."

"Oh, I can assure you he ain't carefree. He'll be paying for injuring Ben by workin' here instead of sittin' in jail. He ain't happy about that at all."

"He deserves a bullet between the eyes."

Chester reaches out for the gun so Beth raises her arm and inadvertently squeezes the trigger. The hammer harmlessly creates a metallic sound but nothing more so Beth lowers the gun to inspect it.

"Dammit! It's empty. What the fu…"

Chester gruffly stops Beth from finishing.

"Beth! Killin' him ain't gonna heal Ben. You'd go to jail and never hold Ben or your daughters again. Go home, take care of Ben."

Chester's remarks soften Beth's glare.

'I'd die if I couldn't hold my family.'

"Fine, but you'd best work him into the dirt."

"Yes, ma'am."

Chester sighs after Beth drives away. Ben sees Beth enter the house holding his gun and writes a note to find out why.

"I went to kill the son of a bitch that hurt you. Chester talked me out of it."

The color drains from Ben's face while he motions Beth to sit down. He writes out how and why he was injured so Beth can learn the truth before she heatedly responds.

"You did what? I almost shot someone. Ben Ross, you should be ashamed of yourself. You know better!"

Ben nods.

"I could've gone to jail."

Beth's disposition changes when Ben writes out two words.

'I'm sorry.'

Beth has long admired Ben's ability to admit when he's wrong.

"Alright, you lovable dumbshit, I'll take good care of you."

Beth hugs Ben and brings a new icepack to numb his jaw. Chester's deliberating his options should Beth return armed again.

'I'm not sure what to do. I have an idea but is it a good one? No one's died yet and I'd like to keep it that way.'

Chester calls Hope with an update.

"Hope, I'm takin' Luke off the ranch for a bit. You'll be able to bring Faith here for the afternoon to see the foal, go swimming, go riding, and relax. The pool's heater is on. Beth was here wantin' to shoot Luke full of holes. We need to talk about Easter as well."

Chester tells Danny to bring Luke in and discovers Luke's ripped up from the fencing. Katie's amazed Luke doesn't flinch while she applies rubbing alcohol to clean his wounds.

'This has gotta hurt but Luke's actin' like it's no big deal.'

Scooter enjoys telling Luke about Beth's deadly intentions.

'Great, two women want to shoot me.'

Cody overhears Scooter and has fun at Luke's expense.

"Y'all gotta be as nervous as a long-tailed cat trapped in a rockin' chair store on kid's day? Hope and Beth know how to shoot a moving target."

Cody shares Luke's misfortune with the others while Luke worries about being a target at the ranch. Anticipating trouble at the bar was easy compared to the challenges the ranch presents with so many variables.

'What do I do if Hope and Beth are here together? Hiding isn't really possible.'

Luke's suspicious when Chester informs him they'll be leaving the ranch for a few hours. Chester identifies Luke's nervous reaction every time they drive beside next to semi-trucks.

"Y'all got a problem with semi's?"

"I don't like them.

"You don't like trucks 'n horses? Y'all got some strange quirks."

"Where are we going?"

"It ain't where ya think. Don'tcha worry, you'll make it back alive. It's a bit of a drive."

Luke's mostly silent during the drive to the mystery destination until passing a road sign indicating they're entering Bastrop.

"How much longer? I wasn't on the bus from Chicago this long."

"We're 'bout there. It can take up to thirteen hours to cross Texas so this drive ain't nothin'."

Chester pays the parking fee when they enter Bastrop State Park and drives along Park Road 1-A to a scenic overlook. Luke notices how quiet it is.

'It's quiet here just like the ranch.'

"There's no noise here. Or at the ranch. I can't stand it."

"That's called peace and quiet. And I prefer it."

Luke follows Chester down a winding gravel path until the shrill calls from a flight of Sandhill Cranes heading in a northerly direction reaches their ears.

"Finally, noise."

'I wish I were going with them. I don't belong here.'

Chester chuckles and continues walking until reaching a particular spot and scans the area around them.

"What do you see here?"

Luke views the sparse forest while various songbirds begin chirping and singing and flit through the branches.

"I'm not impressed with a sorry excuse for a forest."

Luke inspects the meager growth of lighter green saplings mixing with larger dark green pine trees and varying shades of mid-sized trees.

"A fire back in twenty eleven burned a large section of Loblolly pines, Oaks, along with Yaupon Holly and American Beautyberry shrubs. Those are Beautyberries there, with the purple berries. This had been a beautiful forest, it's also known as the Lost Pines because the Loblolly's are usually found in East Texas, but Mother Nature has a way of re-creating life from tragedy. It was a devastating event but life continues after death occurs. Sparks from electrical lines started the fire and yet here we are walkin' through new growth. A single moment can be meaningless or become life-changing if ya let it."

Chester's explanation for Luke brings old emotions and memories to the surface including his parent's funeral. Luke's shoulder's droop and his eyes well up with tears again so he appears weak and vulnerable again.

'What has Luke acting like this? What does Hank know that I don't?'

Luke's quietly haunted by thoughts for the remainder of the walk until finally saying something out of place.

"Can we go home? I'm done being here."

"Yeah, it's about time to head back."

'Interestin', Luke called the ranch home.'

Chester makes a dinner stop and to inform Hope when he'll arrive at the ranch. Chester notices Luke's scratched up hands while he picks at his food.

"I reckon you need better gloves for the fencing."

'Was Luke even trying to be safe in the pasture?'

The sun's setting when they return and Luke clears his throat to get Chester's attention in the truck.

"That was a rude comment I made about your wife. I apologize. It was uncalled for."

Chester sits behind the wheel with his hands on his lap and nods acknowledgement for Luke's apology. Chester remembers Hank's assessment of Luke being more than he shows before joining the others at the fire pit. Luke thinks a hot shower's soothing embrace might wash away the awful memories but sweat is all that rinses down the drain. Luke's shaken to his core trying to transition to Texas and leaves him physically and mentally exhausted. He only knows he feels as if he's in a foreign environment and mindset and attempts to sleep only to wake to his unwelcomed nightmare again.

TWENTY FOUR

ope and Faith arrive shortly after Chester departs with Luke. Faith has a list of names for the foal she shares with Katie.

"My, Faith, you've put a lot of thought into a good name for the foal."

JeniMay and Jubilee reach the ranch expecting to see Luke but reveal disappointed expressions once they find out he's not around.

"You two aren't seriously looking for Luke, are you? Beth came huntin' for him like a diseased cur dog so Chester's taken him somewhere and won't be back for hours. Personally, I hope Chester leaves him there."

They all enjoy riding with the guys before Faith splashes in the pool while Hope continues talking with her friends. Faith overhears Hope complain about Luke again and gets curious.

"Momma, why don't you like that guy? What did he do?"

"Don't you worry none about that, Faith."

Hope leads JeniMay and Jubilee away from the pool after Katie says she'll watch Faith. JeniMay speaks first.

"I wanted to talk to Luke again."

"JeniMay Mitchell! Stop chasin' Luke. That asshole slept with Holly! You don't want her leftovers."

"No, he didn't. Holly was complaining on the phone that Luke passed out right after she took his shirt off. Nothin' happened between them."

Jubilee joins the conversation.

" Luke's hot! Ya gotta admit that. Even you, Hope."

"What's wrong with you two? Luke's violent, boorish, and should be in jail for hurtin' Ben."

Hope's too loud and Faith hears her.

"Why did Luke hurt Ben?"

Hope's frustration is clearly visible that Faith heard her.

"Thanks a lot."

Hope turns towards Faith.

"Don't worry. Ben's gonna be just fine. We'll talk later."

"Boorish? What decade are y'all from?"

"It means ill-mannered, Jubilee."

Jubilee's insulted by Hope's comment.

"I know what it means, Hope. I'm not the blonde one here. I can't remember hearing anyone use that word in the twenty first century."

"Jubilee, you did grow up thinkin' they named Williamson County after you."

"Blame my cousin for that. He thought it was hilarious I believed him and told everyone I met we were the reason for the name."

JeniMay's curious to see how Hope reacts to her comment.

"Luke's kinda cute."

"He's a reprobate."

"Luke's got a sexy smile and seems nice."

"Have you two lost your minds? Rabid coyotes have more manners than him."

Jubilee's nervous to ask her next question.

"Hope, when's the last time you were physical with a guy? When was your last kiss even?"

"I don't want to talk about it."

"I don't recall you even talking about goin' on a date since your divorce."

"Can we change the subject? We don't need to be talkin' 'bout my love life."

"What love life? There doesn't seem to be anything to talk about."

JeniMay and Jubilee realize Hope has spent the last eight years alone raising Faith after divorcing her cheating husband. JeniMay speaks to Hope honestly to state what needs to be said.

"Honestly Hope, I'm surprised you're not dating Colt. I think we all are. He's smart, successful, really good lookin', and you get along. He's perfect for you."

Hope considers JeniMay's assessment.

"I haven't considered Colt dating material in years. We've been friends for so long."

Jubilee adds her own thought.

"That's what can help build a stronger relationship."

"Yeah, I don't know, I've been told that before. I have Faith to think about."

"Wouldn't Faith like a dad?"

Hope's silenced by Jubilee's inquiry.

'What if Jubilee's right?'

Hope looks over at Faith playing with Katie.

"Colt pretends he's a cowboy and chews tobacco when none of the guys do anymore. Their reason is what they call the Chris LeDoux effect. Colt acts like a cowboy but he's a flyboy through and through. The air is his playground except for the training accident with the navy's Blue Angels. I'd need a true cowboy to come along and make me feel something again. Someone born in Texas. I learned my lesson from a poor choice of an Oklahoma transplant for a husband. That seems so long ago."

JeniMay states an obvious fact.

"Because it was.

"It seems like there might be hope for you yet, Hope."

"Hope, I've seen you look at Colt. You must've considered taking a chance. Especially after caring for Colt after the training accident. I have seen you get a peculiar look in your eyes when Luke's name comes up. Don't tell me you haven't checked Luke out. I don't know if you're aware of it."

JeniMay's statement shocks Jubilee before Hope cuts off further speculation.

"What? No! Definitely not! Luke's a barbarian, an ogre. He's not Texan which rules him out already."

Jubilee shares her own thoughts.

"Now that I think about it, you did twirl your hair while Luke was around the other day. Luke is easy on the eyes."

"I wasn't doin' it for him. Or because of him."

"You think he's exasperating, maybe, just maybe, you find him exhilarating? He's about the only guy who hasn't chased after you from the get go. Maybe you find that to be a turn on."

"Like you two are experts on men."

Hope's pointed jab about men agitates JeniMay and triggers her to unload hidden feelings.

"Yeah right. You and Holly are lucky with your big boobs and perfect bodies that make guys want to f your brains out all the time. I'm just average so guys don't look at me and I'm so tired of hearin' how hot you are and must've modeled for the perfect hot-lookin' girl silhouetted on the their mud flaps."

Hope cuts JeniMay off after the initial shock of her verbal assault wears off.

"JeniMay! Why are y'all gettin' mad at me?"

"Wade said my crude mouth kept him in bed longer. None of us are saints here so why are you suddenly acting prudish?"

"Faith's here. I don't need her hearing words like that or me gettin' talked about like that. She's only eight. Too many questions I don't want to answer yet."

"Yes, it's always about you."

"JeniMay. You miss Wade. I'm sorry he didn't make it home from Afghanistan. You two would've been married this June."

Silence ensues until Jubilee speaks up.

"How long will Luke be here?"

"I don't know."

"What should we do about him?"

"How 'bout stayin' away from him. Luke only thinks about himself. He wouldn't put someone else first. He's proved that."

"What if he did? Luke might be someone who could take care of you, I mean protect you."

"What the hell are ya talkin' 'bout Jubilee?"

Jubilee's comment piques JeniMay's curiosity.

"Jubilee, Hope can protect herself."

"Colt and Sam got their asses handed to them the other day."

"They aren't Neanderthal's. They don't fight people for no reason. Luke's like getting the best choice of the worst. You still end up with bad."

"Okay, fine, look what Luke did to Ben."

"Exactly, that's why that asshole should be in jail not here on the ranch. I think Chester's mind has finally thrown a horseshoe or two. And sweet ol' Hank too, he's wantin' to talk to Luke for some reason."

Jubilee apprehensively restates a previous comment.

"Hope, I think you've forgotten what it's like to have a man lying on top of you, completely naked, and feeling him deep inside you, repeatedly. The exhilaration, the passion, begging him not to stop. And his eyes havin' the same wanting look for you like you have for him."

"Okay, okay, keep it down. I get what you're saying, Jubilee. Sex is great, unless you've had your heart and dreams torn apart. I don't know if I can ever feel that way again. To want that again."

"You can't if you won't try."

"You sure remember sex vividly for someone without a boyfriend."

"Um, Hope, there's something I need to tell you. I'm dating Cody."

JeniMay and Hope react together.

"What?"

JeniMay speaks first.

"When did that happen? You were hitting on Luke the other day."

"And why haven't you told us?"

"I hugged Luke in front of Cody to force him to finally ask me out. It worked. We thought you'd be mad."

"Why would I be mad? Cody's a great guy."

"Because you're friends with both of us and you won't let anyone in. I didn't want you feelin' like you had to pretend to be happy around us if you're not."

"That's ridiculous! I'm happy for both of you. Don't let me or my choices affect you and Cody. So you didn't really mean what you said about Luke's looks before."

"Oh, I meant it. Luke's hot as a Texas summer day. But I finally have Cody and get to get him naked already. I'm quite happy with him. I just thought someone else…"

Hope snaps back.

"Enough already! Luke's not an option. End of story."

'I feel like life's conspiring against me and my plans.'

TWENTY FIVE

Luke wakes Monday morning to a depressing realization.

"It's only the fifth day here but it feels like forever already."

Luke struggles to adjust to a new routine after years of a stable schedule. He's trying to keep pace with the guys during tasks but overheats in his new attire. He's more exhausted working on the ranch than from any martial arts training or gym workouts. His feet feel like concrete blocks at the end of each day and he's adjusting to the constantly fluctuating heady strength of horse manure. His hands are sore from the barbed wire abrasions.

'I hate being here. I hate me. I hate everything. I feel so alone. I wish I was dead.'

Luke feels a loss of his identity and stripped bare of everything familiar after only a short amount of time. Texas has already begun to subtly redefine him because of confrontations with new people and unusual tasks and challenges create an emotional imbalance. Cody assists Scooter's supervision of Luke to finish cleaning and feeding to make breakfast on time. He fails to impress Luke with his ability to rapidly clean stalls.

"You'll be this good if 'n yur lucky enough. Y'all're slow as molasses."

"I'm good as is. I'll be talking as stupid as you do if I'm here too long."

Cody drops his mucking rake and storms out. Jake, Jesse, Billy, and Jack witness his enraged exit as they enter to help. Scooter's amused by Jake's inquiry.

"What's crawled up Cody's butt and died? Reckon I should forget my first two guesses and go with number three?"

Jake turns to question Luke.

"Luke, how 'bout sharin' some big city wisdom with us country folk."

Luke sneers and responds.

"A blank mind can't absorb wisdom."

Scooter interjects to stop further squabbling.

"Luke, pick up Cody's rake so no one trips on it."

"I didn't drop it so I'm not picking it up. Tell Cody to pick up his own damn rake."

"Pick up the feckin' rake and put it away so we can go eat."

Luke ignores Hank's advice to follow the Cowboy Code and do what needs doing as well as where to draw the line.

'Why am I picking up Cody's stuff?'

Luke slips his foot under the handle and flips it up to his hand and twirls it around before adding speed with every step. He spins the rake around his body and performs stick handling exercises until noticing the others staring at him and drops the rake and also exits the barn. Scooter expresses his confusion.

"What was that?"

Jack responds first.

"I'm not sure."

Luke's demonstration energizes Jake's remarks.

"That was awesome. I wanna do that. Whadda y'all think, Jesse?"

"Jake, you'd beat yourself silly. Luke looked like a cross of Bruce Lee and Jason Statham."

Chester's concerned to hear Scooter's account of Luke's aggressive display.

'Luke's confrontational nature is more deeply imbedded than I figured.'

"Scooter, put Luke on the tractor detail."

'What's Luke really capable of? What does Hank know and would he share threats with me?'

Scooter, Cody, and Jack lead Luke outside after breakfast to learn how to tune up the tractor. Cody attempts to embarrass Luke.

"Hope and Holly can do this."

Jack's comment confuses Luke.

"Who'd sing about tractors bein' sexy? This beast ain't sexy. Josh Abbott's right in 'I'll Sing About Mine'. Some people need to sing about the life they live instead of what they think they know."

Colt's arrival is concealed by the tractors rough running engine. He stealthily sneaks up behind Luke and shoves his pistol into Luke's back. Colt's unaware Luke's expression doesn't change at the unexpected threat. The guys don't know what Colt's done but are shocked by what happens next.

"Hey asshole, you can't hit me and get away with it? I'm gonna…"

Luke spins around to cut Colt's intimidating comment short. He forcefully chops Colt's wrist with his right hand to knock the gun loose. Colt's pain induced yelp ends when Luke's left fist simultaneously rises against his nose sending blood spurting from ruptured veins. Colt drops to the ground and convulses in sheer agony while Luke bends over to pick up the gun and aim it menacingly in Colt's direction. Colt's oblivious to the danger he's in but the guys nervously worry about the potential for Luke to start shooting at them. Luke's gaze replicates a snake's emotionless unblinking stare and appears coldly detached before turning to hand the gun to Scooter.

"Kids shouldn't be allowed to play with guns."

Jack witnesses Luke's feat.

"How'd he disarm Colt so fast?"

Luke's walking to the bunkhouse when Hope pulls up and sees Cody helping Colt to his feet. She rushes over to find out what happened.

"Colt, are you okay?"

Cody studies Hope's worried expression.

'This is gonna get bad quick.'

Hope becomes alarmed to see Colt's face and shirt covered in blood and looks in Luke's direction.

'Yup, Hope's gonna go ballistic.'

Cody knows Hope won't take the news of Luke punching Colt again well.

"We had a little incident."

"Did Luke do this? Jail and this ranch are too good. I'm gonna kill him."

Cody grabs Hope's arm to stop her.

"Whoa, Hope. It wasn't Luke's fault this time."

Cody hurries through his explanation of what happened. Hope looks into Colt's dazed eyes which reveal increasing shame and appears dejected at failing his mission.

"Colt, what were ya thinkin'? You'd go to jail for this."

"Hope, you just threatened to kill him so you'd go to jail also."

"That's different!"

"How's that different?"

Hope comprehends she can't shoot Luke without probable cause. *'I do have Faith to think about.'*

Colt groans and grabs his wrist.

"My wrist hurts. That son of a bitch better not've broken it. I have an important flight tomorrow morning."

Scooter retrieves Luke from the bunkhouse.

"Laddie, there's work to finish unless you wanna deal with the devil."

Luke's answer is cold.

"I've been dealing with the devil for years."

Luke wants to hide in isolation but Scooter forces him to return to the tractor. They pass Hope caring for Colt so Luke expects another tongue lashing but only receives a silent glare.

'Hope's misjudging me again.'

Luke gazes into Hope's green eyes and feels a strange calm sensation overtake him.

'What's wrong with me? I'm so confused. I just got dumped by a heartless woman and this one's trying to kill me. Why do I feel any interest in Hope? I'm not looking for anything with anyone.'

Scooter spots Luke's tore up hands.

'We don't need him getting an infection.'

"Hope, could you look at Luke's hands? For possible infections."

She hesitates but realizes Scooter wouldn't ask if he weren't concerned.

'Great, now I need to help him.'

Luke cautiously holds his hands out so Hope can inspect them.

"I'm able to take care of myself."

"Yeah, whatever, I'm doin' this for Scooter, not you."

Hope gently cradles Luke's hands in hers to examine his wounds. Her eyes travel up to look into his momentarily before continuing her examination and bitterly reporting to Scooter.

"There's no reason he can't work."

'How is he workin' with his hands in that condition? Why did it feel good holdin' his hands? I felt something, but what?'

Luke's shocked after Hope tenderly holds his hands.

'This feels good. Hope's hands are a mix of soft and rough.'

Scooter's voice invades Luke's thoughts ahead of a dump truck's diesel engine.

"Right on time."

Chester orders fresh gravel annually to improve the driveway and instructs everyone to move their vehicles. Diesel exhaust taints the air while the truck dumps the large load of gravel in the sunbaked circular area. Luke notices Chester's evil grin when he glances towards Luke.

'Now what?'

"I have a great idea."

'Here it comes.'

"Normally y'all do this together. This year Luke's gonna do alone."

Scooter's pushing a wheelbarrow, shovel, and gloves towards Luke.

"You can't be serious! I'm not doing this alone! With only those."

"Yup. Keep punchin' people, ya get more tough work."

"I'm not doing this alone! Use the tractor."

"The tractor's gittin' repaired, remember. You get the pleasure of spreadin' this beautiful gravel to make the area look presentable for the guests."

"I'm not working alone in this heat. Someone's helping me."

"I once heard the Lord can move entire mountains, He just may choose to do it a wheelbarrow at a time. You can feel close to God this way."

Chester's sadistic laugh entertains the others regarding Luke's misfortune. He shares another thought before walking away.

"I'll let Hope supervise y'all."

Hope grins while patting her holster. Luke begins the miserable task of shoveling gravel one load at a time. Colt trails behind Hope and Billy to the riding barn so she can monitor his nose and wrist. Luke's workload and agitated state allows Hope to feel evil satisfaction in the moment. Chester keeps tabs on Luke's progress during the rigorous task but finds he's not the only one. Hope occasionally exits the barn to check on the headway Luke's making with the project. She seems fascinated Luke's single-handedly leveling the mound at a fairly rapid pace. Hope's present thoughts observing Luke would shock Chester if he found out.

'Luke's impressing me with how he's doin'. But why am I watchin' him? I'm not interested in him. Except to see him suffer. Damn JeniMay and Jubilee for sayin' anything. I'm not lookin' for another broken heart. And I have my gun to protect me. I don't need a man.'

Hope's odd behavior puzzles Billy. She usually doesn't stop until the work is finished.

'Hope must want to make sure Luke's workin' like he's supposed to.'

Luke's sweat saturates him from head to toe which attracts biting horseflies. Their painful bites leave red blotches on his exposed forearms. Luke finishes in just over three hours but his face and arms are showing signs of sunburn even after applying sunscreen. Luke returns the shovel and wheelbarrow to the rodeo barn with a smug look. He discovers Sam's arrived unseen during his water break. Hope, Billy, and Colt have also entered the barn since Colt's waiting for Hope to take him to the hospital. Luke's eyes don't hide his loathing for Colt's presence when he approaches to confront Luke.

"Take your bloody nose somewhere else, Dick. I thought your sorry ass would've left already."

Hope's ready to verbally interject until Colt interferes.

"We're not done, asshole. And you still can't dress yourself."

"Oh, we're done alright. I'll break your ossicles so you feel more pain."

Luke's intimidating threat shocks Hope.

'Ossicles? Wait, I know those. The bones inside the human ear. How would Luke know about those?'

"Y'all ain't touchin' my testicles. I'll put you six feet under first."

Hope listens to Colt threaten Luke.

'Colt needs to shut up. Luke's already beat him twice.'

"Colt, play nice, you're already hurt."

"I'm done bein' nice."

Sam makes a combative move towards Luke. Hope rolls her eyes along with a sigh.

'Here we go. Testosterone outta control.'

"Do what you're told asshole."

Luke's unimpressed by Sam's attempted reprimand.

"Have you heard of Schadenfreude?"

"That's not even a real word."

"Oh, it's real. It means to take great delight in the misfortune of others. You and Dick here, or would you rather go by pony boy? Both of you are my schadenfreude as long as I get to knock your asses around."

"Just shut your mouth and work like you're supposed to."

"Sam, let me share some advice with you. It's better to keep your mouth closed and be thought a fool instead of opening it and proving it."

Luke's insult invokes laughter from Scooter. Hope makes a mental note about Luke after listening to him.

'Luke might be smarter than I thought.'

Billy re-enters to find Colt and Sam fuming while Scooter's laughing.

'What's goin' on in here?'

Hope walks to Billy's side and hugs him.

"Thanks for your help today, Billy."

Luke's next inquiry irritates Hope.

"Are you dating Billy?"

Colt speaks defensively.

"Hope should be with me."

Sam squirms after Luke's stinging comment still echoes in his head.

'I wanna say somethin' but I don't want to sound stupid.'

Hope regains Luke's attention.

"My life is none of your business."

Hope's not interested to have Luke know anything about her.

"If you ask me, you've got lousy taste in men. Colt wants to make you his filly for a while."

Hope observes Colt's eyes widen fearfully.

"I'm not datin' anyone. Mind your own business."

'Dammit. Why did I answer Luke?'

Luke's opinion about her dating choices offends Hope because she's still clueless about Colt and Sam's derogatory statements about her being the reason he hit them.

"Sam, let's go on a date tonight."

Colt's stunned and Sam needs a moment to overcome his shock.

"Whoa, Hope, we've always had something special. What gives?"

Colt's deeply bothered Sam could have first chance to bed Hope down.

"You need to go to the hospital. We can schedule a date for another day. Jubilee and JeniMay keep telling me I need to get out more. Maybe they're right."

Billy's concerned by Hope's bombshell invitation to Sam.

"Hope, are ya sure 'bout this?"

"I know what I'm doin', I'm a grown woman."

Hope's already getting a queasy feeling in her knotted stomach about a date with Sam.

'Faith's never liked Sam for some reason. She's gonna kill me. Me and my big mouth. Why is Luke getting to me like this? Why did I let him?'

Sam returns to work with a grin and whistling a happy tune. Hope finds it odd to see Luke's dismayed expression when she glances at him.

'What's his deal?'

Billy remembers his original intention for entering the barn.

"Scooter, Chester wants Luke in his office."

"Alright, Luke, let's go see what's next."

Luke's comment is contemptuous.
"Great, more shit from an asshole."
Luke removes the gloves to reveal his bloody hands.
"Aw shit, Luke, you're hands look worse."
Hope sees Luke's hands and scrutinizes him again.
'Does this guy feel pain?'
"Scooter, let Katie take care of him.

TWENTY SIX

Scooter offers Luke some advice outside the barn after he washes his hands off.

"You may wanna think twice about actin' like a cheeky so and so, dipshit. This ranch could be an opportunity to stay outta jail and learn useful skills. And you're wearing a hat from now on while you're outside."

Scooter's recommendations don't interest Luke.

"This is jail for me. Like a chain gang. I guess they still exist around here, right? Less civilized here. I'm not learning anything useful here. And I don't wear hats."

'Can I still win Linda back?'

Scooter resists the urge to punch Luke for his insolent attitude.

'I want to hit him but I'd end up like Ben.'

Scooter enters the house first so Luke's able to let the screen door crash shut. The insufferable noise resounds throughout the house causing Scooter to cringe before knocking on Chester's open office door. Chester eyes rise from the paperwork spread across to old-fashioned cedar desk while music softly plays in the background. His exasperated expression switches to an angered inspection of Luke.

"It'd be real nice if y'all could show us those ears work and your tiny brain understands not to let the door slam shut. And you're interruptin' my Waylon time."

Chester's irritation amuses Luke.

"Do you understand me?"

"I would if I were listening."

"You're like dealin' with a Monday morning attitude on Friday afternoon."

"I've had it with you barking orders at me."

Chester's loud, booming tone delivers his message.

"I am your boss. You will listen and work hard so you can get the hell off my ranch."

Luke taunts Chester again.

"You don't to be my boss. I'll drive you crazy. I already do."

"I hate headaches! And you're a major headache."

Luke's wicked grin spells trouble for Chester.

"I don't get headaches but I'm known to give people headaches, really bad painful ones."

Luke stops to observe Chester's office more closely and notes several written phrases framed on the wall. One reads:

Opportunity is an unlocked door in life
Hope is the hinges it hangs on
Fear is the lock that keeps it closed
Desire is the key which opens opportunity.

A second one states:

You can stand in front of a brand-new mirror and still look old.

The third one proclaims:

To Become A Man Is Like Constantly Revising And Correcting A Written Piece.

Chester's signature appears under each expression. A small Confederate flag hangs on another wall under an American and Texas state flag.

'Figures a cranky old man in Texas has a Confederate flag.'

Luke thinks he knows the reason but has no clue about the truthful purpose. A large hand-carved dark brown glossy wooden cactus stands next to the computer monitor along with more picture frames.

'I wonder who's in those pictures.'

Another Texas shaped Oak clock beautifully adorned with Texas wildflowers hangs on the wall behind Luke. There's a deer head mounted on the wall behind Chester which surprises Luke since it's not a Longhorn.

"I'm gonna work ya harder than you've ever worked in your life. That'll beat the piss poor attitude outta you."

"I'd rather just leave. I'm treated so unfairly here."

Chester's fed up with Luke's complaints.

"Hey jackass, life ain't fair. Hell it ain't always good. Bad shit happens to challenge you to determine whatchur made of. Life tests your character and bad shit makes us appreciate the good times. Sometimes bad happens to change our course when we can't change on our own."

Luke challenges Chester.

"Life's already been plenty unfair to me. I don't need any more shit thrown my way. I've been shit on too much for one lifetime."

"I'm tired of hearin' the same words coming outta your mouth. Quit complainin' life's unfair. Big deal, life shit on you, stand up, wipe your ass and take charge of your life. Change what needs changin' to make your life better."

"I can't till I leave here."

"How 'bout changin' that attitude here and bring it somewhere else?"

"You sound like Hank."

Chester returns his attention to Scooter feeling like he's won if Luke's comparing him to Hank.

"How are the repairs goin'? I've been stuck here."

Scooter's eyes drift towards Luke.

"Despite several setbacks we're still on schedule somehow."
Chester notices Luke feigning like he's dozing off.
"Are we boring you, Luke?"
Luke responds sarcastically.
"Not at all, Chester. Ranch business is riveting."
Chester furiously slams his hand on the desk.
"You'll address me as Mr. Kinkead, or Sir, you little shit. What's wrong with you? Are y'all that stupid? You can't honestly be as dumb as a box of rocks, can you? Keep actin' up and you'll be stayin' here longer unless I press charges against you on behalf of Ben. You can rot in jail for all I care. I'm so bowed up 'cause y'all ain't seein' the big picture."
'Bowed up?'
Chester's term for feeling angry confuses Luke.
'I have to find new ways to irritate this old coot or I'll be stuck here forever.'
Luke's expression conveys his understanding of this fact and feels irritated he's losing control to aggravate Chester without consequence. Chester in turn grasps this fact.
"You're beginnin' to get my drift. Change your tune, you hear me?"
Luke's frustrated to lose the upper hand.
"I hear you loud and clear."
Chester confronts Luke with a low, angered tone.
"You hear me loud and clear, what?"
Luke's confused at first.
"I hear you loud and clear, sir."
"That's more like it, and look, it didn't kill you to show some respect, even if it wasn't heart-felt."
Chester slyly grins now that the battle with Luke has turned in his favor.
'Maybe this jackass'll lose his rebellious attitude now.'
Scooter wonders if this crippling blow will stop Luke's verbal assaults against the guys.
"Chester, what's with the paperwork? Shouldn't you be working on the computer?"
Chester responds to Scooter's query with moderate irritation.

"The damn thing's acting up and my accountant's out of town. He knows how to fix this."

Luke absent-mindedly asks a question.

"What's the problem?"

"It's not workin'. What difference does it make to you?"

"Did you try rebooting it?"

Chester stares disbelievingly at Luke.

"You want me to kick the computer?"

Luke raise his hands passively while Chester stands up behind his desk.

"No, that's not what I mean."

'This idiot doesn't know re-booting means to restart a computer, not kick it.'

"Would you care to explain yourself?"

"I could but showing you would be better."

Chester snorts indignantly.

"You think you're gonna teach me something?"

Luke's first impulse is to leave but grasps this could help him leave the ranch sooner.

"It's better if I talk you through each step while you write it down."

Chester has his reservations about letting Luke near his computer.

'This guy can't do a lick of work here but offers to help with this.'

"I'll shoot your ass if I think you're up to somethin'."

"Trust me. You'll understand what to do if it happens again."

Chester's bushy eyebrows rise.

"Trust you? After your behavior on my ranch? You haven't been payin' attention, have you?"

"This will get your computer working again, sir."

'He's either a fast talker or fast learner.'

Chester motions Luke around the desk.

'Luke's awful sure of himself. Hank said he has a strong personality and can assert himself like a leader would. Maybe this is what he meant.'

"Alright, show me how to fix this."

Scooter observes a difference in Luke's attitude.

'Luke's supportive and helpful. He's not provoking trouble at all.'

"Write down the steps as I explain them and then do it on the computer. I'll watch."

"Alright, stand here but don't touch anything unless I tell ya to."

Luke studies the pictures momentarily. There's one of Holly standing next to a horse but Luke's drawn to two others. A much younger pudgy version of Hope wearing overalls and pigtails sits next to one of Hope racing a horse around a barrel with her hair flying wildly behind her. Luke's attention shifts to helping Chester.

"Holy shit! It's working again. You fixed it."

"Yep, the computer can annoy you instead of me."

"You're not totally worthless after all."

"Thanks for such a ringing endorsement."

"Don't be thinkin' you're an expert. I don't trust anyone who thinks that way. So-called experts don't know what they think they know."

A female's soft, angelic voice chastises Chester's off-putting remark from the hallway before Hope enters the office.

"You think that way 'bout my care for your horses? Not a strong vote of confidence."

Hope catches Chester off guard. He watches her smile disappear when she spots Luke.

"Why's he here still? Vermin belong outside, dead."

Hope's nasty attitude and hatred for Luke quickly reappear.

"Get him outta here. I can't stand to be so close to rats."

"Hold on, Hope. Luke's actually useful."

"Terrific. Throw a parade then exterminate the vermin."

Luke sarcastically mimics Hope while rolling his eyes to further frustrate her.

'Sam can't match Luke's level of annoyance with Hope.'

Luke's also assessing Hope.

'Hope's just like Chester. Always trying to act in charge at all times. She's cold, distant, mean-spirited and seemingly uncaring and always unhappy.'

Hope mirrors Chester's attitude to make Luke's life miserable while he's at the ranch. Luke's yet to verbally attack Hope like he does everyone else though. He irritates Hope by mimicking her or using a condescending tone but hasn't crossed over to vocally attacking her. Luke finds Hope beguilingly attractive even with her off-putting attitude.

'Hope's eyes are magical. No one but Hank knows that.'

Luke stops to ask Hope a patronizing question.

"Why are you here?"

Chester swiftly interjects.

"Hope's here for my scheduled checkup."

Chester's reasoning perplexes Luke.

"Um, okay. Old people up north go to regular doctors since they need them a lot. It really is different here in Texas."

Hope can't hold back a giggle after Luke's humorous observation. Chester becomes infuriated causing Hope to laugh more while he stands.

"Not for me, you idiot! Hope's here for the horses. You know that already. You can't be that thick-headed to actually think that."

Chester's angry eruption turns Hope's suppressed giggle turns into full, hearty laughter. His reaction to Luke's comment is hilarious and Hope finds it a bonus Chester's yelling at Luke. Scooter struggles to remember hearing Hope laughing so animatedly without Faith being a part of it. Luke notices Hope's changed out of her scrubs.

'Wow! Hope's a knockout in jeans.'

Scooter and Chester note Luke's expression softens at the sight of Hope in her Wrangler jeans which accentuate her long slender legs, shapely hips, and petite waist. Hope's a buxom beauty like Holly, only taller. Her scrubs no longer conceal her curvaceous body. A teal button-down shirt and black cowboy boots complete her outfit. She wears her favorite weathered straw cowboy hat with the hawk's feather in the hat band. Her hair flows freely into long, silky, eye-catching ebony waterfall curls cascading down to her waist. Her black hair and tanned facial features accent her attractive green eyes to create the illusion she can see through the person she looks at. Hope's always noticed when entering rooms by men and women however the women's jealousy of Hope's natural eye-catching beauty is clearly on display. Hope doesn't care a whit about their thoughts because her life is busy and full of troubles and unwanted worries. Hope could have become a professional model at sixteen when an agent spotted her at a rodeo. She refused his offer because she was determined to earn a living using her brain instead of a bikini. Holly tried taking her place but the agent had enough blondes already. Chester originally thought it was a mistake for Hope to refuse another way to earn money for school. Hope told Chester she found the guy offensive and was proved correct six months later when he was arrested for raping several of the models. Chester declared he'd trust her decisions from that point on. Luke's pulled from his trance when Hope speaks again.

"I have a couple errands in town. I'll return to finish up before Faith and I go to the gym."

Chester chooses to seek revenge for Hope laughing at Luke's check-up comment.

'This'll teach Hope to laugh at me like that.'

"Bring Luke to help ya carry everything."

Luke and Hope simultaneously express their astonishment.

"What? No way!"

"Yep, he'll be your helper dude."

"I'm not being her dude."

"That's not a compliment. A dude here means inexperienced rider or a guy from the city."

Luke's unhappy to hear Chester's explanation.

'I should've known those asshole's weren't being nice.'

"Y'all've lost your mind! I have two stops. I certainly don't need help from a convict. He's liable to run away."

Luke casts an indignant look at Hope.

"Convict? I'm not a convict."

"You spent time in jail. That makes you a convict. You wore an orange jumpsuit, right? What if this convict tries stealing my truck?"

Luke rolls his eyes.

"Shoot 'im."

Chester's lips curl into a mischievous smile.

"Shoot 'im dead. You've wanted to since missin' him the first time."

Hope frowns at Chester's perceived jab about missing her target. Luke overlooked the fact Hope's wearing her gun.

"Hold on! Wait a minute! She'll shoot me and make up an excuse later. I'm not going anywhere with her."

Chester's amused Luke seems threatened by Hope and her gun now.

"Hope's a crack shot. Don't get any ideas of runnin' off. She can shoot you if you act up. Oh, and for the record, Hope only misses when she wants to."

Hope's pleased when Chester winks at her since she's proud of her expert level shooting skills. She's still agitated Chester's forcing Luke to go with her. Holly strolls into the office as carefree as can be which intensifies the room's stress level immediately.

"Grand-daddy, I don't have any work to do so I'm gonna see a movie with the girls tonight."

Holly examines the unhappy faces staring back at her.

"Okay, nobody act so happy, please. Who stepped on whose boots in here?"

Chester gruffly addresses Holly.

"You can see the movie but none of this goin' out afterwards. You understand me?"

Holly steps closer to Luke.

"Yes, Grand-daddy, I understand."

Holly smiles seductively and holds Luke's hand.

"Could I bring Luke? He needs some fun too."

Luke's struggling not to look at Holly's half exposed chest since her shirt's halfway unbuttoned.

'Holly's braless to show everything off.'

Luke looks away and sees Hope's disgusted expression.

"Is he one of your buckle bunnies?"

"Not yet."

Hope's spoken contempt for Luke drips like gravy from a ladle.

"Do I really have to take him with me?"

"Yes, it might be better now."

Hope knows it's futile to argue the point with Chester. Luke has a thought cross his mind.

'I'd rather take my chances with Hope now. Chester's threat to kill me for getting close to Holly seems truthful.'

"Can I ask one favor?"

Luke's question annoys Chester.

"What?"

"Can I wear my sneakers instead of these boots, they're killing my feet and giving me blisters."

"Fine! Get your damn gym shoes and go enjoy your date with Hope."

Hope glares at Chester.

"It's definitely not a date!"

"I agree. Not a date."

Luke sighs while changing into his sneakers before emerging from the bunkhouse.

'I feel so much better now.'

Hope sits in her truck gunning the engine feeling more frustrated when she sees Luke walking her way.

'Misfortune strikes again.'

She wants to leave Luke behind but won't go against Chester's wishes.

'I don't want this asshole runnin' errands with me.'

TWENTY SEVEN

Luke's not expecting Hope to hit the accelerator when he opens the passenger door. She makes a hard, fast left turn to cause Luke's foot to slip off the rail. He's barely hanging on to the door's armrest and doorframe while his feet drag behind him. Hope's sending dust and gravel everywhere during the tight turn. Chester groans as the scene unfolds.

"Aw, c'mon. Hope couldn't leave the new gravel in place for one day. Luke actually did a good job and she's gone and wrecked it."

Scooter shakes his head while Hope's truck fishtails down the driveway. Both men are relieved when Luke successfully pulls himself into Hope's truck and closes the door.

"Lord willing and the creek don't rise Luke'll return to your work detail later. If Hope don't kill 'im first."

"That's a mighty big if. You did give Hope permission to shoot him."

"That might've been a mistake."

Laughter breaks out in the barn when Scooter enters alone. Cody questions Chester's decision.

"Chester did what?"

Jake cheerfully declares his thought.

"We won't be seein' Luke again, will we?"

Cody answers.

"Not alive. Hope's been itchin' to shoot Luke all week. She might finish him off today."

Luke's new misadventure entertains the group until Jake shares a thought for their input.

"What if we gang up on Luke and dish out some range justice?"

Cody's quick to respond.

"He's a pain in the ass and deserves a taste of his own medicine for what he did to Ben."

Scooter shares his thought.

"Don't cross the line with Chester over Luke. Have at it but leave me out of it though."

Luke's lividly catching his breath inside Hope's careening truck.

"You obviously don't know how to drive. That stupid stunt almost killed me."

"I'll try harder next time."

"I'm not giving you another chance."

Hope unleashes her full wrath on Luke.

"Shut up asshole! Just shut up! I hate you. I wish you were dead."

Hope's consumed by her rage which affects her driving and gets pulled over by the sheriff.

'I feel like everything's unraveling.'

Hope's aggravated response matches the look in her eyes but Luke's curious Bob seems upset to see him in the passenger seat.

"This is Chester's idea, not mine."

Bob listens to Hope's explanation and lets her go with a verbal warning.

"Slow down. Be safe, Hope. I wouldn't want anything happen to you, alright. Where're y'all goin' in such a hurry anyway?"

"H E B first then Tractor Supply, then back to the ranch to get rid of a convict rat."

Luke's tired of Hope's constant comparison of him to a diseased rodent.

"Alright, slow down and be more careful."

"Sorry Bob, I will."

Luke finds it odd the sheriff would be unhappy to see him in Hope's truck.

'I don't understand why Bob seemed surprised I'm here.'

He looks back to see the sheriff taking out his phone to make a call. Luke turns to face forward again and notices the gold necklace and pendant Hope's wearing when sunlight reflects off it.

"That's a pretty necklace and twin heart pendant."

Hope instinctively reaches for the pendant without acknowledging Luke's compliment.

"Did you buy that or was it a gift?"

"None of your business. And don't think of stealing it either."

"Why would I, oh, never mind? You said you're not dating anyone. So you're married? Your husband gave it to you then."

Luke's incorrect guess provokes a heated response from Hope.

"Ex-husband. And no. Chester gave this to me. The hearts represent me and my daughter being connected for life. Something I doubt you know anything about."

"Um, okay. It's sweet you share a special bond with your daughter."

"Whatever."

'Huh, Luke's actually capable of saying something nice.'

Luke's trying Hank's suggestion to open up instead of remaining silent.

"Sorry I asked."

Hope feels compelled to further explain her necklace.

"Chester bought this when Faith was born. He said it will always remind me the special bond shared between a parent and their child."

Luke detects a new scent.

"Something smells nice."

"It ain't you, that's for sure."

Luke considers another question but Hope tries to shut him down.

"Quit stickin' your nose in my business. You don't need to know anything about me."

Luke's overwhelmed by curiosity.

"Why did Chester raise you on the ranch? What happened to your parents?"

Luke's question hurts Hope deeply so she lashes out.

"Shut up! Just shut up! Stop askin' questions or I will shoot you and leave you on the side of the road for the vultures."

Hope goes quiet until surprising Luke with an answer.

"I was dumped on Chester's doorstep. My parents didn't love me. Chester and Millie raised me like their own daughter. They're the closest I've had to family. As well as Holly and the guys at the ranch."

Hope's voice possesses a distinct sorrow.

"So that's why Faith calls Chester Grand-daddy? I've heard the guys talking."

Hope recognizes she's discussing very personal stuff with Luke and turns nasty again.

"Don't speak my daughter's name again. You're not worthy to. You probably don't know the first thing about kids anyway."

Luke responds with a straight face.

"I know everything I need to know about kids. No bright lights. Don't get them wet. And never feed them after midnight."

Hope's unsure if Luke's serious before coldly speaking.

"What? No! You're an idiot! My daughter's not a gremlin. I'm sure y'all'd make gremlins if you have kids."

'That was sort of funny.'

Luke's grin reveals he knows he touched a nerve.

"No more talk about me and my daughter or you'll suffer severe consequences."

"Sorry. Someone recommended a different approach. It's not like I'm asking you for a date. I have a strict rule not to start a relationship with anyone who shoots at me."

Hope scoffs at Luke's comments.

"A date? A relationship? Don't make me laugh. You'll get neither from me."

Luke adds another comment.

"Relationships are heartaches waiting to happen and I don't need any more of that shit in my life."

Hope hears a similar hint of sorrow during Luke's reply and sadly echoes his answer.

"On that, we can agree."

Hope approaches a semi-truck and Luke reveals a fearful look while nervously leaning towards her. Hope arrives at the H-E-B parking lot and pulls into the employee section.

"That's the grocery store? The whole building? We're going to park near the door, right?"

Hope's plan is to make Luke carry everything.

"Are your legs broke?"

"No, aren't we able to park up front? There's so many open spots."

Hope answers sternly while unbuckling.

"Y'all can walk on your two good legs."

Luke's happy to wear his gym shoes again while walking next to Hope. She halts abruptly stops near the large two story steel framed glass enclosed store entrance.

"Shit! My gun. Grab two buggies while I stow my weapon in the truck. I'll meet you inside. Don't even think of runnin'. My aim is perfect."

"Buggies?"

"Shopping carts, idiot."

Luke spots the sign prohibiting weapons in the store while Hope returns to her truck.

"Hmmm, I thought Texans carried their guns everywhere."

Luke chooses a magazine about southern living off the rack to shield his face from suspicious stares regarding his shabby appearance. Luke's feeling self-conscious until a cart girl frantically runs into the store yelling for help.

"Someone's bein' attacked in the parking lot!"

Luke's first thought forces him to hesitate.

'Hope'll shoot me if she thinks I'm running away.'

Luke's world changes with the girl's next words.

"A lady with long black hair's in trouble."

Luke drops the magazine and sprints through the open sliding glass doors at full speed in the direction of Hope's truck. Luke's forced to perform a cartwheel over the hood of a passing car and turn it into a backflip. He lands on his feet and immediately shifts to avoid an oncoming car heading the opposite direction. A dark blue windowless van is stopped near Hope's truck with the sliding door open. Several men surround Hope while one has her in a bear hug. Luke contemplates an idea after a second glance at the van while Hope wildly kicks her feet into the air and screams.

'*Why does that van look familiar?*'

TWENTY EIGHT

Hope finishes stowing her pistol in her quick access truck safe before a grubby, portly man approaches from a plain blue van. She thinks it's an employee walking to a nearby car until he grabs her and yanks Hope towards the van. She fights to escape his grasp but he easily overpowers her.

'I wish I had my gun.'

Hope yells to get the cart girl's attention only to see her turn and run away.

'She's worthless. What do I do now?'

Three unkempt men of mixed ethnicities exit the van's open sliding door. Their eyes display an unmistakable look of malice and all appear tough and repulsive. The last one out holds a burlap sack.

"We're gonna have fun with her."

Hope screams and kicks her feet into the air again while panic sets in.

'Oh God, Faith needs me.'

Hope's paralyzed by the thought of abduction or worst taking her away from Faith. Her cherished straw hat falls to the ground which produces a nonsensical comment.

"My hat, I can't lose my hat and the feather."

'Please Lord, let me see Faith again. She needs me and I need her.'

Hope's distraught no one seems willing to come to her aid and starts crying at the thought Faith will grow up without her. Hope's forgotten Luke came with her until two of the men turn to shout a warning.

"Watch Out!"

'I wish I hadn't threatened to shoot Luke. He might've been able to help but I'm sure he's waiting in the store like I told him to.'

Luke flashes by Hope and knocks one guy off his feet with a smashing blow to his cheek.

'Luke's here? But he's only one person.'

The man howls in pain while rolling around on the ground. Luke's rapid approach carries him past the group by several long strides before he pivots to face Hope's assailants. Luke steps towards the men which mystifies them. Luke's unknowingly sizing up the motley group during his advancement. They wear jeans or overalls with t-shirts and leather vest with intimidating patches. The driver steps out after watching Luke's aggressive behavior. Hope feels woefully unprepared for this life-threatening situation and recalls Luke's question about the parking spot. She remembers Jubilee's comment about needing someone's protection also.

'Was parking out here really necessary? Damn Jubilee for maybe bein' *right. What am I tryin' to prove?'*

The dazed man's struggling to stand on wobbly legs and move between Luke and Hope. The men wear violent tattoo sleeves to warn others they're dangerous.

'These guys must have depraved ideas about Hope. They've chosen the wrong target today.'

The thug holding Hope growls out a command.

"Beat him dead. J-man'll owe us extra."

Luke scans the area for other threats before refocusing on the brutish quartet surrounding him.

'Why is Luke so calm?'

Luke analyzes each man's movements and expressions for signs which will most likely start the fight. Years of his sensei's intensive training allows Luke to feel at ease and tune out unnecessary distractions.

Several large black birds raucously patrol the parking lot in search of food nearby. Luke baffles Hope.

'We're about to die and Luke's actin' like nothing's happening. Where is anyone else?'

Luke cavalierly addresses the thugs.

"Let's dance."

Luke lets the four men move first before erupting against them with incredible violence. The force of Luke's crushing blows shocks Hope as much as the men he attacks. Irrefutably etched looks of shock and pain indicates how incapable these men are against Luke's assault. Luke's fists, feet, and elbows strike viciously against his adversaries.

'They can't defend themselves against Luke.'

Hope watches the largest guy move first against Luke. Luke's fist smashes into the guy's face before spinning around and thrusting his elbow against the thug's chest. The merciless impact knocks the air out of his lungs and doubles him over while blood gushes from his nose and mouth. Luke returns his focus to the first guy he hit to deliver a combination of punches to his face and body. He finishes with a flying roundhouse kick to the guy's head to knock him out. The third guy, now on Luke's right side is next to receive a kick to the shin which produces an animalistic howl before going silent after Luke's fist fractures his cheekbone and renders him unconscious. Luke's attention shifts back to the guy still bent over and gasping to use a power packed upper cut into his face quickly followed by a ferocious front kick. This fourth thug is thrown backwards and falls to the ground out cold from the fury of Luke's attack. Luke's swift assault appears carefully choreographed with a combination of punches, elbows, and kicks which victimize the four men. Hope's mystified by what she's witnessed.

'What just happened?'

Luke's superior strength and fighting skills negated the size and number of Hope's assailants. The fifth man's shocked Luke's decimated his friends so easily. He stares down at the asphalt where they lie silently and motionless. Luke's unleashed fury succeeds in creating a list of unknown injuries. The final thug standing tightly wraps his arm around Hope's neck to choke her. She gasps for air while straining to loosen his grip until he angrily shakes her like a ragdoll.

"I'll squeeze her head right off if you move an inch."

Hope's face is turning red and her struggling lessens quickly while losing the ability to breath. Fear is plainly seen in her eyes. Luke resolutely steps towards them.

"Back off asshole! I'll drop you right here, right now."

Hope stares into Luke's hazel-colored eyes blazing with a fiery rage and shudders uncontrollably.

'Luke resembles a predator stalking its prey. Is this what I see last?'

Hope's more terrified when the thug issues another threat against Luke's life. His vocal tone seems less certain this time since he's used to people cowering when threatened. Luke continues to fearless approach.

"You're a dead man! You just don't know it yet."

Luke's left eyebrow rises after hearing the third threat.

"I died a long time ago."

Luke's coldly delivered statement confuses Hope.

'What does Luke mean?'

Luke crouches slightly and leans forward before charging without warning and forcibly shoves Hope to the ground with his right arm. The move allows Luke to grab the thug's right wrist with his left hand and dig his thumb into the pressure point which prevents the guy from firing his gun. Luke creates an unbearable pain with his steel trap grip while pushing the assailant's arm upwards. He strikes with a brutal upper cut into the guy's jaw to nearly knock him out as he crumbles into a broken heap. The thug attempts to aim his gun at Luke until Luke delivers a ruthless kick alongside his head which fractures the guy's jaw and cheekbone and knocks him out. Luke puts the gun on Hope's truck hood.

'Hope's abused me all week and even shot me but she didn't deserve this.'

Deep down, Luke knew he doesn't want Faith to grow up without parents like he did.

'No child should know the nightmare I've dealt with for over twenty years.'

Hope lies on the ground mostly unscathed physically but is severely shaken by the ordeal. Luke moves in to kneel down and gently touch his hand on her shoulder to help her sit up. He feels Hope trembling and speaks with a soft reassuring tone.

"Are you okay? You're safe now. I won't let anyone hurt you."

Hope shudders when Luke's hand touches her shoulder. She nods and rubs the sore area on her neck after the potentially lethal choke hold. Luke surprises Hope when he shifts to hug her to comfort her so she knows the danger is truly over. Hope leans her head back slightly to look into Luke's eyes before pressing her lips against his for a sizzling kiss until realizing what she's doing. Her gaze is mixed with passion, confusion, and embarrassment when their eyes meet again.

'What is happening to my life?'

Blaring sirens from converging police vehicles prevents further interaction.

'I haven't heard sirens in nearly a week. I usually hear them every day. Why did Hope kiss me?'

Luke voluntarily stands and raises his arms to indicate he's not a threat.

'Why is Luke surrendering? He saved me.'

Officers approach to help Hope with guns drawn. Two officers forcibly drag Luke towards a squad while a third trains his gun on Luke due to his unkempt condition. More officers arrive but Hope feels alarmingly unprotected since Luke's unseen behind a SUV squad. She struggles to recall what actually happened during Luke's absence and becomes more frightened to realize the full truth.

'It all seems like a terrifying blur.'

Hope's mind wants to block the horrible attack but one fact becomes increasingly sharper.

'The fight only lasted a couple minutes. That's why it seemed like the police took so long to respond.'

Another fact occurs to her.

'Luke wasn't punched once by those guys. How is that possible if I was able to punch him? He could've overpowered me at any point to escape. No wonder Ben got hurt so bad. Luke's a force to be reckoned with.'

Hope ponders Luke's tenderness, concern, and honest compassion revealed in his eyes and voice while kneeling next to her compared to his aggressive side.

'Why did Luke save me? Why did I kiss him? And why did I get chill bumps when he touched me?'

TWENTY NINE

Bob spots Luke face down with his arms spread across the hood of a squad with two officers questioning him and a third holding a weapon on him. He hasn't received any updates about Hope's condition so he rushes at Luke. Bob pulls Luke off the hood and spins him around to smash his hand into his chest.

"Where's Hope? Is she alive? What did y'all do? I should've shot you the other day."

Bob's aggressive action and accusation confuses the officers.

"Whoa, Sheriff Fisher, back down. We don't bring that aggression into a contained scene unless necessary. Why are you here? Your patrol doesn't usually include this area."

"I heard the call and knew a friend was in the vicinity. Is this the man who caused the problem?

An officer interrupts Bob to explain what's actually happened.

"Sheriff, this man subdued multiple suspects attempting to abduct that woman over there."

Bob glances towards Hope while a female office wraps a blanket around her.

"The woman's statement corroborates his explanation of a possible kidnapping. Or worse."

Luke seethes with anger while Bob backs away looking perplexed at the clarification. Bob's unfounded accusation infuriates Luke and one officer observes Luke making a fist and issues a command.

"Stand down. Don't do anything ill-advised now."

Bob notices Luke's clenched hand.

"Try it, I dare you."

Luke defiantly stands his ground while Bob asks an odd question.

"So Hope's not dead?"

"No sir, as you can see she's safe."

Luke contemplates Bob's peculiar question.

'Does Bob expect Hope to be dead?'

"One alleged attacker apparently never had a chance to use his gun."

Luke injects a fiery response.

"He had chances. He failed to take them and paid dearly. He's no alleged attacker. He was an actual attacker."

Bob doesn't like Luke's response.

"Lose the attitude, asshole."

Bob approaches Hope and sees the fright remaining in her eyes while pulling the blanket tighter as if it'll provide imaginary comfort and protection. The impenetrable wall Hope's hidden behind for years has been shattered like a baseball bat striking a fragile wine glass. Hope's newfound vulnerability leaves her feeling weak and unprotected and shivers uncontrollably even though it's a warm sunny day. Bob's shocked by Hope's first question.

"Where's Luke?"

Bob fumbles for an answer while stepping in to comfort Hope only to watch her turn away. He's offended she rejects his sympathetic gesture.

"Um, well, Luke's giving a statement to the officers. More importantly, how are you? Are you hurt?"

"Bob, he saved me from…"

Hope, you're safe. That's what matters. Don't worry 'bout him. Luke'll get what he deserves for lettin' this happen."

Hope stares disbelievingly at Bob.

"What? You think Luke had something to do with this? How? He doesn't know anyone here."

"We don't know anything about Luke. He could've set this up for all we know."

Luke's keenly scrutinizing Bob's body language while he talks to Hope.

'It's odd but Bob seems disappointed Hope's safe. Maybe I'm reading that wrong.'

"Bob, I've been so nasty to Luke since he arrived but I don't see how he planned this out. He didn't even know he was coming with me until we left the ranch."

Bob realizes their conversation isn't going the way he wants so he redirects the focus.

"Let's get you back to the ranch, okay."

"Yeah, okay. Luke could've run and no one would've known. Last week I nearly shot him for hurtin' Ben. I've been so mean to him at every chance."

Bob's aware how Ben's injury happened but recognizes Hope still doesn't know the truth.

'Hope doesn't need to know anything if it means she'll stay mad at Luke. It'll help matters out.'

The suspects are getting cuffed when it becomes obvious they're suffering severe injuries and get transported to a nearby hospital for treatment. Bob instructs an officer to drive Hope's truck and a second to follow behind in his squad.

"Luke'll sit up front so I can sit behind him. Hope'll sit in back with me. Don't try anything or it'll be the last thing you do."

'Why is Bob sayin' that to Luke?'

Bob gets a call and learns the injuries Luke's dispensed to Hope's attackers.

"Hope's alleged assailants'll be staying at the hospital thanks to you."

Luke coldly remarks.

"They got what they deserved."

Bob details the injuries for the officer and Hope listens to what Luke's attack inflicted on the five men. Luke silently stares out the windshield attempting not to lose control of his inner rage.

'Bob's wrongly blamed me twice now.'

Luke relives the captivating sensation he experienced touching Hope and perplexed by her kiss. It's all a mystery he's unable to solve and the accompanying turmoil keeps him from turning around to look at Hope.

'I don't want to meet anyone, especially here, right?'

Hope's facing her own confused state after Luke's kind actions.

'Luke risked his life to save me. Have I misjudged him?'

She continually glances at Luke for signs there could be answers to her questions.

'I'm at a loss for words to explain Luke's decision to face danger instead of escaping.'

Bob tactically apologizes to Luke in front of Hope for unprofessionally accusing him before knowing the facts.

'Bob accused Luke for the attack on me before knowing what happened. That's not like him.'

Hope feels some degree of sympathy for Luke while her thoughts continue to drift to Luke's tender touch.

'Why did I get chill bumps when Luke touched me? And what made me kiss him? I don't like him. I'm not lookin' for anyone, especially not someone like him. Right? Luke's Holly's type, not mine.'

THIRTY

Luke studies the Twisted Live Oak Ranch's impressive oversized black metal gate rolling open. He's ignored it on previous excursions. Luke notices the large star inside the outline of the state of Texas before they pass the Live Oak tree with its three twisted trunks rising from the ground. Legend tells of a tornado creating the knotted tree which gives the ranch its name. Both sights greet visitors to the ranch along the long winding red gravel driveway.

Chester's house, the bunkhouse, and the rodeo barn are located where the drive ends but guest housing and the riding barn are situated further in on the ranch. A dirt road replicating the old west traveler's pathway leads to those structures in an open grassy area.

Chester waits apprehensively on his deck until Hope's truck comes into view after Bob's call. He hurries across the roughed up gravel section to arrive next to her truck before it comes to a full stop. Luke glances at everyone gathered to welcome Hope including Sam and Colt. Chester forced Sam to take Colt for medical aid hoping they'd stay gone but returned for Colt's car. Chester opens the door and pulls Hope into a comforting hug.

"Are you alright? You're safe. Everything's okay."

Chester sheds several tears causing Hope to tremble uncontrollably when reality sinks in that she's safely back at the ranch.

'God, please let this be real and not a dream.'

Hope takes in a deep breath and lets it out slowly and feels relieved to know she's protected by the ranch once more. Chester leads Hope around the truck where Katie, JeniMay, and Jubilee wait to bring her inside. The four women take several steps before Luke emerges for Chester to catch sight of him. Hope turns after Chester charges Luke and clamps his hand on Luke's throat to shove him against the truck. Luke's head impacts the metal with a resounding thud. Chester shocks everyone when his voice projects a rage more intense and never heard by anyone before.

"What the hell happened out there today? Where were you? Why did you let Hope get attacked?"

Chester's final question forces Hope to reconsider Bob's insinuation Luke's responsible for the attack.

'Chester's never been so angry. He's also implying Luke planned this.'

Luke struggles to breathe but resists breaking free while Hope steps towards Chester until Katie pulls her back.

"Let's get away from this."

Luke remains submissive and allows Chester to slam his head twice more until Bob reaches out to take Chester's hand off Luke's throat.

"Luke helped Hope."

Hope's worried Luke will retaliate but remains passive during Chester's aggressive action.

'Why doesn't Luke break loose? I can't figure him out. He's lettin' Chester choke him but beat the shit outta five guys. Who's the real Luke?'

Sam and Colt laugh how Chester's easily roughing Luke up. Sam shares a thought with Colt when Hope's close.

"The jackass ain't so tough after all, is he Colt?"

"Guess not."

Sam steps towards Hope to console her until Katie's austere expression and Hope's indignant glare stops him. Katie's processing newly learned information which forms new thoughts based on what she's observed about Luke while guiding Hope inside.

'Luke's hidin' who he is. There's a lot more to him than we've seen. I've seen a kinder side the others haven't. But this is far beyond that. This is out of character with his pain in the ass routine. He was selfless and maybe even reckless for Hope's sake after she's made his life miserable here. Why did he save Hope? I'll be watchin' him closely to see what I can learn.'

Jubilee and JeniMay join Hope on the couch while Katie gets a glass of sweet tea to soothe her nerves. Katie steps outside to check on the still unfolding scene and notes Sam's smug look.

"Luke saved Hope from five guys tryin' to do something unspeakable. Would you do that for a complete stranger who's been nasty to you for a week?"

Sam shrugs and heads inside to check on Hope. Luke watches the wranglers converge on the house like one big family. Katie received a call from a friend at H-E-B after she gathered information from officers she knew. Katie in turn informs Hank since news crews are covering the story.

"Howdy Hank. Hope's been involved in a crazy situation but she's alright. The news may make it seem otherwise later."

"What happened?"

"Hope was attacked but Luke was there to save her."

Luke saved Hope. Ya don't say. And they're both safe?"

"Yup. Hope's shaken but in one piece."

"Good. I have a favor to ask."

Katie hangs up after listening to Hank's request. She walks inside to hear Jack asking a question.

"You said five guys attacked you? That can't be right. Luke didn't stop that many guys?"

Hope confirms the number is correct.

"It was five guys."

All the guys look at each other.

"We're the ones who shoulda been with ya. Nothin' would've happened then."

"I appreciate that but I am capable of takin' care of myself."

Jubilee looks at JeniMay while Hope's voice trails off and tugs at the blanket around her before Katie strongly states her opinion.

"Nobody should go through what you did, Hope."

Katie remembers Luke's Superman comment and wonders if Hope displayed that invincible complex after Hope states she can take care of herself.

'What if Luke's right? Hope's tough but she might overrate her survival skills. Could she have been reckless today and invited trouble to happen? Luke might read Hope better than we do.'

Hope looks exhausted after her ordeal so Katie chases everyone out.

"Hope could use some quiet rest. Everyone back to work."

Billy lags behind to share a thought with Hope.

"Maybe you just found a white knight after all. Even if he is a pain in the ass."

"Luke's no white knight."

Jubilee and JeniMay hear a shaky tone in Hope's voice.

"I think what Luke did is romantic."

"Please don't start, Jubilee, not now."

"Jubilee's right 'bout one thing. Luke did protect you."

"Both of you, just stop."

Bob removes Chester's hand from Luke's throat.

"Let me fill you in on a walk."

Chester steps back while disbelief replaces anger.

"Luke helped Hope?"

Luke's wheezing and coughing and laboring to regain his regular breathing rhythm. Chester's grip had potentially deadly intentions if he continued squeezing Luke's throat much longer or tighter. A red mark remains after Chester releases Luke and walks away. Bob apathetically glances at Luke.

"I suspected Luke after seeing his expression in Hope's truck. I'm not proud of how I reacted."

Chester's gathering his thoughts and realizes Luke acted different after this encounter.

'Luke seems shaken and withdrawn. He wasn't arrogant and tough, why is that?'

Bob continues talking.

"Luke whooped 'em pretty bad. It looks like a random attack."

Holly runs from the house and throws her arms around Luke while he's alone by Hope's truck.

"Luke, are you alright? Are hurt you? I'll take care of you."

'At least Holly's concerned about me. Hope's so cold and uncaring she hasn't even thought about thanking me. Saving her life means nothing since it's me.'

Holly notices Chester looking and kisses Luke's lips and hugs him tighter. Chester turns to Bob shaking his head. Luke thinks another thought.

'Not that it matters anymore but would Linda act like Holly or Hope?'

Sam approaches Luke and Holly with a smug grin.

"It's time to get ready for my date with Hope. She'll be needin' special attention after today."

Luke rolls his eyes before Sam adds a poorly thought out jab at Luke which becomes his next verbal blunder.

"There's no way you beat five guys in a fight. Not after seein' Chester throw y'all around. Hope might be delusional after not dating for so long. She needs a real man in her life again. Tonight's her lucky night."

Luke throws one punch against Sam's chin and drops him to the ground. Holly's impressed Luke made it seem effortless. Sam struggles to his feet, dazed and staggers off in the wrong direction until Holly corrects him.

"Um, Sam, your truck's the other way."

Chester chooses not to intervene.

'Phoned in information just bit Sam in the ass to keep him from getting a date tonight. Or ever.'

Bob shares more of Hope's attack.

"A younger officer nearly shot Luke. He mistook Luke for a homeless vagrant attacking Hope. Luke's brutal assault's getting compared to the Texas Ranger motto, 'One Riot, One Ranger'. Chester, Luke's dangerous. Maybe jail's safer until we know more."

Bob answers his phone while Chester considers a thought.

'It was a mistake to send Luke in old clothing. Luke'll need new clothes before guests arrive.'

Bob hangs up and swears.

"Shit! They're all busted up worse than originally reported. Those guys are gonna be in the hospital for days. They've got shattered bones, missing teeth, concussions, the works. One deputy viewed the store video and says Luke knew exactly what he was doin'. He's a black belt and he said he'd lose to Luke. Luke didn't flinch when a gun was pointed at him."

Chester thinks about Luke standing strong against Hope and him aiming guns at him.

"I'm not surprised."

'Why don't guns scare you? Why do you stay calm in dangerous situations? What does Hank know that I don't?'

Chester reconsiders Ben's knockout blow.

"Bob, I thought Luke was as full of wind as a corn-eatin' horse when he said he dropped Ben with one punch. I thought he used a two by four, but now?"

"Luke only had his fists today. Made it look easy too."

Colt approaches Chester and Bob.

"Sheriff, arrest Luke for assault. He broke my arm."

Chester interrupts with an agitated response.

"Don't be a super sensitive worm you twit. Y'all're cluckin' like a wet hen. Take your beatin' like a man. Quit whinin' like a spoiled brat."

"Whoa, Chester, settle down. I think you might be losin' it."

"Keep talkin' like that and you'll get your ass shot off by an angry old man."

"Luke assaulted me. Why are you takin' his side?"

"Suck it up, you're complainin' like a bitter little girl."

Bob's shocked Chester's so abrasive with Colt.

"Somethin' I should know about, Chester?"

"Nope. I'm gonna check on Hope. Colt, it's time for you to leave. Unless y'all want to go another round with Luke?"

Chester enters to Katie pulling him aside to whisper something into his ear before hearing Hope ask to go home.

"I'll take you home, Hope. One of the guys can collect me later."

Hope stands and asks another question.

"Where's Luke?"

Hope's expression and voice soften.

"Let's get you home. Luke's busy."

"I haven't thanked him yet. Find him, please."

Luke's visibly agitated to meet Hope by her truck.

"I haven't thanked you yet. I wouldn't be here if it wasn't for you."

The usual glare has left Hope's eye's to reveal a kinder expression than Luke's accustomed to seeing. Hope notices Luke's neck and watches his eyes drop down and rise up to meet hers again. Hope's caring expression differs from Luke's deadened emotionless gaze to offset his earlier compassion. Luke's tone turns venomous.

"You nearly got me killed today. Next time, park near the damned door. Neither of us is Superman. I'm lucky to be standing even though I'd rather not be on this ranch or near you. You only care about yourself."

Hope and Chester are stunned by Luke's vicious response.

'This is an odd time to attack Hope.'

Hope's demeanor immediately shifts to anger.

"How dare you talk to me like that? I was attacked today. I actually thought I might be wrong about you but you've just proven me right. You really are an asshole. I hate you, I hate you. I should've really shot you last week. I oughta turn you into a gelding right now."

Luke emphatically interrupts Hope.

"If you shot me you wouldn't be here now. You don't recognize real trouble. My two good legs are why you're still here. I stopped five guys from killing us today. You're such an uncaring and inconsiderate bitch."

Luke's been dwelling on the fact he was nearly killed defending a woman who hates him. He's been trained to avoid danger not invite it to happen. Chester's angry at Luke but quiet because he understands Luke's point.

'These two need time apart or Hope might shoot Luke even if he has a valid point.'

"Let's get you home, Hope."

Luke's parting comment irritates Hope.

"Yeah, Hope, go home. Take care of Faith."

Luke's thought is considerably different.

'I'm glad you're still able to raise your daughter.'

Hope spews pure hatred back at Luke.

"Y'all go to hell! You're disgustin'! I hate you!"

"I've been living in hell."

Hope's defiant glare would disappear if she knew Luke's honest concern. Chester informs Hope of a stop before her house when they drive away.

"Hank wants to see ya first. We have time before gettin' Faith."

"Sure, I don't want him worrying."

Hank's waiting by the entry and hugs Hope.

"Thanks for bein' concerned. Some people don't have that ability."

Chester gives them privacy in Hank's room.

"I'm happy you weren't alone today, Hope."

"That's debatable. It was Luke."

"Are ya really okay?"

"Yes, Hank, I'm fine."

"Hope, I need to ask a serious question. Do you think about givin' love another chance? Let go and love again. Let your walls down and let someone in. There might be someone out there."

"I'm sorry Hank, have you met me? You already know my answer. I'm not gettin' disappointed or hurt again."

"What if this time doesn't? What if someone can give you what you're lookin' for?"

"That person doesn't exist, Hank. Unless you've got a time machine? Remember?"

Hank chuckles at Hope's inference.

"What if he does?"

Hope's puzzled after Hank's question until contemplating it further.

"Y'all can't be referring to Luke, right?"

"I'm not sayin' a word. Not one word."

"I nearly shot him on his first day. I grazed him the next day. Hank, he insinuated the attack was my fault."

"You missed though, mostly, right? Hope, walls work for houses and barns but not for hearts. You're only trappin' the pain and shuttin' out any chance for love to enter."

Hope considers Hank's advice.

"Hope, sometimes when you change how you look at life, life also changes. We're allowed to change and work to make the changes last. Let go and love."

Music softly plays in the background while Hope fidgets with her hearts charm.

"I need to pick Faith up."

Hope stands just as Hank William's "Take These Chains From My Heart" begins playing. Hank smiles supportively.

"From God's lips to your ears. Hope, stop lettin' Joe win."

CHAPTER

THIRTY ONE

Luke attempts to regain control of his emotions by isolating in his room as soon as Chester departs with Hope.

'That fight was so different from a tournament or bar fight. I had to save Hope's life. I've never been in that position before.'

Scooter informs Chester what Luke's done and returns to find Luke still meditating on his bed when he enters the room.

"I didn't give you permission to enter."

Chester listens to Luke's indignant tone.

'And he's back. He's found his swagger again.'

"Today traumatized Hope and she's pissed at y'all."

"Hope's tough so she'll recover and shake it off. I get blamed before anyone hears the truth."

'Luke has a strong opinion of Hope. And about himself.'

Luke turns away from Chester.

"Around here it's better to say whatcha mean but y'all don't have to be mean when you say it. Words can have a tougher impact than fists and leave deeper, longer lasting wounds."

Luke recalls his life.

'I learned that long ago.'

Chester continues.

"You never need to apologize for cruel words left unspoken but you'll regret words thoughtlessly said in anger. Remember that. Bob apologized for how he acted today. Hope's loved by a lot of people here."

Chester pauses to emphasize his next point.

"Hope has to be tough. She doesn't have much choice. Here's another expression to remember. If you ain't got anything nice to say, don't say anything at all."

"I'm obviously excluded from that rule here."

"You dish it out you're gonna get it back 'round here."

Luke's annoyed glance indicates he's done talking. Chester approaches and firmly places his hand on Luke's shoulder.

"Thanks for saving my daughter today."

Luke's deep in thought and misses Chester's last statement.

"Holly's the only person to care about me here. Maybe I'll give her a chance despite your threat."

Chester exits quietly. He's lost in his own thoughts and has a call to make. Luke dwells on Chester's comments about Hope.

'What would Hank say about all this? I don't have feelings for Hope. Why did I fight for her? Why didn't I just run? Why does Hope have to be tough?'

Luke's longstanding nightmare wakes him later that night like the previous twenty three years. Troubling thoughts keep him up along with the previous day's events.

'Why can't I stop thinking about Hope? I'm confused. How do I deal with her?'

Luke's unsure of a lot after putting Hope's life ahead of his own.

'Why is a stranger complicating my life? I don't know why I feel this way. Is it because of Hope?'

Luke sneaks outside to find comfort in the pre-dawn darkness. He retrieves a pole to stretch with and perform his martial arts kata's before working through a complicated stick handling routine. Luke returns to his room believing he's gone unseen. Another set of troubled eyes has stealthily watched from a dark location.

'What drives you so relentlessly?'

Luke wonders if Linda misses him.

'She's probably too busy getting naked with Robert. Work and money mattered to her, not me.'

Luke starts comparing Holly to Hope. Both women are physically beautiful but Hope captivates him far more easily.

'Hope has undefined ways to be more appealing and alluring. Hope hates my guts. Holly seems more caring and actually concerned about me.'

Luke's silent during the morning routine which is unsettling to the guys. They become more worried when he doesn't complain about unloading the hay bale delivery alone. Jake questions Scooter.

"What's wrong with him?"

Scooter merely shrugs. Cody finds Luke meditating behind the barn once he's done and happily interrupts him.

"Y'all got a lot more work before ya get to relax."

Jack and Billy are loading fishing poles and tackle boxes into a UTV when Luke enters the rodeo barn.

"Alright Scooter, we're gonna wet a line for a bit at the bass pond."

"Enjoy. Don't fall in."

Jack starts laughing while Billy seems annoyed and embarrassed.

"One time, one time and it's never forgotten."

Luke resents they're leaving.

"Why do they get to slack off? Does Chester know?"

"They've earned it. And we don't tattle on each other. We're not kids. Everyone's responsible for their own actions."

Luke's angry to discover he doesn't receive the same consideration for work breaks. Luke crosses paths with Hope in the riding barn where Jake notices they both have red marks on their necks.

"Y'all look like ya got matchin' major make out marks."

Luke feels a twinge of guilt.

'Maybe I pushed Hope too hard.'

Luke's presence upsets Hope and Jake's comment further irritates her so she separates from them. Luke's callous words echo in her mind while Luke relives the fight. The chance for a romantic spark gets extinguished before it can develop once Luke vindictively aggravates Hope with a cynical observation.

"Wasn't it Eve, a woman, who got Adam, a man, kicked out of the Garden of Eden?"

"What are you implying?"

"Nothing. Except women seem to screw up men's lives."

"Or men are easily misled onto different paths by women."

"Only because the men are trying to be nice and not hurt the woman's feelings."

"You sure don't have that problem."

Chester's informed of their exchange immediately.

'They really need space to cool off. Distance might subdue their animosity so they can work past the incident. I'll send Luke with Billy and Cody to Fort Worth.'

"Billy, Cody, y'all're gonna have one more for the rodeo and Stock show in Cowtown."

"Who's that?"

"Luke."

"Y'all sure 'bout that, boss?"

"Not for a minute. Watch him close."

Billy and Cody aren't happy to bring Luke to Fort Worth but check into the Stockyard's Hotel before walking over to Mule Alley to shop for new ball caps, shirts, and other items. Billy and Cody are amused by the alarmed stares Luke's getting for looking destitute in public. Cody informs Chester about the nervous reactions Luke's attire receives during the walk back to Exchange Avenue. Billy explains what's about to happen.

"We're in time for the Longhorn cattle drive."

Our guests have the opportunity to do this at the Twisted Live Oak Ranch.

"They push their herd twice a day here. Our guests participate in a real Longhorn cattle drive through our pastures."

"Why is the ranch called the Live Oak? Aren't all Oaks alive?"

It amuses Billy and Cody that Luke doesn't know about Live Oaks.

"Live Oaks are one type of oak tree in Texas.

"Y'all see Live Oaks everywhere here in Texas. They have smaller elongated versions of Oak leaves."

Cody points to several trees when they pass by the Stockyards Museum.

"Those are Live Oaks."

They teach Luke why everyone is working so hard at the ranch and what it represents.

"We're about to open up for the season to show people our way of life."

They tour the John Wayne museum as well as Texas Cowboy Hall of Fame before entering Cattlemen's Steak House for dinner. Cody and Billy bring Luke to the Cowtown Coliseum to watch the rodeo although Luke doesn't understand what's happening except for cowboys flying off horses. Billy and Cody begin a running commentary during each ride. Cody pokes fun at Luke when the announcer invites kids down to the bucking chutes for mutton busting.

"Luke, this event's one you can do."

Luke's upset to find out what mutton busting is but amused to watch kids attempt to ride sheep like the cowboys ride broncs and bulls. Billy suggests the short walk to Billy Bob's Texas when the rodeo ends although they worry Luke may run off. Cody shares his thought with Billy.

"We'll gamble Luke won't run off while we're inside the bar. He's pretty mellow here so far."

Luke's away from all the irritants of the ranch and feels more relaxed while wandering around the Stockyards. He explores Billy Bob's and finds the bull riding arena Jake visits when possible. There's a room filled with guitars from musicians who've played at Billy Bob's. One case houses a guitar destroyed by the artist on stage for not meeting his performance standards. Billy dances with several different girls while a regional act entertains the crowd. Cody and Billy get in several games of pool before returning to the hotel. They all attend the Stock show the next morning before driving three hours south to Austin. Billy notices Luke tense up while they approach the ranch entrance. They dislike Luke but feel trapped between a rock and hard place since he did save Hope. Luke expects more grief when they face him.

"Y'all're a complete pain in our ass but you did save Hope."

"We wanna thank you for that."

"Everyone cares for Hope like a sister and we look out for her."

Luke's shocked by their kind words.

'Did I only save Hope so Faith wouldn't lose her mom?'

Luke's focus shifts to Billy.

"Why aren't you dating Hope if she's not married? You two seem close."

Billy laughs at Luke's off-base observation.

"We're all close to Hope. Ben's closest though which is why she's so pissed at you. We've all helped Hope through some tough times."

Cody vigorously clears his throat and shoots Billy an alarmed look. *'Shit, Billy, don't be sayin' anything to get us in trouble with Hope.'*

"What tough times?"

"Nothin'. Never mind. Forget I said anything."

Jake gathers the guys in the riding barn for a meeting before Cody and Billy return with Luke.

"We agree Luke needs an ass-whoopin', right? Let's take him into the pasture and pound the smart-mouthed insults outta him. I texted Billy and Cody. They're in."

Hope enters the barn unseen prior to Jake talking and steps into view after hearing his idea.

"Don't fight Luke."

"What? Oh, howdy Hope. Why not? You hate Luke. You ain't feelin' sorry for him?"

"I don't wanna see any of you get hurt."

"We can take care of ourselves."

"No. Not against Luke."

"Are you sayin' we can't fight?"

Hope pauses before answering.

"You fight like cowboys. Throwin' punches everywhere, hopin' to hit someone."

"We outnumber Luke so we'll beat him even if we do fight like cowboys."

"You won't beat Luke. He's disciplined and well-trained. He hates you. He'll cripple all y'all. Look what he did to Ben."

"Cripple? You're bein' a little dramatic. We're ready. Luke surprised Ben and those guys."

Hope fears she can't stop the guys from fighting Luke and grows more upset.

"You're not ready! Forget your stupid juvenile idea to fight Luke. He'll destroy you."

Billy and Cody drop Luke off with Chester and enter the barn to find Hope looking distressed. Billy walks Hope outside and listens to her plead with him not to fight Luke.

"Billy, it's a bad idea. And dangerous. Luke'll beat all of you."

"Do you really think it's a bad idea?"

"Yes."

"I'll talk to the guys. We're fixin' to put Luke in his place here."

"It's a terrible idea. I don't wanna see y'all gettin' seriously hurt."

"Those guys weren't that big, were they? They were like us, right?"

Hope stares into Billy's eyes before responding.

"They were bigger and Luke beat the tar outta them. He saved me but I'm still not sure why."

"Hope, are ya sure you ain't found a knight in shining armor?"

"Luke's no knight in shining armor, not even close."

"Hope, Joe threatened you for divorcing him. Maybe Luke's here for a reason."

"I have all of you and I have this."

Hope pats the gun strapped to her hip.

"Luke's leavin' when Chester tells him to go."

"Possibly. But we weren't with you and you didn't have your gun out there today. Luke was there almost like it was meant that way."

"Drop it Billy. Don't go there."

Billy re-enters the barn to discuss Hope's warning with the guys.

"Hope's got me thinkin' we may want to rethink our ass-whoopin' idea. We could wind up on the wrong end of the beatin' if Hope's right. And I don't have a reason to doubt her."

Jake surprisingly agrees with Billy.

"Hope hates Luke but if she's tellin' us not to fight him, then I'm wonderin' 'bout what he did in that parking lot."

"This guy could be more intimidatin' than we thought."

The attack worsens Luke's demeanor. He becomes more edgy and withdrawn when Hope's around. Chester toughens Luke's workload to wear him out by assigning him to unload the lumber arriving for the final preseason project. Luke's behavior reminds Chester how he was returning from the war.

'We were as ornery and emotionally uncontrollable. Millie brought stability to my life. Luke's more confrontational and even more defensive now. Its peculiar Luke doesn't talk about himself like people are prone to do. He doesn't even boast 'bout his fightin' skills like the guys always do. It's odd Luke complains about bein' on the ranch but not the actual workload. New hires quit because of the never ending tasks. Easter's in a few days and it's supposed to be happy, how's that gonna go now?' Is Hank holdin' back information I need?'

Billy watches Luke around Hope and sees anger but also detects a somewhat protective attitude as well.

THIRTY TWO

Cody's comment about Luke's shabby attire on the Fort Worth trip forces Chester to acknowledge the only remedy for the situation. *'Luke's gonna need nicer clothes for the season.'*

Chester calls Luke into the office to find Luis waiting to bring him to Cavender's Western Outfitter.

"Luis, my longest serving ranch hand's gonna help ya get a new wardrobe to be presentable for guests."

Luis hunches slightly and limps from old rodeo and ranching injuries. He wears a white t-shirt under an untucked and unbuttoned long-sleeved shirt along with his cowboy boots and hat. He's worn, gritty, and real which is far from the polished Hollywood movie cowboy.

"I don't want more stupid cowboy clothes."

"Git! Luis has my list. Make sure Luke gets everything. The boots, jeans, shirts, all of it, especially the one I've circled."

A flirtatious young woman gathers the requested items while dragging Luke around the store. Chester greets Luke with a terror inducing order when he returns.

"We're goin' ridin'. Change into new clothes and meet me in the ridin' barn."

Luke's voice cracks with fear.

"I don't ride horses."

"You will today. We ride horses 'round here, in case you've forgotten."

Luke challenges Chester's demand.

"I don't like horses and they don't like me."

"We'll end that misunderstanding today. And how do you explain Bullet?"

"What if I say no?"

"The sheriff'll make a short visit and leave with one more than he arrived with, if you catch my drift. Now git!"

Chester's stern expression projects his message. Luke stares at the stack of Wrangler jeans, assorted colored button-down shirts, T-shirts on his bed. Two white straw and two black felt cowboy hats rest on his dresser and several pairs of boots and work boots are on the floor. A Longhorn baseball cap was also added at the last minute. Chester had specifically requested a dark green button-down shirt without explaining why. Luke stares into the full-length mirror and doesn't like what he sees.

"I look stupid. I'm not a cowboy. I can't wait to leave this place."

Chester and Luis wait for Luke next to two saddled horses. Luke studies Luis again and notices a worn but energetic expression in his eyes. Years of sun and weather have toughened his facial features. The work duties have taken a physical toll but not his passion for the ranch.

"We're riding into the pasture to chat."

"I'm not riding."

"You're gonna."

"I told you, I don't like horses."

"Bullet seems to disprove that."

"I don't know why. I still don't want to ride."

"Tough shit. Mount up."

Luke's childhood pony ride, his dad's promise, and the outcome of that day flash through his thoughts. His hand trembles while reaching for the reins. Luis speaks in a kind manner.

"Don't worry, Dottie knows what she's doin'."

Dottie's a black Morgan with a small white patch on her nose.

"I don't."

Chester interrupts them.

"Hurry up. Waylon's itchin' to go."

Waylon's a young spirited American Quarter Horse and a large muscular Chestnut colored steed. Luis instructs Luke how to mount Dottie so they can head into the pasture. Chester explains why guests come to the ranch.

"The Twisted Live Oak Ranch sits on fifty thousand acres of beautiful Texas soil. I turned my cattle ranch into a Dude ranch years ago to educate and entertain wannabe cowboys and cowgirls. My great grand-daddy moved from the east and built it up to nearly a hundred thousand acres. We've sold portions off to settle old debts but I refuse to sell any more to developers."

Luke's more concerned with not falling off the horse than hearing ranch history or how it operates.

"When can I get my wallet back?"

"No one knows that answer yet."

Hope arrives after Chester and Luke ride out and she finds Scooter in the barn.

"Howdy, Scooter. Where's Chester? I see his truck but can't find him anywhere."

"Chester's riding with Luke. Out there."

"Luke's afraid of horses, right?"

"Yep. Chester's planning to teach Luke to ride to help guests. He was white as a ghost mountin' up."

Hope responds sadistically.

"That asshole deserves to get bucked off, break his neck, and stomped into the ground for hurtin' Ben and for what he said to me after the attack."

Hope's venomous wish for Luke to be harmed disturbs Scooter.

"Hope, you can't mean that. The poor lad didn't think twice about saving you after being put into a bad spot. The mind makes things seem worse than the actual event afterwards."

"Luke saved me but he enjoys fightin'. He's still vermin in my book."

"The news showed Luke was the only one who came to help you. He fought five guys and a gun. I wouldn't run into a dangerous situation to help someone who's been knocking me around like a piñata. You've taken antagonizing someone to new heights with Luke. They have footage of the fight too."

"I've been too busy to watch the news but Katie mentioned Luke turned down interviews."

"By the way, I doubt Luke's in any danger, he's riding Dottie."

"Dottie's usually reserved for kids. Poor girl, she'll need extra treats."

"You've hammered Luke like a pinball and he is a pain in the ass but remember I couldn't do what he did. We don't know him all that well. There might be another side to him."

"Or he's a pain in the ass that did one nice thing to get off the ranch."

"He didn't run. He stayed to help you."

"I'll see y'all later."

Hope leaves the ranch with distressing new thoughts swirling in her head.

'What's goin' on? Am I missing somethin'? Luke? That can't possibly be it. Luke? No way. I'm fine with the way things have been.'

THIRTY THREE

Chester's entertained by Luke's unfounded fear of Dottie since she's the gentlest horse in the stable. He keeps that information close to his vest.

'Let's see how Luke does before I offer any tips.'

Chester finally starts correcting Luke after what seems like an eternity. He tells Luke how to hold the reins and corrects his posture to sit in the saddle and position his legs.

'Luke don't like horses but he's got a natural ability to ride. Interestin.'

"You inform the horse where to go by the way you sit in the saddle and move."

Luke's terror builds on the back of an animal he despises and Chester's interested to know if Luke's able to follow instructions under duress. His next comment is unexpected.

"Specific qualifications'll make a cowboy outta you for my ranch."

Chester's remark makes Luke suspicious.

"I don't want to be a cowboy for your ranch."

"We'll see. There are basics that make a modern cowboy who he is. Proper fittin' clothes, boots, and hats. A good horse. A good dog for company. A pick-up truck helps if y'all stay here long enough."

"I'm not becoming one of your workers."

"You're gonna be here longer than y'all wanna be. Cowboys work off hunches and gut feelings on the range. We ain't always right but generally have a good grasp on life. It's part of the Cowboy Way."

Luke warily studies Dottie.

"Hank was explaining that to me, I think. He called it the Cowboy Code. Does it apply to Hope as well? Or is she exempt to think she's in charge even when she's not."

"Hope's a spitfire, no doubt. She's been fiercely independent from a young age which has been good and bad."

"A spitfire? That was British plane in World War Two?"

"It was. But not what I mean. Hope's got a bit of a temper. Actually, Hope has a fiery temper when pushed too far."

Luke rubs his lip.

"Yeah, so I've learned."

Chester chuckles.

"Yes you have."

Luke slouches and starts looking down too much so Chester advises him to make adjustments.

"Head up and sit straighter. Lean back in the saddle and loosen up on the reins. You guide the horse, not the other way around. Bend your knees a bit."

Luke tries to relax and shifts his position since Dottie hasn't shown any hostile behavior yet. He detects the hum of insects dueling with birds chirping in the peaceful silence. The gentle breeze crossing the pasture brings the fragrant scent of Texas Sage to Luke's nose to mix with the ever present odor of manure. The guys reference it as nature's bouquet when the flowers aren't blooming or the girls aren't prettied up.

"Not bad for a greenhorn."

"A what?"

"There's a lot you don't know. You're kinda old to be a tenderfoot when it comes to life."

Chester stops at a particular spot.

"You see that bird's nest?"

Luke nods.

"You ever watch birds build a nest?"

Luke shakes his head.

"I watched robins build a nest once. They only used their beaks to retrieve everything necessary to build a home for their eggs. Can you build anything with just your mouth? I know I can't. I realized nothing's impossible if you put your mind to it after watching them succeed."

Chester hopes Luke understands his message.

"Mother Nature shows nothin's impossible with a positive mindset. We're powerless against her will and we don't control or influence her. A Texas thunderstorm rollin' in'll give you real perspective."

Chester seeks answers by pushing Luke out of his comfort zone on the back of a horse. The breeze settles and the air becomes calm and stagnant which allows the surrounding silence to engulf Luke. The scene feels rather eerie while he looks at the ever present large whitish-gray clouds floating lazily overhead. The moisture laden air produces puffy clouds resembling cotton balls.

'I'm so disconnected and lost here and so far from the life I knew.'

Chester's using his deep-seated mean streak to break Luke down and learn more to match Hank's preliminary success.

'Knockin' Luke's guard down should make him reveal personal details. Why's he so abusive to my men? He handles pressure while's his feet are on the ground so maybe Dottie'll scare the truth outta him.'

Luke's unaware Dottie's one of the oldest trail horses who enjoys a walking pace for exercise.

'It's fun watchin' Luke squirm in his pool of fears in the saddle.'

"You seem angry at the world. Maybe with good reason. It seems to me y'all've hit rock bottom. That might be a gift. Rock bottom don't mean the end if you realize it's a new foundation to rebuild your life on. It might humble you and be positive if y'all look at it the right way. You've only got one way to go 'n that's up. I've been around a long time and seen a lot. Ya get what I'm tellin' you?"

Chester's confidence level alerts Luke to respond carefully because his statements may contain too much truth to ignore.

"Don't try to get in my head, old man. You don't know the first thing about me. I doubt your cowboy wisdom can help me."

"Time here might change that."

Chester's statement hides truthful objectives.

"You're not my shrink. Hank's already trying that approach."

Chester's frustrated Hank may be more successful.

'Luke seems angry about shrinks by his tone. Why's Luke more open to Hank?'

"Admitting problems exist is the first step to solvin' 'em."

Luke feels like Chester's setting a trap and stays silent.

"Texas could solve your troubles. It's a big state full of inspiration and happiness if you choose to blaze a new trail like my great granddaddy did."

Chester waits for Luke's reaction while wondering if his approach can work as well as Hank's. Luke chooses to survey the green rolling hills with scattered islands of Live Oaks, Cedars, shrubs, cactus, and Agave, also known as Century Plants. Bluebonnets and Indian Paintbrush speckle the landscape as well. A sizeable number of vultures circle overhead off to Luke's right side.

"Looks like somethin's up and died on the ranch again. Those are Turkey vultures and Black vultures up there. The Turkey vultures travel up your way too."

A Road Runner makes a quick meal of a lizard when it bursts into view from under a bush.

"I doubt Texas can help me."

Chester points out several Fire Ant mounds protruding above the somewhat curly, blue-green Buffalograss during their ride.

"Avoid those. And look at you sittin' on a horse not tryin' to buck ya off."

"The ride's not over yet."

True. What's also true is y'all're gonna work your ass off for hurtin' my foreman."

"Don't remind me."

"I won't need to. Your body's gonna feel plenty of deserved aches and pains."

Luke refuses to let Chester know his body already aches from moving hay bales, bags of feed, but especially from spreading the gravel at such a rushed pace. He overloaded his muscles trying to prove how tough he is by accomplishing the task so quickly.

'That was so foolish. I know better than that. Working on the ranch outdoors all day is so different from my two jobs and workouts.'

"I always thought I'd move to Florida if I left Chicago. Lots of pretty girls there."

'Is Luke's guard down? Let's find out.'

"I think Texas women are prettier, in case y'all ain't noticed."

Luke answers without thinking.

"Yeah, I've noticed."

Chester gruffly clears his throat.

"You best not be talkin' 'bout Holly."

"No, I'm not talking about Holly. She is pretty."

'How do I get out of this?'

Chester glares at Luke.

"You understand what I'm sayin'."

"Yeah, I understand."

Chester abruptly asks another question.

"Are you in trouble with the law up north?"

Luke rudely snaps back.

"No!"

"Don't get smart with me! You're in trouble here with nowhere to go, nowhere good anyway."

Chester despises people disrespecting him. He trips Luke up with an unexpected question.

"What's her name?"

"Why? What's it to you?"

Luke's slip up infuriates him. Chester grunts.

"Now we're gettin' somewhere."

"It's none of your damn business."

Luke's unhappy he revealed anything.

"This girl, did ya get her pregnant?"

"What? No!"

"That's good."

Luke doesn't feel like answering any more questions.

"I told you, it's none of your damned business."

"Why did you leave then?"

Luke's frustration grows with Chester's continued questioning.

"You're not listening. It's none of your business."

Dottie snorts and shakes her head when Luke raises his voice which revives a fearful memory.

'Damned horse. If I don't talk, maybe this old buzzard will get the point and drop it.'

Chester's determined to break Luke down.

"Are you gonna explain it to me?"

Luke heatedly answers with one word.

"No!"

"You still think it's none of my business, right?"

Luke glares and nods.

"I've got news for you. Whatever happened up north put you here on my ranch and that makes it my business."

Luke comprehends Chester won't stop badgering him.

"You're going to keep asking questions, aren't you?"

"Yup."

"Fine, you want to know why I left."

"Yup."

"She cheated on me with a guy from her office. Now you know."

'Hopefully that shuts him up.'

"Tough shit. A girl cheated on you. That's what you ran from? Something tells me there's more to the story. Talkin' 'bout it might make ya feel better."

'Maybe Luke'll think I'm tryin' to be nice and helpful and spill his guts.'

Luke replies flatly.

"I seriously doubt it."

"You ran so you obviously didn't think it was fixable or you'd still be there fightin' for her love."

Chester's stinging point silences Luke.

"Boy, let me tell ya somethin', I'm ninety years old and learned more about life than you've thought about yet."

"Alright mister smartest smart guy. Tell me the answers I need to know."

"I'm not givin' y'all a thing. Answer my questions and you might learn something."

"From you? Doubtful."

Chester believes his assault tactic will gain valuable information from Luke.

"Did you love this girl?"

"Of course I did!"

Chester questions Luke in the past tense and notices Luke answers the same way and not with the present tense.

"How long did you two date?"

"We were together for four years."

"Four years? Any talk of marriage?"

"I proposed three times."

'I wasn't expectin' that answer.'

"Three times? Why'd y'all have to ask three times?"

"She turned me down because she's building her career."

"Uh-hmmm. Did you talk about the future?"

"We talked about taking trips and doing stuff together."

"Not what I mean. What about marriage and kids? Or growin' old and living out dreams?"

Luke can't remember conversations like that with Linda since she stayed more focused on work goals.

"I, I, uh, I don't remember."

"Either ya did or ya didn't. You don't forget those conversations."

"Linda wanted a better life than her parents. They haven't been able to retire yet since they helped put her through college."

"Hmff. Sounds more like an excuse not to build a future with someone to me."

Chester's reasoning riles Luke up.

"You don't know what you're talking about."

"This girl, she turned you down three times for marriage. Three times? So she could build her career as you explained it. She might've believed something better was out there but stayed with you for comfort and didn't want to hurtcha."

"You don't know what you're talking about. You're too old to remember what dating is like."

"You might be right but some things don't change. Did she ever talk about wanting kids?"

"Linda didn't even want to get married, why would she talk about kids?"

"Women think about things like that. Us guys, we don't usually have a thought in our head 'bout stuff like that when we're young. She may not've talked about kids with you but she may've been thinkin' 'bout it with someone someday. Hell, she may not've been fully aware if she wasn't lookin' at it the right way. She'll stay focused on work until the right guy comes along to change her mind."

Luke nudges Dottie away from Chester to avoid the truth behind his interpretations.

"I'm done listening."

Luke's defiant snarl indicates Chester's hit a sore spot and pushes for more.

"Millie brought up kids after only two months of dating. I was still coming to grips with surviving the war. Millie had chances to date a couple wealthy guys from the area but chose me instead. She could see a long-term future for us I couldn't imagine at that point."

"I don't give a shit about your life. It doesn't apply to me at all."

"It seems to me like this Linda didn't see a future with you but wanted to spend time with you and maybe did love you. But if she wasn't talkin' 'bout babies, houses, and rockin' chairs after four years she sounds like she was lookin' past ya."

Chester's presumption about Linda sparks new fury from Luke.

"You'll think of any way possible to punish me for beating your dumb-ass guy. I'm done here."

Chester thinks provoking Luke like poking a sleeping bear is the best way to find out more about him.

"Son, I was born and raised in the great state of Texas. I sit high on a horse every day and enjoy life to its fullest. No hour of life is wasted that's spent in the saddle."

"Yeah, well get off your high horse and shut up."

"This wide open land with no one around to interrupt your thoughts helps set a person straight about life's real problems and how to solve them. You figure out what matters and what doesn't and where you stand in life."

"I'm not your son."

Luke's grappling with Chester's barrage of questions and information when Chester poses another question.

"You act like your problems are worse than anyone else's. What makes you so special? I've seen people evaporate in a cloud of smoke and cease to exist except in memory. I've known people who've buried their children and still go on livin' because it's all they can do."

Chester pauses to catch his breath.

"The people at the senior center have endured more than you and still get out of bed every day."

Luke conceals his thought.

'Don't be too sure about that.'

"You haven't lived my life."

"Everyone's got problems. It's how ya deal with 'em is what makes ya who you are and who you become. You either find the strength to solve problems and succeed or continue to get flattened and fail repeatedly. No one's life if perfect even if they try to make it seem that way. Every tomorrow brings a new chance to overcome problems. You may stumble along the way but things have a way of turnin' 'round if you keep your chin up. Learn from your mistakes and make them lessons instead."

Luke testily erupts.

"I'm not telling you my problems. You're just old and useless to me."

'Luke's anger goes deeper than a breakup.'

"You admit y'all got problems."

"I'm done with you."

Chester imparts sincerely compassionate advice for Luke.

"Don't ever hang onto anger, son, it'll eatcha up from the inside out."

Luke's response is bitter and cutting after Chester calls him son again.

"Stop calling me your son. You don't care about me. I had a dad."

Luke's wrath resentfully attempts to invalidate Chester's pretentious concern for his well-being while challenging Chester again.

"You're some kind of anger expert too."

"I do know about holdin' onto anger too long. I also know I'm a good listener when I'm not dishin' out great wisdom."

Chester's wry smile arcs his lips upward.

'Luke won't share details but I think he may've had a tougher life which Hank might know more about already.'

Chester's concern grows about how little he's learned about Luke.

'I need to talk to Hank and see what he knows.'

Chester's grin irritates Luke but the accuracy of his statements generates a fiery rage for how his life's turned out.

"Luke, life's taught me somethin's appreciated more when it's earned but it is okay to ask for help. Especially when you're down on your luck. A positive influence is worth its weight in gold."

Luke's happy when Dottie drifts away from Chester and Waylon.

'I have no idea where I am or where the barn is.'

Chester's aggravated he's not getting anywhere with Luke like Hank is.

'What's Hank doin' that I ain't to get Luke to open up. Hank best not be holdin' back important information from me.'

Chester decides to let Luke off the hook.

"It's time to head back to the barn."

Chester instructs Scooter what Luke's next task is when they return.

"Scooter, Luke needs to learn how to care for the horses for our guests. Teach him how to brush 'em down and lead them to the stalls. Oh, and Luke, you'll be ridin' Dottie every day."

Luke's mind churns through so many thoughts that he appears less fearful of horses. Scooter misreads Luke's distracted state.

'Chester'll make anyone a better rider but to make Luke less afraid, well that's sayin' somethin'.'

Chester heads to his office to figure out what he's learned about Luke.

'Luke got upset a lot, but why? Did anything I say make sense? Does Bullet sense what Luke's dealing with and accept him for it? Bullet's reaction to Luke is baffling but I trust an animal's instincts. Hank's right that Luke sounds like a broken spirit but I'm still not sure about Hope bein' like that. I don't know how long I'll keep Luke here but I need to know more about

him so I know how to handle him. Why won't Hank share information? Luke can make a strong impression when he wants to. So Bullet, what do I do? Punish Luke or help him? Or both. Millie, I wish you were here.'

His phone interrupts his thoughts.

"Howdy, good timin'. Didja find something already? Really! What?"

Chester listens to details about Luke.

"Seriously? That explains a lot. Thanks. Keep diggin' and let me know what else you turn up."

Chester ponders his newly learned information.

'No wonder Luke's so mad and messed up. Maybe fate brought him here. I'm still gonna bust his ass for breakin' Ben's jaw but maybe I can help him too since he saved Hope. How to do that though? Like a fancy two-step. I sure wish Millie were here to help. She'd know what to do like always.'

THIRTY FOUR

Luke's on the verge of a nervous breakdown by the time he reaches his room that night. Chester's words, riding Dottie, bitter memories and fears being dredged up, and Linda's betrayal combine to build a stress Luke's unable to cope with. He finally comprehends the self-destructive path he's on with no positive outcome which weighs heavily on him. Tears flow uncontrollably and Luke curls into the fetal position on his bed trying to find solace from his pain and sorrow.

'God, why am I still alive? I'm so tired of making bad decisions and living a terrible life. I just want to die and be done with all this pain and hopelessness. Why didn't you let me die instead of my parents? Give me a sign I'm supposed to be here, please.'

Hope stops by the next morning to check on Reba and her foal and arrange to bring Faith to the ranch after school.

"I don't want Faith around Luke. You know how Faith is around strangers, especially men."

"Luke'll be workin' on barbed wire fencin' so he won't be anywhere near Faith today."

"Has he gotten any better at it? I told Faith you're punishing a bad man here for hurtin' Ben."

"That's a good way to explain it."

"It's the truth. Y'all're punishin' Luke, right?"

Chester checks the clock.

"You wanna see Reba now? She and her foal are in the barn."

"Sure."

"Let's go."

Hope notices three men exit the barn during their approach. They're dressed in jeans, long-sleeved shirts, and black cowboy hats and head towards guest housing. Hope recognizes Cody and Kyle but the third man's hidden from sight. She asks a question with unmistakable interest.

"Whoa! Who's that with Cody and Kyle?"

Chester doesn't readily clear the mystery up.

"Why?"

Hope inspects the stranger again.

"Well, I must admit, he looks kinda cute from here?"

Hope's statement astonishes Chester.

'Hope ain't been interested in any man for years. Is this a reaction from the attack?'

Luke raises his head and notices Hope smiling in his direction before lowering his head and hurrying to get in front of Cody and Kyle. His eyes reveal the tortured emotional struggle his silence doesn't tell. Hope glances back at Chester and sees his devilish smile and dreads anything he might say next. Hope's eyes flicker with interest even after unwittingly complimenting Luke's new appearance.

'No mistaking Hope's showin' an obvious interest in Luke. But why? Because he saved her?'

"You think Luke's kinda cute, huh? I'll admit he does look better in clothes that fit properly."

Hope responds in a hissed whisper with crimson cheeks.

"Not one more word from you. I haven't eaten breakfast yet. I'm hungry. I don't know what I'm saying. Remember, I've been through something traumatic, it must be affecting me."

"Sure, y'all keep tellin' yourself that."

Chester's grin blends with a mischievous glint in his eyes. Hope worries he may say something to someone else.

"Don't you dare say anything to anyone, or so help me, I'll…I'll, well I don't know what I'll do, but I'll think of somethin'."

Hope's flustered and walks quicker to move farther ahead. Chester ambles slowly behind her, watching her glance at Luke several more times before reaching the barn and disappear inside. Chester cheerfully mumbles to himself before reaching the barn.

"It seems somethin' might be afoot. This summer could be rather entertainin' after all here on my ranch."

Danny and Kyle's jovial outbursts are offset by Luke's quiet, moody disposition while checking and repairing barbed wire all afternoon. Several sections appear to have been tampered with which would allow the Longhorn to enter areas they don't belong.

"Chester thinks someone's tryin' to sabotage his business."

"But how're they gittin' into the ranch?"

Luke quietly listens while inspecting the condition of the damaged barbed wiring.

'This looks a little like the pet store cage issues we had.'

The trio returns to the barn to see Hope's truck driving away.

"Aw, we missed Hope and Faith. We could've played for Faith, especially Willie Nelson."

"And Waylon, the Hag, and Patsy Cline. Faith prefers real country music, traditional sounding country."

"Yeah buddy. Faith doesn't like the bubblegum pop crap Nashville's puttin' out and callin' 'New Country'."

"New country my ass. Dale Watson's got it right with, 'Country My Ass'. Those Nashville corporate suits don't know what real country music sounds like anymore. Hell, even George Strait wouldn't get a record deal now. There's no fiddle or steel guitar or even a twang. Guys wearin' skinny jeans 'n wigglin' their asses instead of Wranglers and stompin' in cowboy boots definitely ain't country. They don't even wear cowboy boots 'n hats most of the time. Thank God Cody Johnson's tryin' to bring country back to Nashville."

"Nashville wouldn't know real country music if it kicked 'em in the balls. Their 'country' sounds like pop music. It's all fluff 'n happy, not real and gritty. Red Dirt and traditional country sings about pain 'n love 'n real life stuff."

Their comments confuse Luke.

"Isn't Nashville where country musicians go to get famous?"

"It used to be but now real country goes to die at the hands of unqualified suits. Aaron Watson's "Fencepost" tells the truth about a Texan with integrity passin' on sellin' his soul."

"Randy Roger and Wade Bowen's "Standards" is another good one. Austin became a country hub for musicians unwilling to give up their souls just for money. Nashville controls the messaging and lacks passion and risk. But hey, if you wanna make a ton of money soundin' like someone else, Nashville works for you. If Nashville musicians honestly said they're in it for the money instead of makin' real country it'd be easier to accept."

"Here in Texas, we wear our boots, belt buckles, jeans, and cowboy hats and have a drawl when we sing. We listen to KOKE-FM 'round here for that reason. They have standards and integrity far more than most stations. Any station that has mandatory Merle 'n Willie Wednesday's is alright in our books."

"Who's Merle?"

"Who's Merle? Whaddaya mean who's Merle? Merle Haggard, the Hag. Only one of the best singer-songwriters of all time."

"We can't work with y'all anymore."

Luke's amused Danny and Kyle are so serious and knowledgeable about music when they're not responsible otherwise. They escape Luke's wrath because the other guys constantly disrespect them. The next morning revolves around sorting lumber for the final upgrade and repairs for the barns and guest housing. Conversation covers a wide range of topics until Danny states an incorrect rodeo fact. The others jump on him mercilessly until Luke speaks up to insult their speech patterns and accents.

Chester texts Scooter that Luke's expected in the riding barn to saddle up Dottie. The guys are glad Luke's being forced to ride a horse since they've learned he's afraid of them. Scooter shakes his head at the thought of Luke's disrupting presence on the ranch during the season. Henry Johnson's returned to the ranch after being away for several days and brings up the idea of whooping Luke's ass. Scooter reminds him of Luke's fighting results.

"Henry, Luke broke Ben's jaw and beat the shit outta five guys who attacked Hope. We need to grin and bear it while Luke's here. By the way, glad you're back with us. How's your mom doin'?"

"She's much better, sir. And it's good to be back. Seems like I've been missin' stuff goin' on here."

Luke exits the rodeo barn and hears Colt's high performance Corvette engine pulling up. He's brought a friend and both grin while getting out of the car.

'What now?'

Katie steps onto the deck with a glass of sweet tea and overhears their banter.

'Luke looks annoyed.'

"Nice cast, pony boy. Want me to sign it?"

"Y'all're gonna pay for this. My friend Sammy's gonna kick your ass all over this ranch."

Luke's examines both men until Sammy speaks.

"I hear y'all think you're a tough guy. I'm gonna show ya what a tough guy looks like."

Sammy demonstrates his impressive martial arts skills with a series of backflips, punches, and kicks while grunting to sound more intimidating.

"Are you done yet?"

Sammy smiles.

"I'm just gettin' started."

Colt smirks when Sammy begins another display. His smile is short-lived during Sammy's second exhibition. Luke shifts in anticipation of Sammy's move to surprise him before evading his punch and strikes with a crushing blow which drops Sammy unconscious. Colt stares at his motionless friend.

"His ballet recital is over. I'll beat you even worse if you pull another stunt like this."

Katie smiles and relaxes after watching Luke drop Colt's friend.

'Sammy never stood a chance. He was only one guy.'

Chester rides up on Waylon while Colt's departing to sarcastically greet Luke.

"You weren't havin' a playdate, were you?"

Luke frowns and worries what Chester saw.

'This is the last thing I need considering what's next.'

"Go saddle Dottie for your ride. Then y'all need to clean the riding barn. The season's 'bout to start and everything's gotta be shipshape for our guests. Oh, and you'll clean the rodeo barn after that."

"What! That'll take hours. I'll miss dinner."

"Supper'll be waitin'. It might be cold."

Luke storms off to saddle Dottie before angrily returning to the riding barn to begin cleaning. He picks up a pamphlet about the ranch and learns more about its history. Waterloo is an enormous bull Longhorn leading Chester's herd for cattle drives. Waterloo was Austin's original name until 1839 when it was changed in honor of Stephan F. Austin who's credited with being the Father of Texas. Luke learns Jesse Chisholm led cattle drives across Texas and New Mexico with a legendary Longhorn named 'Old Blue'. Luke recalls watching westerns which portrayed the dangers cowboys experienced on the drives. Guest lodges have been designed with worn grey barn lumber to appear rustic but have the amenities of a hotel. Visitors experience a cowboy's old west life with the option to ride the open range and push the Longhorn for two days and one night. This is the main draw on the ranch.

A wooden split rail fence patterned after the old west snake rail zig zag configuration surrounds the guest area. The aesthetics create an old west ambiance allowing guests to feel as if they've stepped back in time. Millie encouraged Chester to install a guest pool with natural rock formations including a waterfall built into one end. Various cactus and succulents combine with Sago Palms and Mexican Palms to landscape the surrounding area. Business grew swiftly after Chester updated brochures with newer pictures and distributed to local and distant hotel lobbies and travel agencies.

The menu for cattle drives is listed on the back page so guests understand what to expect during their experience. Brisket, BBQ Chicken, Cowboy beans (Pinto Beans), and Coffee as well as available seasonal options are mainstays for guests. The disclaimer stating chicken was not a usual menu since chickens couldn't keep up with herd evokes a laugh from Luke. He also learns Chuckwagons would carry five hundred pounds of flour, fifty pounds of salt, fifty pounds of sour dough starter and fifty pounds of baking powder for making biscuits in Dutch ovens, five hundred pounds of potatoes, usually boiled for the cowboys, and five hundred pounds of pinto beans. The Chuckwagon cook, often referred to as 'Cookie' could be second in command after the trail boss.

Luke's angry to work alone but thoroughly cleans the riding barn so the horses can't be injured. He knows Faith spends time in the barn with Hope so he doesn't leave anything out of place. Luke's struck by an odd thought on the way to the rodeo barn.

'Was Hope smiling at me? That's not possible. She was smiling at Cody and Kyle. Was that supposed to be a sign?'

It's dark when Luke heads to the kitchen after finishing fully expecting cold leftovers. Katie surprises him with a hot meal instead.

"I was expecting cold leftovers. Thank you Miss Katie. I'll wash dishes now."

Katie knows Luke's exhausted and gives him a break.

"I'll use the dishwasher tonight. Chester won't dare argue with me. Get some sleep. Easter weekend's gonna be busy here at the ranch."

Luke happily heads for the door but stops long enough to comment.

"I'm trapped here. I get yelled at for doing everything wrong, especially by Hope. I'm always in the wrong spot, just being here is wrong to her. She's pretty stuck up if you ask me."

Katie addresses Luke's incorrect assessment of Hope.

Hope's not stuck up. Quite the opposite. Hope's a highly qualified equine vet and has worked hard for the respect she deserves. She expects everyone to give their best effort all the time. Hope had a chance to become a model but turned an agent down. Hope's achieved success with her mind, not her body. You may not believe this but Hope was a bit of an ugly duckling when she was young. That was hard on her growing up with Holly gettin' chased by boys all the time. You know that part though."

Katie's last quip causes Luke to speak defensively.

"Holly chased me, not the other way around."

"Don't judge Hope by what you see now. Hope and Holly competed in barrel racing at rodeos for years. Hope was a champion rider and proudly wears her buckles. Holly could've been a champion too but let boys distract her. Hope stayed disciplined and determined and retired from the rodeo to go to school. Don't make an uninformed decision about Hope until you have all the facts."

"That rule doesn't apply to me. I'm judged without having a chance to defend myself."

Katie views Luke sympathetically.

"Why is that? No one knows a thing about you, do they? Get some sleep and I'll see you in the morning."

'You may've picked up on Hope irresponsibly over-compensating her abilities for not knowin' her that long.'

Katie glimpses Luke's vulnerable side again after knowing he can be considerate even though he keeps it hidden from the others.

'Luke needs to let himself to be polite, responsible, and sensitive more often.'

Luke lets the screen door slam shut to get back at Chester for his delayed dinner. Katie chuckles how Luke's behavior shifts in mere minutes.

'He's polite to me one minute and pugnacious to Chester the next.'

Chester's muttering in his office.

"Bullet or no Bullet, I can't let that little piss-ant get under my skin."

Easter and the upcoming season's start create dilemmas for Chester to deal with because of Luke.

'I can use Luke's good looks with the women who book stays at the ranch. But can I trust him around the guests? Luke could easily say or do something inappropriate and ruin the ranch's reputation.'

Luke's behavior fluctuates during the week following Hope's attack. He swings between periods of silence and hurling hate-filled comments at everyone. Luke's brush with death opens old emotional wounds and memories accompanying the upheaval of his life. New routines restrict his coping skills and Hope's presence acts like a confusing wrench he's unable to manage. She captures his attention far too easily. Chester pushes Luke daily for signs of how he reacts under pressure after the trauma of the attack. Chester's learned Luke's suffered a horrific event through his detective friend's investigation and struggles to balance punishment with advice.

Loneliness and isolation fuel Luke's negative attitude which is magnified by the ranch. He tries ignoring the emotional overload shutting him down but he doesn't have a positive distraction. Hank seems to know how to help Luke feel safe and open up. Luke doesn't want to willingly share his life with anyone at the ranch.

Luke hangs a length of heavy rope from the rodeo barn rafter without Chester's permission. Chester's mad at first until he realizes it seems to soothe Luke after he installs it.

'Why does a length of rope calm Luke down? How's he usin' it?'

Luke won't touch the rope if anyone's around but sits on the ground and repeatedly pulls himself up and down as a way of exercising and relaxing.

Chester meets Luke in the barn Saturday morning.

"Tomorrow's Easter. Everyone's coming here. Hope's ordered me to keep y'all busy and away from Faith, and her. I'll have someone bring food to you during the day."

"Terrific. Happy Easter to me."

THIRTY FIVE

hester's pleased the first week is fully booked.

"Easter's tomorrow, the ranch barbecue is next Saturday, and the season starts in two weeks. Everythin's set. Except Luke."

Early Sunday morning starts with rumbles of thunder and light drizzle and temperatures around sixty degrees.

'Today's supposed to be about eighty and sunny. Chicago's usually cold.'

Luke works in the barns alongside everyone else in order to finish earlier before breakfast. He returns to the rodeo barn after breakfast to watch the guys spread plastic eggs filled with treats once the rain has stopped. Chester plans to keep Luke busy elsewhere but his plans go awry when Hank unexpectedly arrives to watch the fun. Chester greets Hank by the travel van to help him out.

"I thought y'all were comin' for supper."

"I wanted to come watch Faith hunt for eggs and chat with Luke and Hope."

"Hope ain't gonna be happy. She's on her way and doesn't want Faith around Luke. I plan to keep him busy all day."

"I'm well aware Hope doesn't want Faith around unknown men. We've had many conversations about that subject. Let me keep Luke company and I'll join in later."

Hank's aid moves the van to the guest housing area so it's out of sight. Hank stands with Luke in the rodeo barn to watch Hope and Faith arrive and begin the egg hunt.

"Faith's happy searching for eggs outside."

"Yup. She's a good kid."

Hank recognizes Luke's attention remains on Hope standing with Chester and encouraging Faith during the hunt.

"Chicago's usually too cold to do this."

"Luke, I'm told y'all still need to adjust your attitude 'round here. Become more positive and quit hangin' onto negatives if you wanna succeed here, or anywhere. Your life ain't been great but it's more your doin' because of how you react to everything and everyone. Solve problems and move on instead of stayin' stagnant and complainin' 'bout 'em. You'll find happiness that way."

"I'm here because of my decisions, aren't I?"

"Yup."

Luke sighs heavily.

"I need to saddle everyone's horses."

Luke and Hank make their way to the riding barn so Luke can ready the horses for the morning trail ride.

"I'll be riding Dottie later when the others head indoors."

Katie sends Billy with meals so the two men can eat in the tack room.

"Stay outta sight. Hope's sittin' on the deck swing with a cup of coffee."

Hank's curious when Billy calls Luke to the entrance.

"Actually, Luke, sneak a peek at this."

Luke stares at Hope in the distance. Billy notices his steady gaze.

"'Porch Swing Angel' by Muscadine Bloodline. I think Hope inspired the song. Billy plays the song so Luke can understand the context. It's a strong, measured, sultry tune with a powerful message. Luke silently ponders it after Billy leaves. Hank's studying Luke's reaction to the song.

"That's quite a song, huh? How 'bout walkin' me to the house once Hope goes inside."

Jake and Faith burst through the front door while Hank and Luke approach. Faith shrieks and runs towards Hank but stops short with a concerned expression.

"Oh no, that's a bird's egg. It's broken."

Luke steps behind Hank while Jake approaches to inspect the broken egg.

"Looks like a squirrel or bird ate it. Circle of life, Faith."

Hope frantically exits the house in time to hear Jake and spies Luke behind Hank.

Faith's eyes look sad so Hope's about to yell at Luke.

"Momma, Jake says somethin' ate that baby bird."

Hope's angered glare shifts to Jake and watches him shrug.

"What? It's probably true."

"Jake, y'all're so insensitive."

A new voice speaks up to interrupt Hope.

"It's not true, Faith. The broken shell was pushed out to make room for the babies. They're safe in the nest."

Hank watches Hope's glare soften when she sees Faith's saddened expression switch to relief. He speaks up to help solve Hope's impending problem.

"Jake, Faith, help me inside, okay."

Jake's happy to temporarily escape Hope's wrath.

'I stepped in it big time with Hope.'

Hope remains long enough to address Luke. He's already walking away so she need to chase after him.

"Hey, Chester had specific orders for y'all to stay away from Faith today. She doesn't need to be frightened by you on Easter or any other day."

"This wasn't my fault. What's the big deal anyway? Never mind, I have a ton of work to do alone. I guess thanks to you."

Hope growls her next words.

"I'm not done with y'all."

"Yeah, well I'm done with you."

Hope takes a breath and lets it out.

"I appreciate you told Faith the baby bird's safe."

"It's Easter. Time to celebrate joy and rebirth, right? Faith shouldn't be sad."

"Right, that's nice. Thankfully, Faith wasn't upset by you."

'Maybe there is more to you.'

"You're a beautiful woman with a very ugly side. Chester did warn me to stay away from you and Faith. I was helping Hank. I have work to do so I don't get chewed out by him too."

Luke stomps off fuming and leaves Hope to dwell on his comment.

'Luke called me beautiful and ugly. And then walked away. That's a first. I don't have an ugly side. He can't handle a strong woman. Hopefully he stays away from Faith now.'

Hank examines Hope's perplexed expression when she enters the house.

Chester finalizes plans for the ranch barbecue. Guests enjoy ranch life from April through October and the barbecue is the last time wranglers can relax for months. Chester's grown The Twisted Live Oak into a thriving enterprise allowing people from all over to experience the thrilling sensation of a cattle drive and authentic cowboy living. The adventure creates lifetime memories for guests to reconnect with their inner child. Hope informs Chester she'll be gone all week after gaining a sizable new client.

"I'll be back in time for the barbecue. Faith's stayin' with Ben and Beth."

"Good luck, see you when y'all get back."

Hope's frazzled on her first day when the older gentleman invades her personal space without permission. He strokes her cheek with his hand which catches her off guard.

"You're a very beautiful woman. You could be happy and well cared for with me, darlin'. You wouldn't need to work anymore."

Hope steps back and lashes out angrily.

'Who does this guy think he is?'

"Let's get somethin' straight right now. I'm here for your horses and I can take care of myself. And I prefer men more my age."

Hope immediately thinks about Luke.

"Guys your age don't appreciate a beautiful woman like you."

"Could you protect me against five guys?"

'Luke did.'

"Find another vet if y'all're lookin' for cheap thrills."

"No. I'm told you're the best around. I only want the best."

"I have my own practice. I take care of myself. Your crass assumption women need a man like you to take care of us is full of shit."

Hope recalls reacting to Luke's touch and the unanticipated appeal of his presence.

"My apologies ma'am. I'm not trying to insult you. I thought I'd offer you a chance for a better life.

"My life is how I've planned it."

Luke crosses her mind again.

'Why am I thinkin' 'bout Luke? I can't stand bein' around him.'

'Ma'am, I've planned out my life only to watch life get in the way and change everything."

His comment irritates Hope because it echoes other people's repeated comments. Hope watches a young couple holding hands while walking towards the stables which sparks a thought.

'I may not need a man in my life but maybe I do want a man in my life.'

Holly had shockingly abided Chester's order to leave Luke alone until her friend Jazlynn convinces her to go after Luke. Luke stresses this new development will impede his ability to successfully leave the ranch as soon as possible. Holly shamelessly throws herself at Luke every chance she gets. She finds Luke alone in the riding barn and removes her shirt to fully expose her breasts.

"I'm all yours to play with. These make great toys and turn me on when you caress them."

Luke fearfully tenses up someone will find them while Holly's shirtless. Holly's pleased Luke's unable to take his eyes off her naked torso. He stares at her chest then down to her belly button piercing and notes her tattoo of a cobalt blue butterfly with black detailing on the small of her back when she spins around. Luke shakes his head to clear his mind of wanton thoughts.

"You're going to get me shot."

"No one'll know, Luke. I know places we'd never be found. Your eyes tell me y'all want me naked to have your way with me. I've never understood why Hope's not more like me with her looks. She's got a kid so she knows how to spread her legs. She let her heart get in the way of havin' fun. Not me."

Suggestively undressed images of Hope enter Luke's mind.

"You'd have the best sex of your life if we hook up. I'm willin' to do anything and everything. Nothing's off limits."

"I won't see the sun rise if we hook up. You're beautiful and tempting…"

"Luke, we can live out all our wildest desires together naked and tangled up. Your eyes tell me it shouldn't be long before you find out I'm fun to bed down."

Luke hears a sound and escapes the barn while Holly pulls her shirt on. He sighs and feels relieved no one saw Holly half-naked with him.

'Holly's right. I do want to touch her body. Too much time here and I may risk giving in. But then there's Hope also.'

Luke's inexplicably more irritable during Hope's absence. He's increasingly more aggressive each time the guys upstage him to make him feel more pathetic. Chester's put into a tough situation because of Luke's presence.

'This is a quandary. I need to find out if anyone wants Luke at the barbecue.'

Chester faces resistance about Luke attending the barbecue.

'I can't make anyone babysit Luke and miss the fun.'

Some mention jailing Luke for the day. Chester's shocked when Jake offers a workable solution.

"How 'bout Luke works some tasks alone to miss part of the barbecue?"

"Jake, that's actually a good idea."

"Thanks, Chester. Hey, wait a minute. You say that like I don't have good ideas."

Chester chuckles when Jake realizes his point.

"Jake, your boots are held together with duct tape."

"These are my favorite boots. They're broke in just right. I got my engineerin' degree from DTU. Duct Tape University. I'd be okay if Luke does some of my work."

Jake's imaginary college education makes everyone laugh.

"I'll assign a few tasks Luke can do alone to wear him out before joining the party."

Chester calls Luke into the office Friday afternoon and hands him a clipboard with several projects for Saturday.

"Who's working with me?"

"You're working alone tomorrow."

"You don't want me at the party, do you? Is this part of my punishment? Should I go to my room without dinner and think about my behavior?"

Chester leans forward on his desk but refuses to let Luke rile him up.

"Joke all you want. Actually, Jackass, my wrangler's decided you'd work alone before joining the barbecue."

Chester's announcement dumbfounds Luke.

"You're gonna lose tryin' to compete against life with a poor attitude. You'll only end up bitter. Most things start off difficult until you challenge yourself to change and improve."

Chester's not so subtle messaging attempt to inform Luke to change his attitude doesn't go unnoticed. Chester's irritated Luke rebels against authority without reason and constantly retaliates against people who outperform him on a task.

'Luke's content to remain angry, negative and unproductive to an uninformed observer. But is it really linked to the tragedy of losing his parents?'

Chester ruminates how to help Luke without ending his punishment.

'Luke needs to search within himself like Hank and I did and solve his troubles. Saving Hope may have exposed something he didn't intend to reveal. Maybe that's his true self.'

Chester hopes the investigation will provide answers about Luke's life.

'I need find a way to punish Luke and help him at the same time in a way he doesn't catch on.'

Holly enters wearing another skimpy outfit to remind Luke of their topless encounter which causes Chester to erupt for multiple reasons.

"Stop lookin' at her that way!"

Chester slams his hand down on the desk.

"And you, quit wearin' clothes that look like moths have eaten most of it. Where's the rest of those shorts and shirt."

"Grand-daddy, there's no guests yet so I'll dress how I like until then."

Chester barks an order to Luke.

"Get back to work! Now!"

Luke keeps eye contact with Holly during his hasty departure. She frowns since her desire to get Luke into her bed grows daily.

'Luke's eyes 'n hands'll be on my body tomorrow at the party.'

Luke overhears Chester reprimanding Holly.

"Find more suitable clothing or I'll shoot that boy dead."

Chester understands Luke's inability to look away from Holly.

'Holly draws attention to herself easily. But she's not good for Luke. Hank could be right about Hope in some ways though.'

Luke closes the screen door gently and returns to the barns. He'd rather deal with horses than Holly's seductive behavior and Chester's wrath. Cody and Kyle are tasked with teaching Luke how to repair barbed wire fencing without getting ripped up.

"We can't let the Longhorn get into the guest areas."

Luke retrieves the clipboard from the office after dinner. He looks it over on his way to the bunkhouse before glancing at the decorated pool area.

'I may not even make it to the party.'

"It's their loss, not mine."

THIRTY SIX

Saturday morning begins with the regular routine before Luke splits off to head out to the pasture to repair fencing. He's fully aware this task is meant to take longer than normal alone and spends several hours struggling to fix sections of broken fence. Katie's packed a cooler for Luke to keep him fed while working. He hears a UTV approaching around one o'clock and sees Kyle appear over a ridge.

'Kyle must be bringing more fencing to keep me out here.'

Kyle dismounts and straps his work belt on before putting on gloves and grabs his pliers and heads for Luke.

"I'll help ya get this done sooner but you can't let Chester know. He might shoot me or fire me depending on his mood. Heck, he might shoot me and then fire me."

Luke's confused by Kyle's gesture so he merely nods and resumes working until the task is completed.

"I was never here. This is all you. I need time to get back before y'all come in too, okay."

"Yeah, sure."

'Why did Kyle help me?'

Repairing the screen door is second on the list. The lower portion had been ripped and letting insects indoors until someone put tape over it. Chester finds it unsightly and wants it properly repaired before guests arrive. Billy's simplified explanation made it seem repairs are easy to accomplish alone. Luke removes the hinge pins and takes the door off its frame to lay it down on the deck. He pulls the old screening and splining out.

'So far so good.'

Luke's confidence grows until he tries installing the new screen and spline into the frame. Frustration overtakes him when he realizes Billy may have lied to him.

'I'll make Billy pay for this.'

Barbecue wafts lazily to fill the warm air to remind Luke Katie has more food prepared in the kitchen. He retrieves a large sandwich to satisfy his hunger and returns to struggling with the door. The urge to throw the door one way and everything the other direction overtakes him.

'Billy definitely left certain details out.'

The sun shining on the deck is suddenly obstructed so Luke looks around to see Ben standing over him. Luke jumps to his feet and Ben realizes Luke must think he's trying to sneak up on him and steps back. It's Ben's first visit to the ranch since their altercation and his jaw is still wired shut. He raises his hands to indicate he means no harm before writing a note on a pad of paper and gives it to Luke.

'Let me help you with this.'

Ben writes another note to ease Luke's suspicions.

'It's easier with two people.'

Ben knows several tricks to make the project easier while the two men work together to fix the screen. They face each other after rehanging the door and Ben extends his arm to shake hands with Luke before writing another note. He tears the page and hands it to Luke and leaves before Luke reads the message.

'I was wrong to sit you on Bullet. I'm sorry. Thank you for saving Hope. She's like my little sister.'

Luke looks up before finishing what Ben's written.

'Don't let Chester know I helped you.'

Luke groans at the next task until a thought stops him.

'I did save Hope, didn't I?'

Chester's permitted the guys to leave the barns disorganized so Luke has extra work to consume plenty of time. Repairs to the rodeo barn kept the guys busy all morning but now Luke listens to them enjoying the party while cleaning their mess. He stores the tools in the tack room and shifts lumber to properly safe areas instead of being scattered everywhere. Luke grumbles and stomps around before stopping to complain to a horse until laughter stops him. Scooter steps out of the shadows.

"Grumblin' to the horses won't help ya finish sooner."

Scooter closes the gap to help clean the barn.

"For the record, I was opposed to leaving the barns messy and endanger the horses. I'm helping for that purpose."

Scooter's been on the ranch long enough to recognize when Chester's trying to help someone even if he's punishing them at the same time. Chester's rough exterior hides his soft caring side to offer second chances. Luke hears occasional meowing above him and tries finding the cat hiding overhead. A Northern Mockingbird's perched on a rafter and mimics a cat. Scooter educates Luke.

"Northern Mockingbirds imitate sounds. So if you hear yourself grumbling and your mouth ain't moving, you'll know why. Don't go telling anyone I'm helping you or we'll both be looking down the wrong end of Chester's shotgun."

Scooter pauses at the door once they finish the work.

"Wash up. Get some food. Behave tonight."

Scooter settles in with a Guinness and ponders Chester's decision to allow Luke to join the festivities.

'Was helping Luke the right choice?'

Chester's final task has Luke wearing his new dark green button-down shirt and black felt cowboy hat. Luke's unaware the shirt request is Hope's favorite color. The rich forest green shade will remind Hope of the East Texas Piney Woods she loved on childhood vacations.

'I'm not crossing swords with Chester today.'

Chester's working with Hank's hunches even though he still has his doubts.

THIRTY SEVEN

Luke notices a pair of cooing Mourning Doves while approaching the pool entrance.

'It's like these birds are following me.'

Luke realizes he's about to enter hostile territory which reminds him of being unwanted in his youth.

'Why did Ben, Scooter, and Kyle help me to come to this party? I've made life miserable for everyone here.'

Chester examines the timing of Luke's entrance.

'It's earlier than I thought.'

Chester wonders if Luke will disrupt the barbecue's festive atmosphere before waving him over to his table.

"That's your chair for the night."

Luke would be facing away from the activities like he's in a timeout. He turns around to scan the people there but doesn't see Hope or Holly.

'I don't see Hope. I'll be safer if Holly's not here.'

Luke wants to apologize to Hope for what he said after the attack. Chester's question diverts his attention.

"Think you can behave yourself?"

"Yeah, I think so, unless…"

Chester abruptly cuts him off.

"Nope. No 'unless'. It's a 'Yes sir'. Understand me?"

Luke compliantly answers.

"Yes sir"

Chester states a thought for Luke to think about.

"Changin' your address don't solve your problems. Distance doesn't outrun issues whether people are involved or not. It's better facin' situations head on so they don't get worse."

Luke's in no mood to hear any more of Chester's life wisdom since it all hits too close to home. Everyone acting like one big family at the barbecue reminds Luke what he's lost and magnifies his isolation and loneliness. Luke stands to turn his chair and starts sitting again when Hope appears from the pool's guest house with Faith. He does a double take and misjudges the chair's position and nearly falls to the ground. Hope looks stunning in a one-piece skin tight black bathing suit which accentuates her alluring curves. Luke's admiring Hope when she locks eyes with him and smiles. She turns away but glances back at Luke again and brushes her hair behind her ear and lightly bites her lower lip.

'Hope is smiling at me. Why? What can that mean?'

Hope's brilliant green eyes shine while examining Luke's appearance. Chester notices her gaze.

'Hank might actually know somethin' here. What's Hope thinkin'? Where is Hank, he should see this.'

Luke's outfit captures Hope's full attention.

'Whoa, Luke's rather handsome in that dark green shirt and black cowboy hat.'

Hope's breath-taking beauty has captivated Luke. His eyes express a wanting even loving appearance.

'I've forgotten a man could look at me that way and enjoy it.'

Hope recalls her rodeo days and a holding a certain bronc rider's gaze. She blushes and turns away and feels exposed without her work attire. She glances back at Luke again before Faith gets her attention.

'I really need to apologize to Hope for my selfish behavior. I only thought about myself when she was the one attacked.'

"Y'all're gonna catch flies if ya don't close your mouth."

Hope's appealing new appearance leaves Luke speechless. His mind is spinning while facing Chester again. His heart's beating energetically. Hank observes everything unfold from the pool entry with great interest.

'I knew they had a connection.'

Hank joins Chester and spies Hope and Luke stealing glances at each other.

"Are you seeing what I see?"

Luke doesn't comprehend Chester hasn't ordered him to stop looking at Hope.

"Did you say Hope was related to you?"

Chester coughs after Luke's question.

"I've said Hope's like a daughter to me."

"That's what you said after the attack."

Chester's concerned he's revealed something better left unsaid and leaves the table. Luke doesn't think twice about it but Hank's curiosity has him pondering thoughts. Luke whispers to Hank.

"Saving Hope was the most intense fight I've ever had. No tournament bout or bar fight even comes close."

Hank detects Luke's anxiety.

"You've never saved anyone before, have you? You've never been responsible for someone else. Saving Hope is much different than drunks or opponents."

'I see it now. Savin' Hope's life shook Luke.'

Luke reveals more to Hank.

"I miss feeling wanted and needed by someone. I haven't fit in anywhere or belong someplace."

"What if y'all ain't supposed to fit in?"

"What?"

"Maybe you're supposed to stand out. Ever thought of that? Maybe you've finally found the right place to belong and be wanted. The Good Lord'll send y'all signs if you watch for 'em. He'll help ya build your own path with good, positive choices."

Holly had been at the party but left to change once she found out Luke would be arriving. She re-enters to flaunt her tanned voluptuous body scantily clad in a tiny white bikini. She struts around for everyone to see, especially Luke. Many of the visiting men hunger to hold Holly's nearly naked figure and stare with desire in their eyes. Holly notices Luke's eyes drift between her and Hope. Holly's confident smile fades to a somewhat frustrated frown.

'Hope's never been competition before.'

JeniMay and Jubilee enter the party but stop to admire Luke in proper fitting clothing. They head for Hope and Faith in the shallow end of the pool.

"Luke's lookin' mighty fine."

"Definitely hotter than Texas in August."

Hope ignores their remarks but re-examines Luke's new outfit.

'Luke does look good.'

JeniMay notices Hope's softer gaze during her subtle glance at Luke. Luke's unaware Jubilee's dating Cody when he notices the three women looking his way. Cody and Jake are out buying additional alcoholic choices from Spec's and also stop at Sprouts for lemons, limes, and a few dinner necessities for Katie. Luke compares the four women and wonders why Hope captivates him more.

'Hope nearly killed me. Then she nearly gets me killed in a parking lot. Why is she more alluring than Holly or the others?'

Hank's hints and Chester's reference that Texas could heal him haven't changed Luke's intention to leave when possible.

'I risked my life for Hope. Why? She's verbally abused me for even breathing.'

Holly tempts Luke like the devil in her eye-catching bikini and struts over to straddle his lap and passionately kiss him. JeniMay watches from the pool.

"Hope, I think I'm gonna give Holly competition for Luke."

"What? No way. JeniMay, find someone else, anyone else."

'Luke's obviously interested in Holly.'

Chester's ready to angrily explode and throw Luke out.

'This was a mistake. I can't let this go on.'

Chester realizes he can't make a scene and ruin the party. He's surprised Holly's annoyed by other men's attention since she's normally the center of their focus. Luke wonders guys aren't hitting on Hope.

'Hope's beautiful. Why don't those guys talk to her too?'

Hope's reputation for destroying men's advances and egos is well-known. Hope masks glimpses at Luke as if she's randomly observing people in his vicinity and finds Luke's looking her way. Chester and Hank find it interesting Luke's attention is directed towards Hope even after Holly's kiss. Hank quietly shares a profound thought with Luke.

"God answers prayers when the time's right."

Hank redirects Luke's attention towards Hope and Faith.

"Hope shot at me. I don't consider that God's way of answering someone's prayers."

"He's got quite the sense of humor for gettin' your attention. Jini's in the past but that can help you recognize a new better future. That is, if'n y'all want to know what real love feels like."

"Hope hates me. Why are you telling me this?"

"You can't convince your heart somethin's real and you can't deny your heart when it's tellin' ya when it's real. Give Hope a chance. She may like you more than she's willin' to admit, even to herself."

"I'm leaving as soon as possible."

"You can change your mind, your path, and your plan."

Luke's eyes shift back to Hope to find her already glancing at him until their eyes meet.

'Could Hope like a guy like me?'

"Hank, I'm complicit for my own demise with my negative attitude, aren't I? I've dealt with life and people all wrong. My path has been crooked, unpaved, unmarked, and unplanned."

"Sometimes the road seems like it's ending when it simply changed direction. Forgive yourself and turn with the road to find happiness again. You can't fight the past or change it. That's an unwinnable war. Build a better future."

"You don't know me so why do you seem to know what to say to me?"

"I was you once. Until I changed my approach. I'd like somethin' strong to drink. So git goin'."

Jubilee approaches Luke while he walks to the bar to make a comment after Hope's repeated glances in his direction.

"Maybe y'all might find a reason to stay 'round here. Sometimes home ain't where you're born. For some maybe but other's find home in a place they never expected to."

Jubilee's eyes twinkle which misleads Luke's thoughts before he callously responding.

"No thanks. I'd rather return to civilization."

Jubilee huffs indignantly and walks away but stops long enough to see Luke peering over at Hope.

'What am I missing? This ranch and some of these people seem to think I should stay here. And Hope. What's going on there?'

JeniMay intercepts Luke before he can bring Hank his drink.

"Be honest with me."

"If I'm able to."

"Do y'all like what you see?"

JeniMay's hand motions up and down to bring attention to her bikini-clad body. Luke views her body before his eyes dart to Hope instead of remaining on JeniMay.

"You seem nice JeniMay but I'm gone when Chester cuts me loose."

Luke's attention momentarily returns to JeniMay before drifting back to Hope.

"Thanks a lot, Luke. You've answered my question without words."

JeniMay heads directly for Colt and his buddies. Colt doesn't pay attention until JeniMay whispers into his ear and takes his hand into hers. Colt leads JeniMay towards the exit with a smile. Hope overhears his comment.

"Where'd y'all park?"

Chester questions Hank during Luke's absence.

"Y'all'd be tellin' me things I need to know and watch out for, right? You and Luke act like two peas in a pod."

"I'd mention any real concerns. Luke's needed someone to talk to, someone he can trust. He's smart but doesn't show it. Luke's buried so much for so long. He's lost his identity and who he is. This ranch is helpin' him remember what's important. And maybe it's not just the ranch."

Hank nods towards Hope.

"Luke's searchin' for somethin' and it could be he's found it here."

"Such as? He ain't nothing but a Texas-sized bad attitude. I know he had a tragic childhood. There's more to his story. What aren'tcha tellin' me?"

"What do you know?"

"He lost his parents young."

"How do you know that? I promised Luke I wouldn't divulge anything we talk about unless he gives me good reason to. So far, he hasn't."

"Y'all ain't implyin' Hope has something to do with Luke changin' his attitude."

"Not just Hope."

THIRTY EIGHT

Jubilee's announcement about her relationship with Cody influences JeniMay's decision to reconsider her life.

'I don't want to write men off like Hope has. I'd like to feel a man touchin' me again. I may have to settle from now on.'

"Colt, I know you date around. I know you want Hope. Hell, every guy wants Hope. I have an offer I hope you say yes to."

"What's that, JeniMay?"

She leans in and whispers into his ear.

"I wanna have sex with you, now. In my Jeep. The windows are tinted so we won't be seen or bothered."

JeniMay puts Colt's hand on her breast. Colt takes her hand and leads her out of the party.

"I accept. Where'd y'all park? Let's get outta here."

Colt takes JeniMay's hand and they head out to her Jeep. She enjoys his kisses and hands wandering overs her body. He slides his hand under her bikini top to caress her breast before removing her top. Colt's hand descends downward into her bikini bottom and his finger tip feels the telling moisture of her desire. JeniMay inhales excitedly and rises up to help pull her tiny suit off before stripping Colt as well.

JeniMay spreads her legs and explicitly begs him to plunge deep inside her immediately.

"I want you inside me now."

They fulfill each other's desires during a long steamy explicitly shameless sexual encounter.

"Colt, I needed that more than I knew."

"Darlin', let me know whenever y'all wanna hook up. I'll be inside you as quick as you'll let me. Bangin' you was better than I expected. I never knew you were such a wild kitty in bed or anywhere else."

"I'm quite good in bed. I never refused Wade for any position or how many times he wanted me. Maybe you'd like to find out, too?"

"That sounds good to me."

"I'm always willing."

"Alright, we'll go back to the party for a while but hook up again later."

"I'd like that. I'm not done gettin' wet with you."

Hope's dismayed to see JeniMay re-enter with Colt after both disappeared for quite some time and intercepts JeniMay.

"What's goin' on here? Between you and Colt."

JeniMay's harsh response stuns Hope.

"It's none of your business."

Hope doesn't press further at the party. JeniMay's untidy hair indicates what occurred with Colt. Jubilee runs into Cody's arms to hug and kiss him when he and Jake return. Luke sees them and rethinks his earlier interaction with Jubilee.

'Oh, Jubilee wasn't hitting on me.'

The dinner bell rings to alert everyone to change for dinner. Hope and Faith change in Hope's bedroom in the house. Faith's chosen matching outfits for them to wear.

"Faith, I like your decision we should match."

"Momma, we look good in our jeans and black and white flannel shirts, don't we?"

"Yes we do. Alright Pecan, let's go enjoy supper."

Hope's free flowing hair highlights her long waterfall curls underneath a black felt cowboy hat. She stops at the pool guest house to pull her hair into a pony tail and tugs long strands of hair free to hang down along her cheeks in front of her ears. Hope's naturally gorgeous appearance and facial features are enhanced by this hairstyle. Faith picks out seats on the opposite end from Chester and the vets. The festivities, JeniMay, and recovering from her newest client leave Hope distracted from the fact Luke and Faith are in close proximity. Luke is shielded from view for the time being. Cody and Jubilee sit across from Hope. Holly re-emerges skimpily dressed in a short jean skirt and stylish black lacy but revealing cropped top much to Chester's chagrin. Most male eyes follow her until she sits with Jubilee and Cody. Luke leans back and is immediately captivated by Hope's arousing appearance. He's nearly overwhelmed to give in to the urge to approach Hope.

'I'd really like to kiss Hope. I don't stand a chance with her so why would I even think this way about her? Especially when Holly's throwing herself at me.'

Hank shares an opinion with Luke.

"Whoever said if you love someone you should set them free and if it's meant to be they'll return is an idiot and the advice is a bunch of bullshit. If you love someone, tell 'em every day, don't let 'em go. It brings couples closer."

"I told Linda I loved her every day. She still cheated on me."

'I wonder if I can still win Linda back.'

Hank adds another pearl of wisdom.

"You've hid behind walls thinkin' you're shielded from harm butcha ain't. It's okay to let people in since you decide who stays and who goes. Y'all'll get hurt sometimes but that's how you grow and find new possibilities and maybe find love along the way."

Luke recalls the psychiatrist's words from long ago about pain and healing.

'Hank's saying something similar to that asshole. Was he actually right?'

Luke, truth hit me at a hundred miles an hour and crushed me but it forced me to face reality. I started healin' and movin' forwards again. This ranch can help ya with that too."

Jubilee and Holly exchange telling glances after scrutinizing Hope's hairstyle. JeniMay also approaches with a questioning expression.

'Hope only wears her hair that way when she's interested in a man. She hasn't styled it this way since her divorce. It's a subconscious signal she sends out.'

The ladies wonder why Hope would add an undeniable sexiness to her appearance for the party. Beth's also noticed and searches for potential candidates other than Colt and Sam. Faith regains everyone's attention with a new topic.

"Momma got me a hamster I call Hoppy."

Jubilee's curious about the name.

"Why do you call your hamster, Hoppy?"

"I want a rabbit but Momma says I can have a hamster for now. So I call him Hoppy."

Luke listens to Faith's explanation.

'Faith communicates clearly for being so young.'

"Hoppy likes to pee and poop where he sleeps and eats."

Cody chuckles.

"Hamsters are cute and cuddly but not that smart."

Jubilee pokes fun at Cody.

"That sounds just like you, honey."

Cody slumps down and feigns a frown while everyone laughs at him.

"But I still love you sweetie."

Luke also laughs and adds his own remark.

"The young lady set you up for that insult."

Hope panics when it dawns on her that Faith and Luke are near each other.

'Oh shit, I got so distracted I forgot Luke's here with Faith. Her fear of strangers could ruin the evening for us. Why does Chester have Luke here? This is gonna get bad quick.'

Hope has many doubts about Luke and still wants to separate Faith from Luke. Faith was unaware of Luke's presence until his response. She hesitantly stands to examine Luke from her spot.

'That's the mean sad man I saw at church.'

Faith slowly walks towards Luke and everyone is shocked by what happens next. Luke smiles authentically and replaces his usual dark brooding expression while his eyes shine brighter. Faith's presence seems to erase Luke's moody behavior. Hope jumps to her feet to rescue Faith from an impending fright-filled situation. Faith's only experience with her father happened when she was a year and a half and ended badly. Joe was dreadfully cruel to Faith and left her scarred concerning unfamiliar men. Hope vividly remembers how long it took to console Faith which left her with a deeper bitterness towards all men not belonging to the ranch. Faith sounds calm after cautiously studying Luke.

"Y'all talk funny. Where are ya from?"

Hope's embarrassed by Faith's honesty.

"Faith, that's not polite. I didn't raise you that way. Apologize right now."

Luke chuckles before responding.

"It's okay. I probably do sound funny to Faith."

Luke has no idea the crowd's expecting a fearful shriek. He covers his mouth with his hand and changes his voice to talk like an alien robot inside a tin can.

"Hello Faith, how are you? My name is Luke."

Faith brings her hands to her mouth and giggles before repeating her question.

"Where'd y'all come from?"

Luke leans in and points at the sky and watches Faith's blue eyes widen.

"I'm kidding. I'm from Chicago."

Luke gently taps Faith's nose with his fingertip. She crinkles her nose and giggles again.

"You're funny. I like you."

Faith reaches for Hope's hand but looks back at Luke.

"Why would you hurt Ben?"

Luke stares into Faith's eyes.

"I did hurt Ben but he did something to me first. Ben might explain it better to you."

Luke's also watching for Hope's reaction and hears her voice carry an angry tone.

"C'mon Faith, let's go sit down."

Hearing Luke admit hurting Ben reignites her hatred for him.

"Momma, I like him. He's funny, and nice."

Hope's confused Faith giggled when Luke touched her nose.

'Faith's never laughed for a stranger.'

Hank's taken back by Faith's acceptance of Luke.

'I wasn't expecting that from Faith. She showed no fear. Faith had Luke smiling and laughing too. Why?'

Hope worries Luke will still frighten Faith somehow.

'Why isn't Faith afraid of Luke? She seemed comfortable around him.'

Hope wrestles with doubts and suspicions while re-examining Luke.

'Why did Chester keep you here? Who are you? How were you able to make Faith laugh?'

Hope's irritated by questions without instant answers. She prefers knowledge to explain events and people to eliminate the unknown. Hope's exceptional vet skills stem from constantly seeking out information and solutions. Luke re-evaluates Faith's long curly blonde hair and pretty blue eyes.

'Faith resembles Holly not Hope.'

Katie's also intrigued by Faith's fearless reaction to Luke.

'That's amazin'.'

Chester's confused by Faith's interaction with Luke.

'First, Bullet's bonded with Luke. Then Hope tried carin' for him and now Faith's not afraid of him. This is rather puzzling.'

Hank nudges Luke to break his gaze from Hope and Faith.

"Maybe you've found what you're lookin' for. Believe in yourself and others will too. You've wandered through life but maybe makin' good decisions will help ya stop fightin' ghosts. Be present and accept reality. You've been preoccupied with hidin' and escapin' you ain't allowed yourself to live in the moment. Even now, you're more focused on leavin' instead of learnin'. You're missin' what the ranch and the people here have to offer because y'all're lookin' past it all. To what? Nothin'? The unknown? This is your life and you're wastin' it."

"What am I fighting? Wouldn't you want to escape my life too?"

"That there is your real problem. You focus on the negatives. Focus on positives and solve problems."

Chester stands to address the group.

"Welcome everyone to another wonderful preseason barbecue."
Jack's wife, Rosa, bluntly asks the question on everyone's mind.
"Why isn't that guy in jail for hurtin' Ben?"
Chester glances at Luke.
'Funny, Luke's causin' trouble for just sittin' quiet.'
"Luke's here to pay his debt instead of sittin' in a jail cell. He'll regret injurin' Ben, I promise you that much."
Ben and Beth imperceptibly shift in their chairs while Luke's groan is loud enough to be heard.
'I think Chester just invited everyone to add to my pain.'
Chester's instructed Ben and Beth not to reveal what really happened. Holly smiles invitingly at Luke before interrupting Chester.
"I'll help punish Luke for you, Grand-daddy."
Chester gruffly answers Holly.
"I'll handle it. You've your own work to do."
'Luke ain't gettin' cuddled or coddled.'
Luke notes Holly's speaking up.
'Maybe I should start something with Holly. Even if it can't last.'
Hope asks a suspicion laced question after seeing Holly's yearning expression.
"How long is Luke stayin' here?"
A twinge of jealousy shakes Hope after Holly's seductive suggestion.
'Holly just wants to take care of her own wants with Luke.'
Emotions buried deep seem to be waking and create a myriad of troublesome thoughts for Hope to fight through.
'Why am I jealous? Why do I feel anything because of Luke?'
"There's no answer to that question yet."
Hope's eyes dart between Chester and Luke. Luke's appealing to her emotional side which distresses her significantly. Chester recognizes Hope's expression indicates she's struggling with a problem.
'I've put all my time and energy into Faith and work. I don't need anyone turning everything upside down or causing me heartache.'
Hope feels confused about a man for the first time in years.
'Joe's cheatin' devastated me.'

Hope locks eyes with Chester and makes him consider an old expression.

'Maybe the eyes are the window to the soul.'

Chester dwells on Hank's analysis of Hope while Hope's processing her situation.

'Has Hank been right all along?'

Hank discloses another thought with Luke.

"Don't let anyone else define who you are. Be open and honest with yourself. See what happens."

"What if you deserve to hurt? How do you heal yourself?"

Ben's approach prevents Hank from answering. He hands Luke an apology note for Beth nearly shooting him. Luke' suspicious since Ben's prank is why he's stuck on the ranch.

'This might be from guilt.'

Every eye is on Luke while he walks over to Ben and Beth's table after contemplating the note.

"Beth, I apologize to you for hurting your husband."

Luke's conciliatory act surprises Beth.

"Thank you, that means a lot."

"You're welcome."

Luke looks at Ben.

"I'm still not sorry for hitting you for what you did."

Ben reaches out for Beth's arm when she stands to confront Luke. He shakes his head and scribbles another note and shows her before handing it to Luke.

'I respect that you stood up for yourself. I would've done the same thing.'

Beth utters one word.

"Men."

Hank and Chester watch Luke intently when Ben stands to extend his hand. They're relieved Luke shakes hands without comment. Katie smiles knowing Luke's revealing a little more of himself. Ben and Beth heard about Luke's rude behavior but witness a genuinely civil act.

"Could I borrow your pad and pen?"

Luke writes a single word and shows Ben. He tries laughing through his wired jaw. Beth grabs the notepad away from Ben.

"What?"

She reads Luke's comment.

'Women!'

"Ha Ha. Funny, very funny."

Hope's shocked Ben and Beth seem to be forgiving Luke.

'What the hell is wrong with them? I'm still so angry at Luke.'

Chester informs the DJ dance music can begin once dinner ends. The first request is Charlie Robison's 'El Cerrito Place'. The wrangler's prefer his original version to any cover done later. Holly pulls Luke out to slow dance with her presses her body against his with a tight hug. Holly dedicates Sunny Sweeney's 'Better Bad Idea' to Luke and tries two stepping with him. A few women gather to line dance to the song. Holly knows Chester won't make a scene after staying quiet when she kissed Luke earlier. Hope sees Luke smile in Holly's arms.

'Holly's probably told Luke she's his dessert tonight.'

Holly's aware Luke's eyes travel between her and Hope.

'Why does Luke bother lookin' at Hope? He'll get lucky with me tonight, not her.'

The DJ announces the next song.

"Someone's requesting Dalton Domino's 'Corners' next for inspiration."

Hank nudges Luke.

"This song is written for you. Listen closely."

Luke partially listens until hearing a line about becoming a stranger in front of a lover's eyes.

'Did that happen to me and Linda?'

The song's message mentions finding freedom by surrendering to what was needed all along and how some people need to live in hell to know if heaven would be worth it. The song also conveys taking on unanswered questions and finding purpose by praying for acceptance and understanding if forgiveness doesn't happen. The singer sings about dying a different person and realizing blame lies with the singer and not the devil all along.

'That's my life in song. Except he has hope for a better future.'

Jake asks for the next song but gets a warning before the DJ plays Randy Rogers and Wade Bowen's, 'Hold My Beer'.

"No startin' a fight to this, Jake."

The next song is fun so Faith pulls Hope up for a silly dance by the table. The following song is sultry to bring the women out for a line dance. Holly encourages Hope to join them.

"C'mon, Hope, show 'em how this is done."

"No way. I ain't danced in years."

"I'm not takin' no for an answer. Y'all still got it."

Faith cheers Hope on.

"Momma, go dance."

"I'll dance one dance for you, Pecan, alright."

Hope seductively moves her hips in unison with the other women and fully captures Luke's attention. The men whistle and holler and Hope realizes Luke's gazing at her and blushes. Jubilee wonders why until spotting Luke's focus is solely on Hope.

'Luke's watchin' Hope even though Holly's danced with him.'

Several people scrutinize Luke's behavior until Hope sits down again. Jake walks up just as Faith asks a question.

"Momma, can I have more lemonade?"

Hope's response is unusual.

"Oh, Pecan, you're in charge now. I refuse to adult anymore today. You can get your own drink."

"Momma, I'm only eight. I don't even have a credit card."

Jake promptly adds his own comment.

"I refuse to adult today, too."

"Jake, you refuse to adult every day."

He pretends Hope's accusation offends him before acknowledging her.

"True. Life's good for Jake."

Jake grins.

"That was some mighty fine dancin', Hope. Where'd y'all learn to move like that?"

Hope blushes after Jake's query.

'I can't believe I danced like that around Faith.'

"Momma, you're a good dancer."

"Thanks, Pecan, but I think dancin's best put behind me now so I can spend time with you."

Jubilee requests a song and the DJ nods.

"Cody, this song's for you from Jubilee. And Hope, this goes out to you as well. It's 'Arms' by Christina Perri."

The song's about a woman hiding from love until a certain man puts his arms around her and breaks down her walls. Luke sees Hope excuse herself to leave and returns several minutes later and glances at him with misty eyes.

'Lord, why did Luke save me? Why's he here? Who is he? Did you send him?'

THIRTY NINE

Holly loudly reprimands someone to disrupt the festive atmosphere. "Who do y'all think you are to touch me like that?" Holly moves away from Colt's friend.

"Darlin', y'all got a reputation for wantin' to be touched there, a lot."

"When I ask for it, not because you decide to. Get out! Leave before I shoot your ass off."

Luke overhears Holly tell JeniMay what happened while the guy jokes with Colt before heading towards the exit. Luke's standing near the exit and sees baseballs and mitts lying on the ground from an earlier game of catch. Luke allows the guy to slip through the gate before picking up a ball while the guys find out what happened. Cody leads them to chase after Colt's friend. Luke lets them pass before throwing the ball at the fleeing target. The guy mysteriously falls to the ground and remains motionless. Jake's puzzled to see the ball lying nearby when they reach him.

"Didn't we pick up all the baseballs?"

Cody scans the area and finds the culprit when he spots Luke smirking outside the fence. Hope learns Luke knocked the guy out.

'So Luke defended Holly. Why do I feel jealous? Luke seems interested in her anyway. She's obviously his type. Why am I even thinkin' or feeling this way? Holly's always had the guys chasin' her.'

Luke requests a song.

"Mr. Kinkead's gotta okay that one."

Chester puts a headset on to hear Luke's song choice.

"Who asked for this?"

"That guy over there."

The DJ points at Luke.

"He said it's for a special woman here. I've never heard it before."

"Steelheart, 'I'll Never Let You Go (Angel Eyes).'"

"It ain't like anything else I'll play tonight."

"Go ahead, play it. Let's see what happens."

"You're the boss."

"This next song goes out a special woman here tonight."

Luke's heard the song played on the bar's jukebox but never thought of anyone while listening to it. Hope's eyes inspire him to remember the song and request it.

'Hope's brilliant green eyes and devastating smile are angelic like the song says.'

People whisper complaints after the song's begun and several complain directly to Chester including Beth.

"It's not country. It's not something we even like. Why is the DJ playing this?"

JeniMay asks the DJ to restart the song and concentrates on the words. She scans the crowd while listening to the words and comes to a conclusion once the song ends.

'None of Colt's friends knew that song. Luke's gotta be the one who requested it. He hasn't stopped lookin' at Hope. Only Hope. Not Holly.'

Hope and the guys toast life with a shot of whiskey and a beer after the song. She's drinking sweet tea otherwise since she wants to set a good example for Faith. Jake comments first.

"Thank God that's over. What was that?"

JeniMay approaches Hope.

"Hope, can we talk? Alone."

"Now you want to talk?"

"Get off your high horse, Hope."

"I ride a tall horse, not a high horse."

"I know who requested that song. And who for."

Hope seems out of sorts returning to Faith's side while Hank's spinning a tale for Faith. Luke's listening as well.

"We ate dirt and drank from puddles when I was your age."

Faith's expression reveals her doubt.

"Mr. Hank, y'all're pullin' my leg aren'tcha?"

"Yes ma'am, I am. You're too smart to get fooled by an old man's tale."

Chester readily comments.

"Hank still eats dirt and drinks from puddles."

"Yup, whenever you cook."

Hank's response elicits laughter.

"Y'all can leave now, Hank."

A guest walks up and asks Hope to dance only to get turn down.

"C'mon baby, we can get acquainted during a dance or two here then get better acquainted later in a different dance if y'all know what I mean."

"I'm done dancing."

"Oh darlin', you got a lot more from what I've seen."

Luke steps in front of Hope.

"The lady said she's done. Leave her alone."

Hope responds brusquely.

"I can take care of myself."

Hope looks down.

'Why did I say that? Why didn't Chester say anything?'

Chester's thinking a similar thought about Luke.

'Why did Luke say anything?'

Luke dejectedly returns to his seat before the man walks away.

'Wow. Hope's still Superman.'

Hank focuses Luke on the next song.

"This song describes Hope. It's called 'That Rock Won't Roll' by Restless Heart. She needs the right man to come into her life the way the song explains."

Luke finally seeks Hope out once the barbecue winds down after leaving her alone during the evening. Hope spotted Luke dancing with Holly several more times and even watched JeniMay dance with him a couple times. Hope seems irritated Luke's dancing with them while standing with the guys. Chester notices Luke's demoralized expression whenever Hope laughs with the guys.

"I still want to apologize to Hope.'

Luke walks up behind Hope and speaks to get her attention before moving closer. Her smile remains after turning around to see Luke standing there. Hope recognizes Luke's respecting her personal space.

"Hope, could we talk? I need to say something but I'm not sure how."

Luke steps closer and stammers until Hope speaks authoritatively.

"Say what you need to. I need to take Faith home."

"Um, oh okay. I was inconsiderate after you were attacked. I'm sorry. I was wrong to say what I did. It was rude."

Luke's apology surprises Hope.

'Luke sounds a lot like Ben. He apologizes when he's wrong. I'm impressed Luke's able to say sorry to me. That always gets high marks in my book.'

Ben taught Hope good men apologize when wrong and how to tell if their sincere. Hope studies Luke's eyes and detects the humbleness in his voice. She reaches out to touch Luke's upper arm before taking his hand. She glances at her hand touching Luke's arm before realizing Luke's looking deep into her eyes.

"I'm sorry too."

"You are?"

"I put you in a bad spot."

"I'm not sure what to say."

Hope's soft sweet drawl mesmerizes Luke while her actions shock him. The soft touch of her hand is warm and electrifying and makes Luke's heart beat faster and even skip a beat.

"Watch out! Here I come."

Hope lets go of Luke's hand to ready herself after Faith's yell while she runs towards them.

"Faith's about to do her crash and hug."

Faith surprises Hope and maneuvers past her and jumps up at Luke. He catches Faith which allows her to briefly rest her head on his shoulder before squirming loose.

"That was fun, can I do it again?"

Hope crouches down.

"No, Pecan. It's time to go."

Hope redirects her mystified stare to Luke. He's silhouetted against the clouds tinted pink and purple to contrast the pale blue background of the evening sky's setting sun. Luke misreads Hope's startled expression.

'I'm in trouble again.'

"I'm sorry."

Hope raises her hand.

"It's okay. I didn't know Faith would do that. Y'all're okay."

Hope's attention returns to Faith.

"Faith, why did you do that with Luke?"

Faith looks at Luke with innocent blue eyes.

"I knew Luke would catch me. He's a nice man, Momma."

"Oh."

Hope's bewildered eyes study Luke again.

"Faith, it's time to get you home to bed."

"But I'm not tired…"

Faith's yawn escapes to join the naturally harmonious evening song created by insects and tree frogs.

"C'mon, let's get you home."

Hope reaches out to touch Luke's shoulder. Her eyes momentarily follow her hand.

"I appreciate what you said, thank you."

Faith discloses a thought with Hope.

"Momma, Luke gives very good hugs. You should get one too."

'I've had a very good hug from Luke.'

Ben observes Faith trust Luke and Hope uncharacteristically reach out to Luke.

'Faith doesn't trust many people with a crash and hug. And Hope never physically touches a stranger other than a handshake. She touched

Luke twice which is not like her. I'll need to watch Luke closer when I return. For Hope's sake possibly.'

Holly witnesses Luke and Hope together and walks up to Luke and paints his lips scarlet with a possessive kiss to discourage Hope.

'Of course, what was I thinking? Luke's wants Holly.'

Luke stands in the warm evening air not knowing he's experienced a life changing moment.

FORTY

A late season cold front briefly chills temperatures down to the upper forties and the daytime only reaching the lower sixties. Everyone else layers up for church and work but Luke's comfortable wearing less than normal. Chester's sipping coffee on the deck when Luke passes on his way to the barns.

"Luke, come sit for a spell. We need to talk."

Luke's wary Chester's invitation has a catch.

'Shit, Chester found out about the baseball. Or is this about Holly?'

Luke only has two positives in his favor, saving Hope and solving the computer issue so he cautiously approaches the deck.

"Yes sir."

'Huh, does Luke know how he addressed me? The ranch could be rubbin' off after all.'

Luke yawns while settling into a rocker.

"Pardon me. I didn't sleep much last night."

"I ain't givin' ya enough work?"

"Yes sir, Mr. Kinkead. It's not that. I don't sleep much, or well."

'Is that why Luke always looks tired?'

"I ain't slept good since '45. Don't expect any sympathy from me."

Luke dwells on Chester's comment.

"You still think about the war, don't you? Is that why you don't sleep well?"

Chester stops rocking.

"My sleepin' habits are none of your damned business. Runnin' this ranch comes with stress and worry."

'How'd Luke connect that? Only Millie and my war buddies know and understand. Luke sounds honestly concerned.'

Luke's inquiry about the war's impact on Chester's mental state is thought out.

"Returnin' to why I called ya over. Your attitude still needs improvin'. Y'all are learnin' some and becoming useful 'round here. Make more improvements and we'll figure out a timeframe for your departure."

Luke's testy response backfires.

"I'm just trying to survive around your farm boys."

Luke sounds immature indicating he hasn't yet learned to responsibly accept his punishment for Ben's injury. Chester's eyes burn with anger after Luke's insulting comment.

"We raise girls to be women, boys to become men, and everyone with manners. Respect is earned not given. Call my wranglers farm boys again and I'll throw y'all in jail and forget to return. Your big city mindset is arrogant and condescending. I trust my men with my life."

Luke realizes he's escalated an otherwise calm situation.

'I need to defuse Chester's anger or I'll never leave.'

Luke's confrontational reaction is sparked by Chester's constant jail threat. His rebellious retaliations are his only weapons left to battle with.

"Your men don't want me here anymore than I want to be here."

Chester's silence allows Luke to reconsider the people who've recently helped him.

"I'll try harder to get along with your men, sir."

Chester speaks with closed eyes.

"Good. Get back to work. I want my peace and quiet back."

'Luke defended Holly last night. He also stood up for Hope.'

The guys are mad Luke's late.

"Chester stopped me to talk."

Jake, Cody, and Billy are finishing the final phase and irritated Luke's not working before his scheduled ride on Dottie. Chester demands Luke be comfortable around horses ahead of helping guests. Luke's fear of horses is subsiding but still needs to be forced to ride. Cody detects a slight change in Luke's demeanor.

'Is Chester finally breakin' Luke's attitude?'

Luke's changes aren't due only to Chester's influence. Hank's having an impact through conversations but Hope's presence is also shifting his outlook. Chester's curious why Luke hides his true self.

'Luke doesn't talk about himself like most people. Information slips out accidently.'

Chester's discreet investigation into Luke's life has revealed the accident which killed his parents.

'I'll discover Luke's murky past.'

Hope decides to bring Faith to the ranch for dinner.

'For some reason, Faith doesn't seem to be afraid of Luke.'

Hope and Faith head for the riding barn with apples for the horses while Luke's working in the rodeo barn. Luke's alarmed when he enters to find Patsy lying on the ground.

'Shit! Hope's horse. What happened? I'll get blamed somehow.'

Luke moves closer and is stunned to find Hope lying next to her horse. Her long wavy hair is pulled across the front of her body and her hat's upside down next to her. Faith appears from the tack room with apples for the horses.

"Howdy Luke. See Momma and Patsy. Pretty cool, huh? They trust each other a whole bunch."

"I trust you and Patsy heart and soul."

They finish feeding apples and leave while Luke works which allows him to dwell on Hope's not so subtle message. He enters the kitchen to find his place isn't set. Katie enters behind him.

"You're eatin' in the dining room tonight."

"Should I ask Chester where I'm sitting?"

"Nope. A higher ranked person has picked your spot."

Katie's sly grin makes Luke dread entering the dining room. He sees Hope appearing upset which alarms him before Faith catches sight of him.

"Luke, I've been waiting for you."

Faith runs at Luke without warning and jumps into his arms again.

"Y'all're sittin' next to me."

Beth's amazed Faith's not afraid of Luke. She also sees Hope's dismayed reaction.

"Hope, are y'all okay?"

Ben had shared what occurred between Hope, Faith, and Luke at the barbecue. Hope seems depressed Faith's actually accepting Luke.

'I won't be won over that easy. Or at all.'

"Beth, I'm worried Luke'll hurt Faith. I don't want her gettin' attached to someone who's leaving."

"Don't get ahead of yourself. Faith just met Luke. You can't worry 'bout what may not happen."

Hope's deeply wounded by heartbreak and scarred by her experiences. Faith leads Luke around the table so they can sit alone. Luke's concerned Hope's unhappy he's there and watches for signs of her disapproval.

'Hope's hard to read.'

Chester enters and gives Faith a playful order.

"Alright Faith, your attention belongs to me now."

Luke's stunned to see Chester's gruff exterior vanish and be replaced by a jovial demeanor so unlike his Marine persona. Chester's kinder gentle grandfatherly version of himself entertains Faith until she returns to Luke's side for dinner. Everyone studies the pair like a social experiment is happening and confused why Faith's not afraid of Luke. Everyone heads to the family room to watch television while he washes dishes. A loud cheer erupts to make Luke wonder what they're watching. Katie sends him in with a dessert tray.

'Hockey? I thought they'd be watching a rodeo.'

Faith reveals her reason to watch hockey.

"I wanna skate like them. It looks fun."

Luke speaks without thinking.

"It is fun, Faith. I was your age when I learned."

"Can you teach me to skate?"

Faith's pleading eyes contrast Hope's eyes distressed fury. Luke feels a pit developing in his stomach while backing out of the room.

'Hope's definitely mad at me.'
Hope's grappling with Faith accepting Luke.
'I don't want anything to do with him.'
Hope's unsure she believes herself in the moment even though Luke represents possible heartache. Chester watches Luke's face pale due to Hope's angered state.
'Luke stepped in it again with Hope.'
Luke stops long enough to address Faith again.
"You need to talk with your mom about that. She probably wants a real coach. Are there ice rinks around here?"
Beth answers while the others laugh.
"Yes, we have ice rinks in Austin. Hockey's gettin' popular 'round here."
"Please let Luke teach me, Momma. I trust him."
"I don't know if I trust Luke, Pecan."
Luke's reluctant to speak but wants Faith to understand the truth.
"Faith, skating's harder than it looks. They've been skating since they were your age and make it look easy."
Hope realizes all eyes are on her after Luke's unwanted interference. Her irate expression has been fully aimed at Luke and he knows he'll be dealing with Hope's wrath again.
'I wish I could disappear right now. This feels like my childhood.'
"Faith, I need to think about this. I don't know if it's a good idea. I don't skate."
"Momma, Luke could teach both of us. That would be fun."
"Faith, I said I need to think about it."
Luke recognizes he's put Hope in a tough spot.
"Faith, let your mom think about it. She needs to find someone trustworthy. I'm a stranger. Respect your mom's decision, okay."
"Okay, Luke."
Hope hears the same soft caring tone in Luke's voice like the day of her attack in the room's silence.
'Luke sounds sincere.'
Hope studies Luke's tender gaze until Beth stands up.
"Hope, can I see you in the kitchen."

Luke overhears their conversation from the dining room and pauses before clearing the last of the silverware.

"Hope, why are you opposed to Luke teachin' Faith to skate?"

"I don't trust Luke with Faith."

"I don't think he's a threat to Faith. Be honest. You don't wanna be around Luke, right?"

"Beth, I've seen what he can do."

"Yeah, save your mistrusting ass. Faith's comfortable around Luke. Faith might try skating and hate it."

"Whose side are y'all on? I thought you'd back me up. I don't want Faith around a dangerous man."

Beth laughs.

"That's how you think about the guy who saved you. He could've died protectin' y'all. He ain't Joe."

"Luke's not Joe but he only did one thing for me."

Beth relents to Hope's debate.

"Luke did one majorly good thing. Good luck tellin' Faith Luke won't be teaching her to skate."

"Luke should've kept his mouth shut instead of meddling in my life."

'Why did Luke offer anyway?'

Luke hears Hope's bitter tone through the door before entering and timidly mumbles while they leave.

"I'm sorry I offered to teach Faith before getting your permission. I know you don't trust me."

Luke's distressed display confuses Beth.

'Why is Luke cowering from Hope as if he's afraid of her?'

Faith bursts into the kitchen and jumps in place next to Luke while he finishes the last dish.

"Momma says you can teach me to skate. But she'll be there too."

Faith breathlessly pulls Luke back to the family room. Hope locks eyes with Luke who looks confounded by Faith's announcement. Chester's heavily influenced her decision to allow Luke to teach Faith to skate. His reasoning is in turn influenced by Hank's comments.

"Y'all best not hurt my daughter in any way or so help me God. I'll show you what real pain is."

Luke's response is direct yet cryptic.

"I'd never hurt a child, especially someone as special as Faith. For the record, I've known real pain for years."

There's a profoundly deep agony in Luke's voice that only Chester understands. Luke smiles at Faith and exits the room. Hope's left feeling unsure how to react to Luke's final words.

'What did Luke mean he already knows pain?'

FORTY ONE

Katie intercepts Luke before lunch the next day.

"Hope's picking you up later to give Faith a skating lesson."

Her message confuses.

"Faith can't wait another day and Hope has time after school."

"I look forward to teaching Faith."

Chester enters the kitchen.

"Y'all take care of Faith or Hope's not the only one you'll answer to."

"Nothing bad will happen. I promise."

"Don't make promises y'all can't keep. I've had people make promises to me they didn't keep."

Luke remembers his dad's promise the day he died and momentarily looks at the floor.

"I'm not making a promise I won't keep."

"Work till I send for ya."

Luke cautiously steps into in Hope's truck when she picks him up.

"Get in already. Y'all act like you forgot how to get into a truck."

'Faith's the reason I'm getting in easy this time.'

Hope surprises Luke when she sets her cherished cowboy hat on the truck's dash after parking. Her long hair flows unrestricted while walking towards the rink. Faith hugs Luke at the entrance.

"Thank you, Luke."

The smell of frozen water strongly permeates the air inside the skating rink once the trio enters. Luke inhales deeply and recalls fond memories of his youth. The icy air fills Hope's lungs fill to chill her so she zips up her tan Carhartt winter coat and pulls out a thick fuzzy white knit cap topped with a large fluffy tuft. Luke gazes at her uncommon appearance.

'Hope can't look anything but gorgeous.'

Hope notices Luke staring at her.

"What?"

"Nothing."

Hope and Faith stand by the wall while Luke skates around to test the ice.

"Luke's a good skater, right Momma?"

"It seems so, Pecan."

Luke returns to lead Faith onto the ice while glancing at Hope.

"Hold my hands, Faith."

"Faith, be safe but have fun. But be careful, okay."

"I will, Momma."

"There's a couple rough spots."

"Faith, don't try too much too quick."

"Yes, Momma."

"Here's how you move your feet."

Luke demonstrates while keeping Faith balanced before skating behind her.

"Okay, you try."

Faith's frustrated she's not able to skate like everyone else.

"I can't do this, forget it, let's go home."

Hope sees Faith's getting upset.

'Luke better not screw this up for Faith.'

Hope watches Luke motion a young girl over.

"Hi, how long have you been skating?"

"Five years. Sir."

"Have you always been this good?"

"Heck no! I fell a lot at first. I nearly quit. My dad helped me and I got better."

"So practicing made you better?"

"Yep."

"Thank you. Have fun with your friends."

Faith appears to reconsider her decision about quitting.

"Luke, do you think I can learn to skate?"

"I do. You know why?"

"Why?"

"Because you're here and not by your mom."

Luke's smile is reassuring.

"Faith, I still fall sometimes."

"You do?"

"Sure. It's part of skating. Nobody starts off good."

"Okay, let's try again."

Faith holds Luke's hands and awkwardly moves her feet.

"Relax, move each foot slowly for balance."

They skate together for several minutes.

"Can I try alone?"

"Sure. And remember, falling is part of skating. I'm here to help you."

Faith lets go and falls almost immediately.

"It's okay. It's your first try."

Faith feels embarrassed while looking around.

"Try again."

Faith peers into Luke's reassuring eyes before her second attempt which doesn't much longer.

"We'll work together again."

"Okay."

Luke supports Faith while they practice together again so she becomes more confident on skates.

"Great job. Let's keep going."

"Can I try alone again?"

"Alright."

Faith wobbles to the wall and grabs the ledge and looks back.

"I did it!"

Luke's proud smile matches Faith's while he approaches her.

"Faith, you're a natural!"

Luke hugs Faith while Hope watches with envy of their shared actions.

'I'm usually getting Faith's hugs and attention.'

Hope's watching from across the ice.

'Luke seems to have patience with Faith. And he encourages her to keep trying.'

Hope feels her concerns dissipating which curls her lips into a small smile.

'Faith's doin' better than I thought she would today.'

Hope's smile disappears when Faith falls again until she gets up and attempts to skate off undauntedly.

'Faith's determined to succeed.'

Hope's eyes tear up with joyful pride along with a tinge of jealousy developing.

'I should be teachin' Faith, not Luke. But I can't skate, he can.'

Luke brings a walker out so Faith can continue practicing alone.

"This'll help you learn quicker."

Faith grins and skates to Hope."

"Momma, this is fun. C'mon, join me."

"I don't think that's a good idea."

Luke skates backwards and then turns around to skate off until he hears Faith's next comment.

"Luke'll help ya."

Faith reveals her irresistible expression.

"No, Faith, that's not fair. You know I can't say no to that look. This is your day."

"Have fun with me. We do everything together because we're a team, right?"

Luke recognizes Hope's eyes silently communicate her fear.

"I've never worn skates before."

Luke skates closer to reassure Hope it will be okay.

"I promise I won't let you fall."

Hope surrenders to Faith's irresistible expression and her words. Hope nervously puts skates on and stumbles to the ice.

"I'm not sure about this. I can't even walk in these so how am I supposed to skate?"

"Trust me and hold my hands, okay. I'll keep you safe."

"That sounds mean and underhanded after our parking lot incident."

Hope hesitantly reaches out for Luke's outstretched hands.

"This is a bad idea."

Hope feels chill bumps rise when she touches Luke's hands so he can pull her onto the ice.

'Just like when Luke touched me after the attack.'

The gentle strength in Luke's grip is oddly calming to Hope.

"Look into my eyes. Don't look down. Keep your feet closer together. I'll pull you around so you get the feel of skates under you."

Luke's captivated by Hope's dazzling green eyes and has to shake his head and blink to break his gaze.

'Hope is so beautiful.'

Hope leans too far forwards and loses her balance and falls against Luke. He reaches his arms around her to hold her up. They stare into each other's eyes for several seconds before separating slightly.

"I don't wanna fall 'n get hurt."

'Hope smells incredible.'

"You leaned too far forwards. Bend your knees but stand a little straighter, like riding a horse."

'Luke must feel like this riding.'

Hope subconsciously tightens her grip.

"I can't work if I hurt myself."

"I won't letcha get hurt. Relax. Breathe. I've already filled my quota for hurting anyone on the ranch."

Hope shoots an evil look at Luke so he changes the subject.

"Faith's a quick learner. She'll be skating on her own soon."

"Faith's naturally athletic. Her real fear is strangers, especially men."

Hope's irritated to reveal that information to Luke.

'So that's why everyone seemed shocked Faith came near me.'

Luke's expression tells Hope he's connecting things together. *'Dammit, why did I say anything?'*

"I'm going to bring ya over to the wall for a moment. But we're not done, okay."

"Okay."

Luke wraps his arm around Hope's waist and guides her off the ice and skates out to Faith.

"Faith, you're getting better. Let's skate together again."

"Okay."

Luke has Faith skate the walker over to Hope.

"Luke, do y'all think I'm ready?"

"Let's find out. You won't know until you try."

Faith skates in front of Luke and falls. An older boy skates by and laughs at her down on the ice. Hope's ready to yell at the boy and Faith's about to cry until the boy trips and falls and crashes into the wall. The boy lets out a frightened yelp.

"Serves him right."

Luke looks back at Hope and grins.

"Momma Bear."

Hope's proud Luke's admitting her protective nature properly. Luke helps Faith up while the boy's friends laugh at him.

"You're okay. See, that boy fell after laughing at you and has his friends making fun of him now."

The boy yells back at his friends after getting up and skating away feeling embarrassed. Faith releases Luke's hands to skate further before falling again and gets up by herself and continues trying until she reaches Hope.

"I did it, Momma. Did you see me skate on my own?"

"I'm so proud of you. I'll watch you if you wanna skate some more."

"Or you could skate with me."

"Maybe next time. You're so much better 'n me."

Luke skates nearby during Faith's attempt to convince Hope to skate with her.

"Luke, help Momma skate next to me."

Luke sees the same fear in Hope's eyes before closing in.

"I'm not sure your mom wants to skate any more today."

Hope speaks up.

"Luke can help me one time around, alright."

"Okay, Momma."

Luke moves beside Hope to put his arm around Hope's waist and hold her hand for added support.

'I've forgotten what having a man hold me like this feels like.'

"How long have y'all been skating?"

Luke's a bit surprised Hope wants to learn something about him.

'Is Hope really interested?'

"I've been skating since I was seven. I'm in a hockey league now but I prefer swimming."

The trio skates several more circuits until Hope and Faith whimper.

"Our feet and ankles are getting sore."

"We'll call it a day then. You need to build up your endurance."

Hope sheds her coat and cap outside and puts her favorite cowboy hat on once they reach the truck.

Faith happily shares details of their fun outing with Chester at the ranch. Hope's dwelling on Luke and the physical connection between them.

'I've haven't had a man make me feel so alive in a very long time. It felt so good to let Luke hold me close.'

Faith hugs Luke before he heads to the barns.

"Thank you, Luke. That was so much fun. Can we do that again?"

"Your welcome, Faith. That's up to your mom."

Faith literally pulls Hope from her thoughts with a tug on her arm.

"Momma, I wanna skate again."

Hope glances at Luke and Chester.

"We'll look at the calendar and see what works, okay."

Hope's clueless Beth had been observing from the stands. She's shocked to see Hope's willingness to allow Luke to hold her and lead her around the ice in an intimate way. Beth shares her interpretation with Chester and Ben.

"It's like Hope and Luke were on a date today. And Luke was so good with Faith."

FORTY TWO

The Twisted Live Oak Ranch springs to life when two limousine buses bring the entire first group of guests. Eddie Arnold's, "Cattle Call" creates ambiance for the beginning of an authentic cowboy adventure. Chester portrays the happy, old-time Texas cowboy wearing an oversized red bandana around his neck along with spurs and chaps. He holsters a replica.45 caliber 1873 Colt Single action Army revolver, commonly known as the Peacemaker against his leg. Luke watches Chester entertain guests with welcoming stories during check-in.

The women gush over the handsome cowboys wearing jeans, boots, and hats to help carry luggage to the cabins. Holly enjoys the men's flirtations and being their eye candy. Hope arrives to assist with opening day and politely deals with several men hitting on her.

'Where's Luke when I need him? Why am I thinking 'bout Luke instead of havin' Ben chase these guys off?'

Chester's scheduled a trail ride for after lunch to start the week off. Hope overhears Jake complain several pretty women hit on Luke instead of him.

'Did Luke flirt with them? Why do I care?'

Hope checks the foal to ensure it's not stressed by the increased activity. Luke happens to be helping an attractive brunette while she brazenly flirts with him.

"Help me into the saddle, cowboy."

She maneuvers so Luke's hand lands on her butt when he's ready to push her upwards. Luke admits inwardly it feels good to have intimate physical contact with a woman.

'I wish this was someone else.'

"I knew a cowboy would handle me properly."

Luke tips his hat and smiles respectfully until glancing to see Hope off to the side.

'Why's Hope here?'

Luke and Hope briefly lock eyes.

"Look elsewhere, this cowboy's mine."

Hope relives Luke's touch at the rink and feels jealous while he leads the woman and horse from the barn.

'Would I let Luke hold my hand again? Would I let him touch me like her? And like it?'

Luke's presence tugs at Hope's long forgotten yearnings.

'Do I miss a man's touch more than I'm willing to admit?'

Hope's left alone with another thought.

'Why am I wishin' Luke was still here with me? Was that desire in his eyes? Am I feelin' that too?'

One of the male guests arrives with Cody and immediately hits on Hope. Cody's shocked when Hope throws a punch and drops the guy to the ground and looks at Cody.

"What, I don't work here. Take care of him."

'Not the right guy.'

Luke's assigned to trail rides as well as shopping excursions to the Hill Country and Austin proper with Holly. He's not prepared for cattle drives yet so Holly plots how to ensnare Luke with her beauty while enjoying her special duty.

'Chester's serving Luke up on a platter for me to get tangled with him soon and often.'

Hope and Holly help guide trail rides also. Cody eavesdrops when Holly and several women talk about the cowboys after the trail ride.

'They can talk as degrading about men as good or better than guys about women. I'm impressed and disturbed.'

Hope joined the first ride and gives a death stare to the guy she punched and a worried look towards Luke surrounded by women. Scooter discovers Luke climbing the heavy rope later that night.

'So that's what it's for.'

Luke sits on the ground and climbs to the rafter in an L position with only his arms and slowly lowers to repeat the exercise multiple times. Scooter informs the guys so they attempt the feat and fail miserably.

'Luke made it look easy.'

Chester hears about Luke's exercise at breakfast.

'Somehow the rope's a calming distraction for Luke. He's not as abusive now.'

Luke comprehends the guys have discovered his secret when they don't put the rope back properly.

'Chester better not take the rope away. It's my only way of intimidating the guys still.'

Hope drops Faith off at the ranch for Beth to pick up while she answers a call regarding an ailing horse. Faith asks Chester if she could go riding.

"Sorry Faith, Waylon and I have a private trail ride now."

Waylon's a big spirited horse at seventeen hands tall and behaved around Chester and experienced riders but unruly around children still. Faith's been feeding apples to win Waylon over and decides to climb into his saddle.

"Grand-daddy, look, I can ride Waylon now. I've been feeding him treats."

Chester's concerned Faith's on Waylon.

"Faith, dismount Waylon now, please."

Waylon starts acting skittish before Faith climbs off. Chester fears Faith's behind Waylon's annoyed state before he rears up and whinnies. Beth enters while Waylon drops down only to rear up again and hears Faith's terrified scream. She holds the saddle horn tightly to keep from falling off after Waylon's front hooves barely touch the ground before he lurches up again. Faith's sliding off the saddle and risks the serious chance of being stomped on or kicked. Luke's closest to Faith and Waylon and brushing a horse that's returned from a trail ride. He drops the brush and rushes in to grab the reins and strongly pulls Waylon down. He reaches out to yank Faith off and sets her down so she can move to safety. Waylon's able to rise up and his front hoof strikes Luke's shoulder and knocks him to the ground. Cody's moved in to pull Faith away and Billy scrambles to pull Luke to safety. Luke's memory of the pony throwing and biting him quickly surfaces and leaves him visibly shaking.

'*This proves why I still don't trust horses. They're mean.*'

Chester also seems shaken but no one can imagine why. The group becomes focused on an armadillo scampering into view followed by several cats pursuing it.

'*So what really spooked Waylon?*'

Luke checks on Faith to make sure she's safe and unharmed before exiting the barn. Chester pulls Faith into a strong hug.

'*Lord, thank you for keeping Hope from knowing my pain.*'

Beth chases after Luke as he leaves the barn.

"Luke, thank you so much for saving Faith. Hope would be devastated in anythin' happened to her. I'd never be able to live with myself for being late to pick Faith up."

Luke's ashen shaded face exposes his unmitigated fear. The incident reminds Luke of the final day he saw his dad alive. Beth returns to barn while Luke continues to the bunkhouse.

"Chester, I'll take Faith home and let Hope know what happened and everything's okay."

Beth greets Hope in the driveway to explain the earlier events away from Faith.

"Faith tried ridin' Waylon today and nearly got bucked off. She's fine. In fact, she's better than fine."

Hope's face and voice expose her instant panic.

"What? Where is she?"

"Faith's fine. Better than fine, actually."

"Thank God the guys were there to keep Faith safe."

"Yeah, about that. Luke's the one who protected Faith. He pulled her off Waylon. I think he got kicked for it too."

"Luke saved Faith?"

"Yeah buddy. He seemed real shaken afterwards."

"Oh."

"Now y'all have proof Luke's no threat to Faith."

Hope calls to update Chester after settling Faith in and feeding her supper.

"Chester, Faith's unfazed, she believes an armadillo spooked Waylon."

"That's good news and she might be right."

"Please thank Luke for takin' care of Faith."

The next morning Luke's timidly agitated while prepping horses.

'I'm so tired of being around horses that remind me my dad's dead because of me.'

The corporate outing scheduled for the second week gets postponed due to a flu outbreak. The cancellation allows Chester to test Hank's idea out about putting Hope and Luke into a social setting off the ranch.

'Luke has performed well during this first week so far. This weekend could be perfect to try out Hank's suggestion. Luke responded responsibly around guests and even showed a hint of leadership.'

Luke's observed Hope's admiration of the guys' dedication to the ranch and do what's asked without complaint.

'Nothing's beneath them. I get why Katie was mad at me. Cowboys do what's needed whenever it needs to be done.'

Hope's had to admit Luke's conduct has been different during the first week around guests and Faith.

'I don't think Luke's the same person he was when he got here.'

CHAPTER

FORTY THREE

Chester extends his annual invitation to take Hope and Faith to Spring Lake in San Marcus to enjoy the glass-bottomed boats. Hope frowns to sees Luke in the front seat and stays quiet during the hour long drive.

'Dammit, I really need to talk to Chester about Faith's school situation.'

Hope's irritated because the matter is time sensitive.

'I can't talk to Chester with Luke here.'

Hope's reaction to Luke's presence concerns Chester.

'Hank might be off on this one. I can't tell if Hope's upset or distracted, or both.'

Hope's emotional barriers haven't been breached for years and now Luke shows up and leaves Hope unsure how to handle the chaotic upheaval. Hope has no idea Luke's suffering through similar doubts about her presence in his life as well. Chester's studying Hope and Luke's behavior.

'Hank could be wrong 'bout seein' how they respond to each other. It ain't lookin' good so far.'

Hank shared thoughts and his perception of Hope and Luke with Chester at the barbecue. Luke recognizes Hope's upset he's there and remains quiet except when Faith explains where they're going.

'Luke's so receptive to Faith. He treats her so well. Why, she's my daughter, not his.'

Chester reveals Texas State University was built next to the lake and college students work and learn at the facility as he pulls into a parking spot. Several college-aged boys lean against the truck next to Chester's spot and one rudely addresses him.

"Watch it old man, hit us or scratch my truck 'n I'll bust ya up."

Chester remains uncharacteristically quiet which shocks Hope.

'Why ain't Chester goin' full blown Marine on this asshole?'

"Y'all're too old to drive. Git back to the retirement home."

Hope steps out to glare at them.

"Show some respect."

"Lady, I've got somethin' big and pleasin' to show you."

"Grow up little boy."

"Whatever."

Luke has only one thought in the moment.

'Hope still thinks like Superman.'

Hope's next heated outburst is cut short when Luke emerges from the truck.

"You boys seem to need a lesson how to talk to women and elders."

Luke's imposing stance and intimidating expression frightens the boys off.

'Boy howdy. Luke's gittin' more useful each day.'

Hope notices Chester's pleased expression in the side mirror.

'He's up to somethin'.'

Hope glances at Luke.

'I do feel safer around Luke. I can't admit that though. I'd never hear the end of it.'

Faith leads Luke to their boat so he can sit next to her while Hope reconsiders her actions in the parking lot.

'That wasn't safe or smart to do in front of Faith.'

Faith directs Luke's attention to the transparent hull.

"You can see the fish and turtles swimmin' 'round."

"I've never been on a glass-bottomed boat. And the water's so clear."

Hope's upset Faith's sitting with Luke instead of her.

'Why does Faith seem happy with Luke? I still worry he could upset her.'

Hope sits across from Luke and Faith with Chester.

'Faith normally sits between me and Chester.'

Chester watches Hope during the outing and marvels at Faith acting thrilled to sit with Luke.

'Hope clearly has somethin' on her mind, but what?'

Luke's watching Hope and Chester as well.

'I don't think they trust me with Faith.'

Hope's unsure what to make of Luke's behavior with Faith.

'Luke seems so relaxed with Faith like he's cared about her forever. And Faith's happier around Luke just like she is with the guys at the ranch.'

Luke learns Spring Lake is man-made after a dam was built for a grist mill over a hundred years ago. The underground springs gurgled up to moisten the surface originally but now the submerged bubbling springs stir up the sandy lake bottom.

"Hey, maybe a mermaid's hiding down there, what do you think, Faith?"

"Mermaids live in the ocean, silly."

"Could we consider you an itsy bitsy mermaid here?"

Faith's expression reveals Luke's description bothers her.

"I'm not itsy bitsy."

Hope's ready to reprimand Luke for upsetting Faith.

"Sorry Faith, I'm not trying to make you small or sad. I only meant you're not a big pretty mermaid like your mom."

Hope's baffled by Luke's words.

'Luke apologized to Faith. Did Luke just compliment me?'

Faith ponders Luke's explanation.

"Oh, you might could call me bitsy."

"Only if you're okay with it."

"It's okay. But only you can call me that, deal?"

Luke smiles.

"Deal."

Luke's next move shocks Hope.

"Pinky swear?"

"Pinky swear."

Hope's apprehensive to watch Faith pinky swear with Luke.

'Faith only pinky swears with me.'

Hope's demeanor around Luke worries Chester.

'Hank mentioned Hope felt confused about Luke. The divorce shut her down.'

The return trip is just as quiet until Chester offers to bring Hope and Faith to Inner Space Caverns and Blue Hole Park in Georgetown. Faith quickly asks for Luke to come too.

"Sorry, Luke's scheduled to be with the wranglers tomorrow."

A slight smile reveals Hope's mood lightens after hearing Chester disappoint Faith.

'Great, I'll be able to talk with Chester tomorrow.'

Chester arrives alone the next morning.

"No Luke?"

"Luke's spending the day with the ranch hands."

Hope grasps Chester's devious ploy after noticing several Twisted Live Oak cowboys near the Inner Space entrance.

"What's goin' on Chester?"

Hope's disgusted expression is quite evident while Luke watches her step out of the truck before Faith runs to hug him.

"You're here. Yippee! I can show you the caverns today."

Hope erupts and scolds Faith as if she's misbehaving.

"No! This is our day."

"But Momma."

"Today, it's you and me. Am I clear?"

"Did I do somethin' wrong, Momma?"

Faith's question crushes Hope.

'Why am I mad at Faith? She hasn't done anything wrong. It's Chester and Luke I'm mad at.'

Hope's angered scolding and Faith's heartbroken reaction confuses everyone. Luke remembers bitter memories how his family treated him similarly when he was young.

'Hope still hates me.'

Beth whispers to Ben.

"What gives? Hope let Luke teach Faith to skate and he did rescue Faith from Waylon."

Luke separates from the group during Hope's prolonged glare at him. Jack and Jesse drop back. Jack examines her scowl.

"Why's Hope madder 'n a rattler in a busy wagon wheel rut?"

Luke's response is somber and tormented.

"Me. I shouldn't be here."

Luke feels guilty Faith's sad while Hope steadfastly holds her hand.

"I'm not going anywhere, guys."

Jesse rejoins the others but Jack remains with Luke. Luke learns how the caverns were discovered and focuses on rock formations to take his mind off Hope's fury and Faith's dejected expression. Several women cover their heads when the guide points out bats hanging from the rocky ceiling which gets Luke to chuckle. The temperature hovers around seventy two degrees but feels like eighty since the humidity is ninety eight percent. Prehistoric animals were unearthed by construction crews and are now displayed in the lobby. Jack observes Hope's expression turn passive during several glances at Luke. Faith pleads with Hope to let Luke walk with them.

"Momma, please, Luke feels left out."

Hope can't answer Faith without facing facts she's trying to avoid.

'It is touching Faith wants to include Luke.'

Hope and Faith enter the souvenir shop not knowing Luke's already scanning the items for sale. Jack's trailing behind Luke and watches Hope buy a gift for Faith. Luke spots something on a display case and turns to Jack.

"Chester has my wallet and my money. Could you buy this and he can repay you?"

Jack comments on Luke's choice.

"Wade Bowen has a signature song about that type of ring."

Luke carries the gift bag to Hope while she takes Faith's picture under the Wooly Mammoth head.

"This'll tell me how far to stay away."

Luke's unlikely gesture puzzles Hope. She's more confused when Faith hands her gift to Luke.

"This'll help you remember me after you leave."

Faith holds out a beautiful quartz geode rock.

"Thank you, Faith. But this is yours. And I'd always remember you if I leave."

"Keep it. You mean a lot to me, Luke."

Hope listens to Faith while warily opening the small wooden ring box and views a mood ring and the chart's black symbol circled which indicates anger or stress.

'Wait. Did Luke say if?'

Beth sees Hope's baffled expression and approaches her.

"Wanna talk?"

Hope's order is stern.

"Faith, go stand with Chester."

"Yes, Momma."

"Hope, what's goin' on? Why are you mad at Faith?"

"Faith's gettin' too close to Luke. He's leavin' once Chester releases him. I don't want Faith gettin' hurt."

"Luke might be helpin' Faith be less afraid of strangers. It would be a life lesson if he leaves. Faith thinks you're mad for no reason, Hope. That's not fair to her."

"Life would be easier if Luke hadn't shown up. Beth, I'm not sure what to do."

"Your life hasn't ever been easy, Hope. Not by a long shot. What if Chester keeps Luke around longer? What then? Does Luke look like he's favorin' his left arm?"

"Chester won't keep Luke here."

"Luke could be here all season accordin' to Ben. Luke's not your type so it doesn't matter. He's Holly's type, you like the brainy guys."

Hope looks at the ring in her palm.

"My life ain't what I thought it would be. I'm startin' to wonder what's really meant to be anymore."

CHAPTER

FORTY FOUR

Blue Hole Park is a short drive north on I-35 near Route 29 and Austin Boulevard and attached to the San Gabriel River. People swim, talk, and laugh over the sounds of multiple music sources. Everyone wore swim suits under clothing for an easy change. Hope pulls an oversized Longhorn t-shirt over her suit to conceal her figure from onlookers. Luke crosses the shallow portion of the river on a path of rocks jutting above the surface after removing his boots and socks. He sets his foot down near shore and discovers the river bed is smooth rock instead of sand or mud. Jack follows and comments before continuing upriver.

"The water's clear now. It gets murky during summer. Those rocks get algaed up and slippery."

Luke watches people from a rocky perch. Several jump off the surrounding Limestone bluffs into the deeper area to his right.

'I wish I could swim as well.'

A waterfall gently cascades over a cement wall separating the deeper upper section from the shallow lower area. A rock formation on the north side of the wall creates a natural waterslide enjoyable with or without an inner tube. Hope and Faith remain in the shallow portion. Beth splits her time between them and the guys up top. Holly arrives and does a strip tease to show off her tiny red bikini. A number of men compete for her attention until she heads straight for Luke and settles into his lap to kiss him before he can react. Holly shoots a sideways glance at Hope afterwards to see if she's watching. Luke's arms are wrapped around Holly only to keep her from falling over.

'I wish I could be more like Holly. Carefree and claim a man for her own when she wants one. I guess I don't have a future with Luke anyway.'

Hope's confused when Luke stands and leaves Holly appearing visibly upset. Luke crosses the river and locks pain-filled eyes with Hope and weakly smiles.

'Holly's gonna get me shot. Hope's made it clear she doesn't want me here. Someone said there's a scenic path here. I can't swim so I'll walk off my frustrations. And I've seen enough guys hitting on Hope already.'

Chester's watched Hope grow more irritated by the steady stream of men bothering her while he reads a book. Chester sees Luke glance back at Hope before entering the wooded pathway.

'Luke ain't goin' far. That look says he'll be back.'

Chester turns back and notices Hope looking in Luke's direction.

'Why doesn't Luke hit on me like these guys? Holly's gotta be the reason.'

Billy's flirting by the waterfall and notes Chester's lack of concern that Luke's walking away but gets confused after Hope frantically searches the area by the pathway. Billy calls Beth over after watching Hope's strange behavior.

"Any idea what that's about?"

The guys close in to listen. Beth stares back at them.

"I don't know. Hope's actin' odder by the day."

The guys stare at Beth.

"Whaddy'all think?"

"Fine, I'll see if I can get an answer."

Luke discovers the path leads to University Avenue, also Route 29, which leads to the ranch.

'A bus stop. I don't want to see another bus for a long time.'

Luke returns to the river where Beth's concern grows because of Hope's inexplicable actions.

"Are you okay, Hope? Did you lose something? I'll help you look."

Hope shakes her head to answer Beth's second question. Beth mistakes Hope's response for her first question.

"What's wrong? Tell me."

Hope's blank stare alarms Beth while Ben approaches.

"What's wrong?"

Beth shrugs her shoulders.

"I don't know."

Ben's name is called out by a group of people led by a man slightly larger than Ben. His hostile tone warns of impending danger.

"Three women standin' in the river. Heard y'all got knocked out and busted up, Ben."

Beth intercepts the lead aggressor.

"Grow up, Bo. Y'all never had a shot with me."

"Lettin' your woman fight for you now? Ya got soft, Ben. A good ass-whoopin' would toughen you up again."

"Ben, your jaw's still healin'."

Beth regrets revealing Ben's injury. He's clearly agitated by her blunder. The other guys are quickly closing the distance and Luke's return goes unnoticed. Luke remains concealed while observing the unfriendly interaction develop. He evaluates when the possibility of a physical altercation may occur. Bo's body language indicates it's fast approaching. Hope recognizes the fiery glare in Luke's eyes as he approaches them.

'Luke looks like a predator stalking its prey again.'

"Beth, Jubilee, JeniMay, get over here now. We need to move to safety."

"Safe from what?"

"Momma, is Ben gonna get hurt?"

"No, Pecan, he'll be fine."

Luke closes in behind the ranch group.

"Hey asshole, bother someone else."

Bo's toothy grin indicates he's not intimidated.

"Never corner somethin' meaner 'n you and don't bother somethin' that ain't botherin' you."

Hope suddenly relaxes during the building tension which confuses Beth.

'Why's Hope calm when Bo's threatenin' Ben? Hold on! Hope settled down when Luke showed up. What's up with that?'

Hope's eyes twinkle when Bo steps closer to Luke.

'Wrong choice.'

"I'm gonna crush you into the ground."

Luke's smirk annoys Bo.

"Is that a threat? Please, underestimate me so I enjoy this."

"You won't enjoy the beatin' I'm gonna give ya."

"If you touch me."

Hope's smile widens during Luke's taunts which baffles Beth.

'Is Hope happy Bo's gonna beat the shit outta Luke?'

The guys are entertained Luke's insulting Bo instead of them. Bo's a trouble maker with a reputation to throw punches and fight the cowboys. Few stand up to him and only Ben's beaten him. Hope's considered Luke to be prehistoric until now.

'Luke's different from Bo. He doesn't instigate fights like Bo does even though he has an attitude.'

Bo shifts to throw a punch aimed for Ben's jaw. Luke stops Bo's fist with a strong grip.

"Ooooh. Bad choice."

Luke shoves Bo's fist down and steps in front of Ben.

"You lied. You said you'd crush me. Is that all you got?"

Beth's impressed by Luke's action.

'Luke defended Ben.'

Bo's done with Luke's goading and retaliates with an easily read punch. Luke dodges it and counters with a sharp kick to Bo's shin. Bo groans in agonized pain while bending over which sets him up for Luke's crushing upper cut to Bo's cheek. The force stands Bo up for Luke's brutal front kick to the chest. Bo is sent sprawling backwards into his friends. Several people also fall before Bo staggers to his feet and swings wildly until Luke uses a well-placed round house kick to knock Bo out.

"The Twisted Live Oak people are off limits. Unless you want a beating too."

Luke impresses Chester.

'Maybe they did bury the hatchet.'

Everyone's shocked Bo's been knocked out. Everyone but Hope. *'I knew Luke would do that.'*

Bo's helped to a distant spot downriver so he can recover. The guys witness Luke's brutality up close and comprehend Hope's insistence not to fight him. Beth swats Ben's arm and points at Hope.

"Hope's lookin' happy Luke beat Bo like an old dirty rug."

"She does look proud of him, like you do for me."

"Hope's been actin' peculiar since Luke got here."

"Beth, do you think Luke's got somethin' to do with that?"

"Hope babysat our kids because she's always been mature and logical. Now she's nonsensical."

Beth's aggravated Luke dismissively walks away and ignores her attempt to thank him for defending Ben.

'I'm not picking up Ben's workload again or having Hope blame me.'

Hope notices Luke's favoring his left arm but also wonders why he doesn't celebrate like the guys do.

'Luke looks unhappy. Hank did say something 'bout Luke wantin' to avoid conflict when possible. He may not start fights like I thought but he certainly can end 'em.'

Faith follows Luke to ask a question.

"Come swim with me? We might could chase fish around."

"I don't have a swim suit. I can't swim like this, can I?"

Faith shakes her head.

"Get over here, Faith."

Faith questions Luke with a child's honest innocence while Hope approaches.

"Why is Momma so mad at you?"

Hope hears Faith and listens to Luke's answer.

"She must have her reasons. Be good and listen to your mom, okay."

"Okay Luke, I will."

Hope's envious Faith hugs Luke and kisses his cheek.

'Why isn't Faith afraid of Luke?'

Luke's developing feelings for Hope frustrates him. His view of the ranch is changing too.

'The ranch is starting to feel like home, why? I feel a connection to Texas. And Hope and Faith too.'

Jake reaches Hope before Faith returns.

"Thanks for warnin' us not to fight Luke. We'd've gotten our asses whooped."

"Yep."

Jake realizes Luke hears him.

"Luke didn't hear that, did he?"

"He did."

"We're in deep shit."

Hope reveals a sly half grin.

"Probably."

"You're not helpin', Hope."

"Not tryin' to, Jake. Hey Jake, is Luke hurt?"

"Yeah, his shoulder's black 'n blue from Waylon's hoof."

'Beth was right. Waylon kicked Luke when he saved Faith.'

Hat Creek Burger Company is walking distance north of the river for food and a place to change. Faith enjoys the tunnel slide and outdoor play area with the guys. The guys take breaks at picnic tables placed under several Live Oaks between chasing Faith around. Luke recognizes the noisy black birds are the same ones in H-E-B's parking lot. Jack sees Luke studying the birds.

"Those are Great-tailed Grackles. They'll swoop down to steal unguarded food. We can't stand their screeching."

Luke's time in the pet store leaves him unfazed by the noise while leaning against a post watching the activity. Faith walks over to him.

"Come play with me, Luke."

"Your mom's mad at me."

Faith considers Luke's statement before walking over to Hope and returns several minutes later.

"Momma said it's okay to play with me."

Luke glances at Hope and notes her small approving nod. Beth detains Hope while she's alone.

"What's with you lately?"

Beth's seeking answers to eliminate concerns regarding Hope's mindset.

'Is Ben onto something? Does Luke have anything to do with Hope's behavior?'

Hope divulges her guarded information to Beth.

"Faith's failin' math. She'll be kept in second grade if she doesn't pass."

Luke observes Hope's troubled expression.

'Hope's upset but I don't think it's with me.'

"It'll humiliate Faith."

Luke keeps an eye on Hope and Beth while playing with Faith.

'Does Hope really want me playing with Faith?'

Beth returns to Ben so Luke attempts a risky decision.

'This might end badly for me.'

Luke approaches Hope while she's alone.

"Hope, pardon me, is something else bothering you today, besides me?"

Hope studies Luke's hazel eyes.

"Sorry, it's none of my business. But you seem more troubled than yesterday."

'How would Luke know that? I only just told Beth. Why would he even ask?'

Hope's prolonged silence alarms Luke.

"Never mind. None of my business, I know. I didn't mean to bother you."

"Faith'll have to repeat second grade if she flunks math."

Luke's stunned Hope shares personal information with him.

"I'm good at math. I could help Faith. But you don't trust me."

Hope's quiet pause is filled by other's conversations, laughter, and music.

"Why do you care? Why help Faith? She's not your kid."

'What's Luke's angle for bein' nice to Faith?'

"You're raising a good daughter. Faith might need to learn a different way. I can help her."

"Y'all're bein' honest, arencha?"

"Yes."

"Faith seems to trust you. I'm willing to let you, if you're serious."

"I'm sure Chester needs to okay this, right?"

"I'll take care of that."

Beth returns to Hope's side once Luke heads back to Faith.

"You seem happier after talkin' with Luke. Why? What's goin' on between you two?"

Hope reacts defensively.

"Nothing. Why would you ask that?"

"You've been awfully different around Luke."

"What? No! Y'all're off base. I don't like Luke. He's got nothin' to do with anything."

"I didn't say you liked Luke."

'Wow! Hope's touchy about that.'

"You're just different, that's all."

Beth's speculation angers Hope.

"I don't have time for a man, especially someone like Luke."

"I didn't say that. Hope, I'm not tryin' to start an argument."

"I'm not arguing, I'm loudly sayin' you're wrong."

Hope's verbal protest against liking Luke prompts Beth to consider another possibility.

'Is Luke affectin' Hope somehow? Have we missed somethin'?'

Chester overhears their conversation.

'Hank may be on to something after all.'

Danny shares a thought with Hope during the return to their trucks.

"Hope, y'all know which note is the hardest to find?"

"No, Danny, what note is that?"

"Apolo-G."

"What's that supposed to mean?"

Danny's worried about Hope's sour tone.

"Hope, we're confused why you've been so tough on Faith today."

"Don't tell me how to parent Faith."

Hope storms off leaving Danny fearful she'll retaliate later. Faith further infuriates Hope when she hugs Luke again.

"Luke, I missed spending today with you."

"It's okay. You shared time with your mom, Chester, and the guys."

All eyes turn to Hope after Luke's answer to Faith's heartfelt comment. The group wonders why Hope seems determined to separate

Luke and Faith anymore. Hope becomes more uncomfortable battling uncontrollable emotions re-emerging along with their judgmental stares.

'I need to protect Faith. But is Luke really a threat? I did just ask him to help Faith with math.'

Hope's attempt to justify her reasons forces her to rethink everything which creates new doubts.

"Beth, can you explain I don't want Luke hurtin' Faith if they get close and he leaves. She'd feel abandoned again."

"Sure, I'll tell everyone that for ya."

'I'm not sure Hope's believin' her own words anymore.'

FORTY FIVE

Luke waits in the living room for Hope and Faith to arrive the next day with paper and pencils on the table. He greets Faith with a smile.

"Howdy Faith. Ready for some fun?"

Hope hasn't told Faith their true reason to visit yet.

"Faith doesn't know yet."

"That explains Faith's confused expression."

"Momma, aren't we here to ride?"

"Faith, Pecan, Luke's offered to help you with your math."

A high performance engine pulls up and shuts off.

"Momma, my teacher's already helping me."

Luke calmly interjects.

"I'm gonna teach you a better way."

"Can you really help me?"

"Yep. Second grade was the best three years of my life."

Hope frowns at Luke's comment.

"Not funny."

"C'mon, it's a little bit funny."

"No, not one bit, not even a little."

Chester notices Faith smiles after Luke' joke.

'Faith's apprehension disappeared when Luke made his joke.'
"I've got this."
Colt enters the living room which makes Faith worry again.
"Is Colt helpin' me too?"
"What's goin' on here?"
"Luke's teachin' me math."
"Hope, I'm a pilot, we do math all day. You should've asked me to help Faith. Not him."
Chester notices Faith's sour expression after Colt offers to help.
'Why didn't Hope ask Colt?'
"Alrighty. Hope, Colt, follow me to my office. Luke, start teaching Faith."
"Yes sir."
Hope's nervously pacing and Colt grows more annoyed.
"Why didn't you ask me? Hope, ya don't even know this guy."
Hope glances at Chester.
"Chester, did I make a mistake?"
"First, stop pacing, you're stressing me out. Second, no, Luke knows math."
"You seem awfully sure of that. Why?"
"I'm older 'n smarter than you."
'He's helped with the ranch billing and grocery shopping.'
"You think Luke'll help Faith?"
"I know I can help Faith, Hope. You wouldn't be worried with me."
Hope peeks around the door to see Luke stand and head for the kitchen.
"Sit tight, Faith. I have an idea."
'Maybe Luke's not able to teach Faith.'
Katie follows Luke and gives out while he carries a box of cereal to the table.
"Don'tcha dare ruin supper for Faith."
Luke's entertained by Katie's motherly tantrum.
"Don't worry. This ain't for eating. Mostly."
Katie's frustrated while returning to the kitchen.

The quartet curiously watches Luke use the cereal to teach Faith math problems from their locations.

"Hope, this is ridiculous."

"Shut up Colt, I'm curious to see how Luke plans to succeed."

Luke and Faith begin periodically giggling which puzzles Hope.

'Luke's not takin' this seriously.'

"Hope, that idjit's not teachin' Faith anything. Let me help her."

"Stay put, Colt. Hope's got it right. So does Luke."

Chester's comment surprises Hope.

Faith cheers after realizing she's completed the math without her usual complications.

"Thank you, Luke."

Chester bluntly addresses Colt.

"Hope, see Colt to the door. We need to feed our happy, hungry mathematician."

Hope's shocked by Chester's brusque dismissal towards Colt. Hope walks Colt to the door and Luke sees Colt try to kiss Hope's lips until she turns her head. Colt appears frustrated Hope rejected his kiss and that Luke witnessed it. Hope's thrilled to enjoy a delightful meal instead of Faith's usual argumentative attitude like so many other evenings.

'Luke helped Faith. How? I like her cheerful disposition.'

Hope pulls Luke aside afterwards.

"What did you do that her teacher couldn't do? Faith's struggled all year."

"I showed Faith how to sort out important information to easily solve problems."

"But how?"

"Faith's smarter than she thinks. I used a different technique so she understood the correct formula to use. I made it fun like my dad did with me."

Luke quietly looks down.

'Why does Luke look so sad?'

"I'm sure Faith's teacher does a great job. Separating key information from filler brings quicker success."

"I don't know what to say except thank you."

Hope reaches out to hug Luke which induces him to wrap his arms around her also. Hope melts into Luke's firm, soothing hug and presses her lips against his cheek. Luke doesn't expect any affection from Hope.

'Luke seems to care about Faith. And I do like his hugs.'

"If Faith needs more help, let me know."

"Luke, how's your shoulder?"

"It's fine. Why?"

"No reason."

Hope recognizes Luke's guy speak as not wanting to talk about it. Katie spies their interaction.

'Huh. That's new for Hope.'

Faith calls Chester the following day.

"Grand-daddy! Grand-daddy! I got an A on my math test today! I got an A."

"I'm so proud of you. Your momma must be proud too."

"She is. If I get another A I'll go to third grade. Luke made me smart at math."

"Wonderful. Can I talk to your mom?"

Faith hands the phone to Hope.

"Luke did what he promised. Faith's actually excited about math."

"Let's celebrate."

"Faith's got homework. Let Luke know Faith got an A. And thank him for me."

"Will do."

Chester informs Luke about Faith's grade at dinner.

"I knew Faith could do it. She just needed a different way to look at problems."

"Sounds like good advice for someone else to use as well."

Luke initially misses Chester's intended message but frowns after realizing it's aimed at him. His smile returns knowing Faith succeeded.

June bustles with activity which requires Chester to intensively train Luke for cattle drives.

"Y'all need to understand and anticipate the Longhorn's movement."

Every week in June runs at full capacity and guests participate in Austin's summer offerings along with ranch events. Luke's fear of horses diminishes once he learns to appreciate the animals better. He's surprisingly turning into a skilled rider under Chester's tutelage which impresses the wrangles as well as Hope. Ben shares some Texas history with Luke after another training session with Chester.

"Chester's our own version of legendary horse trainer Buster Welch."

"Who?"

"Buster's regarded as one of the gods of Texas. He trained cuttin' horses and won championships."

Chester sends for Luke one afternoon and sees a step ladder leaning against the wall outside the office.

'Chester must want this returned to the barn.'

Luke grips the ladder before hearing Chester call him inside.

"I didn't call you here for that. Here's tomorrow's trail ride list. You'll need to match up riders to horses based on skill level, or lack thereof."

"Okay, I'll bring the ladder also and save you a trip."

'Naw, I wanna visit Waylon."

Faith and Hope enter the office and Faith immediately jumps into Luke's arms to kiss his cheek.

"Thank you, Miss Faith. That always makes my day better."

Chester chuckles.

"Faith, that was the proper thing to do."

Hope's suspicious of Chester's comment.

"What are you talkin' about?"

Chester looks up and back to Hope. She peers upward to see a fresh sprig of mistletoe hanging above her. And Faith. And Luke.

"Why's that there? Christmas is over and it's too early for our Christmas in July party."

Chester's Cheshire cat smile alarms Hope before he pours fuel onto a spark.

"Its bad luck if y'all don't kiss who you're with under the mistletoe. You don't want any bad luck, do ya?"

Chester's announcement frightens Faith.

"Momma, please kiss Luke so you don't have any bad luck."

Luke adds a comment.

"Faith, that's not true. People blame bad luck when things go wrong. Mistletoe doesn't have anything to do with it. Hope can kiss you for it to count."

Chester's authoritative tone reinforces his theory.

"Bubba, you're way off base. Don't listen to them, Faith. It's true about bad luck. I know a man who didn't kiss someone once and he kept falling off his horse after that. Oh, and a girl needs to kiss a boy in this case."

Hope's stunned to hear Chester call Luke 'Bubba' since it's a term used only on his son. She's more flustered by Faith's reaction to his story about the mistletoe.

"Chester's fibbin', Faith."

Faith fearfully pleads with Hope again.

"Momma, please, just kiss Luke."

Hope's growing irritated Faith's not accepting a plausible explanation thanks to Chester.

"If, and I do mean if I kiss Luke, it means nothing, got it."

'How has my life come to this?'

Hope hesitates before leaning in so her lips barely touch Luke's lightly and briefly. Luke feels an overwhelming desire to pull Hope close and kiss her longer until Faith breaks into the moment.

"Wait, Momma, I want a picture of you kissing Luke to have proof so no bad luck will happen to y'all."

"Oh, Pecan, that's not necessary."

Chester interjects.

"You're absolutely right, Faith. A picture'll keep your mom safer."

Hope glares at him.

"What are y'all doin'?"

Luke also questions Chester's motives.

"Yeah, what are you up to? This is a new one on me."

"Faith, use my phone to take a picture and I'll send it to you, alright."

"Momma, one more kiss for a picture, please."

Hope wavers about the prospect of a second kiss but relents to Faith's request to quell her fears.

"Fine."

Hope's uncertain about the outcome from a second kiss with Luke while looking into his expressive eyes.

'Do I really need Faith to push me for another kiss? I'm feeling emotions and desires I haven't felt for a long time.'

"This is for Faith, no other reason."

'No other reason I'll tell anyone.'

Luke allows Hope to initiate the kiss so Faith can take a picture.

'Is this really happening? I want to kiss Hope again. And longer too.'

Hope moves closer and leans against Luke's body and rests her hands on his well-developed chest. She replicates her first kiss and barely presses her soft lips against Luke's. Long suppressed yearnings surface and intensify Hope's inner desires. She thrusts her lips firmly against Luke's lips and slightly opens her mouth to invite a more passionate kiss to occur. Luke surrenders to his own longing to affectionately kiss Hope and reaches his arms around her to pull her closer into an arousing lover's kiss. Hope slides her arms around Luke and holds him tightly until a jolting shudder sharply shakes her body. The electrifying sensation of this second kiss causes Hope to let go and push away from Luke. He utters one word.

"Wow."

Hope's emerald eyes shine brilliantly while wordlessly gazing at Luke as shock sets in about the effects of their second kiss. Luke speaks again.

"That wasn't terrible, was it?"

Hope can only whisper.

"No. Not at all."

Faith adds tension to the moment.

"Momma, you kissed Luke, like really, really kissed him. You'll be real lucky now."

Hope blushes and turns away before glancing at Chester. He's also stunned by Hope's passionate kiss.

'I'm not sure Hope ever kissed Joe like that. She never seemed that romantically inclined.'

"Luke's not stayin' much longer, right?"

"Bob informed me I can hold Luke here for six to twelve months for assaulting Ben."

"What? That can't be right."

Luke speaks up.

"You're not keeping me here that long."

Hope vigorously expresses her frustrations.

"I need to go riding. Now!"

Chester recognizes Hope's stressed frame of mind.

"Take Waylon, he needs the exercise."

Riding has been Hope's therapeutic escape for highly stressful situations. Luke struggles with his own emotional roller coaster during Hope's rapid exit and touches his lips after she leaves the office.

'Do I really want to leave? Kissing Hope felt better than any kiss I've ever had. What do I do now?'

EPILOGUE

COWBOY WITHIN
CHALLENGES AND REWARDS

Faith grabs Luke's hand to pull him from the office.

"C'mon Luke, we need to make sure Momma's alright."

Hope's hunkered down in the saddle while Waylon's galloping into the pasture. Her long black hair wildly flows from under her hat while they disappear behind distant Live Oaks.

"Is Momma okay?"

Luke tries to sound reassuring.

"I sure she's fine, Faith."

"Momma's never acted this way or kissed like that before."

Luke's blank expression conceals jumbled thoughts.

'Hope's kiss is the best I've ever had but is that a reason to stay here? Shouldn't I try to return to Chicago to win back Linda and show her I can be someone better? I'm no cowboy but I feel like I do fit in here more now or should I go back to what I used to know? So many questions. This ranch, Texas, Hope and Faith, they're all changing me. Who am I anymore?'

Luke looks down at Faith.

'What would life look like if I stay in Texas? Do I have a purpose here?'

Luke scans the horizon and glances at Faith again.

'Chester's turning me into a cowboy. Faith's got me feeling something I've never felt. And Hope.'

Luke relives the stirring feelings of Hope's kiss charged with the energy of a lightning strike.

'Hope's so alluring. Why? She's gorgeous, yes, but it's more than that. What's Hope thinking and feeling right now? Does she still hate me? Is that why she left so quickly?'

Luke leads Faith back to the house once Hope's vanished beyond the horizon. Chester's studying their approach.

'They look natural together. Holdin' hands, walkin' side by side. These two act like they've known each other forever.'

Hope halts Waylon's sprint by a special place near the bass pond and dismounts.

'Of all places to stop, this is where I got my first kiss. Is that supposed to mean something? How can someone I barely know wreak this kind of havoc on my life? Why did I enjoy Luke's kiss and hug so much? Why did I kiss him like that? I've never kissed anyone like that. Do I want more from Luke? With Luke? He's not stayin'. What if I want him to stay? I've been fine with it bein' just me and Faith, what changed? His touch?'

Hope and Luke simultaneously sort through emotional confusion and turmoil regarding their individual futures. Neither knows what's in store or what trials and tribulations await. Beth arrives to bring Ben's new leather gloves just after Hope's hasty departure and sees Luke with Faith. Chester's worried expression concerns Beth while listening to what happened in his office.

"Beth, I'm concerned about Hope. I may have pushed somethin' too far. She's more rattled than I've ever seen."

They're relieved when Hope answers Beth's call.

"Hello?"

"Hope, its Beth. Wanna talk?"

"I'm in the east pasture at our girl's hangout spot."

Beth saddles Patsy and finds Hope sitting near Waylon under several Live Oaks.

"How y'all doin'? Chester's worried 'bout you. Did you leave Faith with Luke?"

"Haven't you heard what happened?"

"Chester explained some. How are you?"

"Confused. I'm not sure how to think or feel anymore. My plan is bein' changed. I feel, I feel…"

"That's just it, Hope. You're startin' to feel again. Did you really kiss Luke the way Chester explained? Do you have feelings for Luke? Is that it? That is it, isn't it?"

"I don't know. I'm not sure. I don't want to. What if I do want Luke to stay?"

"Wow, you've tried not feelin' anything for so long, this has gotta be confusin'. Luke's the cause of you feelin' something. You can't convince your heart somethin's real that's not and you can't deny your heart when it's telling ya it's real."

"Beth, I'm confused, I feel lost. This can't be happening. I don't want Faith bein' hurt by a man again. Luke's made it clear he's not staying."

Beth listens to the angst in Hope's voice.

"Hope, this isn't in your control, honey. Luke's here for the season. Be honest, you're afraid a man might hurt you again."

"Luke's complicating my life. And Faith's life. I don't want her heart gettin' broken."

"Is it really Faith's heart you're tryin' to protect? Or yours? What if Luke decides to stay, what then? I thought we'd be havin' this conversation about Colt."

Hope silently scrutinizes Beth.

'I found the right guy, or so I thought. I was wrong. Luke can't be the right one. It's impossible, right? Faith could use a good man to help raise her and teach her and protect her. Luke's willingly done that and he barely knows her. Colt or Sam haven't done that, or anyone else either. What do I do? God, help me, please tell me what I'm supposed to do, please.'